THE SKIN

CURZIO MALAPARTE

The Skin

Translated from Italian
by David Moore

The Marlboro Press
Marlboro, Vermont
1988

Originally published in Italian as
LA PELLE
Copyright 1949

Manufactured in the United States of America

Library of Congress Catalog Card Number 87-63048

ISBN 0-910395-37-3

In affectionate memory
of Colonel Henry H. Cumming,
of the University of Virginia,
and of all the brave, good
and honorable American soldiers
who were my comrades-in-arms
from 1943 to 1945, and who
died in vain in the cause
of European freedom.

● If conquerors respect the temples
and the gods of the conquered, they
shall be saved.

AESCHYLUS, *Agamemnon*

● Ce qui m'interesse n'est pas toujours
ce qui m'importe.

PAUL VALÉRY

CONTENTS

THE PLAGUE

● Naples was in the throes of the "plague." Every afternoon
at five o'clock, after half an hour with the punching-ball and
a hot shower in the gymnasium of the P.B.S. — Peninsular
Base Section — Colonel Jack Hamilton and I would walk
down in the direction of San Ferdinando, elbowing our way
through the unruly mob which thronged Via Toledo from
dawn until curfew time.

We were clean, tidy and well-fed, Jack and I, as we made
our way through the midst of the dreadful Neapolitan mob
— squalid, dirty, starving, ragged, jostled and insulted in all
the languages and dialects of the world by troops of soldiers
belonging to the armies of liberation, which were drawn

from all the races of the earth. The distinction of being the first among all the peoples of Europe to be liberated had fallen to the people of Naples; and in celebration of the winning of so well-deserved a prize my poor beloved Neapolitans, after three years of hunger, epidemics and savage air attacks, had accepted gracefully and patriotically the longed-for and coveted honor of playing the part of a conquered people, of singing, clapping, jumping for joy amid the ruins of their houses, unfurling foreign flags which until the day before had been the emblems of their foes, and throwing flowers from their windows on to the heads of the conquerors.

But in spite of the universal and genuine enthusiasm there was not a single man or woman in the whole of Naples who was conscious of having been defeated. I cannot say how this strange feeling had arisen in the people's breasts. It was an undoubted fact that Italy, and hence also Naples, had lost the war. It is certainly much harder to lose a war than to win it. While everyone is good at winning a war, not all are capable of losing one. But the loss of a war does not in itself entitle a people to regard itself as conquered. In their ancient wisdom, enriched by the doleful experience of many hundreds of years, and in their sincere modesty, my poor beloved Neapolitans did not presume to regard themselves as a conquered people. In this they undoubtedly revealed a grave lack of tact. But could the Allies claim to liberate peoples and at the same time compel them to regard themselves as conquered? They must be either free or conquered. It would be unjust to blame the people of Naples if they regarded themselves as neither free nor conquered.

As I walked beside Colonel Hamilton I felt incredibly ridiculous in my British uniform. The uniforms of the Italian Corps of Liberation were old British khaki uniforms, handed over by the British Command to Marshal Badoglio and — perhaps in an attempt to hide the bloodstains and bullet holes — dyed dark green, the color of a lizard. They were, as a matter of fact, uniforms taken from the British soldiers who had fallen at El Alamein and Tobruk. In my tunic three holes made by machine-gun bullets were visible. My vest, shirt and pants were stained with blood. Even my shoes had been taken from the body of a British soldier. The first time I had put them on I had felt something pricking the sole of my foot. I had thought at first that a tiny bone belonging to the dead man had remained stuck in the shoe. It was a nail. It would have been better, perhaps, if it really had been a bone from the dead man: it would have been much easier for me to remove it. It took me half an hour to find a pair of pliers and remove the nail. There was no gainsaying it: that stupid war had certainly ended well for us. It could not have ended better. Our amour propre as defeated soldiers was undamaged. Now we were fighting at the side of the Allies, trying to help them win their war after we had lost our own. Hence it was natural that we should be wearing the uniforms of the Allied soldiers whom we had killed.

When I at last succeeded in removing the nail and putting on my shoe I found that the Company of which I was to assume command had been assembled for some time past on the barrack square. The barracks consisted of an ancient monastery, which had been reduced by time and the air bombardments to a state of ruin. It was situated in the vicinity of La Torretta, behind Mergellina. The "square" was a cloistered courtyard, bounded on three sides by a portico, which rested on slender columns of gray tufa, and on the fourth by a high yellow wall, dotted with specks of green mould and great slabs of marble, on which were carved long lists of names, surmounted by great black crosses. During some cholera epidemic of centuries before the monastery had been used as a hospital, and the names referred to those who had died of the disease. On the wall was written in large black letters: *Requiescant in pace.*

Colonel Palese had been anxious to introduce me to my soldiers himself in one of those simple ceremonies of which old military men are so fond. He was a tall, thin man, with completely white hair. He clasped my hand in silence and smiled, sighing dolefully as he did so. The soldiers were nearly all very young. They had fought well against the Allies in Africa and Sicily, and for this reason the Allies had chosen them to form the first cadre of the Italian Corps of Liberation. Lined up before us in the middle of the courtyard, they eyed me with a fixed stare. They too were wearing uniforms taken from British soldiers who had fallen at El Alamein and Tobruk, and their shoes were dead men's shoes. Their faces were pale and emaciated; their eyes, which were white and steady, consisted of a moist, opaque substance. They seemed to gaze at me without blinking.

Colonel Palese nodded his head, and the sergeant shouted: "Company — 'shun!" The soldiers riveted their gaze upon me; it was sorrowful and intense, like the gaze of a dead cat. Their limbs became rigid and they sprang to attention. The hands that grasped their rifles were white and bloodless. The flabby skin hung from the tips of their fingers like a glove that is too big.

Colonel Palese began to speak. "Here is your new commanding officer," he said, and while he spoke I looked at those Italian soldiers with their uniforms that had been taken from British corpses, their bloodless hands, their pale lips and white eyes. Here and there on their chests, stomachs and legs were black spots of blood. Suddenly I realized to my horror that these soldiers were dead. They gave out a faint odor of musty cloth, rotten leather, and flesh that had been dried up by the sun. I looked at Colonel Palese, and he was dead too. The voice that proceeded from his lips was watery, cold, glutinous, like the horrible gurgling that issues from a dead man's mouth if you rest your hand on his stomach.

"Tell them to stand at ease," said Colonel Palese to the sergeant when he had ended his brief address. "Company, stand at — ease!" cried the sergeant. The soldiers flopped down on to their left heels in limp and weary attitudes and stared at me fixedly, with a softer, more distant look. "And now," said Colonel Palese, "your new commanding officer will say a few words to you." I opened my mouth and a horrible gurgling sound came out; my words were muffled, thick, flaccid. I said: "We are the volunteers of Freedom, the soldiers of the new Italy. It is our duty to fight the Germans, to drive them out of our homeland, to throw them back beyond our frontiers. The eyes of all Italians are fixed upon us. It is our duty once more to hoist the flag that has fallen in the mire, to set an example to all in the midst of so much shame, to show ourselves worthy of the present hour, of the task that our country entrusts to us." When I had finished speaking Colonel Palese said to the soldiers: "Now one of you will repeat what your commanding officer has said. I want to be sure you understand. You!" he said, pointing to a soldier. "Repeat what your commanding officer said."

The soldier looked at me; he was pale, he had the thin, bloodless lips of a dead man. Slowly, in a dreadful gurgling voice, he said: "It is our duty to show ourselves worthy of the shame of Italy."

Colonel Palese came up close to me. "They understand," he said in a low voice, and moved silently away. Under his left armpit was a black spot of blood which gradually spread over the material of his uniform. I watched that black spot of blood as it gradually spread, my eyes followed the old Italian colonel, with his uniform that had belonged to an Englishman now dead, I watched him slowly move away and heard the squeaking of his shoes, the shoes of a dead British soldier, and the name of Italy stank in my nostrils like a piece of rotten meat.

"This bastard people!" said Colonel Hamilton between his teeth, forcing his way through the crowd.

"Why do you say that, Jack?"

Having reached the top of the Augusteo we used to turn off each day into Via Santa Brigida, where the crowd was thinner, and pause a moment to regain our breath.

"This bastard people," said Jack, straightening his uniform, which had been rumpled by the terrible pressure of the crowd.

"Don't say that, Jack."

"Why not? This bastard, dirty people."

"Hey, Jack! I am a bastard and a dirty Italian too. But I am proud of being a dirty Italian. It isn't our fault if we weren't born in America. I'm sure we'd be a bastard, dirty people even if we had been born in America. Don't you think so, Jack?"

"Don't worry, Malaparte," said Jack. "Don't take it to heart. Life is wonderful."

"Yes, life is a splendid thing, Jack, I know. But don't say that."

"Sorry," said Jack, patting me on the shoulder. "I didn't mean to offend you. It's a figure of speech. I like Italians. I like this bastard, dirty, wonderful people."

"I know, Jack — I know you like this poor, unhappy, wonderful people. No people on earth has ever endured as much as the people of Naples. They have endured hunger and slavery for two thousand years, and they don't complain. They revile no one, they hate no one — not even their own misery. Christ was a Neapolitan."

"Don't talk nonsense," said Jack.

"It isn't nonsense. Christ was a Neapolitan."

"What's the matter with you today, Malaparte?" said Jack, looking at me with his fine eyes.

"Nothing. What do you suppose is the matter with me?"

"You're in a black mood," said Jack.

"Why should I be in a bad mood?"

"I know you, Malaparte. You're in a black mood today."

"I am sad about Cassino, Jack."

"To hell with Cassino."

"I am sad, truly sad, about what is happening at Cassino."

"To hell with you," said Jack.

"It's really a shame that you're bringing such misery to Cassino."

"Shut up, Malaparte."

"Sorry. I didn't mean to offend you, Jack. I like Americans. I like the pure, the clean, the wonderful American people."

"I know, Malaparte. I know you like Americans. But take it easy, Malaparte. Life is wonderful."

"To hell with Cassino, Jack."

"Oh, yes. To hell with Naples, Malaparte."

There was a strange smell in the air. It was not the smell

that comes down at eventide from the alleys of Toledo and from the Piazzo delle Carrette and Santa Teresella degli Spagnoli. It was not the smell from the fried-fish shops, taverns and urinals nestling in the dark and fetid alleys of the Quartieri that stretch from Via Toledo up toward San Martino. It was not that nauseating, stuffy, glutinous smell, composed of a thousand effluvia, a thousand noisome exhalations — mille délicates puanteurs, as Jack put it — which at certain times of day pervades the city and emanates from the withered flowers that lie in heaps at the feet of the Madonnas in the chapels at the corners of the alleys. It was not the smell of the sirocco, which smacks of bad fish and of the cheese that is made from sheep's milk. It was not even that smell of cooked meat which toward evening spreads over Naples from the brothels — that smell in which Jean-Paul Sartre, walking one day along Via Toledo, *sombre comme une aisselle, pleine d'une ombre chaude vaguement obscène,* detected the *parenté immonde de l'amour et de la nourriture.* No, it was not that smell of cooked meat which broods over Naples toward sunset, when *la chair des femmes a l'air bouillie sous la crasse.* It was an extraordinarily pure, delicate smell, dry, light, unsubstantial — the smell of brine, the salt tang of the night air, the smell of an ancient forest from the trees of which paper is made.

Parties of disheveled, painted women, followed by crowds of Negro soldiers with pale hands, were parading up and down Via Toledo, cleaving the air above the thronged street with shrill cries of "Hi, Joe! Hi, Joe!" At the entrances to the alleys loitered the public hairdressers, the capere. They formed long lines, and each stood behind a seat. On the seats, their eyes closed and their heads lolling against the backs or sunk upon their breasts, sat athletic Negroes with small round skulls and yellow shoes that shone like the feet of the gilded statues of the Angels in the church of Santa Chiara. Yelling and calling to one another with strange guttural cries, singing, or arguing at the top of their voices with their neighbors, who looked down from the windows and balconies as though from boxes at the theatre, the capere sank their combs into the

Negroes' curly, woolly hair, drew them toward them with both hands, spat on the teeth to reduce the friction, poured rivers of brilliantine into the palms of their hands, and rubbed and smoothed the patients' wild locks like masseuses.

Bands of ragged boys knelt before their little wooden boxes, which were plastered with flakes of mother of pearl, sea shells and fragments of mirrors, and beat the lids with the backs of their brushes, crying "Shoeshine! Shoeshine!" Meanwhile, with bony, eager hands, they grabbed the Negro soldiers by the edge of the trousers as they went past, swaying their hips. Groups of Moroccan soldiers squatted along the walls, enveloped in their dark robes, their faces riddled with pockmarks, their yellow deep-set eyes shining from dark, wrinkled sockets, inhaling through quivering nostrils the dry odor that permeated the dusty air.

Faded women, with livid faces and painted lips, their emaciated cheeks plastered with rouge — a dreadful and piteous sight — loitered at the corners of the alleys, offering to the passers-by their sorry merchandise. This consisted of boys and girls of eight or ten, whom the soldiers — Moroccans, Indians, Algerians, Madagascans — caressed with their fingers, slipping their hands between the buttons of their short trousers or lifting their dresses. "Two dollars the boys, three dollars the girls!" shouted the women.

"Tell me frankly — would you like a little girl at three dollars?" I said to Jack.

"Shut up, Malaparte."

"After all, it's not much, three dollars for a little girl. Two pounds of lamb cost far more. I'm sure a little girl costs more in London or New York than here — isn't that so, Jack?"

"Tu me dégoûtes," said Jack.

"Three dollars is barely three hundred lire. How much can a little girl of eight or ten weigh? Fifty pounds? Remember that on the black market two pounds of lamb cost five hundred and fifty lire, in other words five dollars and fifty cents."

"Shut up!" cried Jack.

During the last few days the prices of girls and boys had

dropped, and they were still falling. Whereas the prices of sugar, oil, flour, meat and bread had risen and were still on the increase, the price of human flesh was slumping from day to day. A girl between twenty and twenty-five years of age, who a week before was worth up to ten dollars, was now worth barely four dollars, bones included. This fall in the price of human flesh on the Neapolitan market may have been due to the fact that women were flocking to Naples from all parts of Southern Italy. During recent weeks the wholesalers had thrown on to the market a large consignment of Sicilian women. It was not all fresh meat, but the speculators knew that Negro soldiers have refined tastes, and prefer meat not to be too fresh. Yet Sicilian meat was not in great demand, and even the Negroes refused it in the end. Every day there arrived in Naples, on carts drawn by wretched little donkeys or in Allied vehicles, but mostly on foot, parties of sturdily built, robust girls, nearly all of them peasants, attracted by the mirage of gold. They came from the Calabrias, the Apulias, the Basilicata and Molise. And so the price of human flesh on the Neapolitan market had been crashing, and it was feared that this might have a serious effect on the whole economy of the city. (Nothing of the kind had ever been seen in Naples before. It was certainly a disgrace, and the vast majority of the good people of Naples blushed with shame because of it. But why did it not bring a blush to the cheeks of the Allied authorities, who were the masters of Naples?) In compensation, Negroes' flesh had risen in price, and this, luckily, was helping to re-establish a certain equilibrium on the market.

"What does Negroes' flesh cost today?" I asked Jack.

"Shut up," he answered.

"Is it true that the flesh of a black American costs more than that of a white American?"

"Tu m'agaces," answered Jack.

I certainly had no intention of offending him, nor of poking fun at him, nor even of being disrespectful to the American army — the loveliest, the kindest, the most respectable army in the world. What did it matter to me if the flesh of a black American cost more than that of a white American? I like Americans, whatever the color of their skin, and I proved it a hundred times during the war. White or black, their souls are pure, much purer than ours. I like the Americans because they are good and sincere Christians; because they believe that Christ is always on the side of those who are in the right; because they believe that it is a sin to be in the wrong, that it is immoral to be in the wrong; because they believe that they alone are honorable men, and that all the nations of Europe are more or less dishonest; because they believe that a conquered nation is a nation of criminals, that defeat is a moral stigma, an expression of divine justice.

I like Americans for these reasons, and for many others that I have not mentioned. In that terrible autumn of 1943, which brought so much humiliation and grief to my fellow country-men, the Americans' humanity and generosity, the pure and honest simplicity of their ideas and sentiments, and the genuineness of their behavior, instilled in me the illusion that men hate evil, the hope that humanity would mend its ways, and the conviction that only goodness — the goodness and innocence of those splendid boys from across the Atlantic, who had landed in Europe to punish the wicked and reward the good — could redeem nations and individuals from their sins.

But of all my American friends the dearest was Staff Colonel Jack Hamilton. Jack was a man of thirty-eight — tall, thin, pale and elegant, with gentlemanly, almost European manners. On first acquaintance, perhaps, he seemed more European than American, but this was not the reason why I loved him: and I loved him like a brother. For gradually, as I got to know him intimately, he showed himself to be in-tensely and indisputably American. He had been born in South Carolina ("My nurse," he used to say, "was une négresse par un démon secouée"), but he was not merely what is known in America as a Southerner. Intellectually he was a man of culture and refinement, and at the same time

there was about him an almost childlike simplicity and innocence. What I mean is that he was an American in the
noblest sense of the word — one of the most admirable men
I have ever met. He was a "Christian gentleman." How
hard it is for me to express what I mean by the term "Christian gentleman"! All who know and love the Americans will
understand what I mean when I say that the American nation is a Christian naticn, and that Jack was a Christian gentleman.

Educated at Woodberry Forest School and at the University of Virginia, Jack had devoted himself with equal enthusiasm to Latin, Greek and sport, putting himself with equal
confidence in the hands of Horace, Virgil, Simonides and
Xenophon and in those of the masseurs of the University gym-
nasiums. In 1928 he had been a sprinter in the American
Olympic Track Team at Amsterdam, and he was prouder of
his Olympic victories than of his academic honors. After 1929
he had spent some years in Paris as a representative of the
United Press, and he was proud of his well-nigh perfect
French. "I learned French from the classics," he used to say.
"My French tutors were La Fontaine and Madame Bonnet,
the caretaker of the house in which I lived in Rue Vaugirard.
Tu ne trouves pas que je parle comme les animaux de La
Fontaine? It was he who taught me qu'un chien peut bien re-
garder un Evêque."

"And you came to Europe," I would say to him, "to learn
that? Un chien peut bien regarder un Evêque in America
as well."

"Oh non," Jack would reply, "en Amérique ce sont les
Evêques qui peuvent regarder les chiens."

Jack was also well acquainted with what he called "la ban-
lieue de Paris," in other words Europe. He had journeyed
through Switzerland, Belgium, Germany and Sweden in the
same spirit of humanism and with the same thirst for knowledge as the English undergraduates who, before Dr. Arnold's
reform, used to journey across Europe during their summer
Grand Tour. After his travels Jack had returned to America

with the manuscripts of an essay on the spirit of European civilization and of a thesis on Descartes, which had earned him an appointment as Professor of Literature in a great American university. But academic laurels do not flourish on an athlete's brow as Olympic laurels do; and Jack could not get over the fact that a muscular strain in the knee prevented him from running again in the international contests for the honor of the Stars and Stripes. In an attempt to forget his misfortune Jack would repair to the changing-room of the University gymnasium and read his adored Virgil or his beloved Xenophon, surrounded by that odor of rubber, soaking towels, soap and linoleum which is peculiarly associated with classical culture in the universities of the Anglo-Saxon countries.

One morning I came upon him unawares in the changing-room — deserted at that hour — of the Peninsular Base Section's gymnasium, deeply engrossed in Pindar. He looked at me and smiled, coloring slightly. He asked me if I liked Pindar's poetry, adding that the Pindaric odes written in honor of the athletes who had triumphed at Olympia do not convey any idea of the long, hard drudgery of training, that those divine verses resound with the yells of the crowd and the triumphal applause, not with the hoarse whistling and the rasping sound that comes from the mouths of athletes when they make their last terrible effort. "I know all about it," he said, "I know what the last twenty yards are. Pindar is not a modern poet. He is an English poet of the Victorian era."

Although he preferred Horace and Virgil to all other poets because of their serene melancholy, Greek poetry and ancient Greece filled him with a sense of gratitude — not the gratitude of a scholar, but that of a son. He knew by heart whole books of the *Iliad*, and tears would come into his eyes when he declaimed, in Greek, the hexameters on the "funeral Games in honor of Patroclus." One day, as we sat on the bank of the Volturno, near the Bailey Bridge at Capua, waiting for the sergeant guarding the bridge to give us the signal to cross, we discussed Winckelmann and the concept of beauty among the ancient Hellenes. I remember Jack's telling me that the gloomy, funereal, mysterious imagery of ancient Greece, so raw and barbaric, or, as he put it, Gothic, appealed to him less than the joyful, harmonious, clear imagery of Hellenistic Greece, which was so young, vivacious and modern, and which he described as a French Greece, a Greece of the eighteenth century. And when I asked him what, in his opinion, was the American Greece, he replied with a laugh: "The Greece of Xenophon"; and, still laughing, began to paint a remarkable and witty picture of Xenophon — "a Virginia gentleman" — which was a disguised satire, in the style of Dr. Johnson, of certain Hellenists of the Boston school.

Jack had an indulgent and mischievous contempt for the Hellenists of Boston. One morning I found him sitting under a tree, with a book on his knees, near a heavy battery facing Cassino. It was during the sad days of the Battle of Cassino. It was raining — for a fortnight it had been doing nothing but rain. Columns of trucks laden with American soldiers, sewn up in white sheets of coarse linen cloth, were going down in the direction of the little military cemeteries which were to be seen here and there beside the Via Appia and the Via Casilina. To keep the rain off the pages of his book — an eighteenth-century anthology of Greek poetry with a soft leather binding and gilt edges, presented to him by the worthy Gaspare Casella, the famous antiquarian bookseller of Naples and a friend of Anatole France — Jack was sitting with his body bent forward, covering the precious book with the edges of his mackintosh.

I remember his saying to me with a laugh that in Boston Simonides was not considered a great poet. And he added that Emerson, in his funeral panegyric of Thoreau, declared that "his classic poem on *Smoke* suggests Simonides, but is better than any poem of Simonides." He laughed heartily. "Ah, ces gens de Boston! Tu vois ça? Thoreau, in the opin-

ion of Boston, is greater than Simonides!" he said, and the
rain entered his mouth, mingling with his words and his
laughter.

His favorite American poet was Edgar Allan Poe. But
sometimes, when he had drunk a whisky more than usual,
he would confuse Horace's verses with Poe's, and be deeply
astonished to find Annabel Lee and Lydia in the same Alcaic.
Or he would confuse Madame de Sévigné's "talking leaf"
with one of La Fontaine's talking animals.

"It wasn't an animal," I would say to him. "It was a leaf
— a leaf from a tree."

And I would quote the relevant passage from the letter
in which Madame de Sévigné wrote that she wished there
was a talking leaf in the park of her castle, Les Rochers, in
Brittany.

"Mais cela c'est absurde," Jack would say. "Une feuille
qui parle! Un animal, ça se comprend, mais une feuille!"

"For the understanding of Europe," I would say to him,
"Cartesian logic is useless. Europe is a mysterious place, full
of inviolable secrets."

"Ah, Europe! What an extraordinary place it is!" Jack
would exclaim. "I need Europe, to make me conscious of
being an American."

But Jack was not one of those Américains de Paris — they
are found on every page of Hemingway's *The Sun Also Rises*
— who round about 1925 used to frequent the Select in Mont-
parnasse, who disdained Ford Madox Ford's tea parties and
Sylvia Beach's bookshop, and who are said by Sinclair Lewis,
alluding specifically to certain characters created by Eleanor
Green, to have been like the intellectual fugitives who frequented the Rive Gauche round about 1925, or like T. S. Eliot,
Ezra Pound or Isadora Duncan — "iridescent flies caught in
the black web of an ancient and amoral European culture."
Nor was Jack one of those decadent transatlantic youths who
formed the *Transition* clique. No, Jack was neither a déraciné
nor a decadent. He was an American in love with Europe.

He had for Europe a respect compounded of love and admiration. But in spite of his culture and his affectionate familiarity with our virtues and our faults his attitude to Europe, like that of nearly all true Americans, was conditioned by a subtle species of "inferiority complex," which manifested itself not, to be sure, in an inability to understand and forgive our misery and shame, but in a fear of understanding, a reluctance to understand which was due to a certain delicacy of feeling. In Jack this inferiority complex, this ingenuousness and wonderful delicacy of feeling, were perhaps more apparent than in many other Americans. Whenever, in a Neapolitan street, in a village near Capua or Caserta, or on the Cassino road, he happened to witness some distressing incident which typified our misery, our physical and moral humiliation, and our despair (the misery, humiliation and despair not only of Naples and Italy, but of all Europe), Jack would blush crimson.

Because of that way he had of blushing I loved Jack like a brother. Because of his wonderful delicacy of feeling, so profoundly and truly American, I was grateful to Jack, to all General Clark's G.I.s, and to all the men, women and children of America. (America — that luminous, remote horizon, that unattainable shore, that happy, forbidden country!) Sometimes, in an attempt to hide his delicacy of feeling, he would say, blushing crimson: "This bastard, dirty people." On such occasions I used to react to his wonderful sensitiveness with bitter and sarcastic words, accompanied by uneasy, malicious laughter, which I immediately regretted, and remembered with remorse all night long. He would perhaps have preferred it if I had started to cry: my tears would certainly have seemed to him more natural than my sarcasm, less cruel than my bitterness. But I too had something to hide. We too, in this miserable Europe of ours, are afraid and ashamed of our delicacy of feeling.

It was not my fault, however, if the price of Negroes' flesh was increasing every day. A dead Negro cost nothing; he cost much less than a dead white man — even less than a live

Italian! He cost pretty much the same as twenty Neapolitan children who had died of hunger. It was indeed strange that a dead Negro should cost so little. A dead Negro is very handsome. He is glossy, massive, immense, and when he is stretched out on the ground he occupies almost twice as much space as a dead white man. Even if a Negro, when he was alive in America, was only a poor Harlem bootblack, or a worker whose job was to unload coal in the docks, or a fireman on the railways, in death he took up almost as much space as the huge, magnificent corpses of the Homeric heroes. At heart I was pleased to think that the corpse of a Negro took up almost as much ground as the corpse of Achilles, Hector or Ajax would have done. And I could not resign myself to the idea that a dead Negro should cost so little.

But a live Negro cost a small fortune. Within the last few days the price of live Negroes had risen in Naples from two hundred to a thousand dollars, and its tendency was to increase. It was only necessary to see the hungry expressions with which the poor people eyed a Negro — a live Negro — to appreciate that the price of live Negroes was very high, and was still rising. The dream of all the poor people of Naples, especially the street arabs and the boys, was to be able to hire a "black," if only for a few hours. Hunting Negro soldiers was the favorite sport of the boys. Naples, to them, was a vast equatorial forest, redolent with a warm, heavy odor of sweet fritters, where ecstatic Negroes promenaded, swaying their hips, their eyes fixed upon the heavens. When a street arab managed to seize a Negro by the sleeve of his tunic and drag him along behind him from bar to bar, from inn to inn, from brothel to brothel, all the windows, doorsteps and street corners in the maze of alleys that constitutes Toledo and Forcella would fill with eyes, hands and voices crying: "Sell me your black! I'll give you twenty dollars! Thirty dollars! Fifty dollars!" This was what was called the "flying market." Fifty dollars was the maximum price that was paid for the hire of a Negro for a day, that is for a few hours — the time needed to make him drunk, to strip him of everything he had on, from his cap to his shoes, and then, after nightfall, to abandon him naked on the pavement of an alley.

The Negro suspects nothing. He is not conscious of being bought and resold every quarter of an hour, and he walks about innocently and happily, very proud of his shoes, which glitter as though made of gold, his smart uniform, his yellow gloves, his rings and gold teeth, his great white eyes, viscous and translucent like the eyes of an octopus. He walks along with a smile on his face, his head inclined on his shoulder and his eyes lost in contemplation of a green cloud drifting far away through the sea-blue sky, his sharp, dazzlingly white teeth seeming to cut like scissors the blue fringe of the roofs, the bare legs of the girls leaning against the railings of the balconies, the red carnations that protrude from the terra-cotta vases on the window sills. He walks like a somnambulist, savoring with delight all the smells, colors, tastes, sights and sounds that make life sweet: the smell of fritters, wine and fried fish, a pregnant woman sitting on her doorstep, a girl scratching her back, another girl looking for a flea in her bosom, the crying of a baby in its cradle, the laughter of a street arab, the flashing of the sunlight on a windowpane, the music of a gramophone, the flames of the papier-mâché Purgatories in which the damned burn at the feet of the Madonnas in the chapels at the corners of the alleys, a boy who with knifelike teeth, snow-white and dazzling, produces from a curved slice of melon, as from a mouth organ, a half-moon of green and red sounds that sparkle against the gray sky of a wall, a girl combing her hair at a window, singing "Ohi Marí" and gazing at her image reflected in the sky as in a mirror.

The Negro does not notice that the boy who holds his hand and strokes his wrist, talking to him softly and looking up at him with mild eyes, from time to time changes his identity. (When the boy sells his "black" to another street arab he slips the Negro's hand into that of the buyer and loses himself in the crowd.) The price of a Negro on the flying market is based on the lavishness and recklessness of his expenditure, on his avidity for food and drink, on the way in which he smiles, lights a cigarette or looks at a woman. A hundred expert, eager eyes follow the Negro's every gesture, count the coins that he draws from his pocket, observe his pink-and-black fingers with their pale cuticles. There are boys who are very expert at the precise and rapid calculation which the traffic entails. (In two months Pasquale Mele, a boy of ten, earned from the purchase and resale of Negroes on the flying market about six thousand dollars, with which he acquired a house in the vicinity of the Piazza Olivella.) As he wanders from bar to bar, from inn to inn, from brothel to brothel, as he smiles, drinks and eats, as he caresses the arms of a girl, the Negro is oblivious of the fact that he has become a medium of exchange, he does not even suspect that he has been bought and sold like a slave.

It was certainly not dignified, the position of the Negro soldiers in the American army — so kind, so black, so respectable — who had won the war, landed at Naples as conquerors, and now found themselves being bought and sold like unfortunate slaves. But in Naples this kind of thing has been happening for a thousand years. Such was the experience of the Normans, the Angevins and the Aragonese, of Charles VIII of France, and of Garibaldi and Mussolini themselves. The people of Naples would have perished of hunger centuries ago if every so often they had not been lucky enough to be able to buy and resell all those, Italians and foreigners, who presumed to land at Naples as conquerors and overlords.

If the cost of hiring a Negro soldier on the flying market for a few hours was only twenty or thirty dollars, the cost of hiring him for one or two months was high, ranging from three hundred to a thousand dollars or even more. An American Negro was a gold mine. The owner of a Negro slave possessed a sure income and a source of easy gain. He had solved the problem of making a living, and often grew rich. The risk, certainly, was great, since the M.P.s, who understood nothing about the affairs of Europe, nourished an inexplicable aversion to the traffic in Negroes. But in spite of the M.P.s the Negro trade was held in high honor in Naples. There was not a family in the city, however poor, which did not possess its Negro slave.

A Negro's master treated his slave as an honored guest. He offered him food and drink, filled him with wine and fritters, let him dance with his own daughters to the strains of an old gramophone, made him sleep, along with all the members of his family, male and female, in his own bed — one of those vast beds which occupy a large part of every Neapolitan basso. And the Negro would come home every evening with gifts of sugar, cigarettes, spam, bacon, bread, white flour, vests, stockings, shoes, uniforms, bedspreads, overcoats, and vast quantities of caramels. The "black" was delighted by the quiet family life, the decorousness and warmth of his welcome, the smiles of the women and children, the sight of the table laid for supper beneath the lamp, the wine, the pizza cheese, the sweet fritters. After a few days the fortunate Negro, having become the slave of this poor, warmhearted Neapolitan family, would become engaged to one of his master's daughters; and he would return home every evening laden with gifts for his fiancée — cases of corned beef, bags of sugar and flour, cartons of cigarettes, and treasures of every kind, which he filched from the military stores, and which the father and brothers of his fiancée sold to dealers on the black market. It was also possible to buy white slaves in the jungle that was Naples; but they showed little return, and so cost less. Still, a white soldier from the P.X. cost as much as a colored driver.

Drivers were the most expensive of all. A black driver cost up to two thousand dollars. There were drivers who presented their fiancées with complete vehicles laden with flour, sugar, tires and cans of gas. One day a black driver gave his fiancée, Concetta Esposito, of the Vicolo della Torretta, situated at the end of the Riviera di Chiaia, a heavy tank — a Sherman. In two hours the tank, which had been hidden in a yard, was stripped of all its bolts and dismantled. In two hours it disappeared: not a trace was left of it save for a patch of oil on the flagstones of the yard. One night a Liberty ship, which had arrived from America a few hours before in convoy with ten other ships, was stolen from Naples harbor. Not only was the cargo stolen, but the ship itself. It vanished, and was never heard of again. All Naples, from Capodimonte to Posilipo, rocked with tumultuous laughter, as if convulsed by an earthquake. The Muses, the Graces, Juno, Minerva, Diana and all the Goddesses from Olympus, who in the cool of the evening appear among the clouds above Vesuvius and look down on Naples, could be seen laughing and clasping their bosoms with both hands, while Venus made the heavens shimmer with the flashing of her white teeth.

"How much does a Liberty ship cost on the black market, Jack?"

"Oh, ça ne coûte pas cher, you damned fool!" Jack would reply, turning red.

"You were right to post sentries on the bridges of your battleships. If you aren't careful they'll steal your fleet."

"To hell with you, Malaparte."

When, each evening, we came to the end of Via Toledo and arrived outside the famous Caffè Caflisch, which the French had requisitioned and turned into their foyer du soldat, we used to slacken our pace in order to listen to General Juin's soldiers talking French among themselves. It was a pleasure to us to hear the French language articulated by French voices. (Jack always spoke French to me. When, immediately after the Allied landing at Salerno, I was appointed liaison officer between the Italian Corps of Liberation and General Headquarters of the Peninsular Base Section, Jack, Staff Colonel Jack Hamilton, had at once asked me if I spoke French, and at my "Oui, mon colonel" he had flushed with joy. "Vous savez," he said to me, "il fait bon de parler français. Le français est une langue très, très respectable. C'est très bon pour la santé.") At every hour of the day a small crowd of soldiers and sailors from Algeria, Madagascar, Morocco, Senegal, Tahiti and Indochina would be standing about on the pavement outside the Caffè Caflisch, but their French was not that of La Fontaine, and we could not understand a word they said. Sometimes, however, if we strained our ears, we were lucky enough to catch a few French words pronounced with a Parisian or Marseillais accent. Jack would flush with joy, and seizing me by the arm would say: "Ecoute, Malaparte,

écoute, voilà du français, du véritable français!" We would
both stop, deeply moved, and listen to those French voices,
those French words, with their Ménilmontant or La Canne-
bière intonation, and Jack would say: "Ah, que c'est bon!
Ah, que ça fait du bien!"

Often, each lending the other courage, we would cross the
threshold of the Caffè Caflisch. Timidly Jack would go up
to the French sergeant who ran the foyer du soldat and ask
him with a blush: "Est-ce que, par hasard . . . est-ce qu'on a
vu par là le lieutenant Lyautey?"

"Non, mon colonel," the sergeant would reply, "on ne l'a
pas vu depuis quelques jours. Je regrette."

"Merci," Jack would say. "Au revoir, mon ami."

"Au revoir, mon colonel," the sergeant would say.

"Ah, que ça fait du bien, d'entendre parler français!" Jack
would say, red-faced, as we walked out of the Caffè Caflisch.

Jack and I, accompanied by Captain Jimmy Wren, of Cleveland, Ohio, used often to go and eat hot taralli, fresh from
the oven, in a baker's shop situated on the Pendino di Santa
Barbara, that long, gently sloping flight of steps which leads
up from the Sedile di Porto in the direction of the Monastery
of Santa Chiara.

The Pendino is a dismal alley. It owes its character not
so much to its narrowness, carved out as it is between the
high, mildewed walls of ancient, sordid houses, or to the
eternal darkness that reigns within it even on sunny days, as
to the strangeness of its inhabitants.

In point of fact, the Pendino di Santa Barbara is famous
for the many female dwarfs who reside in it. They are so
small that they barely come up to the knee of a man of aver-
age height. Repulsive and wrinkled, they are among the
ugliest of their kind in the world. There are in Spain female
dwarfs of great beauty, with well-proportioned limbs and
features. And I have seen some in England who are truly
exquisite, pink-skinned and fair-haired, like miniature Venuses. But the female dwarfs of the Pendino di Santa Barbara

are frightful creatures. All of them, even the youngest, look like very old women, so wizened are their faces, so creased their foreheads, so thin and faded their disheveled locks. The most astounding thing about that noisome alley, with its horrible population of dwarf women, is the handsomeness of the men, who are tall and have very dark eyes and hair, leisurely, noble gestures, and clear, resonant voices. There are no male dwarfs to be seen on the Pendino di Santa Barbara, a fact which encourages the belief that they die in infancy or that this lack of inches is a monstrous legacy inherited only by the women.

These dwarf women spend the whole day sitting on the doorsteps of the bassi or squatting on tiny stools at the entrances to their lairs, croaking to one another in froglike voices. Their shortness of stature seems prodigious against the background of the furniture that fills their dark caverns — chests of drawers, vast cupboards, beds that look like giants' couches. To reach the furniture the dwarf women climb on chairs and benches; they hoist themselves up with their arms, making use of the ends of the high iron beds. And anyone climbing the steps of the Pendino di Santa Barbara for the first time feels like Gulliver in the Kingdom of Lilliput, or a servant at the Court of Madrid among Velasquez's dwarfs. The foreheads of these female dwarfs are scored with the same deep wrinkles as furrow the foreheads of the horrible old women portrayed by Goya. Nor should this Spanish analogy be thought arbitrary, for the district is Hispanic in character and still alive with memories of the long years when Naples was subject to Castilian domination. There is an air of old Spain about the streets, alleys, houses and mansions, the strong, sweet smells, the guttural voices, the long, musical laments that echo from balcony to balcony, and the raucous strains of the gramophones that issue from the depths of the dark caverns.

Taralli are little cakes made of sweet pastry; and the bakery halfway up the steps of the Pendino, from which at all hours of the day there emanates the appetizing smell of fresh, crisp taralli, is famous throughout Naples. When the baker thrusts his long wooden shovel into the red-hot mouth of the oven the dwarf women run up, stretching out their little hands, which are as dark and wrinkled as the hands of monkeys. Uttering loud cries in their raucous little voices they seize the dainty taralli, all hot and steaming, hobble rapidly to different parts of the alley, and deposit the taralli on shining brass trays. Then they sit on the doorsteps of their hovels with the trays on their knees and wait for customers, singing "Oh li taralli! oh li taralli belli cauri!" The smell of the taralli spreads all through the Pendino di Santa Barbara, and the dwarf women, squatting on their doorsteps, croak and laugh among themselves. And one, a young one perhaps, sings at a little window high up, and looks like a great spider poking its hairy head out of a crack in the wall.

Bald, toothless dwarf women go up and down the slimy stairway, supporting themselves with sticks or crutches, reeling along on their little short legs, lifting their knees up to their chins in order to mount the steps, or drag themselves along on all fours, whimpering and slobbering. They look like the little monsters in the paintings of Breughel or Bosch, and one day Jack and I saw one of them sitting on the threshold of a cavern with a sick dog in her arms. As it lay on her lap, in her tiny arms, it seemed a gigantic animal, a monstrous wild beast. Up came a companion of hers, and the two of them seized the sick dog, the one by the hind legs, the other by the head, and with great difficulty carried it into the hovel. It seemed as if they were carrying a wounded dinosaur. The voices that ascend from the depths of the caverns are shrill and guttural, and the wails of the dreadful children, who are tiny and wrinkled, like old dolls, resemble the mewling of a dying kitten. If you enter one of these hovels you see, in the fetid half-light, those great spiders with enormous heads dragging themselves across the floor, and you have to take care not to crush them beneath the soles of your shoes.

Occasionally we saw some of these dwarf women climbing the steps of the Pendino in the company of gigantic American soldiers, white or colored, with moist, shining eyes. Tugging them along by the trouser legs they would push them into their lairs. (The white soldiers, thank God, were always drunk.) I shuddered when I visualized the strange unions of those enormous men and those little monsters, on those high, vast beds.

And I would say to Jimmy Wren: "I am glad to see that those little dwarfs and your handsome soldiers like each other. Aren't you glad too, Jimmy?"

"Of course I'm glad too," Jimmy would answer, furiously chewing his gum.

"Do you think they'll get married?" I would say.

"Why not?" Jimmy would answer.

"Jimmy is a nice guy," Jack would say, "but you mustn't provoke him. He flares up easily."

"I'm a nice guy too," I would say, "and I'm glad to think that you have come from America to improve the Italian race. But for you those poor dwarfs would have remained spinsters. By ourselves, we poor Italians couldn't have done anything about it. It's a lucky thing that you people have come from America to marry our dwarf women."

"You will certainly be invited to the wedding breakfast," Jack would say. "Tu pourras prononcer un discours magnifique."

"Oui, Jack, un discours magnifique. But don't you think, Jimmy," I would say, "that the Allied military authorities ought to encourage marriages between these dwarf women and your handsome soldiers? It would be an excellent thing if your soldiers married those little dwarfs. As a race you are too tall. America needs to come down to our level, don't you think so, Jimmy?"

"Yes, I think so," Jimmy would answer, giving me a sidelong glance.

"You are too tall," I would say, "too handsome. It's immoral that the world should contain a race of men who are so tall, so handsome and so healthy. I should like all the American soldiers to get married to those little dwarfs. Those 'Italian brides' would score a tremendous hit in America. American civilization needs shorter legs."

"To hell with you," Jimmy would say, spitting on the ground.

"Il va te caresser la figure, si tu insistes," Jack would say.

"Yes, I know. Jimmy is a nice guy," I would say, laughing to myself.

It made me feel sick at heart to laugh in that way. But I should have been happy, truly happy, if all the American soldiers had one day gone back to America arm in arm with all the little dwarf women of Naples, Italy and Europe.

The "plague" had broken out in Naples on October 1, 1943 — the very day on which the Allied armies had entered that ill-starred city as liberators. October 1, 1943, is a memorable date in the history of Naples, both because it marks the beginning of the liberation of Italy and Europe from the anguish, shame and sufferings of war and slavery, and because it exactly coincided with the outbreak of the terrible plague which gradually spread from the unhappy city all over Italy and all over Europe.

The appalling suspicion that the fearful disease had been brought to Naples by the liberators themselves was certainly unjust; but it became a certainty in the minds of the people when they perceived, with a mixture of amazement and superstitious terror, that the Allied soldiers remained strangely immune from the contagion. Pink-faced, calm and smiling, they moved about in the midst of the plague-stricken mob without contracting the loathsome disease, which gathered its harvest of victims solely from among the civilian population, not only in Naples itself, but even in the country districts, spreading like a patch of oil into the territory liberated by the Allied armies as they laboriously drove the Germans northward.

But it was strictly forbidden, under threat of the severest penalties, to insinuate in public that the plague had been brought to Italy by the liberators. And it was dangerous to repeat the allegation in private, even in an undertone, since among the many loathsome effects of the plague the most loathsome was that it engendered in its victims a mad passion, a voluptuous avidity for delation. No sooner were they stricken with the disease than one and all began to inform against fathers, mothers, brothers, sons, husbands, lovers, relations and dearest friends — but never against themselves. Indeed, one of the most surprising and repulsive characteristics of this extraordinary plague was that it transformed the human conscience into a horrible, noisome ulcer.

The only remedy which the British and American military authorities had discovered for the disease was to forbid the Allied soldiers to enter the most seriously infected areas of the city. On every wall one read the legends "Off Limits" and "Out of Bounds," surmounted by the aulic emblem of the plague — a black circle within which were depicted two black bars in the form of a cross, similar to the pair of crossed shinbones that appears beneath a skull on the saddlecloth of a funeral carriage.

Within a short space of time the whole of Naples was declared "off limits" with the exception of a few streets in the center of the city. But the areas most frequented by the liberators were in fact those which were "off limits," i.e., the most infected and therefore forbidden areas, since it is in the nature of man, and especially of the soldiers of all ages and every army, to prefer forbidden things to those that are permitted. And so the contagion, whether it had been brought to Naples by the liberators, or whether the latter carried it from one part of the city to another, from the infected areas to the healthy, very soon reached a terrible pitch of violence, rendered abominable, almost diabolical, by its grotesque, obscene manifestations, which were suggestive of a macabre public celebration, a funereal kermis. Drunken soldiers danced with women who were almost or completely naked in the squares and streets, in the midst of the wreckage of the houses that had been destroyed in the air raids. There was a mad orgy of drinking, eating, gaiety, singing, laughing, prodigality and revelry, amid the frightful stench that emanated from the countless hundreds of corpses buried beneath the ruins.

This was a plague profoundly different from, but no less horrible than, the epidemics which from time to time devastated Europe during the Middle Ages. The extraordinary thing about this most modern of diseases was that it corrupted not the body but the soul. The limbs remained seemingly intact, but within the integument of the healthy flesh the soul festered and rotted. It was a kind of moral plague, against which it seemed that there was no defense. The first to be infected were the women, who in every nation constitute the weakest bulwark against vice, and an open door to every form of evil. And this seemed an amazing and most lamentable thing, inasmuch as during the years of slavery and war, right up to the day of the promised and eagerly awaited liberation, the women — not only in Naples, but throughout Italy and Europe — had proved, amid the universal wretchedness and misfortune, that they possessed greater dignity and greater strength of mind than the men. In Naples and in every other city of Europe the women had refused to give themselves to the Germans. Only the prostitutes had had relations with the enemy, and even they had not done so openly, but in secret, either to avoid having to endure the sharp revulsion of popular feeling or because they themselves considered that to have such relations was to be guilty of the most infamous crime that a woman could commit during those years.

And now, as a result of this loathsome plague, which first corrupted the feminine sense of honor and dignity, prostitution on the most appalling scale had brought shame to every hovel and every mansion. But why call it shame? Such was the baneful power of the contagion that self-prostitution had become a praiseworthy act, almost a proof of patriotism, and all, men and women, far from blushing at the thought of it, seemed to glory in their own and the universal degradation. True, many, whose sense of justice was warped by despair, almost made excuses for the plague, implying that the women used the disease as a pretext for becoming prostitutes, and that they sought in the plague the justification of their shame.

But a more intimate knowledge of the disease subsequently revealed that such a suspicion was mischievous. For the first to despair of their lot were the women; and I myself have heard many bewailing and cursing this pitiless plague which drove them, with an irresistible violence their feeble virtue was powerless to withstand, to prostitute themselves like bitches. Such, alas, is the nature of women, who often seek to buy with tears forgiveness for their deeds of shame, and pity too. But in this case one must perforce forgive them and have pity on them.

If such was the lot of the women, no less piteous and horrible was that of the men. No sooner were they infected than they lost all self-respect. They lent themselves to the most ignoble transactions and committed the most sordid acts of self-abasement; they dragged themselves on all fours through the mire, kissing the boots of their "liberators" (who were disgusted by such extreme and unasked-for abjectness), not only to obtain pardon for the sufferings and humiliations which they had undergone during the years of slavery and war, but so that they might have the honor of being trampled underfoot by their new masters; they spat on their own country's flag and publicly sold their own wives, daughters and mothers. They did all this, they said, to save their country. Yet those who seemed on the surface to be immune from the disease fell sick of a nauseating malady which made them ashamed of being Italians and even of belonging to the human race. It must be admitted that they did all they could to be unworthy of the name of men. Few indeed were those who remained free from taint, their consciences seemingly impervious to the disease; and they went about in fear and trembling, despised by all, unwelcome witnesses of the universal shame.

The suspicion, which later became a conviction, that the plague had been brought to Europe by the liberators themselves had filled the people with profound and heartfelt grief. Although it is an ancient tradition that the vanquished hate their conquerors, the people of Naples did not hate the Allies. They had awaited them with longing, they had welcomed them with joy. Their thousand-year-long experience of wars and foreign invasions had taught them that it is the habit of conquerors to reduce those whom they have vanquished to slavery. Instead of slavery, the Allies had brought them freedom. And the people had immediately loved these magnificent soldiers — so young, so handsome, so well groomed — whose teeth were so white and whose lips were so red. In all those centuries of invasions, of wars won and lost, Europe had never seen such elegant, clean, courteous soldiers. Always they were newly shaven; their uniforms were impeccable; their ties were tied with meticulous care; their shirts were always spotless; their shoes were eternally new and shining; they had never a tear in their trousers or at their elbows, never a button missing. Such were these wonderful armies, born, like Venus, of the sea foam. They contained not a soldier who had a boil, a decayed tooth, even a pimple on his face. Never had Europe seen soldiers who were so free from infection, without the smallest microbe either in the folds of their skin or in the recesses of their consciences. And what hands they had — white, well looked after, always protected by immaculate shammy-leather gloves! But what touched the people of Naples most of all was the kindliness of their liberators, especially the Americans: their urbane nonchalance, their humanity, their innocent, cordial smiles — the smiles of honest, goodhearted, ingenuous, overgrown boys. If ever it was an honor to lose a war, it was certainly a great honor for the people of Naples, and for all the other conquered peoples of Europe, to have lost this one to soldiers who were so courteous, elegant and neatly dressed, so goodhearted and generous.

And yet everything that these magnificent soldiers touched was at once corrupted. No sooner did the luckless inhabitants of the liberated countries grasp the hands of their liberators than they began to fester and to stink. It was enough that an Allied soldier should lean out of his jeep to smile at a woman, to give her face a fleeting caress, and the same woman, who until that moment had preserved her dignity and purity, would change into a prostitute. It was enough that a child should put into its mouth a caramel offered to it by an American soldier, and its innocent soul would be corrupted.

The liberators themselves were terrified and deeply affected by this dire scourge. "It is human to feel compassion for the afflicted," writes Boccaccio in his introduction to the *De-*

cameron, with reference to the terrible plague which swept Florence in 1348. But the Allied soldiers, especially the Americans, faced with the pitiable spectacle of the plague of Naples, did not only feel compassion for the unhappy people of that city: they felt compassion for themselves as well. The reason was that for some time past the suspicion had been growing in their ingenuous and honest minds that the source of the terrible contagion was in their frank, timid smiles, in their eyes, so full of human sympathy, in their affectionate caresses. The source of the plague was in their compassion, in their very desire to help these unfortunate people, to alleviate their miseries, to succor them in the tremendous disaster that had overtaken them. The source of the disease was in the very hand which they stretched out in brotherhood to this conquered people.

Perhaps it was written that the freedom of Europe must be born not of liberation, but of the plague. Perhaps it was written that, just as liberation had been born of the sufferings of war and slavery, so freedom must be born of the new and terrible sufferings caused by the plague which liberation had brought with it. The price of freedom is high — far higher than that of slavery. And it is not paid in gold, nor in blood, nor in the most noble sacrifices, but in cowardice, in prostitution, in treachery, and in everything that is rotten in the human soul.

On that day too we crossed the threshold of the foyer du soldat, and Jack, going up to the French sergeant, asked him timidly, almost in confidence, "si on avait vu par là le lieutenant Lyautey."

"Oui, mon colonel, je l'ai vu tout à l'heure," replied the sergeant with a smile. "Attendez un instant, mon colonel, je vais voir s'il est toujours là."

"Voilà un sergent bien aimable," said Jack to me, flushing with pleasure. "Les sergents français sont les plus aimables sergents du monde."

"Je regrette, mon colonel," said the sergeant, coming back

after a few moments, "le lieutenant Lyautey vient justement de partir."

"Merci, vous êtes bien aimable," said Jack. "Au revoir, mon ami."

"Au revoir, mon colonel," replied the sergeant with a smile.

"Ah, qu'il fait bon d'entendre parler français," said Jack as he went out of the Caffè Caflisch. His face had lit up with childish joy, and at such moments I felt that I really loved him. I was glad to like a better man than myself. I had always despised or felt bitter toward better men than myself, and this was the first time I had ever been glad to like such a man.

"Let's go and look at the sea, Malaparte."

Crossing the Piazza Reale, we descended the Scesa del Gigante and leaned on the parapet at the bottom. "C'est un des plus anciens parapets de l'Europe," said Jack, who knew the whole of Rimbaud by heart.

The sun was setting, and little by little the sea was turning the color of wine, which is the color of the sea in Homer. But in the distance, between Sorrento and Capri, the water and the high rugged cliffs, the mountains and their shadows were slowly taking on a flame-bright coral hue, as if the coral reefs which cover the bottom of the gulf were slowly emerging from the depths of the sea, tinging the sky blood-red with their reflected glory, as of old. Far away the barrier of Sorrento, thick with orchards, rose from the sea like a hard slab of green marble, which the sun, as it sank below the farther horizon, smote with its weary, oblique rays, bringing out the warm, golden glory of the oranges and the cold, bluish glitter of the lemons.

Like an ancient bone, thin and worn smooth by wind and rain, Vesuvius rose, solitary and naked, into the vast cloudless sky. Little by little it began to glow with a pink, furtive light, as if the fires within its womb were showing through its hard, pallid lava crust, which shone like ivory: until the moon, like an egg shell, crossed the edge of the crater, and rose clear and ecstatic, marvelously remote, into the blue abyss of the evening. From the farthermost horizon, as if borne on the wind, the first shadows of the night climbed into the sky. And whether on account of the magical limpidity of the moonlight, or of the cold cruelty of that unreal, ghostly scene, the moment had in it a delicate, fleeting sadness, like a presage of a happy death.

Ragged boys, seated on the stone parapet which rose sheer from the sea, sang with their eyes turned to the sky, their heads tilted slightly on to their shoulders. Their faces were pale and thin, their eyes blinded by hunger. They sang as the blind sing, their faces uplifted, their eyes fixed upon the heavens. Human hunger has a wonderfully sweet, pure voice. There is nothing human about the voice of hunger. It is a voice that arises from a mysterious level of man's nature, wherein lie the roots of that profound sense of life which is life itself, our most secret, most intense life. The air was clear and sweet to the lips. A light breeze, redolent of salt and seaweed, blew from the sea. The mournful cry of the gulls rippled the golden reflection of the moon upon the waves, and far away, low on the horizon, the pallid ghost of Vesuvius sank little by little into the silver mist of the night. That cruel, inhuman scene, so insensible to the hunger and despair of men, was made purer and less real by the singing of the boys.

"There is no kindliness," said Jack, "no compassion in this marvelous Nature."

"It is malignant," I said. "It hates us, it is our enemy. It hates men."

"Elle aime nous voir souffrir," said Jack in a low voice.

"It stares at us with cold eyes, full of frozen hatred and contempt."

"Before it," said Jack, "I feel guilty, ashamed, miserable. It is not Christian. It hates men because they suffer."

"It is jealous of men's sufferings," I said.

I liked Jack because he alone, among all my American friends, felt guilty, ashamed and miserable before the cruel, inhuman beauty of that sky, that sea, those islands far away on the horizon. He alone realized that this Nature is not

Christian, that it lies outside the frontiers of Christianity, and that this scene was not the face of Christ, but the image of a world without God, in which men are left alone to suffer without hope. He alone realized how much mystery there is in the story and the lives of the people of Naples, and how their story and their lives are so little dependent on the will of man. There were, among my American friends, many intelligent, cultured and sensitive young men; but they despised Naples, Italy and Europe, they despised us because they believed that we alone were responsible for our miseries and misfortunes, our acts of cowardice, our crimes, our perfidies, our infamies. They did not understand what mystery and inhumanity there is behind our miseries and our misfortunes. Some said: "You are not Christians: you are pagans." And there was a hint of scorn in their voices as they uttered the word "pagans." I liked Jack because he alone realized that the word "pagan" does not in itself reveal the deep-seated, historic, mysterious causes of our suffering, and that our miseries, our misfortunes, our infamies, our way of being miserable and happy, the very reasons for our greatness and our degradation, are outside the realm of Christian ethics.

Although he called himself Cartesian, affecting to put his trust wholly and always in reason and to believe that reason can probe and explain everything, his attitude to Naples, Italy and Europe was one of affection tempered both with respect and with suspicion. To him, as to all Americans, Naples had been an unexpected and distressing revelation. He had believed he was setting foot in a world dominated by reason and ruled by the human conscience; and he had found himself without warning in a mysterious country, where men and the circumstances that make up their lives seemed to be governed not by reason and conscience, but by obscure subterranean forces.

Jack had traveled all over Europe, but he had never been to Italy. He had landed at Salerno on September 9, 1943, from the deck of an L.S.T. — a landing barge — amid the din and smoke of the explosions and the hoarse cries of the soldiers as they hobbled rapidly across the sands of Paestum under the fire of German machine guns. In his ideal Cartesian Europe, the "alte Kontinent" of Goethe, governed by mind and reason, Italy was still the land of his beloved Virgil and Horace. It suggested to his imagination the placid green and blue panorama of his own Virginia, where he had completed his studies and spent the better part of his life, and where he had his home, his family and his books. In the Italy of his heart the peristyles of the Georgian houses of Virginia and the marble columns of the Forum, Mount Vernon and the Palatine combined in his mind's eye to form a familiar scene, in which the brilliant green of the fields and woods blended with the brilliant white of the marble under a limpid blue sky like that which stretches in an arch above the Capitol.

When, at dawn on September 9, 1943, Jack had leapt from the deck of an L.S.T. on to the beach at Paestum, near Salerno, he had seen a wonderful vision rising before his eyes through the red cloud of dust thrown up by the caterpillars of the tanks, the explosions of the German grenades and the tumult of the men and machines hurrying up from the sea. On the edge of a plain thickly covered with myrtles and cypresses, to which the bare mountains of Cilento, so like the mountains of Latium, provide a background, he had seemed to see the columns of the Temple of Neptune. Ah, this was Italy, the Italy of Virgil, the Italy of Aeneas! And he had wept for joy, he had wept with religious emotion, throwing himself on his knees upon the sandy shore, as Aeneas had done when he landed from the Trojan trireme on the sandy beach at the mouth of the Tiber, opposite the mountains of Latium, with their sprinkling of castles and white temples set amid the deep green of the ancient Latin woods.

But the classical setting of the Doric columns of the temples of Paestum concealed from his eyes a secret, mysterious Italy. It concealed Naples, that terrible, wonderful prototype of an unknown Europe, situated outside the realm of Cartesian logic — that *other* Europe of whose existence he had until that day had only a vague suspicion, and whose mysteries and secrets, now that he was gradually probing them, filled him with a wondrous terror.

"Naples," I told him, "is the most mysterious city in Europe. It is the only city of the ancient world that has not perished like Ilium, Nineveh and Babylon. It is the only city in the world that did not founder in the colossal shipwreck of ancient civilization. Naples is a Pompeii which was never buried. It is not a city: it is a world — the ancient, pre-Christian world — that has survived intact on the surface of the modern world. You could not have chosen a more dangerous place than Naples for a landing in Europe. Your tanks run the risk of being swallowed up in the black slime of antiquity, as in a quicksand. If you had landed in Belgium, Holland, Denmark, or even in France, your scientific spirit, your technical knowledge, your vast wealth of material resources might have given you victory not merely over the German army, but over the very spirit of Europe — that *other,* secret Europe of which Naples is the mysterious image, the naked ghost. But here in Naples your tanks, your guns, your machines provoke a smile. They are scrap iron. Jack, do you remember the words of the Neapolitan who, on the day you entered Naples, was watching your endless columns of tanks passing along Via Toledo? *'What beautiful rust!'* Here, your particular American brand of humanity stands revealed in all its nakedness — defenseless, dangerously vulnerable. You are only big boys, Jack. You cannot understand Naples, you will never understand Naples."

"Je crois," said Jack, "que Naples n'est pas impénétrable à la raison. Je suis cartésien, hélas!"

"Do you think, then, that Cartesian logic can help you, for instance, to understand Hitler?"

"Why particularly Hitler?"

"Because Hitler too is an element in the mystery of Europe, because Hitler too belongs to that *other* Europe which Cartesian logic cannot penetrate. Do you think, then, that you can explain Hitler solely with the help of Descartes?"

"Je l'explique parfaitement," replied Jack.

Then I told him that Heidelberg Witz which all the students in the German universities laughingly pass from one to the other. At a conference of German scientists held at

Heidelberg, all present found themselves agreed after lengthy discussion in asserting that the world can be explained with the aid of reason alone. At the end of the discussion an old professor, who until that moment had remained silent, with a silk hat jammed down over his eyes, got up and said: "You who explain everything — could you tell me how on earth this thing has appeared on my head tonight?" And, slowly removing the silk hat, he revealed a cigar, a genuine Havana, which was projecting from his bald cranium.

"Ah, ah, c'est merveilleux!" said Jack, laughing. "Do you mean, then, that Hitler is a Havana cigar?"

"No, I mean that Hitler is *like* that Havana cigar."

"C'est merveilleux! un cigare!" said Jack; and he added, as though seized by a sudden inspiration, "Have a drink, Malaparte." But he corrected himself, and said in French: "Allons boire quelque chose."

The bar of the P.B.S. was crowded with officers who already had many glasses' start on us. We sat down in a corner and began to drink. Jack looked into his glass, and laughed; he banged his fist on his knee, and laughed; and every so often he exclaimed: "C'est merveilleux! un cigare!" — until his eyes grew dim and he said to me, laughing — "Tu crois vraiment qu'Hitler . . ."

"Mais oui, naturellement."

Then we went in to supper, and sat down at the big table reserved for senior officers of the P.B.S. All the officers were in a merry mood, and they smiled at me sympathetically because I was "the bastard Italian liaison officer, that bastard S.O.B." At a certain point Jack began telling the story of the conference of German scientists at Heidelberg University, and all the senior officers of the P.B.S. looked at me in amazement, exclaiming: "What? A cigar? Do you mean that Hitler is a cigar?"

"He means that Hitler is a Havana cigar," said Jack, laughing.

And Colonel Brand, offering me a cigar across the table, said to me with a sympathetic smile: "Do you like cigars? This is a genuine Havana."

THE   VIRGIN

OF   NAPLES

● "Have you ever seen a virgin?" Jimmy asked me one day as we came out of the baker's shop on the Pendino di Santa Barbara, crunching the lovely hot, crisp taralli between our teeth.

"Yes, but only from a distance."

"No, I mean close up. Have you ever seen a virgin close up?"

"No, never close up."

"Come on, Malaparte," said Jimmy.

At first I was unwilling to follow him. I knew that he would show me something distressing and humiliating, some appalling evidence of the depths of physical and moral humiliation to which man can sink in his despair. I do not like to witness the spectacle of human baseness; it is repugnant to me to sit, as judge or as spectator, watching men as they descend the last rungs of the ladder of degradation. I am always afraid they will turn round and smile at me.

"Come on, come on, don't be silly," said Jimmy, walking ahead of me through the maze of alleys that is Forcella.

I do not like to see how low man can stoop in order to live. I preferred the war to the "plague" which, after the liberation, had defiled, corrupted and humiliated us all — men, women and children. Before the liberation we had fought and suffered *in order not to die*. Now we were fighting and suffering *in order to live*. There is a profound difference between fighting to avoid death and fighting in order to live. Men who fight to avoid death preserve their dignity and one and all — men, women and children — defend it jealously, tenaciously, fiercely. The men did not bow the knee. They fled into the mountains and the woods, they lived in caves, they fought like wolves against the invaders. They were fighting to avoid death. It was a noble, dignified, honest fight. The women did not throw their bodies onto the black market in order to buy lipsticks, silk stockings, cigarettes or bread. They suffered the pangs of hunger, but they did not sell themselves. They did not sell their men to the enemy. They were willing to see their own children die of hunger rather than sell themselves or their men. Only the prostitutes sold themselves to the enemy. Before their liberation the peoples of Europe suffered with a wonderful dignity. They fought with their heads high. They were fighting *to avoid death*. And when men fight to avoid death they cling with a tenacity born of desperation to all that constitutes the living and eternal part of human life, the essence, the noblest and purest element of life: dignity, pride, freedom of conscience. They fight to save their souls.

But after the liberation men had had to fight *in order to live*. It is a humiliating, horrible thing, a shameful necessity, a fight for life. Only for life. Only to save one's own skin. It is no longer a fight against oppression, a fight for freedom, for human dignity, for honor. It is a fight against hunger. It is a fight for a crust of bread, for a little fuel, for a rag with which to cover the nakedness of one's own children, for a handful of straw on which to lie. When men are fighting in order to live, everything, even an empty jar, a cigar stub, a piece of orange peel, a crust of dry bread rescued from the rubbish heap, a meatless bone — everything has for them an enormous, decisive value. To live, men will perform the meanest actions; to live, they will stoop to every sort of infamy, every sort of crime. For a crust of bread we are ready, all of us, to sell our own wives, our own daughters, to defile our own mothers, to sell our brothers and our friends, to prostitute ourselves to other men. We are ready to go down on our knees, to grovel, to lick the boots of any who can assuage our hunger, to bend our backs beneath the whip, smilingly to wipe our cheeks when men have spat upon us; and all this with a humble, gentle smile, with eyes full of a ravenous, animal hope, a stupendous hope.

I preferred the war to the plague. Within the space of a day, within a few hours, all — men, women and children — had been infected by the horrible, mysterious disease. What amazed and terrified the people was the sudden, violent, fatal character of that fearful epidemic. The plague had been able to achieve more in a few days than tyranny had done in twenty years of universal humiliation, or war in three years of hunger, grief and atrocious suffering. These people who bartered themselves, their honor, their bodies and the flesh of their own children in the streets — could they possibly be the people who a few days before, in those same streets, had given such conspicuous and horrible proof of their courage and fire in face of German opposition?

When, on October 1, 1943, the liberators reached the first suburban houses in the Torre del Greco district, the people of Naples, in a ferocious battle which lasted four days, had already chased the Germans from the city. The Neapolitans had previously risen against the Germans at the beginning of September, in the days that followed the armistice; but that first revolt had been suppressed with implacable ferocity amid a welter of blood. The liberators, whom the people awaited with eager longing, had at some points been hurled back into the water; at others, near Salerno, they resisted tenaciously with their backs to the sea; and the Germans had fought on with renewed heart and fury. Toward the end of September, when the Germans had begun to kidnap the menfolk in the streets, herding them into their vehicles with the intention of carrying them off to Germany as slaves, the people of Naples, goaded on or led by bands of infuriated women who uttered cries of "Not the men!" had fallen unarmed upon the Germans and had cornered and massacred them in the alleys, crushing them beneath an avalanche of tiles, stones, articles of furniture and boiling water dropped from roof tops, balconies and windows. Groups of courageous boys hurled themselves at the panzers, raising aloft with both hands bundles of flaming straw, and died in the act of setting fire to those steel tortoises. Innocent-looking little girls smilingly displayed bunches of grapes to the thirsty Germans, cooped up in the bellies of their sun-scorched tanks; and as soon as the Germans raised the turret tops and leaned out to receive the grapes so kindly offered parties of boys, who had been lying in ambush, exterminated them with a shower of hand grenades taken from their dead foes. Many were the boys and girls who lost their lives in the execution of these cruel but selfless stratagems.

Trucks and trolleys, overturned in the streets, blocked the passage of the German columns as they rushed up to lend support to the troops resisting at Eboli and Cava dei Tirreni. For the people of Naples did not assail the Germans in the rear as they retreated. They faced them, without weapons, while the Battle of Salerno was still in progress, though it was madness for unarmed citizens, weakened by three years of hunger and fierce, continuous air raids, to resist the passage of the German columns as they drove through Naples on their way to attack the Allied invaders who had landed at Salerno.

The boys and women were the most to be dreaded during those four days of strife, in which no quarter was asked for or given. I myself saw the corpses of many German soldiers, still unburied two days after the liberation of Naples, with lacerated faces and throats mangled by human teeth; and the tooth marks could still be seen on the flesh. Many had been disfigured by scissors. Many lay in pools of blood with long nails driven into their skulls. For lack of other weapons the boys had driven those long nails into the Germans' heads, knocking them in with large stones, while ten or twenty infuriated lads pinned their victims to the ground.

"Come on, come on, don't be silly!" said Jimmy, walking ahead of me through the maze of alleys that is Forcella.

I preferred the war to the plague. In a few days Naples had become an abyss of shame and sorrow, an inferno of degradation. And yet the dread disease could not destroy that wonderful sentiment which the Neapolitans preserved in their hearts after countless centuries of hunger and slavery. Nothing can ever destroy the Neapolitans' historic, wonderful sense of pity. They did not only pity others: they pitied themselves too. No people can nourish a sense of freedom if it lacks a sense of pity. Even those who sold their own wives and daughters, even the women who prostituted themselves for a package of cigarettes, even the boys who prostituted themselves for a box of caramels pitied themselves. It was an extraordinary sentiment, a wonderful kind of pity. Because of this sentiment, only because of their historic, undying sense of pity, they will one day be free — free men.

"Oh, Jimmy, they love freedom," I said. "They love freedom so much! They love American boys, too. They love freedom, American boys, and cigarettes too. Even the children love freedom and caramels, Jimmy, even the children pity themselves. It's a splendid thing, Jimmy, to eat caramels instead of dying of hunger. Don't you think so too, Jimmy?"

"Come on," said Jimmy, spitting on the ground.

So I went with Jimmy to see the "virgin." The scene of her

activities was a basso at the end of an alley near the Piazza Olivella. A small crowd of Allied soldiers was loitering outside the door of the hovel. There were also three or four American soldiers, a few Poles, and some English sailors. We joined the queue and waited our turn.

After a wait of about half an hour, during which we moved forward a yard every two minutes, we found ourselves at the entrance to the hovel. The interior of the room was screened from our gaze by a red curtain, patched and grease-stained. At the entrance stood a middle-aged man, dressed in black. He was very thin, with a stubbly, pale face. A dingy black felt hat was set at a meticulous angle on his thick gray hair. His two hands were clasped together on his chest, and between his fingers he clutched a bundle of bank notes.

"One dollar each," he said. "A hundred lire each person."

We entered and looked about us. It was the usual Neapolitan interior: a windowless room with a small door at the end, a vast bed against the wall facing us, and along the other walls a dressing table, a rough iron washstand enameled white, a chest of drawers, and, between the bed and the chest of drawers, a table. On the dressing table was a large glass bell, under which stood a number of colored wax statuettes representing the Holy Family. The walls were covered with cheap oleographs depicting scenes from *Cavalleria Rusticana* and *Tosca*, a picture of Vesuvius surmounted by columns of smoke, like a horse decked with plumes for the Piedigrotta carnival, and photographs of women, children and old men, not, to be sure, taken from life, but after death, with their subjects stretched out on their deathbeds and festooned with flowers. In the corner between the bed and the dressing table stood a miniature altar with a statue of the Virgin upon it, lit by a small oil lamp. The bed was draped with an enormous sky-blue silk counterpane, whose long gilt fringe touched the green and red clay floor. On the edge of the bed sat a girl, smoking.

She sat with her legs dangling from the bed, and smoked silently, lost in thought, her elbows resting on her knees, her face buried in her hands. She looked very young, but she had rather lacklustre eyes, the eyes of an old woman. Her coiffure conformed to the baroque style cultivated by the capere of the poorer quarters — a style modeled on the characteristic headdress of Neapolitan Madonnas of the seventeenth century. Her curly, lustrous black hair was filled out with horsehair and ribbons and stuffed with tow. It rose from her head like a castle, creating the illusion that she had a tall black miter resting on her brow. There was something Byzantine about the long, narrow, pale face, whose pallor was visible through a thick layer of paint. Byzantine too was the set of the large, slanting, jet-black eyes beneath the deep, smooth brow. But the fleshy lips, magnified by a vivid splash of rouge, lent an air of sensuality and insolence to the exquisite, statuesque melancholy of the face. She wore a red silk dress, discreetly low at the neck, and flesh-colored silk stockings, and her small, plump feet, which were encased in a pair of gaping, formless black felt slippers, swung idly to and fro. Her dress had long sleeves, narrow at the wrists, and at her throat hung one of those necklaces of pale pink coral, mellowed with age, which are the pride of every poor Neapolitan girl.

She smoked in silence, looking fixedly in the direction of the door, with a haughty air of detachment. In spite of the insolent character of her red silk dress, her baroque hair style, her thick fleshy lips and her gaping slippers, her vulgarity was quite impersonal. It seemed rather to be a reflection of the vulgarity of her environment, of that vulgarity which surrounded her on all sides yet scarcely touched her. Her ears were very small and exquisite, so white and translucent that they seemed artificial, as if they were made of wax. When I entered she fixed her eyes on my captain's three gold pips and smiled contemptuously, turning her face with an almost imperceptible movement toward the wall. There were about ten of us in the room. I was the only Italian spectator. No one spoke.

"That is all. The next in five minutes," came the voice of the man standing at the entrance, behind the red curtain.

Then he thrust his head into the room through a gap in the curtain and added: "Ready?"

The girl threw her cigarette on the floor, grasped the fringe of her petticoat with the tips of her fingers and slowly raised it. First her knees appeared, gently gripped by the silk sheath of her stockings, then the bare skin of her thighs. She remained for a moment in this posture, a sad Veronica, her face severe, her mouth half-open in an expression of contempt. Then, slowly turning on her back, she lay at full length on the bed.

"She is a virgin. You can touch. Don't be afraid. She doesn't bite. She is a virgin. A real virgin," said the man, thrusting his head into the room through the gap in the curtain.

A Negro stretched out his hand. Someone laughed, and seemed to repent of it. The "virgin" did not move, but stared at the Negro with eyes full of fear and loathing. I looked about me. Everyone was pale — pale with fear and loathing.

The girl raised herself up with a jerk, pulled down her dress, and with a rapid movement of the hand snatched the cigarette from the mouth of an English sailor who was standing near the edge of the bed.

"Get out, please," said the man's head, and we all slowly filed out through the little door at the end of the room, shuffling across the floor, overcome with shame and embarrassment.

"You people ought to be well satisfied to see Naples brought to this pass," I said to Jimmy when we were outside.

"It certainly isn't my fault," said Jimmy.

"Oh, no," I said, "it certainly isn't your fault. But it must give you all great satisfaction to feel that you have conquered a country like this," I added. "Without such scenes how would you make yourselves feel that you were conquerors? Be frank, Jimmy: you would not feel that you were conquerors without such scenes."

"Naples has always been like that," said Jimmy.

"No, it has never been like that," I said. "Such things have never been seen in Naples before. If you didn't like such things, if scenes like that didn't amuse you, they wouldn't happen in Naples. Such sights wouldn't be seen in Naples."

"*We* didn't make Naples," said Jimmy. "We found it ready made."

"*You* didn't make Naples," I said, "but it has never been like this before. If America had lost the war think of all the American virgins in New York or Chicago who would show themselves for a dollar. If you had lost the war there would be an American virgin on that bed, instead of that poor Neapolitan girl."

"Don't talk nonsense," said Jimmy. "Even if we had lost the war you wouldn't see things like that in America."

"You would have seen worse things in America if you had lost the war," I said. "To make himself feel that he is a hero every conqueror needs to see these things."

"Don't talk rubbish," said Jimmy.

"I would rather lose the war and spend my time sitting on that bed like that poor girl than go and inspect her for the pleasure and glory of feeling that I was a conqueror."

"You came to see her too," said Jimmy. "Why did you come?"

"Because I am a coward, Jimmy, because I too need to see such things, so that I may feel that I am one of the defeated — that I am one of the unfortunate ones."

"Why don't you go and sit on that bed too," said Jimmy, "if it gives you so much pleasure to feel that you are on the side of the conquered?"

"Tell me the truth, Jimmy — would you be willing to pay a dollar to come and see me?"

"I wouldn't even pay a cent to come and see you," said Jimmy, spitting on the ground.

"Why not? If America had lost the war I should immediately go over there to see Washington's descendants showing themselves in front of the conquerors."

"Shut up!" cried Jimmy, forcibly gripping my arm.

"Why wouldn't you come and see me, Jimmy? All the

soldiers of the Fifth Army would come and see me — even General Clark. Even you would come, Jimmy. You would pay not one dollar, but two or even three, to see a man unbutton his trousers. All conquerors need to see these things, to convince themselves that they have won the war."

"You're all a lot of mad swine, in Europe," said Jimmy, "that's what you are."

"Be frank with me, Jimmy — when you go back to America, to your home in Cleveland, Ohio, it will give you pleasure to tell about that poor Italian girl."

"Don't say that," said Jimmy in a low voice.

"Forgive me, Jimmy — I hate it for your sake and for mine. It isn't your fault or ours, I know. But it makes me sick to think of some things. You shouldn't have taken me to see that girl. I shouldn't have come with you to see that horrible thing. I hate it for your sake and for mine, Jimmy. I feel miserable and cowardly. You Americans are fine fellows, and there are some things that you understand better than many other people. Isn't it a fact, Jimmy, that there are some things that you understand too?"

"Yes, I understand," said Jimmy in a low voice, gripping my arm tightly.

I felt miserable and cowardly, as I had done on the day when I climbed the Gradoni di Chiaia, in Naples. The Gradoni are that long flight of steps leading up from Via Chiaia to Santa Teresella degli Spagnoli, the miserable quarter where once were the barracks and places of amusement of the Spanish soldiers. The sirocco was blowing, and the clothes hanging out to dry on the lines which stretched from house to house flapped noisily in the wind like flags: Naples had not thrown its flags at the feet of the conquerors and the conquered. During the night a fire had destroyed a large part of the magnificent palace of the Dukes of Cellamare, situated in Via Chiaia, not far from the Gradoni; and the warm humid air was still pervaded by a dry odor of burnt wood and cold smoke. The sky was gray; it seemed to consist of dirty paper, covered with specks of mould.

On days when the sirocco prevails Naples, huddled beneath that scabious, mouldy sky, assumes an appearance that is at once both miserable and arrogant. The houses, the streets and the people exhibited a self-conscious air of abject, baleful insolence. In the distance, above the sea, the sky was like the skin of a lizard, mottled green and white, dripping with the cold, dull moistness peculiar to the skin of reptiles. Gray clouds with greenish edges flecked the dirty blue of the horizon, on which the warm squalls of the sirocco left a trail of oily yellow streaks. The sea was green and brown in color, like the skin of a toad, and the smell of the sea was pungent and sweet, like the smell of a toad's skin. From the mouth of Vesuvius belched forth a dense yellow smoke, which, re-pelled by the low vault of the cloudy sky, opened out like the foliage of an immense pine tree, interspersed with black shad-ows and large green cracks. And the vineyards dotted about the purple fields of cold lava, the pines and cypresses rooted in the deserts of ashes, amid which the greys and pinks and blues of the houses that clung to the sides of the volcano stood out with sombre prominence, took on gloomy, deathly tints in that panorama, which was bathed in a greenish half-light broken by vivid yellows and purples.

When the sirocco blows the human skin perspires, the cheekbones sparkle in faces dripping with grimy sweat and overlaid with a black down which leaves a dirty moist shadow about eyes, lips and ears. Even voices sound thick and lazy, and words have an unwonted meaning, a mysterious signifi-cance, as though they belonged to a forbidden jargon. The people walk in silence, as though oppressed by a secret an-guish, and the children pass long hours seated mutely on the ground, nibbling crusts of bread or fruit black with flies, or looking at the cracked walls on which can be seen the motion-less outlines of lizards, embedded by mildew in the ancient plaster. The air is heavy with the perfume of the brilliant carnations which stand in terracotta vases on the window sills. The voice of a woman, singing, ascends now from this side, now from that: the song echoes slowly from window to window, coming to rest on the sills like a weary bird.

The odor of cold smoke from the fire in the Cellamare palace pervaded the dense, sticky atmosphere. Sadly I inhaled that odor of a captured city, sacked and consigned to the flames, the ancient odor of an Ilium enveloped in smoke from burning buildings and funeral pyres, prostrate on the shore of a sea crowded with enemy ships, under a mould-specked sky, beneath which the flags of the conquering peoples, who had hurried forward from all the corners of the earth to take part in the long siege, grew mouldy in the wind that blew in hoarse, steamy, fetid gusts from the far horizon.

I walked down Via Chiaia in the direction of the sea, surrounded by crowds of Allied soldiers who thronged the pavements, jostling and pushing one another and shouting in a hundred strange, unfamiliar tongues, as they made their way along the banks of the raging river of vehicles which flowed tumultuously through the narrow street. And I felt amazingly ridiculous in my green uniform, which was riddled with bullets from our own rifles, and had been stripped from the corpse of an English soldier who had fallen at El Alamein or Tobruk. I felt lost in that hostile throng of foreign soldiers, who pushed me on my way with violent shoves, used elbows and shoulders to thrust me to one side, and turned back, looking contemptuously at the gold braid on my uniform and saying to me in furious voices: "You bastard, you son of a bitch, you dirty Italian officer."

And I thought to myself as I walked: "Who knows how one says 'You bastard, you son of a bitch, you dirty Italian officer' in French? And how one says it in Russian, in Serb, in Polish, in Danish, in Dutch, in Norwegian, in Arabic? Who knows, I thought, how one says it in Brazilian? And in Chinese? And in Indian, in Bantu, in Madagascan? Who knows how one says it in German?" And I laughed as I thought that that conquerors' jargon must certainly translate very well into German too — even into German — because German too, compared with Italian, was the language of a victorious people. I laughed as I thought that all the languages of the earth, even Bantu and Chinese, even German, were the languages of

victorious peoples, and that we alone, we Italians alone, in
Via Chiaia, Naples, and in all the streets of all the cities of
Italy, spoke a language which was not that of a victorious
people. And I felt proud of being a poor "Italian bastard," a
poor "son of a bitch."

I looked about me in the crowd for someone who, like me,
felt proud of being a poor "Italian bastard," a poor "son of a
bitch." I looked hard into the faces of all the Neapolitans I
met, lost like me in that noisy crowd of conquerors, pushed
like me on one side with violent shoves, with elbow thrusts in
the ribs: poor wan, emaciated men, women with thin white
faces hideously restored to life with rouge, skinny children
with enormous eyes, ravenous and fearful; and I felt proud of
being an Italian bastard like them, a son of a bitch like them.

But something in their faces, in their expressions, made me
feel humble. There was something about them that wounded
me deeply. It was an insolent pride, the vile, horrible pride
of hunger, the arrogant and at the same time humble pride of
hunger. They did not suffer in their souls, but only in their
bodies. They suffered no kind of pain other than bodily pain.
And suddenly I felt lonely and strange in that crowd of conquerors and poor starving Neapolitans. I was ashamed that
I was not hungry. I blushed because I was only an Italian
bastard, a son of a bitch, and nothing worse. I felt ashamed
that I too was not a poor starving Neapolitan; and elbowing
my way along the street I escaped from the press of the crowd
and set foot on the first step of the Gradoni di Chiaia.

The long flight of steps was cluttered up with women,
seated one beside the other, as on the tiers of an amphitheatre,
and it seemed that they were there to enjoy some wonderful
spectacle. They laughed as they sat, talking among themselves in high-pitched voices, or eating fruit, or smoking, or
sucking caramels, or chewing gum. Some were leaning forward, their elbows on their knees, their faces buried in their
clasped hands; others lolled back with their arms on the step
above them; others yet rested lightly on their sides; and all

were shouting and calling one another by name, exchanging voices and formless oral sounds rather than words with their companions seated lower down or higher up, or with the shrieking attendant crowd of disheveled, repulsive old women on the balconies and at the windows overhanging the alley, who, their toothless mouths agape with obscene laughter, were waving their arms and hurling gibes and insults. The women seated on the steps were straightening one another's locks, which in every case were gathered together and built up into a lofty edifice of hair and tow, reinforced and supported by hairpins and tortoise-shell combs, and adorned with flowers and false tresses, in the style of the wax Madonnas in the little chapels at the corners of the alleys.

This crowd of women sitting on the steps, which resembled the ladder of the angels in Jacob's dream, seemed to have come together for some celebration, or for some play in which they were at once actresses and spectators. At intervals one of them would sing a song, one of these melancholy songs of the Neapolitan people. This would at once be drowned by outbursts of laughter, raucous voices, and guttural yells which sounded like appeals for help or cries of pain. But there was a certain dignity about those women, about their varied postures, now obscene, now comic, now solemn, about the very disorder of the tableau which they presented. A certain nobility even, revealed in some of their gestures, in the way they raised their arms to touch their temples with the tips of their fingers, to straighten their hair each with her two plump and dexterous hands, in the way they turned their heads and inclined them on their shoulders, as though the better to hear the voices and the obscene words which floated down from the balconies and windows above, and in the very way in which they spoke and smiled. Suddenly, when I set foot on the first step, all became mute, and a strange palpitating silence, like an immense variegated butterfly, settled lightly on the packed stairway.

In front of me walked a number of Negro soldiers in their close-fitting khaki uniforms, swaying on flat feet encased in thin shoes of yellow leather which shone as if they were made of gold. Slowly they climbed, in that sudden silence, with the lonely dignity of the Negro; and as they advanced up the steps, through the narrow passage left free by that mute crowd of seated women, I saw the legs of those unfortunates slowly open, and splay apart in horrible fashion. "Five dollars! Five dollars!" they suddenly began to cry all together, in hoarse, strident voices, but without gestures; and this absence of gestures added obscenity to their voices and their words. "Five dollars! Five dollars!" As the Negroes ascended, so the clamor increased, the voices became shriller, hoarser and hoarser grew the cries of the termagants on the balconies and at the windows, as they goaded the Negroes on and joined in the chorus of yells: "Five dollars! Five dollars! Go, Joe! Go, Joe! Go, go, Joe, go!"

But no sooner had the Negroes gone by, no sooner had their gilded feet moved from a step, than the legs of the girls who were sitting on that step slowly closed again like the pincers of brown crabs, and the girls turned round, gesticulating, shaking their fists and shouting obscene insults at the Negro soldiers, beside themselves with intense, savage fury, until first one Negro, then another, then yet another stopped, seized as he passed by ten or twenty hands. And I continued to climb the triumphal ladder of the angels, which rose straight into the sky, into that festering sky from which the hoarse sirocco tore fragments of greenish skin, and scattered them over the sea.

I felt far more miserable and cowardly than I had done on September 8, 1943, when we had had to throw our arms and our flags at the feet of the conquerors. They were old, rusty arms, it is true, but they were precious family mementos, and all of us, officers and men, were attached to those precious family mementos. They consisted of old rifles, old sabres, old cannon of the period when women wore crinolines and men tall stovepipe hats, dove-gray redingotes and high boots with buttons. With those shotguns, those rust-covered sabres, and those bronze cannon our grandfathers had fought alongside Garibaldi, Victor Emmanuel and Napoleon III against the Austrians, for the freedom and independence of Italy. The flags too were old and démodé. Some were very old: they were the flags of the Republic of Venice, which had flown from the masts of the galleys at Lepanto and from the towers of Famagosta and Candia; the ensigns of the Republic of Genoa and those of the Communes of Milan, Crema and Bologna, which had flown from the carroccio [1] in the battles against the German emperor Frederick Barbarossa; the standards painted by Sandro Botticelli, which Lorenzo the Magnificent had given to the archers of Florence; the standards of Siena, painted by Luca Signorelli; and the Roman flags of the Capitol, painted by Michelangelo. In addition, there was the flag presented to Garibaldi by the Italians of Valparaiso, and the flag of the Roman Republic of 1849. There were also the flags of Vittorio Veneto, of Trieste, of Fiume, of Zara, of Ethiopia, of the Spanish War. They were glorious flags, among the most glorious of the earth and the sea. Why should only the British, American, Russian, French and Spanish flags be glorious? The Italian flags are glorious too. If they were not, what pleasure should we have derived from throwing them in the mud? There is not a nation in the world that has not once at least had the pleasure of throwing its flags at the feet of conquerors. It falls to the lot of even the most glorious flags to be thrown in the mud. Glory, what men call glory, is often thick with mud.

It had been a wonderful day for us, September 8, 1943 — the day on which we had thrown our arms and our flags not only at the feet of the conquerors, but also at the feet of the conquered; not only at the feet of the British, the Americans, the French, the Russians, the Poles and all the rest, but also at the feet of the King, Badoglio, Mussolini and Hitler. We had thrown them at the feet of all, victors and vanquished — even at the feet of those with whom it had nothing whatever

---

[1] A car drawn by horses or oxen, on which the standards of the Communes were flown in time of war. (Translator's note.)

to do, and who sat back enjoying the spectacle. We had even thrown them at the feet of the passers-by, and of all those whom the spirit moved to assist at the unusual, diverting spectacle of an army throwing its arms and its flags at the feet of the firstcomer. Not, indeed, that our army was any worse or any better than countless others. In that glorious war — let us be fair — it had not fallen to the lot of the Italians alone to turn their backs on the enemy: that experience had been shared by all — by the British, the Americans, the Germans, the Russians, the French, the Jugoslavs — by all, victors and vanquished. There was not an army in the world which in that splendid war had not, on some fine day, had the pleasure of throwing its arms and its flags in the mud.

The Order signed by the King's Gracious Majesty and by Marshal Badoglio actually contained the following words: "Officers and men of the Italian Army, throw your arms and your flags like heroes at the feet of the firstcomer." There was no possibility of error. The actual phrase used was *like heroes*. Even the word *firstcomer* was written with great distinctness, so that there might be no room for doubt. To be sure, it would have been far better for all, victors and vanquished, and far better for us too, if we had received the order to throw down our arms not, indeed, in 1943, but in 1940 or 1941, when it was the fashion in Europe to throw one's arms at the feet of the conqueror. Everybody would have said "Well done!" It is quite true that everybody had said "Well done!" on September 8, 1943. But they had said it because, in all honesty, they could not say anything else.

It had been in truth a most beautiful spectacle — a diverting spectacle. All of us, officers and men, vied with one another to see which of us could throw our arms and flags in the mud most "heroically." We threw them at the feet of everyone, victors and vanquished, friend and foe, even at the feet of the passers-by, even at the feet of those who, not knowing what it was all about, stopped and looked at us in amazement. Laughingly we threw our arms and our flags in the mud, and immediately ran to pick them up so that we could start all over again. "Long live Italy!" cried the enthusiastic crowd, the good-natured, laughing, noisy, gay Italian crowd. All — men, women and children — seemed drunk with joy, all clapped their hands, crying: "Encore! Well done! Encore!" And we, weary, perspiring, breathless, our eyes sparkling with manly pride, our faces alight with patriotic fervor, heroically threw our arms and flags at the feet of victors and vanquished, and immediately ran to pick them up so that we could throw them in the mud once more. Even the Allied soldiers, the British, the Americans, the Russians, the French, the Poles, clapped their hands and threw large handfuls of caramels in our faces, crying: "Well done! Encore! Long live Italy!" And we, with sickly smiles, threw our arms and flags in the mud, and immediately ran to pick them up so that we could start all over again.

It had been truly a glorious spree, an unforgettable spree. In three years of war we had never had such a feast of entertainment. By evening we were dead tired, our faces ached from our Homeric laughter, but we were proud because we had done our duty. The celebration over, we formed a column, and just as we were, without arms, without flags, set off for new battlefields, seeking to win at the side of the Allies that same war which we had already lost at the side of the Germans. We marched with heads high, singing, proud at having taught the peoples of Europe that in these days the only way to win wars is to throw one's arms and one's flags heroically in the mud, "at the feet of the firstcomer."

THE WIGS

● The first time I felt afraid that I had caught the contagion,
that I too had been stricken by the plague, was when I went
with Jimmy to the "wig" shop. I felt humiliated by the loathsome disease in the very part of my anatomy which in an
Italian is most sensitive. The genitals have always played a
very important part in the lives of the Latin peoples, especially in the lives of the Italian people and in the history
of Italy. The true emblem of Italy is not the tricolor but
the sexual organs. The patriotism of the Italian people is
all there. Honor, morals, religion, the cult of the family —
all are there. No sooner had I crossed the threshold of the
"wig" shop than I felt that the plague was humiliating me in
what, to every Italian, is the only, the true Italy.

The vendor of "wigs" had his shack near the Ceppo di Forcella, in one of the most miserable and sordid quarters of Naples.

"You are all rotten, in Europe," said Jimmy to me as we walked through the maze of alleys which wraps itself, like a coil of intestines, round the Piazza Olivella.

"Europe is the land of men," I said. "There are no more virile men in the world than those who are born in Europe."

"Men? You call yourselves men?" said Jimmy, laughing and slapping his thigh.

"Yes, Jimmy, there are no nobler men in the world than those who are born in Europe," I said.

"A lot of dirty bastards, that's what you are," said Jimmy.

"We are a wonderful race of conquered men, Jimmy," I said.

"A lot of dirty bastards," said Jimmy. "At heart you're glad you've lost the war, aren't you?"

"You're right, Jimmy, it's a real stroke of luck for us that we've lost the war. The only thing that irks us a little is that it will be our job to rule the world. It is the defeated who rule the world, Jimmy. It's always like that after a war. It's always the defeated who bring civilization to the victorious countries."

"What? Do you really think that you're going to bring civilization to America?" said Jimmy, looking at me with amazement and fury in his eyes.

"That's just the way of it, Jimmy. Even Athens, when she had the good fortune and the honor to be conquered by the Romans, was forced to bring civilization to Rome."

"To hell with your Athens, to hell with your Rome!" said Jimmy, looking at me askance.

Jimmy walked through those filthy alleys, in the midst of that miserable populace, with an elegance and a nonchalance which only Americans possess. No one on this earth save the Americans can move about with such easy, smiling grace among people who are filthy, starved and unhappy. It is not a sign of insensibility: it is a sign of optimism and at the same time of innocence. The Americans are not cynics, they are optimists; and optimism is in itself a sign of innocence. He who is blameless in thought and deed is led not, to be sure, to deny that evil exists, but to refuse to believe in the necessity of evil, to refuse to admit that evil is inevitable and incurable. The Americans believe that misery, hunger, pain and everything else can be combatted, that men can recover from misery, hunger and pain, that there is a remedy for all evil. They do not know that evil is incurable. They do not know, although they are in many respects the most Christian nation in the world, that without evil there can be no Christ. "No love, no nothin'." No evil, no Christ. The less evil there is in the world, the less of Christ there is in the world. The Americans are good. Faced with misery, hunger and pain, their first instinct is to help those who suffer hunger, misery and pain. There is no people in the world that has so strong, so pure, so genuine a sense of human solidarity. But Christ demands from men pity, not solidarity. Solidarity is not a Christian sentiment.

Jimmy Wren, of Cleveland, Ohio, a lieutenant in the Signal Corps, was, like the great majority of the officers and men of the American army, a good fellow. When an American is good, there is no better man in the world. It was not Jimmy's fault if the people of Naples suffered. That terrible spectacle of grief and misery offended neither his eyes nor his heart. Jimmy's conscience was at rest. Like all Americans, by that contradiction which characterizes all materialistic civilizations, he was an idealist. To evil, misery, hunger and physical suffering he ascribed a moral character. He did not appreciate their remote historical and economic causes, but only the seemingly moral reasons for their existence. What could he have done to try and alleviate the appalling physical sufferings of the people of Naples, of the peoples of Europe? All that Jimmy could do was to take upon himself part of the moral responsibility for their sufferings, not as an American, but as a Christian. Perhaps it would be better to say not only as a Christian, but also as an American. And that is the real reason why I love the Americans, why I am profoundly grateful to the Americans, and regard them as the most generous, the purest, the best and the most disinterested people on earth — a wonderful people.

Jimmy had certainly not achieved an understanding of the obscure moral and religious considerations which led him to feel partly responsible for the sufferings of others. Perhaps he was not even aware that Christ's sacrifice incidentally imposes on each individual, on each one of us, a responsibility for the sufferings of humanity, that our Christianity obliges each of us to regard himself as the Christ of all his fellows. Why should he have known these things? Sa chair n'était pas triste, hélas! et il n'avait pas lu tous les livres. Jimmy was an honest fellow, socially of the middle class, and of moderate culture. In civil life he was a clerk in an insurance company. His culture was of a standard far lower than that of any European of his station. It was certainly not to be expected that a little American clerk, who had landed in Italy for the purpose of fighting the Italians and punishing them for their sins and their crimes, should set himself up as the Christ of the Italian people. It was not even to be expected that he should know certain essential facts about modern civilization — for instance, that a capitalist society (if one disregards Christian pity, and weariness of and disgust with Christian pity, which are sentiments peculiar to the modern world) is the most feasible expression of Christianity; that without the existence of evil there can be no Christ.

But Jimmy was superior to any European of his station, and, unfortunately, of my station too, in this — that he respected the dignity and freedom of man, that he was blameless in thought and deed, and that he felt morally responsible for the sufferings of others.

Jimmy walked along with a smile on his lips, but my face felt cold and sombre.

A clean northeast wind was blowing from the sea, and a fresh salt tang cut the fetid air of the alleys. One seemed to hear, echoing across the roofs and balconies, that trembling of leaves, that prolonged whinnying of foals, that laughter of countless little girls, those thousand youthful, happy sounds which skim over the crests of the waves when the nor'easter blows. The clothes hanging out to dry on the cords which stretched across the alleys bellied in the wind like sails. On every side one heard a beating of pigeons' wings, a fluttering of quails in the corn.

Seated on the doorsteps of their hovels, the people watched us in silence, following us into the distance with their eyes. There were almost naked children, there were old men whose skin was white and transparent as the fungus that grows in cellars, there were women with swollen bellies and thin, ashen faces, and pale, emaciated girls with withered breasts and narrow flanks. All around us was a glint of eyes in the green shadow, a muted laughter, a flashing of teeth, and a silent gesticulation which clove the rays of light that filter into the alleys of Naples at sunset, a light the color of dirty water, the ghostly light of an aquarium. The people watched us in silence, opening and closing their mouths as fishes do.

Sleeping men, dressed in ragged military uniforms, lay in heaps on the pavement outside the doors of the hovels. They were Italian soldiers, many of them Sardinians or Lombards; nearly all were airmen from the neighboring flying field at Capodichino who, after the collapse of the army, to avoid falling into the hands of the Germans or the Allies had sought refuge in the alleys of Naples, where they lived on the charity of the people, who are as poor as they are generous. Stray dogs, attracted by the pungent odor of sleep, that familiar odor of dirty hair and coagulated sweat, went about sniffing the sleepers, nibbling their gaping shoes and tattered uniforms and licking the shadows thrown flat against the walls by their bodies as they lay huddled in sleep.

Not a voice was to be heard, not even the crying of a child. A strange silence brooded over the starving city, moist with the pungent sweat of hunger. It was like that wonderful silence which pervades the poetry of the Greeks, when the moon climbs slowly from the sea. And indeed the moon, pale and transparent as a rose, was even now climbing above the line of the distant horizon, and the sky was fragrant as a garden. From the doorsteps of their hovels the people lifted their heads to watch the rose as it climbed slowly from the sea, embroidered upon the blue silk quilt of the sky. On one side of the quilt, a little way down to the left, was embroidered a likeness of Vesuvius in yellow and red, and high up, a little to the right, above the vague shadow of the island of Capri, were embroidered in letters of gold the words of the prayer, *Ave Maria maris stella.* When the sky resembles his own beautiful quilt of blue silk, covered with embroidery like the mantle of the Madonna, every Neapolitan is happy: it would be so lovely to die on so clear and calm an evening.

Suddenly we saw a black cart pull up at the entrance to an alley. It was drawn by two horses covered with silver saddle-cloths and plumed like the steeds of the Paladins of France. Two men were sitting on the box. The one holding the reins cracked his whip, the other rose to his feet, blew into a curved bugle, which gave forth a harsh, piercing lament, then in a hoarse voice cried "Poggioreale! Poggioreale!" — the name of the cemetery and also of the prison of Naples. I had many times been confined in Poggioreale Jail, and the name struck a chill into my heart. The man repeated his cry several times, until a vague murmur, which gradually swelled into a deafening uproar, arose from the alley, and an ear-splitting wail spread from hovel to hovel.

It was death's hour — the hour when the carts of the Municipal Cleansing Department, the few carts spared by the terrible, ceaseless air raids of those years, went from alley to alley, from hovel to hovel, to collect the dead, just as, before the war, they used to go to collect the garbage. The misery of the times, the public disorder, the high death rate, the greed of the speculators, the negligence of the authorities and the universal corruption were such that to accord the dead Christian burial had become almost an impossibility, the privilege of the few. To take a dead man to Poggioreale on a cart drawn by a little donkey cost ten or fifteen thousand lire. And since we were still in the early months of the Allied occupation, and the populace had not yet had time to scrape together a few soldi by illicit dealings on the black market, they could not afford the luxury of giving their dead that Christian burial of which, though poor, they were worthy.

For five, ten and even fifteen days the corpses remained in the houses waiting for the garbage cart. Slowly they decomposed on the beds, in the warm, smoky light of the wax candles, listening to the familiar voices, to the bubbling of the coffee urn and the pot of kidney beans on the glowing range which stood in the middle of the room, to the cries of the children as they played, naked, on the floor, to the groans of the old men crouched on the chamber pots amid the warm, sticky odor of excrement, an odor like that which emanates from corpses that are already in a state of dissolution.

At the cry of the monatto, at the sound of his bugle, there arose from the alleys a murmuring, a frantic shouting, a raucous hymn of woe and supplication. A crowd of men and women emerged from their den bearing on their shoulders a rough box (there was a dearth of timber, and the coffins were made of old unplaned tables, the panels of cupboards, and worm-eaten shutters). They came running out, weeping aloud and shouting, as though some grave and imminent peril threatened them, crowding round the coffin in jealous frenzy, as if afraid that someone might come and dispute their possession of the corpse, and snatch it from their arms and from their affections. And their running, their shouting, their jealous fear, the way they turned round and stared with suspicion in their eyes, as though they were being pursued, made that strange funeral seem in some obscure way like an act of theft, and endowed it with the character of an abduction, with a quality of lawlessness.

Down one of the alleys, carrying in his arms a dead child wrapped in a sheet, there came, almost at a run, a bearded man, followed and hemmed in by a horde of women, who were tearing their hair and their garments, violently beating their breasts, bellies and thighs, and uttering a loud, broken lament, more animal than human, like the howl of a wounded beast. People appeared in the doorways, shouting and waving their arms, and through the wide-open doors one could see, getting up and sitting on their beds or lying with their faces turned toward the door, frightened children, terribly disheveled and emaciated women, or couples still locked in an obscene embrace; and all were following the noisy funeral cortège with wide eyes as it passed down the alley. Meanwhile, the already overloaded cart had become the center of a tussle between the latest comers, who were fighting among themselves to secure a little space for their own dead. And as the brawl developed the miserable alleys of Forcella were filled with the sounds of tumult.

It was not the first time that I had witnessed a brawl over a corpse. During the terrible raid to which Naples was subjected on April 28, 1943, I had taken refuge in the vast cave which opens into the side of Mount Echia, behind the old Albergo di Russia, in Via Santa Lucia. The cave was packed tight with an enormous, yelling, unruly mob of people. I found myself near old Marino Canale, who for forty years had been skipper of the little steamer that plies between Naples and Capri, and Captain Cannavale, also from Capri, who during the last three years had been going to and fro between Naples and Libya on the troopships. Cannavale had returned that morning from Tobruk, and he was now going home on leave. I felt afraid of that terrible Neapolitan mob. "Let's get out of here. It's safer out in the open, under the bombs, than in here among all these people," I said to Canale and Cannavale. "Why? The Neapolitans are fine people," said Cannavale. "I don't say they're bad," I answered, "but any crowd is dangerous when it's afraid. They'll crush us to death." Cannavale gave me a strange look. "I have been sunk six times, and I haven't died at sea. Why should I die here?" he said. "Ah! Naples is worse than the sea," I answered. And I went out, dragging Marino Canale along by the arm, while he shouted in my ear: "You're mad! You want me to be killed!"

The bare, deserted street, in which nothing moved, was bathed in that ghastly, cold, slanting light which sometimes illuminates scenes in documentary films. The azure of the sky, the green of the trees, the blue of the sea, the yellow, pink and ochre of the house fronts were obscured. Everything was black and white and overlaid with a gray dust, which resembled the ashes that rain slowly down on Naples during eruptions of Vesuvius. The sun was a white spot in the middle of a vast, dirty gray canvas. Several hundred Liberators were passing high over our heads, bombs were falling in various parts of the city with a dull thump, houses were collapsing with a terrifying roar. We had started to run down the middle of the street in the direction of Chiatamone when two bombs fell behind us, one after the other, right in the entrance to the cave which we had left a few moments before. The blast from the explosion threw us to the ground. I turned on my back, following the Liberators with my eyes as they made off in the direction of Capri. I looked at my watch: it was a quarter past twelve. The city was like a lump of cow dung that has been squashed by the foot of a passer-by.

We sat down on the edge of the pavement, and for a long moment were silent. A terrible cry could be heard coming from the cave, but it was faint and far away. "Poor fellow," said Marino Canale, "he was going home on leave. A hundred times in three years he had crossed the sea between Italy and Africa, and now he's died of suffocation underground." We rose and set off for the mouth of the cavern. The roof had collapsed, and muffled yells came from beneath the ground. "It's murder in there," said Marino Canale. We lay on the ground and put our ears against the débris. No cries for help arose from that vast sepulchre, but the din of a ferocious brawl. "It's murder! It's murder!" cried Marino Canale, and he wept, hammering his fists against the heap of earth and stones. I sat down on the pavement and lit a cigarette. There was nothing else to do.

Meanwhile swarms of terrified people were arriving from the Vicolo del Pallonetto. They threw themselves on the débris, digging with their fingernails like a pack of dogs looking for a bone. Finally help arrived in the shape of a company of soldiers, who had no implements but, in compensation, were armed with rifles and machine guns. The soldiers were dead tired; they were dressed in worn-out uniforms, and there were holes in their shoes. Cursing, they threw themselves to the ground, and fell asleep.

"What have you come to do?" I asked the officer in command of the company.

"Our job is to preserve law and order."

"Ah, good. You'll shoot them all, I hope, when they pull them out — those blackguards who've got buried in there."

"Our orders are to keep the crowd away," replied the officer, looking at me hard.

"No, your orders are to shoot the dead as soon as they pull them out of that tomb."

"What do you expect *me* to do?" said the officer, passing his hand over his brow. "It's three days since my men have closed their eyes, and two since they've had anything to eat."

At about five o'clock a Red Cross ambulance arrived with a few orderlies, and a company of sappers with picks and shovels. At about seven the first corpses were dug out. They were bloated, purple, unrecognizable. All bore the marks of strange wounds: their faces, hands and chests were bitten and scratched, and many had knife injuries. A police superintendent, followed by a few constables, approached the dead and began counting them aloud: "Thirty-seven . . . fifty-two . . . sixty-one . . ." while the constables rummaged in the pockets of the corpses, looking for documents. I thought he wanted to arrest them. I certainly shouldn't have been surprised if he had arrested them. His tone was that of a police superintendent who confronts a malefactor with the intention of putting the handcuffs on him. "The documents! The documents!" he shouted. I thought of the annoyance to which those poor corpses would have been subjected if their papers hadn't been in order.

By midnight more than four hundred corpses and about a hundred injured had been dug out. At about one a few soldiers arrived with a searchlight. A blinding shaft of white light penetrated into the mouth of the cavern. At a certain stage in the proceedings I went up to an individual who seemed to be in charge of the rescue operations.

"Why don't you send for more ambulances? One is useless," I said to him.

The man was a municipal engineer — an excellent fellow.

"There are only twelve ambulances left in the whole of Naples. The rest have been sent to Rome, where they don't need them. Poor Naples! Two raids a day, and we haven't even got ambulances. Thousands of people have been killed today: as always, the working-class districts are the worst hit. But what can I do with twelve ambulances? We need a thousand."

I said to him: "Requisition a few thousand bicycles. The injured can go to a hospital on bicycles, can't they?"

"Yes, but what about the dead? The injured can go to a hospital on bicycles, but what about the dead?" said the engineer.

"The dead can go on foot," I said, "and if they don't want to walk kick them in the ass. Don't you agree?"

The engineer looked at me strangely, and said: "You're trying to be funny. I'm not. But it will end as you say. We shall only get the dead to the cemetery if we kick them there."

"They deserve it. They're a real nuisance, the dead. Always corpses, more corpses, and still more corpses! Corpses everywhere! For three years we've seen nothing but corpses in the streets of Naples. And what airs they give themselves — as if they were the only people in the world! Let them lay off, once and for all! Otherwise, boot them to the cemetery, and to hell with it!"

"Exactly. To hell with it!" said the engineer, giving me a strange look.

We lit cigarettes, and began to smoke, scanning the corpses lined up on the pavements in the blinding glare of the searchlight. Suddenly we heard a frightful uproar. The crowd had rushed the ambulance, hurling stones at the orderlies and the soldiers.

"It always ends like that," said the engineer. "The crowd demands that the dead should be taken to a hospital. They think the doctors can revive the corpses with the aid of a few injections or artificial respiration. But the dead are dead — more than just dead! Do you see the state they're in? Their faces are pushed in, their brains are sticking out of their ears, their intestines are in their trousers. But the people are like that. They want their dead taken to hospital, not to the cemetery. Oh, grief makes people mad."

I saw that he was crying as he spoke. He was crying, and it seemed that the tears were not his own, but those of someone else close by. It seemed that he did not realize he was crying, that he was sure there was someone else beside him who was crying for him.

I said to him: "Why are you crying? It's no good."

"It's my only amusement, crying," said the engineer.

"Amusement? You mean consolation."

"No, I mean amusement. Even we have a perfect right to amuse ourselves every now and again," said the engineer, and he began to laugh. "Why don't you try it too?"

"I can't. When I see some things I want to be sick. My amusement is being sick."

"You're luckier than I am," said the engineer. "Being sick relieves the stomach. Crying doesn't. I wish I could be sick too!" And he moved off, elbowing his way through the crowd, who were yelling and cursing in menacing tones.

Meanwhile, summoned by the appalling news of the mass burial at Santa Lucia, hordes of women and boys were arriving from the outlying parts of the city, from Forcella, the Vomero and Mergellina, dragging behind them conveyances of every sort, even wheelbarrows, on which they heaped the dead and the injured without distinction. The procession finally moved off, and I followed in its wake.

Among those unfortunates was poor Cannavale, and I hated the idea of leaving him all alone in the midst of that heap of dead and injured. He was a splendid fellow, Cannavale, he had always had a great liking for me, and he had been one of the few to come to meet me and publicly shake me by the hand when I returned from the island of Lipari. But now he was dead; and can one ever know how a dead man looks at things? He might have borne me a grudge for all eternity if I had deserted him, if I had not stayed near him now that he was dead, if I had not accompanied him to the hospital. Everybody knows what a race of egoists the dead are. They are the only people in the world, no one else counts. They are jealous, and full of envy, and they forgive the living everything save the fact that they are alive. They would like everybody to be like themselves — full of worms, with empty eye-sockets. They are blind, and do not see us; if they were not blind, they would see that we also are full of worms. Ah, the bastards! They treat us like slaves, they would like us to be alongside them, at their beck and call, always ready to be of service to them, to satisfy all their whims, to bow and raise our hats, to say "Your most humble servant." Try to say "No" to a dead man, try to tell him that you have no time to waste on the dead, that you have other things to do, that the living have their own affairs to settle, that they have duties to perform toward the living too, and not merely toward the dead, try to tell him that in these days the dead are dead and the living soon console themselves for their absence. Try to tell a dead man this, and see what happens to you. He will round upon you like a savage dog, and will try to bite you and tear your face with his nails. The police ought to handcuff the dead instead of being in such a frantic hurry to handcuff the living. They ought to shut them up in their coffins with irons on their wrists, and get a strong force of thugs to follow every funeral procession, in order to protect honest citizens from the fury of those savages; for they have a terrible strength, the dead, and they might burst their irons, smash their coffins, and break out and bite and tear the faces of all and sundry, relations and friends. The police ought to bury them with handcuffs on their wrists and, having nailed up the coffins securely, lower them into very deep, specially dug holes, and then tread down the earth above the grave, to prevent those bastards from coming out and biting people. Ah, sleep in peace, you bastards! Sleep in peace if you can, and leave the living undisturbed!

Such were my thoughts as I followed the procession up through Santa Lucia, through San Ferdinando, Toledo and the Piazza della Carità. A pale, ragged crowd of people brought up the rear, weeping and cursing. The women tore their hair and dug their nails into their faces; baring their breasts, they raised their eyes to heaven and howled like dogs. Those whose sleep had been rudely shattered by the uproar appeared at the windows, waving their arms and shouting, and everywhere people were weeping, swearing and calling upon the Virgin and St. Januarius. All were weeping, for in Naples a death is lamented by all, not by one, nor by a few, nor by many, but by everybody, and the grief of the individual is the grief of the entire city, the hunger of one man is the hunger of all. In Naples there is no private grief, no private misery. Every man suffers and weeps for his neighbor, and there is no anguish, no hunger, no outbreak of cholera, no massacre which these goodhearted, unhappy, generous people do not regard as a common treasure, a common legacy of tears. "Tears are the chewing gum of Naples," Jimmy had said to me one day. Jimmy did not know that if tears were the chewing gum not only of the Neapolitans, but also of the American people, America would be a truly great and happy nation, a great nation of human beings.

When the funeral procession finally reached the Ospedale dei Pellegrini the dead and the injured were unloaded haphazard in the courtyard, which was already thronged with tearful people (the relatives and friends of the dead and injured whose homes were in other districts of the city); and from there they were carried bodily into the corridors.

Dawn was already breaking, and a light green mist was forming on the skin of the mourners' faces, on the plaster of the walls, and on the gray blanket of the sky, in which gaps had been torn here and there by the bitter wind of early morning; and through the rents a pinkness was visible, like the new flesh that forms over a wound. The crowd continued to wait in the courtyard, praying aloud, and every so often interrupting its prayers to give expression to its grief.

At about ten in the morning pandemonium broke loose. Weary of the long wait, impatient to have news of their dear ones, to know if they were really dead or if there was any hope of saving them, and fearful of being betrayed by the doctors and orderlies, the crowd began yelling, cursing and hurling stones against the windowpanes; and finally, by sheer weight of numbers, they broke open the doors. As soon as the heavy portals yielded the deafening, ferocious clamor died down as if by magic; and silently, like a pack of wolves, panting, gritting their teeth, every so often peering through doorways, running with lowered heads through the passages of the ancient building, made fetid and filthy by time and neglect, the crowd invaded the hospital.

But having reached the entrance to a cloister, from which dark corridors radiated in every direction, they burst into a terrible cry, and halted, petrified with horror. On the floors, piled up on heaps of garbage, bloodstained garments and damp straw, lay hundreds and hundreds of disfigured corpses, their heads enormous, swollen through suffocation and blue, green and purple in color, their faces crushed, their limbs truncated or torn right off by the violence of the explosions. In a corner of the cloister stood a pyramid of heads with wide-open eyes and gaping mouths. With loud cries, frantic wails and savage laments the crowd threw themselves on the dead, calling them by name in voices that were terrible to hear, fighting for possession of those headless trunks, those torn limbs, those severed heads, those miserable remains which deluded pity and love seemed to recognize.

Surely no human eye ever witnessed a struggle so fierce, nor yet so pitiful. Every scrap of flesh and bone was fought for by ten or twenty of those demented creatures, who were maddened by grief and even more by the fear of seeing their own dead carried off by others, of seeing them stolen by their rivals. And that which the raid had failed to do was finally accomplished by their macabre fury, their mad pity; for every corpse, torn, truncated, rent asunder, ripped to pieces by a hundred eager hands, became the prey of ten or twenty demented creatures, who ran off, pursued by hordes of yelling people, hugging to their breasts the miserable remains which they had succeeded in rescuing from the fierce pity of their fellows. The wild affray spread from the cloisters and corridors of the Ospedale dei Pellegrini into the streets and alleys, and finally spent its fury in the cellars of the city's slums, where the people could at last find an outlet for their pity and love in tears and in the payment of their final homage to the mangled corpses of their dear ones.

The cortège had already vanished into the dark labyrinth of the alleys of Forcella, and by now the lamentations of the family mourners who followed in the wake of the death cart were fading away in the distance. American soldiers glided along beside the walls or loitered in the doorways of the bassi, comparing the price of a girl with that of a package of cigarettes or a can of corned beef. The shadows were filled with whispers and hoarse voices and sighs, and the sound of stealthy footsteps. The moon lit up the edges of the roofs and the railings of the balconies with its silvery beams, though it was still too low to illuminate the depths of the alleys. Jimmy and I walked in silence through the dense and fetid gloom until we arrived outside a half-closed door. Pushing it open, we halted in the entrance.

The interior of the hovel was illuminated by the blinding white light of an acetylene lamp which lay on the marble top of a chest of drawers. Two girls, clad in gleaming, gaudily-colored silk, stood before the little table which was in the middle of the room. On the table lay a heap of what appeared at first glance to be wigs, of every size and shape. They consisted of tufts of long fair hair, carefully combed. Whether they were made of flax or of silk or actually of women's hair I cannot say. Each had a large red satin eyelet in the middle, to which the hair was fastened. And some of the "wigs" were golden in color, some ash-blond, some rust-colored, some of that fiery hue known as titian; and some were curly, others wavy, others yet adorned with ringlets, like the hair of a little girl. The girls were carrying on a lively discussion, uttering shrill cries, and as they talked they stroked those strange "wigs," passing them from one hand to the other and playfully swishing them against their faces, as if they were fly swatters, or horses' tails.

They were a comely pair, those two girls. The darkness of their complexions was concealed beneath a thick layer of paint and snow-white powder, which made their faces stand out in relief against their necks, like chalk masks. Their hair was curly and lustrous, and of a yellowish color which indicated the use of peroxide, but its roots, which could be glimpsed beneath the tinsel of the false gold, were black, as also were their eyebrows. Black too was the down which was visible here and there on their faces. Gray under its sprinkling of powder, it was thicker and darker on the upper lip and continued thus along the jawbone as far as the ears, at which point it suddenly assumed the color of flax, blending with the false gold of the hair. The girls' eyes were bright and very dark, and though their lips were naturally the color of coral, the rouge if anything detracted from their blood-red sheen, giving them a dull appearance. They were laughing, and as we came in sight they turned, dropping their voices as if ashamed; and letting the wigs fall from their hands, they at once assumed an air of studied indifference, smoothing the creases in their dresses with the flat of their hands, and with modest gestures straightening their hair.

A man was standing behind the table. As soon as he saw us enter he leaned forward, resting his two hands on the table and bearing upon them with all the weight of his body, as if to shield his wares. At the same time he raised his eyebrow as a signal to a fat, disheveled woman who was sitting on a chair before a rough stove on which a coffee pot was bubbling. Rising in ponderous haste, the woman with a quick movement gathered the heap of wigs into the edge of her skirt, went swiftly over to the chest of drawers and put them away.

"Do you want me?" asked the man, turning to Jimmy.

"No," said Jimmy. "I want one of those strange things."

"That's for women," said the man. "Only for women. Not for gentlemen."

"Not for what?" said Jimmy.

"Not for you. You American officers. Not for American officers."

"Get those things out," said Jimmy.

The man looked hard at him for a moment, passing his hand over his mouth. He was a small, thin man, dressed entirely in black, with dark, unwavering eyes set in an ashen face. He said slowly: "I am an honest man. What do you want from me?"

"Those strange things," said Jimmy.

"These bastards!" said the man in Neapolitan dialect, never moving his eyes, as though he were talking to himself. "These bastards!" Smilingly he added: "Well, I'll show you. I like Americans. (Bastards, the lot of them!) I'll show you."

Up to that moment I had not said a word. "How's your sister?" I asked him at that point in Italian.

The man looked at me, recognized my uniform and smiled. He seemed glad and reassured. "She's quite well, thank God, Captain," he answered, smiling with a confidential air, as much as to say, "You aren't an American, you are one of us, and you understand me. But these bastards!" And he nodded to the woman, who had remained standing with her back against the chest of drawers, in a defensive attitude.

The woman opened the drawer, took out the wigs, and arranged them carefully on the table. She had a plump hand, which up to the wrist was a bright yellow, saffron color.

Jimmy took one of the "strange things" and examined it closely.

"They aren't wigs," said Jimmy.

"No, they aren't wigs," said the man.

"What are they for?" asked Jimmy.

"They are for your Negroes," said the man. "Your Negroes like blondes, and Neapolitan girls are dark." He turned to one of the girls and added, "You show this bastard."

Laughing, and at the same time shrinking back with a false show of modesty, the girl took the wig which the man was offering her and held it close to her stomach. She was laughing, and so was her companion.

"I don't see what it can be for," said Jimmy, while the two girls laughed, pressing their hands to their lips.

"Show how it works," said the man to the girl.

It was a monstrous object, it really looked like a wig, that tuft of fair hairs which entirely covered her stomach and came halfway down her thighs.

The other girl, who was laughing, said: "For Negroes, for American Negroes."

"What for?" shouted Jimmy, opening his eyes wide.

"Negroes like blondes," said the man. "Ten dollars each. Not expensive. Buy one."

Jimmy, red in the face, doubled up with mirth. Every so often he closed his eyes as if his convulsive laughter made him feel sick at heart.

"Stop, Jimmy," I said.

The wig was not a subject for laughter. It was sad — horrible.

"The women have lost the war too," said the man with a strange smile, slowly passing his hand over his mouth.

"No," said Jimmy, looking at him hard. "Only the men have lost the war. Only men."

"Women too," said the man, half-closing his eyes.

"No, only the men," said Jimmy in a hard voice.

Suddenly the girl jumped up and, looking Jimmy in the face with a sad and malignant expression, cried: "Long live Italy! Long live America!" And she burst into a fit of laughter, which distorted her mouth horribly.

I said to Jimmy: "Let's go, Jimmy."

"That's right," said Jimmy. He thrust the wig into his pocket, threw a thousand-lire note on the table and, touching my elbow, said: "Let's go."

At the end of the alley we met a patrol of M.P.s, armed with their white-enameled truncheons. They were walking along in silence; they were certainly going to cause a fluttering in the dovecotes of Forcella, the home of the black market. And above our heads, from balcony to balcony, from window to window, sped the warning cry of the lookouts as they announced the approach of the M.P.s to the black-market army, spreading the alarm from alley to alley: "Mama and Papa! Mama and Papa!" As the cry arose there was a stir down in the hovels, a scurrying of footsteps, an opening and closing of doors, a creaking of windows.

"Mama and Papa! Mama and Papa!"

The cry sped gaily and lightly through the streets, brilliant beneath the silvery moon, and "Mama and Papa" slipped silently along the walls, swinging their white truncheons in their hands.

At the entrance to the Hôtel du Parc, where the American officers of the P.B.S. had their Mess, I said to Jimmy: "Long live Italy! Long live America!"

"Shut up!" said Jimmy, and he spat furiously on the ground.

When he saw me enter the Mess Colonel Jack Hamilton signed to me to go and sit by him at the large table reserved for senior officers. Colonel Brand lifted his head from his plate to answer my greeting, and gave me a kindly smile. He had a handsome, pink face, crowned with white hair; and his blue eyes, his shy smile, the way he had of looking about him and smiling, gave his serene countenance an ingenuous and good-natured, almost boyish air.

"There's a wonderful moon this evening," said Colonel Brand.

"Truly wonderful," I said with a smile of pleasure.

Colonel Brand thought that Italians are pleased when they hear a foreigner say "The moon is wonderful this evening," because he imagined that Italians love the moon as if it were a part of Italy. He was not a very intelligent man, nor was he very cultured, but he had an extraordinarily kindly disposition; and I was grateful to him for the friendly way in which he had said "The moon is wonderful this evening," because I felt that by those words he had meant to express to me his sympathy with the Italian people in their misfortunes, sufferings and humiliations. I would have liked to say "Thank you" to him, but I was afraid that he would not have understood why I was saying "Thank you." I would have liked to shake hands with him across the table, to say to him: "Yes, the Italians' true country is the moon — it is our only country now." But I was afraid that the other officers who were sitting round our table — all except Jack — would not have appreciated the meaning of my words. They were splendid fellows — honest, simple, genuine, as only Americans can be; but they were convinced that I, like all Europeans, had the bad habit of putting a hidden significance into every word I uttered, and I was afraid that they would have sought in my words a different meaning from the true one.

"Truly wonderful," I repeated.

"Your house on Capri must look a picture in this moonlight," said Colonel Brand, coloring slightly, and all the other officers looked at me with sympathetic smiles. They all knew my house on Capri. Whenever we came down from the sad mountains of Cassino I used to invite them to my house, and with them some of our French, English and Polish comrades — General Guillaume, Major André Lichtwitz, Lieutenant Pierre Lyautey, Major Marchetti, Colonel Gibson, Lieutenant Prince Lubomirsky, aide-de-camp to General Anders, Colonel Michailovsky, who had been Marshal Pilsudski's ordnance officer and was now an officer in the American army; and we would spend two or three days sitting on the rocks, fishing, or drinking in the hall around the fire, or stretched out on the balcony looking at the blue sky.

"Where have you been today? I was looking for you all the afternoon," Jack said to me in a low voice.

"I've been for a walk with Jimmy."

"There's something wrong with you. What's the matter?" said Jack, looking at me hard.

"Nothing, Jack."

From the dishes rose the steam of the usual tomato soup, the usual fried Spam, the usual boiled corn. The glasses were brimming over with the usual coffee, the usual tea, the usual pineapple juice. I felt a lump in my throat, and I did not touch the food.

"That poor king," said Major Morris, of Savannah, Georgia, "certainly didn't expect a welcome like that. Naples has always been very devoted to the Monarchy."

"Were you in Via Toledo today when the king was hooted?" Jack asked me.

"What king?" I said.

"The king of Italy," said Jack.

"Ah, the king of Italy."

"They hooted him today in Via Toledo," said Jack.

"Who did? The Americans? If it was the Americans, they shouldn't have done it."

"He was hooted by the Neapolitans," said Jack.

"They did quite right," I said. "What did he expect — to be pelted with flowers?"

"What can a king expect from his people today?" said Jack. "Flowers yesterday, hoots today, flowers again tomorrow. I wonder if the Italian people know the difference between flowers and hoots."

"I'm glad it was the Italians that hooted him," I said. "The Americans have no right to hoot the king of Italy. They have no right to photograph a Negro soldier sitting on the throne of the king of Italy in the Palazzo Reale at Naples, and to publish the photograph in their papers."

"I can't deny the justice of what you say," said Jack.

"The Americans have no right to urinate in the corners of the throne room of the Palazzo Reale. They have done so. I was with you when I saw them do it. Even we Italians have no right to do such a thing. We have a right to hoot our king — to put him against the wall, even. But not to urinate in the corners of the throne room."

"And have *you* never thrown flowers at the king of Italy?" said Jack with friendly irony.

"No, Jack, my conscience is clear so far as the king is concerned. I have never thrown a single flower at him."

"Would you have hooted him today if you had been in Via Toledo?" said Jack.

"No, Jack, I should not have hooted him. It is a shame to hoot a defeated king, even if he is one's own king. All of us — not only the king — have lost the war, here in Italy. All of us — especially those who were throwing flowers at him yesterday and are hooting him today. I have never thrown a single flower at him. For that reason, if I had been in Via Toledo today I should not have hooted him."

"Tu as raison, à peu près," said Jack.

"Your poor king," said Colonel Brand. "I am very sorry for him." And he added, smiling at me kindly: "And for you too."

"Thanks a lot for him," I answered.

But somehow my words must have rung false, because Jack looked at me strangely and said to me in a low voice: "Tu me caches quelque chose. Ça ne va pas, ce soir, avec toi."

"No, Jack, I'm all right," I said, and I began to laugh.

"Why are you laughing?" said Jack.

"It does one good to laugh now and again," I said.

"I like laughing too, now and again," said Jack.

"Americans," I said, "never cry."

"I had never thought about it," said Jack. "Do you really find that Americans never cry?"

"They never cry," I said.

"Who never cries?" asked Colonel Brand.

"Americans," said Jack laughing. "Malaparte says that Americans never cry."

They all looked at me in amazement, and Colonel Brand said: "What a funny idea!"

"Malaparte is always having funny ideas," said Jack, as if apologizing for me, while everyone laughed.

"It isn't a funny idea," I said. "It's a very sad idea. Americans never cry."

"Strong men don't cry," said Major Morris.

"The Americans are strong men," I said, and I began to laugh.

"Have you never been in the States?" Colonel Brand asked me.

"No, never. I have never been to America," I answered.

"That's why you think Americans never cry," said Colonel Brand.

"Good gosh!" exclaimed Major Thomas, of Kalamazoo, Michigan. "Good gosh! Tears are fashionable in America. The celebrated American optimism would be absurd without tears."

"Without tears," said Colonel Eliot, of Nantucket, Massachusetts, "American optimism wouldn't be absurd, it would be monstrous."

"I think it's monstrous even with tears," said Colonel Brand. "I've thought that ever since I came to Europe."

"I thought it was against the law to cry in America," I said.

"No, it isn't against the law to cry in America," said Major Morris.

"Not even on Sundays," said Jack, laughing.

"If it were against the law to cry in America," I said, "America would be a wonderful country."

"No, it isn't against the law to cry in America," repeated Major Morris, looking at me severely, "and perhaps America is a wonderful country for that very reason."

"Have a drink, Malaparte," said Colonel Brand, taking a small silver flask from his pocket and pouring a little whisky into my glass. Then he poured a little whisky into the others' glasses and into his own and, turning to me with a friendly smile, said: "Don't worry, Malaparte. Here you are among friends. We like you. You are a good guy. A very good one." He raised his glass, and with a friendly wink pronounced the toast of American drinkers: "Mud in your eye!"

"Mud in your eye!" they all repeated, raising their glasses.

"Mud in your eye!" I said, while the tears rose to my eyes.

We drank, and looked at one another, smiling.

"You are strange people, you Neapolitans," said Colonel Eliot.

"I am not a Neapolitan, and I regret it," I said. "The people of Naples are wonderful people."

"Very strange people," repeated Colonel Eliot.

"In Europe," I said, "we are all more or less Neapolitans."

"You get yourselves in a mess, and then you cry," said Colonel Eliot.

"One must be strong," said Colonel Brand. "God helps . . ." and he certainly intended to say that God helps the strong, but he broke off and, turning his head in the direction of the radio set which stood in the corner of the room, said, "Listen."

The radio station of the P.B.S. was broadcasting a melody that sounded like one of Chopin's. But it was not Chopin.

"I like Chopin," said Colonel Brand.

"Do you think it *is* Chopin?" I asked him.

"Of course it's Chopin!" exclaimed Colonel Brand in a tone of profound amazement.

"What do you suppose it is?" said Colonel Eliot with slight impatience in his voice. "Chopin is Chopin."

"I hope it isn't Chopin," I said.

"On the contrary, I hope it is Chopin," said Colonel Eliot. "It would be very strange if it wasn't Chopin."

"Chopin is very popular in America," said Major Thomas. "Some of his blues are magnificent."

"Hear, hear!" cried Colonel Brand. "Of course it's Chopin!"

"Yes, it's Chopin," said the others, looking at me with a reproving air. Jack was laughing, his eyes half closed.

It was a kind of Chopin, but it was not Chopin. It was a concerto for piano and orchestra, as it would have been written by a Chopin who was not Chopin, or a Chopin who had not been born in Poland, but in Chicago or in Cleveland, Ohio, or perhaps as a cousin, or a brother-in-law, or an uncle of Chopin would have written it — but not Chopin.

The music stopped, and the voice of the P.B.S. station announcer said: "You have been listening to Addinsell's 'Warsaw Concerto,' played by the Los Angeles Philharmonic Orchestra under the direction of Alfred Wallenstein."

"I like Addinsell's 'Warsaw Concerto,'" said Colonel Brand, flushing with pleasure and pride. "Addinsell is our Chopin. He's our American Chopin."

"Perhaps you don't like Addinsell either?" said Colonel Eliot to me with a note of scorn in his voice.

"Addinsell is Addinsell," I replied.

"Addinsell is our Chopin," repeated Colonel Brand in a boyish triumphant tone.

I was silent, my eyes fixed on Jack. Then I said humbly: "Please forgive me."

"Don't worry, don't worry, Malaparte," said Colonel Brand, clapping me on the shoulder. "Have a drink." But his silver flask was empty, and with a laugh he suggested that we should go and have something to drink in the bar. So saying he left the table, and we all followed him into the bar.

Jimmy was sitting at a table near the window, surrounded by a group of young Air Force officers, and he was showing something to his friends — something which was light in color, a tuft of hairs which I at once recognized. Jimmy, red in the face, was laughing loudly; the Air Force officers were also red in the face, and were laughing and clapping one another on the shoulder.

"What is it?" asked Major Morris, going up to Jimmy's table, and looking at the wig curiously.

"It's an artificial *thing*," said Jimmy, laughing, "a *thing* for Negroes."

"What's it for?" exclaimed Colonel Brand, bending over Jimmy's shoulder and looking at the *thing*.

"It's for Negroes," said Jimmy, while all around him laughed.

"For Negroes?" said Colonel Brand.

"Yes," I said, "for American Negroes," and snatching the wig from Jimmy's hands I showed him how it worked. "Look," I said, "that's a woman, an Italian woman, a girl for Negroes."

"Oh, shame!" exclaimed Colonel Brand, rolling his eyes in disgust. His face was red with mortification and outraged modesty.

"See what our women have come to," I said, while the tears ran down my cheeks. "That's what women have come to, Italian women. See, the whole of Italy is nothing but a tuft of fair hairs."

"I'm sorry," said Colonel Brand, while they all gazed at me in silence.

"It isn't our fault," said Major Thomas.

"It isn't your fault, I know," I said. "It isn't your fault. The whole of Europe is nothing but a tuft of fair hairs. A crown of fair hairs for your victorious brows."

"Don't worry, Malaparte," said Colonel Brand in a friendly voice, offering me a glass. "Have a drink."

"Have a drink," said Major Morris, clapping me on the shoulder.

"Mud in your eye!" said Colonel Brand, raising his glass. His eyes were moist with tears, and he was looking at me and smiling.

"Mud in your eye, Malaparte," said the others, raising their glasses.

I wept silently, with that horrible thing clutched in my palm.

"Mud in your eye!" I said, while the tears flowed down my cheeks.

THE ROSE

OF FLESH

● At the first news of the liberation of Naples, as if summoned by a mysterious voice, as if guided by the sweet smell of new leather and Virginian tobacco, that smell of blond women which is the smell of the American army, the languid hosts of the homosexuals, not of Rome and of Italy only, but of all Europe, had crossed the German lines on foot, advancing over the snow-clad mountains of the Abruzzi and through the mine fields, braving the fire of the patrols of the Fallschirmjäger, and had flocked to Naples to meet the armies of liberation.

The international community of inverts, tragically disrupted by the war, was reconstituting itself in that first strip of Europe to be liberated by the handsome Allied soldiers. A month had not yet passed since its liberation, and already Naples, that noble and illustrious capital of the ancient Kingdom of the Two Sicilies, had become the capital of European homosexuality, the most important world center of the forbidden vice, the great Sodom to which all the inverts of the world were flocking — from Paris, London, New York, Cairo, Rio de Janeiro, Venice and Rome. The homosexuals who had disembarked from the British and American troopships and those who were arriving in droves, by way of the mountains of the Abruzzi, from all the countries of Europe still under the German heel, recognized one another by their smell, by a tone of voice, by a look; and with loud cries of joy they threw themselves into one another's arms, like Virgil and Sordello in Dante's *Inferno*, making the streets of Naples ring with their mincing, slightly hoarse feminine voices: "Oh, my dear! Oh, my sweet! Oh, my darling!" The battle of Cassino was raging; long lines of wounded men on stretchers were passing down in the direction of the Via Appia; day and night battalions of Negro sappers were digging graves in the war cemeteries; and meanwhile the dainty apostles of Narcissus promenaded in the streets of Naples, swaying their hips and turning to gaze with hungry eyes at the handsome, broad-shouldered, pink-faced American and British soldiers as they forced their way through the crowds, moving with the freedom of athletes who have just left the hands of the masseur.

The inverts who had flocked to Naples by way of the German lines represented the flower of European refinement, the aristocracy of forbidden love, the "upper ten" of the sexual beau monde; and they testified, with a dignity beyond compare, to all that was choicest and most exquisite in the world whose passing was symbolical of the tragic decline of European civilization. They were the gods of an Olympus that was situated outside nature, but not outside history.

They were, indeed, the remote descendants of those splendid apostles of Narcissus who had flourished in the time of Queen Victoria, and who, with their angelic faces, white arms and deep thighs, had formed an ideal link between the pre-

Raphaelitism of Rossetti and Burne-Jones and the new aesthetic theories of Ruskin and Walter Pater, between the ethic of Jane Austen and that of Oscar Wilde. Many of them were included among the strange progeny abandoned on the pavements of Paris by the noble American roturiers who had invaded the Rive Gauche in 1920 and whose faces, bleared by drink and drugs, appear in the portrait gallery of the early novels of Hemingway and in the pages of the review *Transition,* indistinguishable one from another, as in a Byzantine picture. Their emblem was no longer the lily of the lovers of "poor Lelian" but the rose of Gertrude Stein ("A rose is a rose is a rose is a rose").

Their language, the language which they spoke with such wonderful sweetness of voice, with such delicate inflections, was no longer the English of Oxford, which during the years between 1930 and 1939 had already been going out of fashion; nor was it that distinctive idiom which echoes like ancient music through the verses of Walter de la Mare and Rupert Brooke — the English of the last humanistic tradition of Edwardian England. It was, on the contrary, the Elizabethan English of the *Sonnets,* that same English which is spoken by certain characters in the comedies of Shakespeare: by Theseus at the beginning of *A Midsummer Night's Dream,* when he laments the belated passing of the old moon and calls upon the new moon to rise ("O, methinks, how slow this old moon wanes!"); or by Hippolyta when she abandons to the river of dreams the four nights that still separate her from nuptial felicity ("Four nights will quickly dream away the time"); or by Orsino in *Twelfth Night,* when he divines the femininity of Viola beneath her male attire. It was that winged, abstracted, ethereal language, lighter than the wind, more fragrant than the wind that breathes on a meadow in spring, that dreamy language, that sort of rhymed speech, which is characteristic of happy lovers in Shakespeare's comedies — of those wonderful lovers whose "swan-like end, fading in music" arouses the envy of Portia, in *The Merchant of Venice.*

Or else it was that same winged language which flies from

the lips of René to those of Jean Giraudoux, and is the language of Baudelaire himself as we read it in the Stravinskian transcription of Proust — full of those cadences, both tender and sinister, which recall the tepid atmosphere of certain Proustian "interiors," of certain morbid landscapes, the whole of that autumn of which the tired sensibility of modern homosexuals is redolent. Their voices jarred when they spoke in French, not, indeed, like the voices of those who sing out of tune, but like the voices of men who talk in their sleep: they placed their stress between one word and the next, between one note and the next, as do Proust, Giraudoux and Valéry. In their shrill, mincing voices one discerned that kind of jealous hunger which is aroused by the stale smell of withered roses or the taste of overripe fruit. But sometimes there was a certain harshness in their tone, an element of pride, if it be true that the peculiar pride which inverts feel is merely the obverse of humility. Proudly they defy the meekness and submissiveness of their frail feminine natures. They have the cruelty of women, the cruel excess of loyalty which characterizes the heroines of Tasso, that element of pathos and sentimentality, of softness and perfidy, which women contrive surreptitiously to introduce into human nature. They are not content with being, in their natural state, heroes who have rebelled against the divine laws: they aspire to be something more — heroes disguised as heroes. They are like Amazons déguisées en femmes.

The clothes they wore, faded by exposure to wind and weather, torn in the course of their weary journey through the mountain forests of Abruzzo, were in perfect harmony with their deliberately careless elegance — with the way they had of wearing trousers without a belt, shoes without laces, stockings without garters, of disdaining to put on a tie, hat or gloves, of going about with their jackets unbuttoned, their hands in their pockets, their shoulders swaying. They harmonized too with their uninhibited movements — freed, it seemed, not from the discipline of conventional dress, but from almost any moral discipline.

The libertarian ideas which at that time were prevalent throughout Europe, especially in the countries still under the German heel, appeared not to have exalted, but to have humbled them. The flagrancy of their vice had been dimmed. In the midst of the open and universal corruption those young apostles of Narcissus seemed, by contrast, not, perhaps, virtuous, but chaste. A certain characteristic refinement which was in them assumed, amid the brazen unchastity that was the general rule, an appearance of elegant modesty.

If there was something that cast an impure shadow over the gentle, chaste femininity of their conduct, over their languor, and still more over their abject and confused ideas of liberty, peace and brotherly love among men and nations, it was the blatant presence in their midst of youths seemingly of the laboring class — those proletarian ephebes with jet-black, curly hair, red lips and dark, shining eyes who until some time before the war would never have dared to associate in public with these nobles. The presence among them of those young laboring men laid bare for the first time the social promiscuity of the vice, which, as being the most secret element of vice itself, generally chooses to blush unseen, and showed that the roots of the evil are buried deep down in the lowest strata of society, at the very rock-bottom of the proletariat. The contacts, hitherto discreet, that existed between the homosexual haute noblesse and proletarian inverts stood shamelessly revealed. And by their very nakedness they assumed the aspect of a blatant challenge to the decency, the prejudices, the rules, the moral code which inverts of the upper classes, in their relations with Philistines, especially those of humble origin, usually, with jealous hypocrisy, pretend to respect.

From these overt contacts with the secret and mysterious perversions of the proletariat they caught an infection that was social in character, not only as it affected their conduct, but also and above all as it affected their ideas, or rather their intellectual points of view. Those same noble apostles of Narcissus who had hitherto posed as decadent aesthetes, as the last representatives of a weary civilization, sated with

pleasures and sensations, and who had looked to such as
Novalis, the Comte de Lautréamont and Oscar Wilde, to
Diaghilev, Rainer Maria Rilke, D'Annunzio, Gide, Cocteau,
Marcel Proust, Jacques Maritain, Stravinsky and even Barrès
to furnish the motifs of their played-out "bourgeois" aethet-
icism, now posed as Marxist aesthetes; and they preached
Marxism just as hitherto they had preached the most effete
narcissism, borrowing the motifs of their new aestheticism
from Marx, Lenin, Stalin and Shostakovich, and referring contemptuously to bourgeois sexual conventionalism as a de-
based form of Trotskyism. They deluded themselves that
they had found in Communism a point of contact with the
ephebes of the proletariat, a secret conspiracy, a new cove-
nant, moral and social as well as sexual in character. From
"ennemis de la nature," as Mathurin Régnier called them, they
had changed into "ennemis du capitalisme." Who would ever
have thought that among other things the war would have
bred a race of Marxist pederasts?

The majority of these proletarian ephebes had replaced
their working clothes with Allied uniforms, among which they
preferred, because of their distinctive cut, the elegant American uniforms, which were tight round the thighs and even
tighter round the waist. But many of them too wore dungarees, and derived satisfaction from exhibiting their oil-stained
hands. These were the most corrupt and shameless of all; for
there undoubtedly was an element of diabolical hypocrisy or
subtle perversion in their attachment to their working clothes,
which they degraded to the status of a livery or mask. Those
who posed as Communists wore their silk shirts open at the
neck with the collars turned down over the collars of their
tweed jackets, were shod with pigskin moccasins by France-
schini or Hermes, and caressed their painted lips with enormous silk handkerchiefs bearing their initials embroidered in
the Venetian style. They had filled their hearts not only with
a sad, insolent contempt but with a sort of feminine jealousy,
an angry, evil resentment. Not a trace remained in their
make-up of that robust sentiment which impels proletarian
youth to hate and at the same time to despise the wealth,

graces and privileges of others. That virile social consciousness had been replaced by a womanish envy and ambition.
They too proclaimed themselves to be Communists, they too
sought in Marxism a social justification for their sexual affran-
chissement. But they did not realize that their vaunted Marxism was merely an unconscious proletarian Bovary-ism which
had degenerated into homosexuality.

During this same period an obscure Neapolitan printing-
works had issued, under the editorship of a publisher of rare
and valuable books, a collection of war poems written by a
group of young English poets, exiles in the trenches and fox-
holes of Cassino. The "fairy band" of inverts who had flocked
to Naples, by way of the German lines, from all parts of Europe, and the sprinkling of homosexuals in the Allied armies,
had pounced on those poems with an eagerness which revealed that their traditional "bourgeois" aestheticism was not
yet dead; and they used to meet to read them, or rather to
declaim them, in those few drawing rooms of the Neapolitan
aristocracy which one by one were reopening in the ancient
mansions that had been shattered by explosions and despoiled
by looters, or in the hall of the Ristorante Baghetti in Via
Chiaia, which they had turned into their private club. These
poems were not calculated to help them reconcile their still
active narcissism with their new Marxist aestheticism. They
were lyrics of a cold, glassy simplicity, reflecting that sad indifference in face of war which characterizes young men in
all armies, even young German soldiers. The terse, frigid
melancholy of these verses was not obscured or warmed by
hopeful anticipations of victory, its serenity was not disturbed
by the feverish pulse of revolt. After the first wave of their
enthusiasm had passed they forsook those poems in favor of
the latest writings of André Gide (whom they called "our
Goethe"), Paul Eluard, André Breton, Jean-Paul Sartre and
Pierre-Jean Jouve, published sporadically in the reviews of
the French Resistance which were already beginning to arrive
from Algeria.

In those writings they vainly sought the mysterious sign,

the secret word of command that would throw open to them the gates of that New Jerusalem which was undoubtedly arising in some parts of Europe and which, they hoped, would unite within its walls all the young men who were anxious to work with the people, and on behalf of the people, for the salvation of Western civilization and for the victory of Communism. ("Communism" was the name they gave to their homosexual Marxism.) But after a time the need, of which they became suddenly and powerfully aware, to associate more intimately with the proletariat, to seek new means of allaying their insatiable hunger for novelty and "suffering," new justifications for their Marxist postures, prompted them to undertake new quests, to seek new experiences, as an antidote to the ennui to which, in consequence of the prolonged halt of the Allied armies before Cassino, their noble spirits were beginning to fall a prey.

During those days a crowd of young men of miserable appearance used to assemble each morning on the pavements of the Piazza San Ferdinando. They would hang about all day outside the Caffè Van Bole e Feste, only dispersing in the evening, at curfew time.

They were thin, pale young men, clad in rags or in uniforms which they had begged. For the most part they were officers and men of the disbanded and humiliated Italian army who had escaped from the massacres and the shame of the German or Allied prisoner-of-war camps and had sought refuge in Naples in the hope of finding work, or of being enlisted by Marshal Badoglio and thus joining in the fight at the side of the Allies. Consisting almost entirely of natives of the provinces of Central and Northern Italy still under the German heel, and prevented in consequence from reaching their homes, they had done all they could to escape from that humiliating and precarious situation. But having had their services refused at the barracks at which they presented themselves for enrolment, and being unable to find work, their one remaining hope now was that they would not be overwhelmed by their sufferings and humiliations. And meanwhile they were dying of hunger. Dressed in lurid rags — one in a pair of German or American trousers, another in a threadbare civilian jacket or a faded, disintegrating woollen jersey, another in a British combat-jacket — they tried to cheat cold and hunger by walking up and down the pavements of San Ferdinando, waiting for some Allied sergeant to engage their services for work in the docks or for some other arduous labor.

These young men aroused the pity not of the passers-by, who were also miserable and starving, nor of the Allied soldiers, who did not conceal their resentful embarrassment at the sight of such vexatious evidence of the hollowness of their victory, but of the prostitutes who cluttered up the archways of the Teatro San Carlo and the Galleria Umberto and congregated around the pick-up points. Every so often one of those unfortunates would approach the group of starving young men, offering them cigarettes or biscuits or a few slices of bread, which on most occasions were refused with disdainful or shamefaced courtesy.

Among those unhappy men moved the fairies seeking to enrol a few fresh recruits in their band, looking upon it all as a great lark, an incredibly smart and subtle manoeuvre, to try to corrupt those young men who had no roof, no food, and were stunned by despair. Perhaps it was their wild appearance, their shaggy beards, their eyes, bright from fever and lack of sleep, and their tattered garments that awoke in their breasts strange desires and refined longings. Or did the anguish and misery of those unhappy men perhaps furnish that very element of "suffering" which their Marxist aestheticism lacked? The suffering of others must surely serve some purpose.

It was actually in the midst of that unhappy crowd that one day, as I was passing the Caffè Van Bole e Feste, I thought I espied Jeanlouis, whom I had not seen for some months, and whom I recognized not so much by his appearance as by his voice, which was very soft and slightly hoarse. Jeanlouis recognized me too, and ran to meet me. I asked him what he was doing in Naples and where he was staying. He replied that he had fled from Rome about a month previously to evade the inquiries of the German police, and began to describe to me in a charming voice the vicissitudes and perils of his flight across the Abruzzi mountains.

"What did the German police want with you?" I asked him abruptly.

"Ah, you've no idea!" he replied, adding that life in Rome had become hell, that everyone was going into hiding or fleeing through fear of the Germans, that the people were awaiting the arrival of the Allies with longing, that he had found many old friends in Naples, and that he had made many new acquaintances among the officers and men of the British and American armies — "des garçons exquis," he called them. And suddenly he began to talk to me about his mother, the old Contessa B—— (Jeanlouis belonged to one of the oldest and most illustrious branches of the Milanese nobility), telling me that she had taken refuge in her villa on Lake Como, that she had forbidden any reference to be made in her presence to the extraordinary events that were unfolding in Italy and in Europe, and that she continued to receive her friends as if the war were simply a piece of society scandal, at the mention of which visitors to her drawing room were at the most allowed to smile discreetly, with polite indulgence. "Simonetta," he said (Simonetta was his sister), "has asked me to remember her kindly to you." And all of a sudden he fell silent.

I looked him in the eye, and he blushed.

"Leave those poor boys alone," I said. "Aren't you ashamed?"

Jeanlouis fluttered his eyelids, feigning ingenuous surprise. "Which boys?" he answered.

"You ought to leave them alone," I said. "It's shameful to trifle with other people's hunger."

"I don't understand what you mean," he replied, shrugging his shoulders. But he at once added that those poor boys were hungry, that he and his friends had determined to help them, that among his friends he numbered many Britishers and Americans, and that he hoped to be able to do something for those poor boys. "My duty as a Marxist," he concluded, "is to try to prevent those unhappy lads from becoming the tools of bourgeois reaction."

I looked at him hard. Jeanlouis fluttered his eyelids and asked me: "Why are you looking at me like that? What's the matter?"

"Did you know Count Karl Marx personally?" I said.

"Who?" said Jeanlouis.

"Count Karl Marx. A fine name, Marx. It's older than yours."

"Don't make fun of me. Stop it," said Jeanlouis.

"If Marx were not a count, you certainly wouldn't be a Marxist."

"You don't understand me," said Jeanlouis. "Marxism . . . One needn't be a working man, or a bum, to be a Marxist."

"On the contrary," I said, "one needs to be a bum to be your kind of Marxist. Leave those boys alone, Jeanlouis. They are hungry, but they would rather steal than go with you."

Jeanlouis looked at me with an ironical smile. "Either with me or with someone else," he said.

"Neither with you nor with anyone else. Leave them alone. They are hungry."

"Either with me or with someone else," repeated Jeanlouis. "You don't know the power of hunger."

"You nauseate me," I said.

"Why should I nauseate you?" said Jeanlouis. "What fault is it of mine if they are hungry? Do *you* give those boys anything to eat? I help them — I do what I can. We regard it as our duty to help one another. Anyhow, what has all this got to do with you?"

"Hunger has no power," I said. "If you think you can count on other people's hunger you're mistaken. At twenty, men don't suffer because *they* are hungry, but because others are hungry. Ask Count Marx if it isn't true that a man doesn't prostitute himself just because he's hungry. To a young man of twenty hunger isn't a personal matter."

"You don't know the young men of today," said Jeanlouis. "I should like to help you get to know them personally. They are much better, and much worse, than you think." And he told me that he had an appointment with a few of his friends at a house on the Vomero, that he would be very pleased indeed if I would go there with him, that I should meet some most interesting boys there, that he was not sure if I would like them or not, but that in any case he advised me to get to know them personally because an acquaintance with them would more or less enable me to pass judgment on all the rest, and because, in short, I had no right to pass judgment on young men if I didn't know them. "Come with me," he said, "and you will see that after all we are no worse than the men of your generation. We are, at all events, what you have made us."

And so we went to a house on the Vomero where a few young Communist intellectuals, friends of Jeanlouis, were in the habit of meeting. It was an ugly bourgeois house, furnished in the bad taste that is characteristic of the Neapolitan bourgeoisie. The walls were hung with pictures, dripping with thick oil paint and brightly varnished, representative of the Neapolitan school that flourished at the end of the last century. Framed in the window, down at the foot of Mount Echia and beyond the trees of the Parco Grifeo and Via Caracciolo, one saw in the distance the sea, the Castello dell'Ovo, and far away on the horizon the blue ghost of Capri. That seascape, viewed from this vulgar bourgeois interior, harmonized in some absurd way with the furniture, with the pictures and photographs that adorned the walls, with the gramophone, the radio set, and the chandelier of false Murano crystal that swung from the ceiling, directly above the table in the center of the room.

It was a bourgeois scene, too, whose outline was framed in the window — a bourgeois interior rooted in nature and peopled, in the foreground, by young men who sat on the divan

and on the easy chairs with their red satin covers, smoking
American cigarettes and sipping small cups of coffee. They
were talking of Marx, Gide, Eluard and Sartre, their eyes
fixed on Jeanlouis in ecstatic admiration. I had found a seat in
a corner of the room and was watching their faces, hands and
gestures outlined against the background of those distant
prospects of sea and sky. They were all youths of about
eighteen or twenty, seemingly students, and the poverty of
the families from which they came was visible not only in
their garments, which were threadbare, grease-stained and
mended in parts with hasty care, but in their personal slovenliness — in their unshaved beards, their dirty nails, the long,
unkempt hair which covered their ears and hung down over
their necks and inside the collars of their shirts. And I won-
dered how far such slovenliness, which was then, and is to
this day, fashionable among young Communist intellectuals
of bourgeois origin, could be attributed to indigence, and
how far to coquetry.

Among those students were a few youths who seemingly
belonged to the working class. There was also a girl, not
more than sixteen years of age and extraordinarily fat. She
had white skin with red freckles, and for some unknown
reason she seemed to me to be pregnant. She was sitting in
a small armchair beside the gramophone, her elbows resting
on her knees and her broad face sunk in her hands; and she
kept looking from face to face, gazing unblinkingly at each
in turn. I do not remember her taking any part in the discussion during all the time we spent in that room, save at
the end, when she told her companions that they were a lot
of Trotskyists; and that remark sufficed to dispel the general
gaiety and break up the meeting.

These youths knew me by repute, and they naturally affected to despise me, treating me as a contemptible being to
whom not only the world of their ideas and feelings but even
their idiom meant nothing. They talked among themselves
as if they were speaking a language unknown to me, and
on the rare occasions when they addressed me they spoke

slowly, as if struggling to find the right word in an idiom which was not theirs. They kept winking at one another as if there existed among them some kind of secret understanding, and I was not merely an outsider but an unfortunate being, deserving of pity. They talked of Eluard, Gide, Aragon and Jouve as if they were dear friends, with whom they had long been intimate. And I was already on the point of reminding them that probably they had seen those names for the first time in the pages of my literary review *Prospettive,* in which during those three years of war I had been publishing the banned verses of the poets of the French maquis, and of which they now pretended that they no longer even remembered the title, when Jeanlouis began talking about Soviet music and literature.

Jeanlouis was on his feet, leaning against the table, and his pale face, resplendent with that delicate yet virile beauty which is peculiar to the scions of certain of the great Italian noble families, contrasted singularly with the mincing softness of his accent, with his affected grace of manner, with all the wondrous femininity that was perceptible in his demeanor, in his voice, in his very words, with their vagueness and ambiguity. Jeanlouis' was the romantic male beauty which delighted Stendhal, the beauty of Fabrizio del Dongo. He had the head of Antinoüs, carved in marble the color of ivory, and the long ephebic body of an Alexandrine statue. His hands were short and white, his eye proud yet soft, dark and lustrous in its regard, his lips red. His smile was evil: it was the bitter, sorrowful smile which Winckelmann sets as an extreme limit to his pure ideal of Greek beauty. And I asked myself in amazement how on earth my own robust, courageous, virile generation, a generation of men who had been moulded by war, by civil strife, by their resistance as individuals to the tyranny of dictators and of the mob, a masculine generation, not resigned to death and certainly not conquered, in spite of the humiliation and suffering of its defeat, had fathered a generation so corrupt, cynical and effeminate, so calmly and amiably despairing, a generation of which young men like Jeanlouis represented the flower, which bloomed on the extreme fringe of the consciousness of our time.

Jeanlouis had begun talking about Soviet art, and I, from my seat in the corner, smiled ironically as I heard on those lips the names of Prokofiev, Konstantin Simonov, Shostakovich, Essenin and Bulgakov, uttered in the same languid tones as those in which, until a few months before, I had been wont to hear him utter the names of Proust, Apollinaire, Cocteau and Valéry. One of those boys said that the theme of Shostakovich's symphony *The Siege of Leningrad* repeated in an extraordinary way the motif of a war song of the German S.S., the raucous sound of their cruel voices, the cadenced rhythm of their heavy feet as they marched over the sacred Russian soil. (The words "sacred Russian soil," uttered in a mincing, tired Neapolitan accent, sounded blatantly insincere in that smoke-filled room, in the presence of the pallid, ironical ghost of Vesuvius, outlined against the dull patch of sky that was visible through the window.) I observed that the theme of Shostakovich's symphony was the same as that of the *Fifth Symphony* of Tchaikovsky, and all with a single voice protested, saying that naturally I understood nothing of the proletarian music of Shostakovich, of his "musical romanticism," and of his deliberate echoes of Tchaikovsky. "Or rather," I said, "of the bourgeois music of Tchaikovsky." At my words a wave of distress and indignation swept over those youths, and they turned to me, talking all at once in confused tones, each trying to dominate the voices of the rest: "Bourgeois? What has Shostakovich to do with bourgeois music? Shostakovich is a proletarian — he is a true-blue. No one has any right today to have such ideas about Communism. It's scandalous."

Here Jeanlouis rushed to the assistance of his friends, and began to recite a poem by Jaime Pintor, a young poet who had lost his life a few days before while trying to cross the German lines with the object of returning to Rome. Jaime Pintor had visited me at my house on Capri, and we had talked at length of Benedetto Croce, of the war, of Communism, of the rising generation of Italian writers, and of the strange ideas which Croce had on the subject of modern literature. (Benedetto Croce, who had taken refuge on Capri with his family, had just discovered Marcel Proust, and did nothing but talk about *Le côté de Guermantes,* which he was reading for the first time.) "It is to be hoped," said one of those youths, looking at me with an arrogant expression, "that you won't write Jaime Pintor off as a bourgeois poet. You have no right to insult a dead man. Jaime Pintor was a Communist poet — one of the best and truest." I replied that Jaime Pintor had written the poem in question when he was a Fascist and a member of the Armistice Commission in France. "So what?" said the youth. "Fascist or not, Pintor was always a true Communist. One need only read his poems to realize it." I retorted that the poetry of Pintor, and that of many other young poets like him, was neither Fascist nor Communist. "It seems to me," I added, "that that is the finest tribute one can pay him, if one wishes to respect his memory."

"Italian literature is rotten," said Jeanlouis, stroking his hair with his small white hand, the nails of which were pink and glossy. One of the youths said that all Italian writers except those who were Communists were traitors and cowards. I replied that the one real merit of young Communist writers, and of young Fascist writers, was that they were children of their time, that they accepted the responsibilities of their age and environment in that they were rotten like everyone else. "That's not true!" cried the youth venomously, gazing into my face with a wrathful and menacing expression. "Faith in Communism is a safeguard against all corruption: it is, if anything, an expiation." I replied that it was fanatical poppycock. "What?" cried a young working man wearing the blue dungarees of a mechanic. "It's fanatical poppycock," I repeated.

"It's quite clear," said one of the youths, "that you belong to a defeated generation."

"Undoubtedly," I replied, "and I set great store by it. A defeated generation has far more significance than a victorious one. As for myself," I added, "I am not at all ashamed of belonging to a defeated generation, in a defeated and ruined Europe. The thing I regret is having endured five years of imprisonment and exile. And for what? For nothing."

"Your years of hard labor," said the youth, "don't entitle you to any respect."

"And why?" I said.

"Because you didn't endure them in a noble cause."

I replied that I had endured hard labor for the freedom of art.

"Ah, so it was for the freedom of art, then — not for the freedom of the proletariat!" said the youth.

"Isn't it the same thing, perhaps?" I said.

"No, it isn't the same thing," replied the other.

"In point of fact," I retorted, "it isn't the same thing, and that's the whole trouble."

At this point two young English soldiers and an American corporal entered the room. The two English soldiers were very young and shy, and they gazed at Jeanlouis with decorous admiration. The American corporal was a student from Harvard; he was of Mexican extraction, and he talked of Mexico, of the West Indies, of Diaz, the painter, and of the death of Trotsky. "Trotsky was a traitor," said Jeanlouis. I started laughing. "Think of what your mother would say," I said, "if she heard you running down someone you don't know, and a dead man too. Think of your mother!" And I laughed. Jeanlouis flushed scarlet. "What has my mother got to do with it?" he said. "Isn't your mother a Trotskyist?" I answered. Jeanlouis looked at me in a strange way. Suddenly the door opened, and with an affectionate shout Jeanlouis rushed with open arms to meet a young English lieutenant who had appeared in the doorway. "Oh, Fred!" cried Jeanlouis, embracing the newcomer.

Fred's entry had the same effect as the wind does when it changes, stirring up the dead leaves and sending them scurrying hither and thither. All the youths got up and started walking hither and thither about the room, in the grip of a strange excitement; but as soon as they heard the voice of Fred, gaily responding to Jeanlouis' affectionate greeting, they all quieted down and silently resumed their seats. Fred was a Tory member of the House of Lords, and a close friend, it was said, of a cabinet member. He was a tall, fair-haired pink-faced young man, slightly bald. He could not have been more than thirty. He spoke in a slow, serious voice, which every so often rose to a shrill, feminine pitch, and died away into that delicate whisper, or, as Gérard de Nerval says of the voice of Sylvia, that frisson modulé, in which lies so much of the charm of the Oxford accent, now, alas! no longer fashionable.

As soon as Fred had appeared in the doorway Jeanlouis' manner had undergone a sudden change, as had that of his young friends, who seemed cowed and uneasy, and gazed at Fred not so much respectfully as jealously and with ill-concealed fury. To my amazement and annoyance the conversation between Fred, Jeanlouis and myself assumed a "society" tone. Fred persisted in trying to persuade me that I had undoubtedly known his father, that it was impossible that I had never met him.

At a certain point in the conversation Fred turned to Jeanlouis and, speaking in a curiously soft voice, began holding forth about London, actors, obscure happenings in the worlds of the theatre and of fashion, about Noel Coward, Ivor Novello, and G——, and A——, and W——, and L——, interweaving his own initials with the first letters of those mysterious names, and embroidering in the air, as on an invisible canvas, with languid, graceful gestures of his transparent hands, the profiles of personages whom I did not know, wanderers in the mists of a fabulous London, scene of the most extraordinary exploits and the most wonderful adventures. Then, suddenly turning to me as if resuming an interrupted conversation, he asked me whether the supper at Torre del Greco was fixed for tomorrow or for another day. Jeanlouis looked at him meaningly and Fred was silent, flushing slightly and staring at me in amazement.

"I think it's tomorrow, isn't it, Jeanlouis?" I said with an ironical smile.

"Yes, tomorrow," replied Jeanlouis in an agitated voice, giving me an angry look. "But what's it got to do with you? We've only one car — a jeep — and there are already nine of us. I'm sorry, but there's no room for you."

"I'll come in Colonel Hamilton's car," I said. "I'm sure you won't expect me to walk all the way to Torre del Greco."

"You had better walk," said Jeanlouis, "seeing that no one has invited you."

"If you have another car," said Fred with an air of vexation, "there will be room for everyone. Including you there will be ten of us: Jeanlouis, Charles, myself, Zizi, Georges, Lulu . . ." and he continued to count on his fingers, mentioning the names of some celebrated Corydons hailing from Rome, Paris, London and New York. "Of course," he added, "it won't be our fault if you feel — how shall I put it? — an intruder."

"I shall be your guest," I answered. "How could I feel uncomfortable?"

Many times in the past I had heard references to "the confinement," the famous sacred rite which is celebrated secretly every year at Torre del Greco, and is attended by the highest dignitaries of the mysterious sect of the Uranians, who come from all over Europe for the purpose; but it had never been my good fortune to witness that mystic and most ancient rite.[1] Its celebration had been suspended during the war; and now for the first time since the liberation the mysterious ceremony was coming into its own again. Luck was with me, and I was taking advantage of it. Jeanlouis seemed annoyed and almost offended by my impudence, but he did not dare to

[1] The Asiatic cult of Uranianism was introduced into Europe from Persia shortly before the birth of Christ, and during the reign of Tiberius the rite of the "confinement" was already being celebrated in Rome itself in many secret temples, of which the most ancient is in Suburra.

shut the doors of the forbidden temple in my face, feeling that it would be safer if my curiosity were allayed than if it were left unsatisfied. Fred, who had at first taken me for an initiate and now found that I was a layman, seemed amused at his error and showed himself a good sportsman. At heart he enjoyed Jeanlouis' embarrassment and smiled at it with that malignity which is peculiar to his sex and is the noblest sentiment of which the Uranian soul is capable. But Jeanlouis' young friends, who did not know English and so had not grasped the meaning of our words, looked at us with distrust and, so it seemed to me, even hostility.

"Isn't there anything to drink?" said Jeanlouis loudly and with forced gaiety, in an attempt to divert his friends' attention from that vexing incident. The American corporal had brought a bottle of whisky with him, and we all began drinking; but when that first bottle had been emptied the young working man in the mechanic's dungarees turned to Jeanlouis and said with an insolent air, "You're the one with the cash — out with it! We're short of juice!" Taking some money from his pocket Jeanlouis handed it to the youth, bidding him hurry up. The boy went out and shortly afterwards returned with four more bottles of whisky which we hastened to pass from hand to hand and from glass to glass. The youths were very soon merry, their shyness and with it their air of jealousy and spitefulness vanished, and soon they were exchanging smiles, talking and caressing one another openly and shamelessly.

Jeanlouis had seated himself on the divan next to Fred and was talking to him in a low voice, caressing his hand. "Let's dance!" cried one of the youths, and the girl, who until that moment had continued to sit by the gramophone, smoking in silence, never blinking, her elbows resting on her knees and her face between her hands, rose and put a record on the gramophone. The smoke-filled room resounded with the raucous, sugary voice of Frank Sinatra. Fred jumped to his feet, seized Jeanlouis round the waist and began to dance. All the rest followed suit: the young working man in dungarees

put his arm round the American corporal, other couples took
the floor, and so languid were their movements, their smiles,
the swaying of their hips, and the way in which they embraced that they looked like so many pairs of dancing women.

At a certain point in the proceedings there occurred an incident which I had not anticipated, although I had had an
obscure feeling that something of the kind was likely to happen at any moment. The girl, who had resumed her seat beside the gramophone, and was gazing at Jeanlouis with hatred
in her eyes, suddenly leapt to her feet, shouting: "Cowards!
Cowards! You're a lot of cowardly Trotskyists!" — and hurling herself at Fred she slapped his face.

At about eleven o'clock on the evening of July 25, 1943, the
Secretary of the Royal Italian Embassy in Berlin, Michele
Lanza, was reclining comfortably in an armchair near the
open window in the little bachelor apartment occupied by
the Press attaché, Cristiano Ridomi.

It was stiflingly hot, and the two friends, having extinguished the light and thrown the window wide open, were
sitting in the dark room, smoking and chatting. Angela Lanza
had left for Italy with her little girl a few days before, in-
tending to pass the summer in her villa near Lake Como.
(The families of foreign diplomats had left Berlin at the beginning of July in order to avoid not so much the suffocating
heat of the Berlin summer as the air raids, which were becoming heavier each day.) And Michele Lanza, like the other
Embassy officials, had got into the habit of spending his nights
at the homes of various colleagues so as not to be left alone,
shut up in a room, during the hours of darkness, which are
the slowest of all to pass, and so that he might share with
a friend, with a human being, the anguish and dangers of the
raids.

That evening Lanza was in Ridomi's apartment, and the
two friends were sitting in the darkness, discussing the massacre of Hamburg. The happenings described in the reports
from the Royal Italian Consul in Hamburg were terrible.

Whole districts of the city had been set alight by phosphorus bombs, which had claimed a great number of victims. There was nothing strange about that: even the Germans are mortal. But thousands and thousands of unfortunate people, dripping with burning phosphorus, had thrown themselves into the canals which cross Hamburg in every direction, into the river, the harbor, into ponds, even into the basins in the public gardens, hoping thereby to extinguish the flames that were devouring them; or they had had themselves covered over with earth in the trenches that had been dug here and there in the squares and streets to provide immediate shelter in the event of sudden raids. Clinging to the banks and to boats and immersed in the water up to their mouths, or buried in the earth up to their necks, they waited for the authorities to find some antidote to those treacherous flames. For the nature of phosphorus is such that it adheres to the skin like a sticky leprous crust, and burns only when it comes in contact with the air. As soon as those wretched beings stuck an arm out of the ground or out of the water it started to burn like a torch. To protect themselves from the scourge the hapless victims were forced to remain immersed in the water or buried in the earth like the damned in Dante's *Inferno*. Rescue squads went from one to another of them, offering them food and drink, fastening those who were immersed in the water to the bank with ropes lest, overcome by weariness, they should collapse and drown, and experimenting with all sorts of ointments. But their efforts were in vain; for while they were anointing an arm, or a leg, or a shoulder, having momentarily pulled it out of the water or out of the ground, the flames at once flared up again like little fiery serpents, and nothing availed to check the spread of that terrible burning corruption.

For a few days Hamburg presented the appearance of Dis, the infernal city. Here and there in the squares, in the streets, in the canals, in the Elbe, thousands and thousands of heads projected from the water and from the ground, looking as though they had been lopped off by the headsman's axe.

Livid with terror and pain, they moved their eyes, opened their mouths and spoke. Those horrible heads, wedged between the paving stones of the streets or floating on the surface of the water, were visited night and day by their doomed owners' relatives, an emaciated, ragged throng, who spoke in low voices, as if to avoid intensifying their excruciating agony. Some brought food, drink and ointments, others brought cushions to place beneath the heads of their dear ones; some sat beside those who were buried in the ground and fanned their faces to bring them comfort in the heat of the day, while others sheltered their heads from the sun with umbrellas, or mopped their perspiring brows, or moistened their lips with soaking handkerchiefs, or straightened their hair with combs; some leaned from boats or from the bank of the canal or the river and consoled the doomed victims as they clung to their lines and moved to and fro with the current. Packs of dogs ran hither and thither, barking and licking the faces of their interred masters, or jumping into the water and swimming out to help them. Sometimes one of the doomed creatures, seized with impatience or despair, would utter a loud cry and attempt to escape from the water or from the ground, to put an end to the torment of his useless waiting; but immediately his limbs came in contact with the air they flared up, and dreadful scuffles broke out between the desperate victims and their relatives, who punched them with their fists, struck them with stones and sticks, or exerted the whole weight of their bodies in their efforts to push those dreadful heads back into the water or into the earth.

The bravest and the most patient were the children. They did not cry or call out, but looked about them with serene eyes, gazing at the fearful spectacle, and smiled at their relatives, with that wonderful resignation so characteristic of children, who forgive the impotence of their seniors, and pity those who cannot help them. As soon as night fell a whispering arose on all sides, a murmuring, as of the wind in the grass, and those thousands and thousands of heads watched the sky with eyes that were bright with terror.

On the seventh day the order was given for the removal of the civilian population from the localities where the doomed beings were buried in the ground or immersed in the water. The crowd of relatives silently withdrew, urged on gently by the soldiers and orderlies. The doomed victims were left alone. A terrified muttering, a gnashing of teeth, a stifled sobbing came from those horrible heads, which protruded above the water and the ground along the banks of the canals and the river, in the streets and the deserted squares. All day those heads talked among themselves, wept, cried out, with their mouths just above the surface of the ground, making frightful grimaces, putting out their tongues at the schupos on guard at the crossroads; and they seemed to be eating earth and spitting stones. Then night fell: and mysterious shadows moved among the doomed creatures and silently bent over them. Columns of trucks arrived with their lights extinguished, and stopped. From every side arose the sound of spades and shovels, and a splashing, and the dull plop of oars, and cries that were at once stifled, and moans, and the staccato crack of pistols.

Lanza and Ridomi sat talking of the massacre of Hamburg, and Lanza, who was near the window, shivered as he peered up at the dark starry sky. In due course Ridomi got up and switched on the radio, in order to hear the latest news from Rome. A woman's voice was singing in a sonorous, metallic void, to the accompaniment of a number of stringed instruments. The voice was warm, and it vibrated above the cold, strident sound of steel-stringed aluminium violins and violoncellos. Without warning the singing ceased, the instruments stopped playing, and the sudden silence that followed was shattered by a raucous voice: "Attention! Attention! This evening, at six o'clock, by order of His Majesty the King, the Head of the Government, Mussolini, was arrested. His Majesty the King has entrusted Marshal Badoglio with the task of forming the new Government." Lanza and Ridomi leapt to their feet and remained for a few moments in silence, facing each other across the dark room. The voice resumed its singing. Ridomi pulled himself together, closed the window and turned on the light.

The two friends looked at each other. They were pale, breathless. Lanza rushed to the telephone and rang up the Italian Embassy. The official on duty knew nothing. "If it's a joke," he said, "it's a joke in very bad taste." Lanza asked him whether Ambassador Alfieri, who during the last few days had been in Rome for a meeting of the Grand Council, had telephoned the Embassy. The official on duty replied that the Ambassador had telephoned at five o'clock, as he did every day, to know if there was any news. "Thank you," said Lanza, and he telephoned the Propaganda Ministry: Scheffer was not there. He telephoned Reichsminister Schmidt: he was not in. He tried Reichsminister Braun von Stum: he was not in. The two Italian diplomats looked at each other. They must have more definite information; it was necessary to act quickly. If the news of Mussolini's arrest was true the German reaction would be immediate and brutal. They must take refuge in some safe place in order to escape the first wave of violence, which, as always, would be the most dangerous. Ridomi suggested that they should take refuge in the Spanish Embassy or the Swiss Legation. But what if the news were false? They would be the laughingstock of Berlin. Finally the two Italian diplomats decided to ring up a Berlin lady, Gerda von H——, with whom they were both on friendly terms. Gerda knew a lot of people in the foreign diplomatic world and in Nazi circles. Perhaps she would be able to give them some advice and help, and offer them asylum for a few days, a few hours, until the situation was clarified.

"Oh, lieber Lanza," replied the voice of Gerda von H——, "I was just going to ring you up. I've got a few very dear friends here with me, do come — tell Ridomi not to be lazy: we'll have a lovely evening. Come at once: I'm expecting you." Lanza had left his car outside the front door, and the two friends rushed down the stairs, jumped into the vehicle, and set off at high speed in the direction of Gerda von H——'s house. They fled as if the Gestapo were already at their heels. Gerda lived in the West End. The streets were dark and deserted. As they approached the West End suburbs the air became misty, the green foliage of the lime trees floated in the starry sky, the thousand remote sounds of the city dissolved in the blue haze like a drop of colored liquid in a glass of water, and all the while the transparent veil of mist had a light sonorous hue.

Gerda von H—— was wearing a long sky-blue gown, which fell about her bare feet in soft folds, like the grooves in a Doric pillar. With her fair hair swept up above her temples and gathered into a mass on top of her head she looked like Nausicaa emerging from the sea. There was something of the sea, indeed, in her slow, sweeping gestures, in the way she raised her knees as she walked and threw her head back at every step, as if she really were walking along the seashore. Gerda von H—— had remained faithful to the ideal of classical beauty which was in vogue in Germany about 1930. She had been a pupil of Curtius at Bonn, had for some time frequented the little world of intellectuals and aesthetes who were initiated in the cult of Stephan George, and seemed to live and move and have her being in the conventional setting of Stephan George's poetry, in which the neoclassical architectural designs of Winckelmann and the scenes in the second part of *Faust* provide a background for the spectral Muses of Hölderling and Rainer Maria Rilke. Her house, to use her old-fashioned phrase, was a temple, in which she received her guests while reclining at her ease on a pile of cushions, in the center of a group of young women stretched out on thick carpets — *comme un bétail pensif sur le sable couché.* A brilliant smile played about her sad lips. Her eyes were round, their gaze warm and steady.

Gerda von H—— took Lanza by the hand, and walking lightly on her bare feet led the way into the drawing room, in which were assembled five girls. Tall and ephebic of frame, they had lean faces and calm, steady, lustrous blue eyes, which shone forth from under deep brows. Their lips were of a rich ruby color, slightly modified by that faint green tinge which is sometimes discernible in the lips of blond women. Their ears were small and pink, like stems of coral. But there was something indeterminate about their faces, that vague, nebulous quality which is apparent in a face reflected in a mirror, when the contrast with the icy brilliance of the crystal makes the image dull and remote. They wore low-necked evening gowns, which revealed their shoulders — sun-tanned, rounded, smooth, the color of honey. They had some-what thick ankles, as German girls do, but their legs were well-shaped, long and supple, with rather prominent, bony knees. She who appeared the boldest, and looked like Diana among the huntresses, said that they had spent the day boating on the Wannsee, and that they were still drunk from the sun. She laughed, throwing back her head, and the movement revealed her lean throat and her ample, muscular Amazonian bosom.

The champagne was tepid, and as the windows had been closed for the black-out the atmosphere of the room was humid and oppressive, and full of the acrid smell of tobacco. The young women and the two Italian diplomats talked of Rome, Venice and Paris. The girl who looked like Diana had returned from Paris a few days before, and the tone in which she spoke of the French gave Lanza and Ridomi a disagree-able shock: it was a tone in which affection was mingled with bitterness, and jealousy with spite. It seemed that she was in love with France and at the same time hated it. Here was the love of a woman who has been betrayed. "The French hate us," said Gerda von H——. "Why do they hate us?" As Lanza and Ridomi conversed their minds were far away, obsessed by the thought which was troubling them, and every so often they exchanged anxious glances. A dozen times already Lanza had been on the point of revealing to Gerda and her friends the reason for their perturbation, but each time an obscure sense of foreboding restrained him. Meanwhile time was passing, and the uncertainty in the minds of the two Italian diplomats was turning to anguish.

Lanza was already on the point of getting up, of drawing Gerda aside, of telling her the truth, of asking her for advice and help. He was already getting up, he was already going over to her, when she spread out her arms, rested a hand on his shoulder and said: "Would you like to dance?"

"Yes, yes!" cried the other girls, and one of them switched on the radio.

"It's late," said Ridomi. "All the stations have closed down."

But the girl was turning the knob, and in due course she picked up Rome. The sound of a dance orchestra filled the room. "A whole night with you," sang a woman's voice.

"Wunderbar!" said Gerda. "Rome is still singing."

"It'll sing a lot more soon," said Ridomi.

"Why?" asked Gerda.

"Because . . ." answered Ridomi, but he said no more, because of that obscure sense of foreboding which, in his mind and in that of his companion, was gradually ripening into fear.

To the ears of the two Italian diplomats the voice sounded faint and very remote, like a thin mist of sound rolling through the night; and the two friends felt their hearts trembling within them, assailed as they were by the fear that at any moment that tender voice would become raucous and harsh, and proclaim the dread news.

"Dance with my friend," said Gerda, pushing Lanza into the arms of the girl who looked like Diana, and with innocent grace pulling the fat, slow-moving Ridomi toward her by the hand. The other four girls had split up into couples and were dancing languidly, each pressing herself against her partner. Lanza's partner clung tightly to him and gazed into his eyes, smiling and constantly fluttering her eyelids. Lanza felt the vigorous beating of her heart close to his own, felt the motion of her flanks against his, felt her stomach pressing hard against his stomach. But his thoughts were elsewhere, and in his mind was a confused picture of Mussolini, the King and Badoglio indulging in a free fight, getting mixed up together, disengaging themselves, rolling on the floor, and trying to handcuff one another, like acrobats when they engage in a rough-and-tumble on a mat.

Suddenly the music stopped, the tender feminine voice was silent, and a hoarse, breathless voice announced: "Before we read the proclamation by Marshal Badoglio here is a summary of the latest news. At about six o'clock this evening the Head of the Government, Mussolini, was arrested by order of His Majesty the King. The new Head of the Government, Marshal Badoglio, has addressed the following proclamation to the Italian people . . ."

At the sound of that voice, of those words, Lanza's partner broke away from him, repelling him with a shove that seemed to Lanza like a blow of the fist. Each of the other couples disengaged themselves from their embrace, and before the eyes of the two bewildered Italian diplomats there occurred the most extraordinary thing imaginable. The movements, the postures, the smiles, the voices, the expressions of the girls gradually underwent an amazing metamorphosis. Their blue eyes darkened, the smiles died away on their lips, which had suddenly become pale and thin, their voices grew deep and harsh, their movements, which a moment before had been languid, became abrupt, their arms, just now plump and soft, grew hard and wooden, as when the branch of a tree is torn off by the wind, and, with the gradual drying up of its vital sap, loses its bright greenness, the sheen on its bark, that suppleness which is characteristic of trees, so that it becomes hard and rough. But the change which comes over a branch of a tree gradually was wrought in those girls instantaneously. As Lanza and Ridomi stood face to face with the young women they were conscious of the same bewilderment and terror as had seized Apollo when Daphne was transformed from a young girl into a laurel before his eyes. In the space of a few seconds those fair-haired, gentle girls turned into men. They *were* men.

"Ach, so!" said the one who a moment before had looked

like Diana, in a harsh voice, staring at the two Italian diplomats with a menacing expression. "Ach, so! Do you think you can get away with it? Do you think the Führer will let you arrest Mussolini without bashing your heads in?" And turning to his companions, "Let's go to the camp at once," he went on. "No doubt our squadron has already received orders to start. In a few hours we shall be bombing Rome."

"Jawohl, mein Hauptmann," answered the four Air Force officers, clicking their heels loudly. The captain and his companions bowed silently to Gerda von H——, and without deigning to look at the two stupefied Italians departed in great haste with virile strides, making the floor ring with the sound of their heels.

The girl's sudden cry, her words, her gesture, the noise of the slap, were the signal for all the youths to disengage themselves from their partners' embrace. Letting the feminine mask drop from their faces, shaking off their languor, their inertia, the superficial effeminacy of their gestures, expressions and smiles, and becoming men again in the space of a few seconds, they pressed menacingly round the girl. Pale and breathless, she stood in the middle of the room, staring at Fred with eyes full of hatred.

"Cowards!" she repeated. "You're a lot of cowardly Trotskyists, that's what you are!"

"What? What? What did she say?" cried the youths. "We're Trotskyists? Why? What's come over her? She's mad!"

"No, she's not mad," said Fred. "She's jealous." And he burst into a fit of laughter so shrill that I expected every moment to see it turn to tears.

"Ha! ha! ha!" chorused the other youths. "She's jealous! Ha! ha! ha!"

Meanwhile Jeanlouis had gone up to the girl and, caressing her shoulder with a gesture full of tenderness, was whispering something in her ear, to which she, her face deathly white, assented with a slight nod of the head. I had risen, and was surveying the scene with a smile.

"That man — what does that man want with us?" cried the girl suddenly, brusquely repelling Jeanlouis and looking me boldly in the face. "Who let him in? Isn't he ashamed to be among us?"

"I'm not at all ashamed," I said, smiling. "Why should I be ashamed? I like being in the company of fine fellows. Isn't it true that at heart they are all fine fellows?"

"I don't understand what you're referring to," said one of the youths with a provocative air, coming so close to me that he was almost touching me.

"But aren't you fine fellows?" I said, resting the flat of my hand on his chest. "Why, yes — you're all fine fellows. If it weren't for you there would be no one who had won the war." And laughingly I made for the door and descended the stairs.

Jeanlouis caught me up in the street.

He was a little embarrassed, and for a long while we did not speak. In due course he said to me: "You shouldn't have insulted them. They are suffering."

"I didn't insult them," I answered.

"You shouldn't have said that they alone had won the war."

"Didn't they win the war, then?"

"Yes — in a sense, yes," said Jeanlouis. "But they are suffering."

"Suffering? What from?"

"They are suffering," said Jeanlouis, "because of all that has happened during these years."

"You mean because of Fascism, and the war, and our defeat?"

"Yes, because of that too," said Jeanlouis.

"It's a fine pretext," I said. "Couldn't you have found a better pretext?"

"Why do you pretend not to understand?" said Jeanlouis.

"But I do," I said. "I understand you very well. You have

taken to playing the harlot in desperation, because of your grief at losing the war. Isn't that right?"

"No, it isn't quite like that, but it comes to the same thing," said Jeanlouis.

"And Fred? Is Fred suffering too? Has he, perhaps, taken to playing the harlot because Britain has won the war?"

"Why do you insult him? Why do you call him a harlot?" said Jeanlouis with a gesture of petulance.

"Because if he is suffering, he is suffering as a harlot suffers."

"Don't talk nonsense," said Jeanlouis. "You know very well that young men have suffered more than the rest during all these years."

"Even when they applauded Hitler and Mussolini and spat at those who went to jail?"

"But don't you understand that they were suffering? Don't you understand that they *are* suffering?" cried Jeanlouis. "Don't you understand that everything they do is done because they are suffering?"

"It's certainly a fine excuse," I said. "Luckily not all young men are like you. Not all young men play the harlot."

"It isn't our fault if we're reduced to this," said Jeanlouis.

He had slipped his arm through mine, and as he walked at my side he leaned against me with all the weight of his body, just like a woman who wants to be forgiven for something, or a weary child.

"And then, why do you call us harlots? We aren't harlots, and you know it — it's unfair that you should call us harlots."

He was talking in a whimpering voice, exactly like a woman who wants to arouse pity, or a weary child.

"Are you starting to cry now? What do you expect me to call you?"

"It isn't our fault — you know very well it isn't our fault," said Jeanlouis.

"No, it isn't your fault," I said. "If it were only your fault do you think I would say to you some of the things I am saying? It's always the same old story after a war. The young men react against heroism, against rhetorical talk of sacrifice and heroic death, and they always react in the same way. When they get sick of heroism, noble ideals, heroic ideals, do you know what young men like you do? They always choose the easiest form of revolt — degradation, moral indifference, narcissism. They think they're rebels, nihilists, they think they're blasé, emancipated, and really they're only harlots."

"You have no right to call us harlots!" cried Jeanlouis. "Young men deserve to be respected. You have no right to insult them."

"It's a question of the meaning of words. I knew thousands like you after the other war who thought they were dadaists or surrealists, and were really only harlots. You'll see, after this war, how many young men will think they're Communists. When the Allies have liberated all of Europe, do you know what they'll find? A horde of disappointed, corrupt, desperate young men, who will play at being pederasts as they would play tennis. It's always the same old story after a war. Young men like you, when they get sick and tired of heroism, nearly always end up as pederasts. They assume the rôle of Narcissus or Corydon to prove to themselves that they aren't afraid of anything, that they have risen above bourgeois prejudices and conventions, that they are truly free — free men — and they don't realize that this is just another way of acting the hero!" I laughed. "You can never get away from heroism! And their excuse for all this is that they are sick of heroism!"

"If you call all that has happened during these years heroism," said Jeanlouis in a low voice.

"And what *would* you call it? What do you think heroism is?"

"Heroism is your bourgeois cowardice," said Jeanlouis.

"The same thing always happens after proletarian revolutions," I said. "Young men like you think that pederasty is a form of revolutionism."

"If you're referring to Trotskyism," said Jeanlouis, "you're making a mistake. We're not Trotskyists."

"I know you aren't Trotskyists either," I said. "You are poor boys who are ashamed of being bourgeois, and haven't the courage to become proletarian. You think that to become a pederast is just one way of becoming a Communist."

"Stop! We're not pederasts!" cried Jeanlouis. "We're not pederasts, do you understand?"

"There are a thousand ways of being a pederast," I said. "Often pederasty is merely a pretext. A fine pretext, there's no denying it. I don't doubt you'll find someone who will invent a literary or political or philosophical theory to justify you. There's never any shortage of pimps."

"We want to be free men," said Jeanlouis. "Is that what you call being pederasts?"

"I know," I said. "I know you are sacrificing yourselves for the liberty of Europe."

"You're being unfair," said Jeanlouis. "If we're what you say it's your fault. It's you who have made us like this. What were you people capable of doing? A fine example you gave us! The only thing you were capable of doing was to get yourselves thrown into jail by that clown Mussolini. Why didn't you start a revolution, if you didn't want war?"

"War or revolution, it's the same thing. Both are always breeding grounds of poor heroes like you and your friends."

Jeanlouis began to laugh in a malicious, spiteful way. "We aren't heroes," he said. "Heroes make us sick. Mothers, fathers, the national flag, honor, country, glory — they're all stuff and nonsense. They call us harlots and pederasts. Yes, perhaps we are harlots and pederasts, or even worse. But we don't realize it. And that's enough for us. We want to be free, that's all. We want to give a meaning, a purpose to our lives."

"I know," I said in a low voice, smiling. "I know you're fine fellows."

Meanwhile we had descended the hill of the Vomero and

had reached the Piazza dei Martiri. From there we turned
off into the Vicolo della Cappella Vecchia with the intention
of making our way up to the Calascione. The Rampa Caprioli
opens at its lower end into the piazzetta of the Cappella
Vecchia, a kind of large courtyard dominated on one side by
the rugged slopes of the Monte di Dio and on the other by the
wall of the Synagogue and the high façade of the mansion in
which Emma Hamilton passed long years. From that upper
window Horatio Nelson, his brow pressed against the glass,
used to gaze out at the Bay of Naples, the island of Capri,
drifting on the horizon, the mansions on the Monte di Dio,
and the hill of the Vomero, green with pines and vineyards.
Those high windows, which look straight down on to the
Chiatamone, were the windows of Lady Hamilton's apart-
ments. Clad sometimes in the costume of the island women
of Cyprus, sometimes in that of the women of Nauplia, sometimes like the girls of Epirus, in broad red trousers, and sometimes in the Greco-Venetian costume of Corfu, her hair
swathed in a sky-blue silk turban, as we see her in the portrait
by Angelica Kauffmann, Emma used to dance before Horatio,
while the mournful cries of the orange sellers ascended from
the green and blue abyss of the alleys of the Chiatamone.

I had stopped in the middle of the piazzetta of the Cappella
Vecchia and was looking up at Lady Hamilton's windows,
gripping Jeanlouis tightly by the arm. I was unwilling to drop
my eyes and look about me. I knew what I should see, there
in front of us, at the foot of the wall that forms a background
to the courtyard on the Synagogue side. I knew that there in
front of us, a few yards from where I stood — I could hear
the reedy laughter of the children and the raucous voices of
the goumiers — was the child-market. I knew that today, as
on every other day, at this hour, at this moment, boys from
eight to ten years old were sitting half-naked in front of the
Moroccan soldiers, who were observing them closely, picking
them out, and coming to terms with the horrible toothless
women, gaunt-faced, wizened and plastered with rouge, who
trafficked in those little slaves.

Such things had never been seen in Naples in all its centuries of misery and slavery. From time immemorial all kinds of things had been sold in Naples, but never children. All kinds of things had been marketed in Naples, but never children. Never before had children been sold in the streets of Naples. In Naples children are sacred. They are the only sacred thing there is in Naples. The people of Naples are generous people, the most humane people in the world. They are the only people in the world of whom it can be said that even the poorest family brings up among its children, among its ten or twelve children, a little orphan, adopted from the Ospedale degli Innocenti. And that orphan is the most sacred, the best dressed, the best fed of all, because it is the "child of the Madonna," and brings good luck to the other children. One could say anything one liked about the Neapolitans, anything, but not that they sold their children in the streets.

And now the piazzetta of the Cappella Vecchia, situated in the heart of Naples, beneath the noble mansions of the Monte di Dio, Chiatamone and the Piazza dei Martiri, and close to the Synagogue, had become the resort of Moroccan soldiers, who came to buy Neapolitan children at the price of a few soldi.

The children sat in a row beneath the wall, looking into the faces of the buyers. They laughed as they chewed their caramels, but they lacked the usual restless gaiety of Neapolitan children, they did not talk among themselves, they did not shout, they did not sing, they did not make faces or romp about. It was evident that they were afraid. Their mothers, or those strapping, painted women who called themselves their mothers, held them tightly by the arm, as though they feared that the Moroccans would carry them off without paying. Then one of them would take her money, count it and make off, clutching her child tightly by the arm, followed by a goumier, his face pockmarked, his deep-set eyes glinting beneath the edge of the dark cloak that covered his head.

I looked up at Emma Hamilton's windows, and was unwilling to drop my eyes. I looked at the strip of blue sky that fringed the high balcony of Lady Hamilton's house, and Jean-louis at my side was silent. But I felt that he was silent not because he feared my mood, but because an obscure force was at work within him, tormenting him, because the blood was mounting to his temples and choking him. All of a sudden he said: "I really do pity those poor children."

I turned then and looked him in the face. "You're a coward," I said.

"Why do you call me a coward?" said Jeanlouis.

"You pity them, do you? Are you quite sure it *is* pity? Isn't it perhaps something else?"

"What do you suppose it is?" said Jeanlouis, looking at me with an odious, malignant expression.

"You would *almost* buy one of those poor children yourself, wouldn't you?"

"What difference would it make to you if I did?" said Jeanlouis. "Better I than a Moroccan soldier. I would give him food, I would clothe him, I would buy him a pair of shoes, I would not let him want for anything. It would be an act of charity."

"Ah, it would be an act of charity, would it?" I said, looking hard into his eyes. "You're a hypocrite and a coward."

"One can't even have a joke with you," said Jeanlouis. "In any case, what does it matter to you if I am a coward and a hypocrite? Do you think, then, that you have a right to act the moralist — you and all the others like you? Do you think *you* aren't a coward and a hypocrite too?"

"Yes, certainly I'm a coward and a hypocrite too, like thousands of others," I said. "And what of it? I'm not at all ashamed of being a child of my time."

"Well, then, why haven't you the courage to say of those children what you have said of me?" said Jeanlouis, seizing me by the arm and looking at me with eyes that were bright with tears. "Why don't you say that those children have become harlots with Fascism, war and defeat as their excuse? Come on — why don't you say that those children are Trotskyists?"

"One day those boys will become men," I said, "and if God so wills they will push our faces in — your face, and my face, and the faces of all those like us. They'll push our faces in, and they'll be justified."

"They would be justified," said Jeanlouis, "but they won't do it. When they're twenty those children won't break any heads. They'll do as we did, they'll do as you and I did. We were sold too when we were their age."

"My generation was sold at the age of twenty. But the reason wasn't hunger, it was something worse. It was fear."

"The young men of my age were sold when they were still children," said Jeanlouis, "and you won't find them breaking any heads today. Those children there will do as we did: they'll grovel at our feet and lick our boots. And they'll think they're free men. Europe will be a continent of free men, that's what Europe will be."

"Luckily those children will always remember that they were sold because someone was hungry — and they will forgive. But we shall never forget that we were sold for a worse reason — fear."

"Don't say such things. You mustn't say such things," said Jeanlouis in a low voice, gripping my arm. And I felt his hand trembling.

I wanted to say to him, "Thank you, Jeanlouis, thank you for suffering"; I wanted to tell him that I understood the reasons for many things, that I pitied him; and then I chanced to raise my eyes, and saw the sky. It is a shame that there is such a sky anywhere in the world. It is a shame that the sky at certain moments is as it was on that day, at that moment. What made a shiver of fear and disgust run down my back was not the sight of those little slaves leaning against the wall of the Cappella Vecchia; it was not those women, thin-faced, wizened, plastered with rouge, or those Moroccan soldiers with their dark, scintillating eyes and their long, powerful fingers. It was the sky, that blue, limpid sky, above the roofs, above the ruins of the houses, above the green trees, whose boughs were thick with birds. It was that lofty canopy of raw silk, that cold, brilliant blue sky, into which the sea infused a vague, nebulous green luminosity; that soft, heartless sky, which seemed pink and tender as the skin of a child where it hung in a gentle curve over the hill of Posilipo.

But the point at which that sky looked softest and most heartless was directly above the wall at whose foot sat the little slaves. The wall that forms a background to the court-yard of the Cappella Vecchia is high and sheer. Its plaster is all cracked with age and through exposure to the elements, though once, no doubt, it was of the same red color as the houses of Herculaneum and Pompeii, the color which Neapolitan painters call rosso borbonico. Time, sun, rain and neglect have faded and softened that vivid red, giving it the color of flesh, pink here, pale there and, farther off, transparent as a hand before the flame of a candle. And whether on account of the cracks, or of the green patches of mould, or of the white, ivory and yellow tints which were visible in places on the ancient plaster, or of the play of the light, whose constant variations were due to its reflecting the continual, irregular movement of the sea, or to the restless vagaries of the wind, which modifies the color of the light according as it blows from the mountain or from the water — whatever the reason, it seemed to me that that high, ancient wall had life, that it was a living thing, a wall of flesh, in which all the experiences to which human flesh is subject were represented, from the pink innocence of babyhood to the green and yellow melan-choly of life's decline. It seemed to me that that wall of flesh was gradually withering; and on its surface could be seen those white, green, ivory and pale yellow tints which charac-terize human flesh when it is weary, old, scored with wrinkles, and ready for the final, marvelous experience of dissolution. Big flies wandered slowly over that wall of flesh, humming. The ripe fruit of the day was turning soft, decaying, and the sky, that cruel Neapolitan sky, so pure and tender, was filling the weary air, over which the first shades of evening had al-ready cast their blight, with misgiving, with regret, with a sad and fleeting happiness. Once more the day was dying. And one by one sounds, colors, voices, that tang of the sea, that scent of laurel and honey, which are the tang and the scent of the light of Naples, were taking refuge again in the warmth of the night, like stags and deer and wild boars when they seek the shelter of the woods.

Suddenly a window opened in the wall and a voice called me by name. It was Pierre Lyautey, calling to me from the window of General Guillaume's Moroccan Divisional Headquarters. We went up, and Pierre Lyautey, tall, athletic, sturdy, his face cracked by the frosts of the mountains of Cassino, came to meet us on the stairs, spreading his huge arms wide.

Pierre Lyautey was an old friend of Jeanlouis' mother, Contessa B——. Whenever he came to Italy he never failed to spend a few days, or a few weeks, on Lake Como, in Contessa B——'s villa, a remarkable creation of Piermarini. Here were reserved for his use, by ancient prescription, Napoleon's bedroom, the one in the corner which looks out over the lake in the direction of Bellagio, the bed in which Stendhal had spent a night with Angela Pietragrua, and the little mahogany writing desk at which the poet Parini had written his famous poem "Il giorno."

"Ah, que vous êtes beau!" cried Pierre Lyautey as he embraced Jeanlouis, whom he had not seen for some years. And he went on to say that he had left Jeanlouis "quand il n'était qu'un Eros," and now that they were reunited he found "qu'il était un . . ." I was expecting him to say "un héros," but he corrected himself in time and said "un Apollon." It was dinnertime, and General Guillaume invited us to his table.

With his Apollo-like profile, his ruby-red lips, his dark, lustrous eyes, set in a smooth, pale face, and his exquisitely soft voice, Jeanlouis made a deep impression on those French officers. It was the first time they had been to Italy, and for the first time they found themselves confronted with a vision of manly beauty in all the splendor of the ancient Greek ideal.

The Moroccan servants who were busying themselves around the table could not take their enraptured eyes off Jeanlouis. Those eyes, I saw, gleamed with an evil desire. To those men from the Sahara and the Atlas Mountains Jeanlouis was merely a thing of pleasure. And I laughed to myself (I could not help laughing, the impulse was too strong for me; in any case, there was no harm in laughing at so strange and sad an idea) as I imagined Jeanlouis and all the young "heroes" like him sitting in the midst of the other little slaves in the piazzetta of the Cappella Vecchia, propped up against that wall of flesh as it gradually dissolved in the fading light, and little by little was swallowed up in the night like a piece of rotten flesh.

To my eyes Jeanlouis personified the venality which unfortunately characterizes certain choice elements of the younger generation in this Europe that has been not purged but corrupted by suffering, not exalted but degraded by its newly won liberty. Why should they not be venal too? *We* had been sold when we were young. It is the destiny of the young, in this continent of Europe, to be sold in the streets because someone is afraid, or hungry. It is very necessary for the young to prepare to play their part in social and political life, and to accustom themselves to doing so. One day or another, if all goes well, the young will be sold in the streets for some far worse reason than fear or hunger.

As if, under the influence of my lugubrious thoughts, the minds of my table companions had reverted to the same subject, General Guillaume suddenly asked me why the Italian authorities not only did not prohibit the traffic in children, but did not even show any signs of being aware of the scandal. "It's a disgrace," he added. "I've had those shameless women and their unfortunate children chased away a hundred times. A hundred times I've called the Italian authorities' attention to the matter. I've even spoken about it myself to the Archbishop of Naples, Cardinal Ascalesi. All to no purpose. I've forbidden my goumiers to touch those boys. I've threatened to have them shot if they disobey. The temptation is too strong for them. A goumier will never be able to understand that it may be illegal to buy what is sold in the open market. It's up to the Italian authorities to take the necessary steps, to arrest those unnatural mothers and put their children in an institution. There's nothing I can do." He spoke slowly, and I was conscious that it was painful to him to utter such words.

I began to laugh. Arrest those unnatural mothers! Put their children in an institution! There was nothing left in Naples, nothing left in Europe, everything had gone to rack and ruin, everything was destroyed, everything was down to the ground: houses, churches, hospitals, mothers, fathers, sons, aunts, grandmothers, cousins — everything was kaputt. I laughed, and my loud, anguished laughter made my stomach positively ache. The Italian authorities! A bunch of thieves and cowards — until the day before they had been throwing poor unfortunate people into jail in the name of Mussolini, and now they were throwing them into jail in the name of Roosevelt, Churchill and Stalin; until the day before they had lorded it in the name of tyranny, and now they were lording it in the name of liberty. What did it matter to the Italian authorities if there were unnatural mothers who sold their children in the streets? A bunch of cowards, the lot of them, from first to last — too busy licking the victors' boots to be able to concern themselves with trivialities. "Arrest the mothers?" I said. "What mothers? Forbid them to sell their own children? And why? Don't their children belong to them? Do they belong to the State, to the Government, to the police, to the municipal authorities, to the political parties? They belong to their mothers, and their mothers have the right to do with them what they think fit. They are hungry, and they have the right to sell their sons to satisfy their hunger. Better sell them than eat them. They have the right to sell one or two children out of ten to satisfy the hunger of the other eight. And then, what mothers? What mothers do you mean?"

"I don't know," said General Guillaume in profound astonishment. "I am referring to those unfortunate women who sell their children in the streets."

"What mothers?" I said. "What mothers are you referring to? Are they mothers, those creatures? Are they women? And the fathers? Haven't they got fathers, those children? Are they men, their fathers? And we? Are *we* men?"

"Ecoutez," said General Guillaume. "Je me fous de vos mères, de vos autorités, de votre sacré pays. But the children — ah, not that! If children are sold in Naples today, it's a sign that they have always been sold there. And it's a disgrace to Italy."

"No," I said, "children have never been sold in Naples before. I should never have believed that hunger could drive people to such extremes. But the fault is not ours."

"Do you mean that it's ours?" said General Guillaume.

"No, it isn't your fault. It's the fault of the children."

"The children? Which children?" said General Guillaume.

"The children — those children. You don't know what a terrible breed of children flourishes in Italy. And not only in Italy, but throughout Europe. It's they who compel their mothers to sell them in the open market. And do you know why? To make money, so that they can keep their lovers and lead a life of luxury. Today there's not a child anywhere in Europe who hasn't got lovers, horses, cars, castles and a banking account. They're all Rothschilds. You have no idea of the depths of moral degradation to which children — our children — have sunk, all over Europe. Of course, no one likes it to be mentioned. It's against the law to say these things in Europe. But that's how it is. If the mothers didn't sell their children, do you know what would happen? To make money, the children would sell their mothers."

They all looked at me in amazement. "I don't like to hear you talk like that," said General Guillaume.

"Ah, you don't like it when I tell you the truth? But what do you know of Europe? Before you landed in Italy where were you? In Morocco, or in some other part of North Africa. What do the Americans or the British know of it? They were in America, in Britain, in Egypt. What can the Allied soldiers who landed at Salerno know of Europe? Do they think that Europe still contains children — that it still contains fathers, mothers, sons, brothers and sisters? A heap of putrid flesh, that's what you'll find in Europe when you have liberated it. No one likes it to be said, no one likes to be told so, but it's the truth. That's what Europe is today — a heap of putrid flesh."

They were all silent, and General Guillaume stared at me with lackluster eyes. He felt sorry for me, he could not conceal the fact that he felt sorry for me, and for countless others too — for all the others like me. It was the first time that a conqueror, an enemy, had felt sorry for me and for all the others like me. But General Guillaume was a Frenchman; *he* was a European too — a European like me; his own town, somewhere in France, had been destroyed too; *his* home, too, was in ruins; *his* family, too, was living a life of terror and anguish; *his* children, too, were hungry.

"Unfortunately," said General Guillaume after a long silence, "you are not the only one to talk like that. The Archbishop of Naples, Cardinal Ascalesi, says the same as you. Terrible things must have happened in Europe to have brought you to such a pass."

"Nothing has happened in Europe," I said.

"Nothing?" said General Guillaume. "Hunger, air raids, shootings, massacres, anguish, terror — is all this nothing to you?"

"Oh, that's nothing," I said. "Hunger, air raids, shootings, concentration camps are trifles — all trifles, trivialities, ancient history. We've known these things for centuries in Europe. We're used to them by now. These aren't the things that have brought us to our present pass."

"What has brought you to it, then?" said General Guillaume in a slightly hoarse voice.

"Skin."

"Skin? What skin?" said General Guillaume.

"Skin," I replied in a low voice. "Our skin, this confounded skin. You've no idea what a man will do, what deeds of heroism and infamy he can accomplish, to save his skin. This — this loathsome skin, do you see?" (And as I spoke I grasped the skin on the back of my hand between two fingers, and kept pulling it about.) "Once upon a time men endured hunger, torture, the most terrible sufferings, they killed and were killed, they suffered and made others suffer, to save their souls, to save their own souls and the souls of others. They would rise to every form of greatness and stoop to every form of infamy to save their souls — not only their own souls, but the souls of others too. Today they suffer and make others suffer, they kill and are killed, they do wonderful things and dreadful things, not to save their souls, but to save their skins. They think they are fighting and suffering to save their souls, but in reality they are fighting and suffering to save their skins, and their skins alone. Nothing else counts. Men are heroes for the sake of a very paltry thing today! An ugly thing. The human skin *is* ugly. Look! It's loathsome. And to think that the world is full of heroes who are ready to sacrifice their lives for such a thing as this!"

"Tout de même . . ." said General Guillaume.

"You can't deny that in comparison with all the other things . . . In Europe today everything is for sale — honor, country, freedom, justice. You must admit that selling one's own children is a mere detail."

"You are an honorable man," said General Guillaume. "You wouldn't sell your children."

"Who knows?" I replied in a low voice. "It's not a question of being honorable, it means nothing to be a man of principle. It isn't a matter of personal honor. It's modern civilization, this godless civilization, that makes men attach such importance to their own skins. One's skin is the only thing that counts now. The only certain, tangible, undeniable thing is one's skin. It's the only thing we possess, the only thing that's our own. The most mortal thing in the world! Only the soul is immortal, alas! But what does the soul count for now? One's skin is the only thing that counts. Everything is made of human skin. Even the flags of armies are made of human skin. Men no longer fight for honor, freedom and justice. They fight for their skins, their loathsome skins."

"You wouldn't sell your children," repeated General Guillaume, looking at the back of his hand.

"Who knows?" I said. "If I had a child perhaps I would go and sell it so that I could buy myself some American cigarettes. One must be a child of one's time. When one is a coward, one must be a coward through and through."

THE SON

OF ADAM

● Next day Colonel Jack Hamilton drove me in his car to Torre del Greco. The idea of attending a "confinement," the ancient sacred rite of the Uranian cult, amused and at the same time disturbed him. His puritanical conscience made him apprehensive, but I had finally put an end to his scruples. Was he not an American, a conqueror, a liberator? Of what, then, was he afraid? It was his duty to neglect no opportunity of getting to know that mysterious Europe which the Americans had come to liberate.

"Cela t'aidera à mieux comprendre l'Amérique, quand tu retourneras là-bas, chez toi," I told him.

"Comment veux-tu que cela m'aide à comprendre l'Amérique?" answered Jack. "Cela n'a aucun rapport avec l'Amérique."

"Don't be ingenuous," I said to him. "What use would it be to you to have liberated Europe if it didn't help you to understand America?"

Georges had arrived in Naples only a few days before, bringing with him the latest news from Rome and Paris. Unlike all the others, he had not crossed the German lines by way of the Abruzzi mountains, but had come by sea in a British motor launch which had waited for him off the Adriatic coast, outside Ravenna.

I had got to know Count Georges de la V—— many years before in Paris, at the house of the Duchesse de Clermont-Tonnerre, who was then living in Rue Reynouard, Passy. He used to appear there from time to time together with Max Jacob, of whom he was an intimate friend. Georges was one of the most famous Corydons in Europe, and as a young man he had been one of the most beautiful mignons in Paris — one of the sort that we find, in the society chronicles of the young Marcel Proust, peeping out from behind the backs of armchairs in the salons of the Faubourg, like the shepherd boys who, their golden curls adorned with silk ribbons, peep over the shoulders of the Nymphs in the paintings of fêtes champêtres by Boucher and Watteau. Connected, on his father's side, with Robert de Montesquiou, and on his mother's with the Napoleonic nobility, Georges not only reconciled in his person the splendid eighteenth-century tradition of libertinism with that coarse, uncompromising sensuality which originated in the time of the Empire and was transmitted, through Louis Philippe and his offshoots, to the grands bourgeois of M. Thiers, but he almost justified, and in a sense corrected, the excesses of virility that are so frequently apparent in the history of the Third Republic. Such personages, it must be admitted, contribute more to our understanding of the evolution of a community's manners and customs than do politicians. Born during the supremacy of Fallières, growing up at a time when Diaghilev's bright star was in the ascendant, and emerging from adolescence under the sign of Jean Cocteau, he bore witness not to the moral decadence of Republican France but to the extreme splendor, the exquisite intellectual and social refinement, which France would have achieved had there been no Third Republic. Count Georges de la V——, who by now was close on forty, was universally recognized as belonging to that elect band of refined and, it may well be said, uninhibited spirits who, after excusing and mitigating, in the eyes of Europe, the muflerie of the men of the Third Republic, seemed destined to justify the inevitable muflerie of the men of that Fourth Republic which would surely be born of the liberation of France and of Europe.

"Is Georges a Marxist too?" I murmured in Jeanlouis' ear.

"Of course," answered Jeanlouis.

That "of course" left me in a state of perplexity, and somewhat disturbed me. I could not accustom myself to the idea that Marxism was nothing but a pretext serving to justify the moral laxity of the younger generation of Europeans. That pretext must conceal a deeper cause. It is common knowledge that wars and revolutions, like famines and pestilences, are invariably followed by a decline in moral standards. In the case of young men moral corruption is as much an ethical as a physiological question, and easily degenerates into abnormality. Its most frequent manifestation is homosexuality, in the form, normally most prevalent among the young, *d'un hédonisme de l'esprit* — I transcribe here the words of a Catholic writer who has considered the problem with restraint and delicacy — *d'un dandysme à l'usage d'anarchistes intellectuels, d'une méthode pour se prêter aux enrichissements de la vie et pour jouir de soi-même.*

This time, however, the moral corruption of European youth had preceded, not followed, the war. It had heralded and preluded the war; it had, as it were, paved the way for the tragedy of Europe, and had not been one of its consequences. Long before the lugubrious events of 1939 it had seemed that European youth was obedient to a word of command, that it was the victim of a plan, of a program which had been drawn up long since and was administered with cold deliberation by a cynical mind. One would have said that there existed a homosexual Five Year Plan for the corruption of Europe's young men. That air of equivocality which could be detected in their conduct, their demeanor, their speech, in the tone of their friendships, in the promiscuity of the relations between young men of the middle and of the working classes, that marriage of bourgeois and proletarian corruption, were phenomena already known, alas! long before the war, especially in Italy (where, in certain circles frequented by young intellectuals and artists, in particular painters and poets, pederasty was practised in the belief that it was a manifestation of Communism), and already brought to the public notice by observers, scholars and even politicians, who are generally heedless of matters unconnected with political life.

It may, perhaps, be objected that this phenomenon is only apparent, that the Communism of the young, like their vaunted and much publicized sexual inversion, which is, however, an "act" rather than a reality, is nothing but a form of intellectual dandyism, a kind of dilettantism, reflected in their demeanor more than in their actions, a sensational challenge to bourgeois morality and prejudice, and that young men today pose as inverts just as, in the time of Byron and de Musset, they posed as romantic heroes, or, later, as satanic poets and, more recently, as refined Des Esseintes. Nevertheless these thoughts disturbed me, sharpening my desire to attend the confinement — a desire prompted not so much by mere curiosity as by a wish to be able to ascertain how much the evil was to be feared, what was the spirit that informed it, and to what extent that spirit was new.

My surprise knew no bounds when Jeanlouis subsequently revealed to me that Georges was a kind of political personage (or rather, he added, a hero); that during the war he had rendered, and was still rendering, invaluable services to the Allies; that, finding himself in London in the summer of 1940, he had dropped by parachute on to French territory; that three times since 1940 he had succeeded in reaching England by way of Spain and Portugal, and had three times returned to France by parachute in order to accomplish missions of critical importance; and that the Allies thought so highly of him that they had put him in command of the maquis of Europe's inverts.

The idea of Georges descending from the sky, swinging to and fro in the shadow of the vast white umbrella that floated directly above his head, cleaving the blue firmament with convulsive movements of his pink hands and rounded flanks — the idea of that blond Cupid coming down to earth and touching the grass with his ethereal toes, as an angel touches the edge of a cloud, made me — I blush to admit it — made me laugh. It is, I know, irreverent to laugh at a hero: but there are heroes who make one laugh, even if they are heroes in freedom's cause. There are heroes, too, who make one weep; and I know not whether they are better or worse than the other sort. In Europe today we do nothing but laugh at and weep over one another: it is an ugly sign. But I add, by way of self-justification, that happily in my laughter there was no malice.

The inverts who were to be found all over Europe, including, of course, Germany and the U.S.S.R., had shown themselves to be an invaluable element in the British and American intelligence services, having since the beginning of the war discharged a political and military function of a particularly delicate and dangerous character. Inverts, as is well known, constitute a sort of international brotherhood, a secret society governed by the laws of a friendship that is both deep and tender, and not at the mercy of the foibles and the proverbial fickleness of sexual feeling. The love of inverts is, thank God, superior to the sexual feeling of men and women. It would be a perfect sentiment, free from any of the shackles that encumber humanity, from the virtues as well as from the vices that are peculiar to man, if it were not dominated by the caprices and hysterias and by certain sad, ignoble faults that are part and parcel of the old-maidish nature of the homosexual. But a famous, able and hard-hitting American general, of whom Georges had become the right-hand man in all matters connected with the homosexual maquis, had contrived to exploit the very foibles of sexual inverts in such a way as to make of them a wonderful fighting instrument. One day, perhaps, when the secrets of the war can be revealed to the uninitiated, we shall be privileged to learn how many human lives were saved thanks to the secret caresses of the mignons who are to be found in every country of Europe. In this strange and terrible war everything became a means to the end of victory — everything, including pederasty, which accordingly merits the respect of every sincere lover of freedom. Certain moralists, perhaps, will not share this opinion; but it cannot be pretended that the ethics of heroes are always above reproach, or that their sex is always clearly defined. There is no obligatory sex for the heroes of freedom.

The idea of a homosexual maquis had been conceived by Georges; and to him belongs the credit for having organized, in all the countries occupied by the Germans, and even in Germany itself, that réseau of young mignons which has rendered so many and such valuable services to the noble cause of European freedom. During those November days of 1943 Georges had come secretly from Paris to Naples to draw up in collaboration with the Allied Supreme Command at Caserta the plan that was to be put into effect in Italy. It was thanks to Georges that the famous Colonel Dolmann, the true political "brain" of Hitler in Rome, was eventually caught in the net of mignonnerie which Georges had patiently spread about him.

Dolmann was cruel and very handsome — two qualities which made it inevitable that he should fall a victim to the subtle arts of Georges. Smitten with love for a scion of the Roman haute noblesse, he was led by that imprudent passion to become a traitor. It was, in fact, Dolmann who, without the knowledge of Hitler and Mussolini, concluded in Switzerland those secret agreements which saved the industries of Northern Italy from destruction and led to the failure of the resistance, and to the surrender, of the German troops during the Allied offensive of April, 1945, in Italy. In those negotiations Georges played the decisive part, conducting himself like the Cornelian hero that he was and, I hope, still is. For, though he too was deeply enamored of Dolmann's young lover, he was able to sacrifice his love in the cause of European freedom. Of what sacrifices is an invert not capable in freedom's cause!

Georges, who was sitting next to Jack, had laid a hand on his arm and was talking to him of Paris, of France, of Parisian life during the occupation, and painting a picture of the German officers and men walking in the Champs Elysées, or sitting at the tables of Maxim's, Larue's and the Deux Magots. He was holding forth about Paris and its amours, its gossip and its scandals, and every so often Jack would turn to me and say: "Tu entends? On parle de Paris!" Jack was happy to be able to chat in French with a real Frenchman, though sometimes he found himself in the position of François de Séryeuse when confronted by Mrs. Wayne in the *Bal du Comte d'Orgel:* the conversation of Georges was larded with mots which Jack took for errors of French grammar. Georges spoke of the young and beautiful Comtesse de V——, his cousin, with jealous spite, of André Gide with veiled resentment, of Jean Cocteau with affectionate scorn, of Jean-Paul Sartre and his Mouches with feigned indifference, and of the old Duchesse de P—— as a spinster speaks of her dog, saying that she had had "flu," that she was better now, that she did her business regularly, and that she barked in front of mirrors. That old Duchesse de P—— who barked in front of mirrors made a profound impression on Jack, who turned to me every so often and said: "Tu entends? C'est marrant, n'est-ce pas?"

In due course Georges began to talk of the zazous of Paris.

"What?" said Jack. "Les zazous? Qu'est-ce que c'est que les zazous?"

At first Georges laughed at Jack's naïve ignorance; then, his face gradually clouding, he said that the zazous were eccentric young men aged between seventeen and twenty, who dressed in a strange manner, affecting golf shoes, ultra-smart trousers rolled halfway up their shins, very long jackets, often made of velvet, and shirts with high, narrow collars. They plastered their hair down, he said, and wore it long, so that it came down over their necks. Above the forehead and at the temples it was combed in a manner reminiscent of the coiffure of Marie Antoinette. The zazous had begun to appear sporadically in Paris toward the end of 1940, when they were to be found in the greatest numbers in the district known as La Muette, near the Place Victor Hugo (indeed, a bar in that square was their headquarters). Later they had gradually spread in large groups along the Rive Gauche; but they still preferred the fashionable districts of La Muette and the Champs Elysées to all others.

They belonged as a rule to families drawn from the comfortably off middle classes, and they appeared to be free from the various cares which in those days assailed the minds of Frenchmen. They showed no particular interest in art, literature or sport, and still less in politics — if, that is, one may so describe the dirty politics of those years. Toward everything that the word "flirt" expresses or implies they affected indifference, although they were usually accompanied, or rather followed, by female zazous, who were, like them, very young, and, like them, dressed in an eccentric way, wearing long jumpers that came down as far as the hips and short skirts that ended just above the knee. They never spoke aloud in public, but always in subdued voices, as if in confidence, and always about the cinema — not, however, about actors and actresses, but about producers and films. They used to spend their afternoons in cinemas, and in the dark halls nothing could be heard but their subdued chattering, and their staccato, guttural cries as they called to one another.

That there was something furtive about them, and about their secret conclaves and their mysterious comings and goings, might be proved by the fact that their regular haunts were often invaded by the police. "Allez, allez travailler, les fils à papa!" the flics would say good-humouredly, pushing the zazous toward the door. The French police during those years had no great desire to appear shrewd, and the German police did not attach any great importance to the zazous. It is impossible to say whether the attitude of the French police was due to ingenuousness or to a tacit complicity; but it was universally known that the zazous declared themselves, albeit discreetly, to be Gaullistes. As time went on many zazous took to small-scale trading, concerning themselves especially with the black market in American and English cigarettes. And toward the end of 1942 it frequently happened that the police were successful in seizing from the pockets of zazous not only packages of Camels and Player's but handbills containing Gaulliste propaganda, printed in England. "Childish pranks," some said; and this was also the opinion of the French police, who did not want trouble.

Whether or not the zazous were backed by the famous American general it was not easy at that time to establish. Today there can no longer be any doubt in the matter. The zazous formed a réseau which was hand in glove with the American and British Intelligence. But at the time the zazous seemed to the Parisians to be merely young eccentrics who, as a natural reaction against the austerity of life during those years, had started a fashion that was amusing and easy to follow, and against whom the severest reproach that could be leveled was that they posed as social lions and dandies, indifferent alike to the general suffering and anguish and to the arrogance and brutality of the Germans, in an abject and terrified bourgeois society which only desired to avoid trouble either with the Germans or with the Allies, but more so with the former than with the latter. Of the zazous' morals nothing definite, and above all nothing derogatory, could be said. Perhaps their ways and their demeanor were also inspired by that myth of individual freedom which is a major element in the folklore of homosexuals. But rather than their morals, what distinguished them from inverts was their political bias: for the zazous called themselves Gaullistes, whereas the homosexuals declared themselves to be Communists.

"Ah! ah! les zazous! Tu entends?" said Jack, turning to me. "Les zazous! Ah! ah! les zazous!"

"Je n'aime pas les zazous," said Georges suddenly. "Ce sont des réactionnaires."

I began to laugh. "He's jealous of the zazous," I murmured in Jeanlouis' ear.

"Jealous of those imbeciles?" answered Jeanlouis with intense scorn. "While they pose as heroes in Paris we are dying in the cause of freedom."

I was silent, not knowing what to say in reply. One never knows what to reply to people who die in freedom's cause.

"And Matisse? What is Matisse doing?" said Jack. "And Picasso?"

Smilingly Georges replied; and his voice was like the cooing of a turtledove. On his lips every topic of conversation became a pretext for idle gossip; and the mention of Picasso, Matisse, cubism and French painting during the German occupation was the signal for him to paint a wonderful arabesque of gossip and perfidy.

"And Rouault? And Bonnard? And Jean Cocteau? And Serge Lifar?" said Jack.

At the mention of Serge Lifar the face of Georges grew dark, and from his lips there came a muffled groan. His face sank on to Jack's shoulder, with his right hand he made a slow, vague gesture in the air. "Ah, ne m'en parlez pas, je vous en supplie," he said, his voice weak and breaking with emotion.

"Oh, I'm sorry," said Jack. "Est-ce qu'il lui est arrivé quelque malheur? Est-ce qu'on l'a arrêté? fusillé?"

"Pire que ça," said Georges.

"Pire que ça?" exclaimed Jack.

"Il danse!" said Georges.

"Il danse?" said Jack with profound astonishment, unable to

imagine how it was such a grave misfortune for a ballet dancer in Paris to dance.

"Hélas, il danse!" repeated Georges, his voice filled with anguish, regret and bitterness.

"Vous l'avez vu danser?" said Jack in the same tone in which he would have asked: "Vous l'avez vu mourir?"

"Hélas, oui!" answered Georges.

"Il y a longtemps de cela?" asked Jack in a low voice.

"Le soir avant de quitter Paris," said Georges. "Je vais le voir danser tous les soirs, hélas! Tout Paris court le voir danser. Car il danse, hélas!"

"Il danse, hélas!" repeated Jack. "Il danse, tu comprends?" he said in a triumphant voice, turning to me. "Il danse, hélas!"

When we reached Torre del Greco it was four o'clock in the afternoon. We turned off in the direction of the sea, and stopped outside a gate at the end of a narrow lane flanked by high walls, at a point where the vineyards and orange groves stretch right down to the seashore. We pushed open the gate and entered a large orchard, in the middle of which stood a fisherman's house, a mean dwelling with faded red walls like those of the houses of Pompeii. The arch of a loggia opened into the façade of the house, and in front of the loggia was a large pergola, which extended all the way down the orchard and was still covered with vine leaves, now blighted by the first frosts of autumn. Here and there among the red vine leaves were bright clusters of white grapes, gilded by the last fires of the summer that was past. Beneath the pergola a rustic table had been laid. It was covered with a coarse linen cloth, on which were set a quantity of rough majolica crockery, some bone-handled knives and forks, and a few bottles of Vesuvian wine, that white wine which the black lava from the volcano and the limpidity of the sea air endow with a wondrous potency, dry and delicate.

Jeanlouis' friends, who were sitting waiting for us on the ancient marble benches that were scattered about the orchard (the houses, gardens and orchards in that part of the Neapolitan countryside which lies at the foot of Vesuvius are full of blocks of marble unearthed during the excavations at Herculaneum and Pompeii), received Georges, Fred and Jeanlouis with loud cries of joy, and came forward to meet them with open arms, swaying their hips and moving their heads from side to side gently, lovingly. They embraced, they whispered in one another's ears, they looked tenderly into one another's eyes. It seemed as though they had not seen one another for a hundred years, whereas they had parted but a short time — perhaps an hour — before. One after the other they all kissed Georges' hand. He accepted their homage with regal graciousness, all the time smiling proudly and disdainfully. When the ceremonial embraces were over Georges underwent a transformation. He seemed to rouse himself, he opened his eyes, he looked about him with feigned astonishment, he begun to chirrup and shake his feathers, and walked from one to another of his friends with peculiar short, lively steps which made him look like a sparrow hopping on invisible branches. He did in fact hop from one to another of the shadows thrown on the ground by the vine branches of the pergola, and every so often he appeared to peck with birdlike grace at the golden grapes that peeped between the red vine leaves.

Jack and I had sat down by ourselves on a marble bench, so as not to interrupt those honorable and graceful manifestations of love. Jack was laughing and shaking his head. "Do you really think," he said, "tu crois vraiment . . . ?"

"Of course," I said.

"Ah! ah! ah! c'est donc ça," said Jack, "c'est donc ça, ce que vous appelez des héros, en Europe?"

"It is you," I said, "who have made heroes of them. Did you really need our pederasts to win the war? Luckily we *have* got something better in the way of heroes in Europe."

"Don't you think you've got something better in the way of pederasts as well?" said Jack.

"I'm beginning to think that the pederasts are the only victors in the war."

"I'm beginning to think so too," said Jack, shaking his head and laughing.

Meanwhile Georges and his friends were walking about the orchard, whispering among themselves and casting anxious and impatient glances in the direction of the house.

"What are they waiting for?" said Jack. "Do you think they're waiting for someone? I'm beginning to feel apprehensive — I suspect that this story is destined to have a disagreeable ending."

Suddenly I turned my eyes seawards. "Look at the sea, Jack," I said in a low voice.

The sea clung to the shore and stared at me. It stared at me with its great green eyes, panting, clinging like some savage creature to the shore. It gave forth a strange odor, the powerful odor of a wild beast. Far away to the west, where the sun was already sinking toward a misty horizon, were hundreds and hundreds of steamers, bobbing up and down as they rode at anchor outside the harbor. They were enveloped in a dense gray fog, relieved by the brilliant whiteness of the seagulls. Away in the distance other ships furrowed the waters of the bay, looking black against the blue transparent ghost of the island of Capri. A storm was blowing up from the southeast; it was gradually filling the sky with livid clouds, seamed with streaks of sulphur-colored light, unexpected, narrow, green cracks, and dazzling black scars. I had a vision of white sails, fleeing in confusion before the storm, seeking the safety of Castellammare harbor. The scene was sad yet animated, with the ships belching smoke far away on the horizon, the sailing boats fleeing before the green and yellow lightning that flashed across the black storm clouds, and the remote island drifting in the blue abyss of the sky. It was a fabulous panorama; and somewhere at its edge Andromeda, chained to a rock, was weeping, and somewhere Perseus was slaying the monster.

The sea stared at me with its great imploring eyes, panting like a wounded beast; and I shuddered. It was the first time the sea had ever looked at me in that way. It was the first time I had ever felt those green eyes resting upon me with such overwhelming sadness in them, such anguish, such desolate grief. It stared at me, panting; it clung to the shore, looking exactly like a wounded beast; and I trembled with horror and pity. I was weary of watching men suffer, of watching them drip blood and drag themselves groaning along the ground. I was weary of listening to their laments, to those wonderful words that dying men murmur, smiling in their agony. I was weary of watching men suffer, and animals too, and trees, and the sky, the earth and the sea. I was weary of their sufferings, of their senseless, futile sufferings, of their terror, of their interminable agony. I was weary of my horror, weary of my pity. Ah, pity! I was ashamed of my pity. And yet I trembled with pity and horror. Beyond the distant curve of the bay Vesuvius rose, bare and ghostlike, its slopes streaked with fire and lava and bleeding from deep wounds whence issued flames and clouds of smoke. The sea clung to the shore and stared at me with its great imploring eyes, panting. It was covered all over with green scales, like a huge reptile. And I trembled with pity and horror as I heard the hoarse lament of Vesuvius floating through the upper air.

But around us were the leaves of the lemon and orange trees, dark and lustrous, and the olives, silver-spangled in the sea breeze and the murky rays of the now setting sun — a warm, bright oasis of peace in the heart of a chaotic, menacing nature. From the little house came the agreeable smell of fresh fish and newly baked bread, the clatter of plates and dishes, and the gentle voice of a woman talking in subdued tones.

An old fisherman emerged from the house, and turning toward our friends, who were at the bottom of the orchard, conversing among themselves with a mysterious air, shouted that all was ready. I thought he was referring to supper, and sitting down at a table next to Jack I filled our glasses with wine. The wine was strong and had a delicate flavor, which dissolved into a delicious aroma of wild herbs. I recognized

in its flavor and its scent the hot breath of Vesuvius, the tang
of the autumnal wind in the vineyards that have arisen from
the fields of black lava and the lifeless deserts of gray ashes
surrounding Bosco Treccase, on the barren slopes of the volcano. And I said to Jack: "Drink. This wine was squeezed
from the grapes of Vesuvius, it has the mysterious flavor of
the infernal fires, the scent of the lava and ashes that buried
Herculaneum and Pompeii. Drink, Jack — drink this sacred,
ancient wine."

Jack raised his glass to his lips. "What a strange people you
are!" he said.

"A strange, a miserable, a marvelous people," I said, lifting
my glass. But at that moment I noticed that our friends had
disappeared. From inside the house came the sound of subdued voices and a loud, prolonged groan, a sort of intoned
wail, almost a hymn of woe, like the wailing of a woman in
labor attuned to the motif of a love song. Our curiosity
aroused, we got up, noiselessly approached the house, and
entered. The sound of voices and that strange wailing came
from the upper floor. We climbed the stairs in silence, pushed
open a door, and paused on the threshold.

It was a humble room, of the sort one would expect to find
in the home of fisher folk. Much of the space was taken up
by a vast bed, on which there lay, beneath a yellow silk
counterpane, the indeterminate figure of a human being — it
might have been a man or a woman. The head, framed in a
white coif trimmed with lace and fastened beneath the chin
with a broad blue ribbon, rested in the center of a large and
voluminous pillow with a shining white silk cover; it was
like a bodiless head engraved on a silver dish. The large eyes,
which looked out from a face tanned by sun and wind, were
dark and lustrous. The mouth was wide, and a small black
moustache afforded a contrast to the red lips. It was undoubtedly a man — a young man of not more than twenty.
Open-mouthed, he was wailing in a singing voice and moving his head from side to side on the pillow. His muscular
arms, encased in the sleeves of a woman's nightdress, were

outside the bedclothes, and he was waving them about, as
though in the grip of some cruel pain which he could no
longer endure. Every so often, with a melodious cry of "Ohi
misera me!" he pressed both hands to his belly, which was
strangely swollen, exactly like that of a pregnant woman.

Jeanlouis and his friends were grouped around the bed,
restless, solicitous and fearful, as if assailed by the anguish
that grips the relatives of a woman in travail as they stand at
her bedside. One was soothing the patient's brow with soaking cloths, another had poured vinegar and perfume into a
handkerchief and was holding it to his nostrils. A third was
making ready towels, gauze and linen bandages, while a
fourth was busying himself about two washbasins, into which
an old woman with a wrinkled face and unkempt gray hair
was pouring hot water from two jugs, which she raised and
lowered rhythmically, her slow, deliberate gestures contrast-
ing with the anguished movements of her head, her profound,
breathless sighs, and the imploring looks which she repeatedly
directed heavenward. All the others were rushing about the
room with never a pause, crossing one another's paths, bumping into one another, pressing their hands to their heads and
crying "Mon Dieu! mon Dieu!" whenever the "mother-to-be"
uttered a particularly shrill yell or a groan that was more than
usually heart-rending.

In the middle of the room, clutching an enormous wad of
cotton-wool, and solemnly pulling from it large tufts which
he threw into the air, so that they slowly fell around him like
warm snow from a torrid, luminous sky, stood Georges,
looking like the statue of Anguish and Grief. "Ohi misera me!
Ohi misera me!" chanted the "mother-to-be," beating his
swollen belly with his two hands so that it reverberated like a
drum. To Georges there was something utterly inhuman in
the deep booming sound produced by the pommeling of
those strong seaman's fingers on that teeming belly. Pale-
faced and trembling, he shut his eyes and groaned — "Mon
Dieu! ah! mon Dieu!"

As soon as Jeanlouis and his friends perceived us standing
in the doorway, engrossed in that extraordinary spectacle, they

were upon us with one voice. With timid gestures, with chaste violence, with countless manifestations of frenzy and innumerable graceful little movements, with light taps that resembled caresses, accompanied by sighs that seemed to betoken alarm and yet were almost indicative of pleasure, they tried to push us out through the door. And they might have attained their object if a piercing cry had not suddenly reverberated through the room. They all turned, and with a howl of anguish and alarm rushed to the bed.

Pale, his eyes wide open, his two hands pressed to his temples, the mother-to-be was beating his head again and again on the pillow and uttering shrill cries. His lips were beslavered with blood and froth, and large tears rolled down his dark, virile cheeks, forming beads on his black moustache. "Cicillo! Cicillo!" cried the old woman, throwing herself on the bed. She thrust her hands beneath the bedclothes and, puffing and blowing, clicking her tongue, making obscene noises with her lips, rolling her eyes, and uttering deep, gurgling sighs, worked strenuously on that swollen belly, which kept rising and falling grotesquely beneath the yellow silk counterpane. Every so often the old woman would yell "Cicillo! Cicillo! Don't be afraid, I'm here!" It seemed that she had grasped with both hands some loathsome creature that was concealed beneath the clothes, and was trying to throttle it. Cicillo was lying with his legs wide apart, foaming at the mouth and calling upon St. Januarius for help. He kept thrashing his head from side to side with blind violence, while Georges made futile efforts to restrain him, weeping and embracing him with the utmost tenderness, and constantly trying to prevent him from striking his head against the iron frame of the bed.

Suddenly the old woman began pulling something toward her with both hands — something that came from inside Cicillo's belly. Finally, with a shout of triumph, she wrenched it out, raised it aloft and displayed it to all. It was some sort of monstrous abortion, dark in color, with a wrinkled, red-spotted face. At the sight of it they all became delirious with joy. With tears in their eyes they exchanged embraces and kissed one another on the mouth. Jumping and shouting, they pressed round the old woman while she, sticking her fingers into the dark, crinkled flesh of the new arrival, kept lifting it on high, as if she were offering it as a gift to some god. "O blessed one! O miracle child!" she cried, while all, like men possessed, began rushing about the room, behaving after the fashion of newborn babes, screaming and yelling in shrill voices, opening their mouths so wide that they seemed to stretch to their ears and rubbing their eyes with their clenched fists. Torn from the clutches of the old woman, the new arrival passed from hand to hand and eventually came to rest on its "mother's" pillow. The "mother" raised himself up and sat on the bed, his handsome, virile, moustached face lit up by the sweetest of maternal smiles, and opened his muscular arms to receive the fruit of his womb. "My son!" he cried, and seizing the monstrosity he clasped it to his bosom, rubbed it against his hairy chest and covered its face with kisses. For a long while he rocked it in his arms, crooning softly, and finally, with a lovely smile, handed it to Georges.

In the confinement ceremony this gesture signified that the honor of fatherhood belonged to Georges. The latter, receiving the new arrival into his cupped hands, began tossing it about, fondling and kissing it and gazing at it with tears and laughter in his eyes. I looked at the child in horror. It was an old wooden statuette, a roughly carved fetish; it looked like one of those phallic images that are depicted on the walls of the houses of Pompeii. It had a very small, shapeless head, its arms were short, like those of a skeleton, with a swollen stomach. For a long while Georges' eyes dwelt on the monstrosity. He was pale, breathless, dripping with perspiration, and his hands trembled. All the others pressed around him, yelping, lifting their arms and waving them about, and kissing that loathsome object with a jealous, frantic eagerness that was both wonderful and horrible to behold.

Just then a loud voice was heard shouting from the foot of the stairs. "The spaghetti! the spaghetti!" it cried, and simultaneously the room was filled with the odor of baked pastry and tomato sauce. Thereupon Cicillo threw his legs out of the bed, rested one hand on Georges' shoulder, almost embracing him, and with the other modestly clasped the edge of his nightdress to his breast. He rose, put his feet to the floor and, with many a graceful gesture, sighing plaintively and glancing languidly about him, very slowly moved off, supported and urged on by ten loving arms. Swathed in a red silk dressing gown, which the old woman had thrown over his shoulders, he made for the door, groaning as he went. And we all followed him.

Dinner commenced. First came spaghetti, then fried mullet and cuttlefish, then beef alla genovese, and finally a sweet pastiera (a Neapolitan dough-cake made with eggs and soaked in whey). Jack and I sat at the end of the table and, our anxiety far outweighing our amusement, silently observed the behavior of the various characters in that singular comedy, expecting every moment that something extraordinary would happen. They all ate and drank merrily, in the grip of an excitement which was at first subdued, but which gradually mounted, until it became an amorous frenzy, a fever of jealousy. Following a heedless word from Georges, who, red-faced, his brow resting on Cicillo's shoulder, was gazing at his friends and rivals with a malevolent expression, Jeanlouis suddenly began to cry. It seemed to me that his tears were tears of vexation; and my astonishment knew no bounds when I perceived that he was sincerely and acutely distressed, and that his suffering was genuine. I called him by name, and they all turned toward me in surprise and annoyance, as though I had interrupted a scene notable for its expert construction and acting. Jeanlouis went on crying for some considerable time, and showed no sign of regaining his composure until Cicillo, rising languidly from his seat, went up to him and, after kissing him behind the ear, began to stroke his hair, talking to him in a low voice, the tone of which was extraordinarily tender. It was obvious, however, that he did so not so much out of a desire to alleviate Jeanlouis' distress as because he took a malicious delight in arousing the jealousy of his rivals.

When he stood up, and one saw him at close quarters,

Cicillo looked much younger than he appeared when lying in bed. He was a very handsome lad of not more than eighteen. But what disturbed me was the perfect naturalness of his behavior and of his tone of voice, coupled with the impression he gave of being an actor with all the tricks of the trade at his command. Not only did he not seem shy or ashamed because of his strange get-up and of the part he was playing, but he almost appeared proud of his disguise and of his artistic prowess.

After fondling Jeanlouis for a while he resumed his seat at the head of the table. For some reason — possibly the warmth of the food, or the fiery quality of the wine, or the keen sea air — it was not long before he seemed gradually to lose something of — if one may so term it — his feminine modesty. His eyes blazed, his voice grew stronger and assumed a rich, masculine, sonorous timbre. The sinews beneath his sun-burned skin came to life, the muscles of his shoulders and arms rippled. Gradually his hands became virile, his fingers gnarled and tough. I did not like this: it seemed to me that such a transformation placed too unequivocal an emphasis on the disagreeable element in the comedy, on its symbolical meaning, expressed or latent. But, as I learned subsequently, even this unexpected metamorphosis was an integral part of the confinement ceremony — indeed, it constituted its most exquisite moment. The ceremony invariably ended with what we may call the "hand-kissing" ritual.

Cicillo, in point of fact, began in due course to arouse the guests by voice and gesture, seasoning affectionate words and exclamations with scurrilous insults and gibes. Eventually he rose to his feet and with a sweeping, regal gesture removed the coif from his brow as though it had been a crown. He looked haughtily about him and parted his lips in a triumphant, contemptuous smile, tossing his curly black mane. Then, kicking over his chair, he suddenly started to run off in the direction of the house, passed through the doorway, gave a loud, harsh laugh, and vanished. The guests all rose, and with shrill wails of distress and fury pursued him, disappearing inside the house.

"Come on!" shouted Jack, seizing me by the arm and dragging me along at his side. I noticed that he was pale, and that his forehead was bedewed with large drops of perspiration. We rushed upstairs and stopped in the doorway.

Cicillo was lying on his back on the bed. Supporting himself on his elbows, he was gazing at Georges with eyes in which there was an ironical and at the same time a menacing glint. Georges stood before him, motionless, panting hard, almost leaning against his friends, who stood in a cluster behind him, pressing hard against his shoulders with their chests.

Jack gripped my arm with terrible violence, his face white as a sheet. I saw that his lips were trembling, his eyes glazed, his temples bursting. "Go on, Malaparte, go on!" he stuttered. "Oh! go on, Malaparte! Kick him, kick him in the ass, Malaparte! I can't stand it any longer, Malaparte — kick him in the ass! Oh, go on, Malaparte, go on!"

"I can't, Jack," I answered, "I just can't, Jack, I'm only a wretched, defeated Italian, I can't kick a hero. Georges is a hero, Jack, one of freedom's heroes, Jack. I'm only an unfortunate wretch, crushed beneath the conqueror's heel. I haven't the right to kick one of freedom's heroes in the ass, Jack, I haven't the right, I swear to you that I haven't the right, Jack!"

"Ah, you're afraid!" stuttered Jack, forcibly gripping my arm.

"Yes, I'm afraid, Jack — I admit it, I'm afraid. You don't know what that splendid breed of heroes can do! You don't know what a cowardly, evil breed they are! They would get their revenge, they would have me jailed, they would ruin me, Jack. You don't know how cowardly and evil pederasts are when they start posing as heroes!"

"You're afraid! You're a coward too! Go on, you bastard!"

And suddenly, knocking me to one side with a blow in the ribs, he threw himself at Georges and gave him a terrible kick in the buttocks. "Salauds! Cochons!" he cried. He laid about him furiously with his boot, and snatching the wooden monstrosity from Cicillo's hands whirled it about in the air like a club. He seemed to be in such a blinding rage that I feared for his safety. While Georges and his friends, uttering shrill feminine shrieks and loud wails, lay in a heap on the floor at the foot of the bed (the only one who betrayed neither amazement nor fear was Cicillo, who sat on the edge of the bed and looked at Jack with eyes full of admiration, exclaiming "What a lovely man! What a lovely man!"), I seized Jack by the shoulders, clasped him in my arms, and lifting him almost bodily endeavored to drag him back and push him toward the door. Having at last managed to overpower him, I hauled him down the stairs and got him into the car. I sat at the wheel, started the engine, turned, drove into the road, and away we went.

"Oh, Malaparte!" groaned Jack, covering his face with his hands, "on ne peut pas voir ces choses-là, non, on ne peut pas!"

"You're lucky," I said to him. "You're lucky because you're an honorable man, Jack! I like you, I like you very much. You are a splendid, honorable, innocent American, Jack — just that! You are a wonderful American, Jack!"

Jack remained silent, and stared straight ahead.

"I'm sorry, Malaparte," said Jack, blushing. "I shouldn't have done what I did."

"You did quite right, Jack," I said. "You're a splendid chap, Jack."

"Perhaps I had no right to do what I did," said Jack. "I had no right to insult them."

"You did quite right, Jack," I said.

"No, I had no right to do it," said Jack. "I had no right to kick them."

"You are a conqueror," I said. "You are a conqueror, Jack."

"A conqueror?" said Jack, flinging the horrible thing he was clutching through the window. "A conqueror? Don't make fun of me, Malaparte. A conqueror!"

THE BLACK WIND

● The black wind began blowing toward daybreak, and I awoke, dripping with perspiration. I had recognized its sad voice, its black voice, as I slept. I went to the window and searched the walls, the roofs, the surface of the street, the leaves on the trees, the sky over Posilipo, for signs of its presence. The black wind is like a blind man, who gropes his way, caressing the air and barely touching near-by objects with his outstretched hands. It is blind, it does not see where it is going, it touches now a wall, now a branch, now a human face, now the seashore, now a mountain, leaving in the air and on the things that it touches the black imprint of its light caress.

It was not the first time that I had heard the voice of the black wind, and I recognized it at once. I awoke, dripping with perspiration, and going to the window I scanned the houses, the sea, the sky, and the clouds high above the sea.

The first time I heard its voice was when I was in the Ukraine, during the summer of 1941. I happened to be in the Cossack lands of the Dnieper, and one evening the old Cossacks of the village of Constantinovka said to me, as they sat smoking their pipes in the doorways of their houses, "Look at the black wind over there." The day was dying, the sun, low on the horizon, was sinking into the earth. Its last pink, translucent rays were touching the topmost boughs of the silver birches; and it was in that sad hour when the day dies that I first saw the black wind.

It was like a black shadow, like the shadow of a black horse, wandering uncertainly over the steppe, now here, now there, at one moment cautiously approaching the village, at the next fleeing in terror. Something that was like the wing of a night bird brushed the trees, the horses, the dogs that were scattered around the edge of the village, so that they immediately took on a dark hue and were tinged with the color of night. The voices of men and animals seemed like pieces of black paper drifting through the air in the pink light of sunset.

I made off in the direction of the river, and the water was cloudy and dark. I looked up at the foliage of a tree, and the leaves were black and shining. I picked up a stone, and in my hand the stone was black, heavy, opaque, like a bud that opens at night. The eyes of the girls returning from the fields to the long, low sheds of the kolkhoz were dark and shining, the echoes of their gay, carefree laughter rose into the air like black birds. And yet it was still daylight. The trees, the voices, the animals, the men, already so black though it was still daylight, filled me with a vague horror.

The old Cossacks, with their wrinkled faces, each with a large twisted tuft of hair crowning his shaven skull, said: "It is the black wind, the chorny vetier"; and they shook their heads, watching the black wind as it meandered uncertainly about the steppe like a frightened horse. I said: "Perhaps it is the shadow of evening that gives the wind its black tinge." The old Cossacks shook their heads. "No," they said, "it is not the shadow of evening that tinges the wind. It is the chorny vetier, which tinges with black everything it touches." And they taught me to recognize the voice of the black wind, and its smell, and its taste. One of them took a lamb in his arms, blew on the black wool, and the roots of the fleece were seen to be white. Another held a little bird in his hand, blew on the soft black feathers, and the roots of the feathers were seen to be tinged with yellow, red and blue. They blew on the plaster of a house, and beneath the black down left by the wind's caress the white lime could be seen. They sank their fingers into the black mane of a horse, and the reddish-brown hair became visible once more between their fingers. Whenever the black dogs that played in the little village square passed behind a fence or a wall, where they were sheltered from the wind, they assumed that brilliant tawny color which is peculiar to Cossack dogs, and lost it as soon as they got into the wind again. An old man dug up with his nails a white stone that had been buried in the soil, placed it in the palm of his hand and threw it into the teeth of the wind. It looked like a star whose light had been extinguished, a black star sinking into the clear pool of the day. I learned in this way to recognize the black wind by its smell, which is reminiscent of dry grass, by its tang, which is strong and bitter, like the tang of laurel leaves, and by its marvellously sad voice — the voice of Cimmerian night itself.

The next day I was on my way to Dorogo, which is three hours' journey from Constantinovka. It was already late, and my horse was weary. I was going to Dorogo in order to visit the famous kolkhoz which was the breeding ground of the finest horses in the whole of the Ukraine. I had left Constantinovka about five o'clock in the afternoon, and I was counting on reaching Dorogo before nightfall. But the recent rains had transformed the track into a quagmire and had carried away the bridges over the streams, which are very numerous in that region. As a result I was forced to make my way along the undulating bank in search of a ford. And I was still a long way from Dorogo when the sun, which was low on the horizon, sank into the earth with a dull plop. On the steppe the sun sets abruptly; it falls into the grass like a stone, with the plop of a stone hitting the earth. As soon as I had left Constantinovka I had joined a group of Hungarian cavalrymen who were on their way to Stalino, and I had accompanied them for many miles. They smoked long pipes as they rode, and every so often they stopped and talked among themselves. They had soft, musical voices. I thought they were deliberating as to which road they should take, but in due course the sergeant who was in command of them asked me in German if I was willing to sell my horse. It was a Cossack horse, and knew all the smells, all the flavors, all the sounds of the steppe. "It is my friend," I replied. "I don't sell my friends." The Hungarian sergeant looked at me with a smile. "It's a fine horse," he said, "but it can't have cost you very much. Can you tell me where you stole it?" I knew how to answer a horse thief, and I replied: "Yes, it's a fine horse. It runs like the wind all day without getting tired. But it's got leprosy." I looked him in the face and laughed. "It's got leprosy?" said the sergeant. "Don't you believe me?" I said. "If you don't believe me touch it, and you'll find it will give you leprosy." And caressing the horse's flank with the toe of my boot I slowly rode off, never looking back. For quite a while I heard them laughing and shouting and hurling insults at me; then, out of the corner of my eye, I saw that they had turned off toward the river and were galloping along in close formation, waving their arms. After a few miles I met some Rumanian cavalrymen who were out on a marauding expedition. Across their saddles were thrown piles of silk dressing gowns and rams' skins, which they had without doubt stolen from some Tartar village. They asked me where I was going. "To Dorogo," I replied. They would have liked to accompany me, they said, as far as Dorogo, in order to protect me in case of accidents, since the steppe (they added) was infested by bands of Hungarian robbers; but their horses were tired. They wished me bon voyage and made off, looking back every so often to wave to me.

It was already dusk when I discerned, far ahead of me, the glare of fires. It was undoubtedly the village of Dorogo. Suddenly I recognized the smell of the wind, and my heart froze within me. I looked at my hands: they were black and dry; they looked almost like pieces of charcoal. Black, too, were the few trees that were dotted about the steppe; the stones were black, the ground was black; but the atmosphere was still bright, and had a silvery look. The last fires of the day were dying in the sky behind me, and the wild horses of night were rushing toward me at a gallop from the far horizon to the east, raising black clouds of dust.

I felt the black caress of the wind on my face and the black night of the wind filling my mouth. An oppressive, sticky silence covered the steppe; it was like a stagnant, turbid lake. I bent over my horse's neck and whispered in its ear. The horse listened to my words, whinnying softly, and turned its great oblique eye upon me, its great dark eye, in which there shone a light of madness, chaste and melancholy. Night had already fallen, and the fires of the village of Dorogo were near, when suddenly I heard human voices floating high above my head.

I raised my eyes, and it seemed to me that a double row of trees flanked the road at that point, bending their boughs above my head. But I did not see their trunks, or their boughs, or their leaves. I was conscious only of being surrounded by trees, of a strange presence, of an element of strength pervading the black night, of something living that was immured in the black wall of the night. I stopped my horse and strained my ears. Yes, I could hear voices above my head, human voices floating through the blackness high above me. "Wer da?" I shouted. "Who goes there?"

Ahead of me, on the horizon, a faint pink glimmer was spreading into the sky. The voices floated high above my head. They were *human* voices; they spoke in German, Russian, Hebrew. They were conversing in loud, but rather shrill tones. Sometimes they were harsh, sometimes they were cold and brittle as glass, and often at the end of a word they broke with the tinkling sound of glass when it is struck by a stone. Again I shouted: "Wer da? Who goes there?"

"Who are you? What do you want? Who is it? Who is it?" answered several voices, drifting high above my head.

The rim of the horizon was pink and transparent as the shell of an egg. As one looked at the skyline it did indeed seem as if an egg were slowly emerging from the womb of the earth.

"I am a man; I am a Christian," I said.

A shrill laugh rippled across the black sky. It faded away into the distance and was lost in the night. A voice, louder than the rest, shouted: "Ah! A Christian, are you?" I answered: "Yes, I am a Christian." Scornful laughter greeted my words. It drifted high above my head into the distance, and gradually died away in the night.

"And aren't you ashamed of being a Christian?" shouted the voice.

I was silent. Bent over my horse's neck, with my face buried in its mane, I was silent.

"Why don't you answer?" shouted the voice.

I was silent: I was watching the horizon as it gradually lightened. A golden radiance, transparent as an egg shell, was slowly spreading across the sky. It was in truth an egg, that thing which was taking shape on the skyline, gradually appearing from beneath the ground, slowly rising from the deep, dark tomb of the earth.

"Why don't you speak?" shouted the voice.

And high above my head I heard a rustling sound, as of branches shaken by the wind, and a murmuring, as of leaves in the wind. I heard a furious laugh, and harsh words drifting across the black sky, and I felt something that was like a wing brush my face. They were, of course, birds, those creatures up there — large black birds, crows perhaps, that had been roused from sleep and were flying away, flapping their thick black wings as they made off. "Who are you?" I shouted. "For God's sake answer me!" The sky was bathed in the faint light of the moon. It was in truth an egg, that thing which was issuing from the womb of the night, it was in truth an egg that was issuing from the womb of the earth, and climbing slowly above the horizon. I saw the trees which flanked the road gradually emerge from the night and roughly outline themselves against the golden sky, while black shadows stirred high up among the branches.

I stifled a cry of horror. They were crucified men. They were men, nailed to the trunks of the trees, their arms outspread in the form of a cross, their feet bound together and fixed to the trunks with long nails or with pieces of steel wire that had been twisted round their ankles. The heads of some of them were lolling on their shoulders or chests; others, with upturned faces, were gazing at the rising moon. Many were clad in the black caftan that Jews wear. Many were naked, and their flesh shone chastely in the cool, mild light of the moon. Like the teeming egg which the corpses in the cemeteries of Tarquinia, in Etruria, hold up between two fingers as a symbol of fruitfulness and eternity, the moon was emerging from beneath the ground and poising itself in the sky. White and cold as an egg, it lit up the bearded faces, the black eye-sockets, the gaping mouths and twisted limbs of the crucified men.

I rose on the stirrups and stretched out my hands toward one of them. With my fingers I tried to tear out the nails that pierced his feet. But the sound of angry voices arose on all sides, and the crucified man yelled: "Don't touch me, curse you!"

"I don't intend to hurt you!" I shouted. "For God's sake, let me help you!"

A horrible laugh ran from tree to tree, from cross to cross. Here and there I saw heads moving, beards wagging, mouths opening and closing; and I heard a gnashing of teeth.

"Help us?" shouted the voice from above. "And why? Can it be because you pity us — because you are a Christian? Come on — answer: Is it because you are a Christian? Do you think that's a good reason? Do you pity us because you are a Christian?" I was silent, and the voice went on more loudly: "Aren't the men who crucified us Christians like yourself? Are they dogs, or horses, or mice — the men who nailed us to these trees? Ha! ha! ha! A Christian!"

I bent my head over my horse's neck and was silent.

"Come on — answer! What right have you to presume to help us? What right have you to presume to pity us?"

"*I* didnt do it!" I shouted. "*I* didn't nail you to the trees! *I* didn't do it!"

"I know," said the voice, and its tone was ineffably gentle and malignant. "I know. It was the others, it was all the others like you."

Just then a groan was heard in the distance, a loud, wild lament. It was the cry of a young man, a cry cut short by a dying sob. A murmur reached our ears, a murmur that passed from tree to tree. Forlorn voices shouted: "Who is it? Who is it? Who is that who's dying?" And in succession down the line of crosses came other plaintive voices, answering: "It's David, it's Samuel's boy David, it's David, Samuel's son, it's David, it's David . . ." As the name echoed from tree to tree we heard a stifled sob, a hoarse, faint lament, and groans and curses, and howls of pain and fury.

"He was still a boy," said the voice.

Then I raised my eyes, and in the light of the moon, which was now high in the heavens, in the chill white radiance of that egg, poised in the dark sky, I saw the man who was addressing me. He was naked, and his thin, bearded face had a silvery sheen. His arms were outspread in the form of a cross, his hands were nailed to two thick branches which grew out of the tree trunk. He was staring at me with glittering eyes, and suddenly he shouted: "What sort of pity is yours? What do you expect us to do with your pity? We spit on your pity — ya naplivayu! ya naplivayu!" And from all sides there came the sound of furious voices repeating his words: "Ya naplivayu! ya naplivayu! I spit on it! I spit on it!"

"For God's sake," I cried, "don't drive me away! Let me unnail you from your crosses! Don't reject my helping hand: it is the hand of a human being."

The air around us filled with malignant laughter. I heard the branches groaning above my head, and a horrible rustling sound spread among the leaves.

The crucified man roared with laughter. "Did you hear?" he said. "He wants to take us down from our crosses! And he isn't ashamed! You filthy Christians — you torture us, you nail us to trees, and then you come and offer us your pity! You want to save your souls, eh? You're afraid of hell! Ha! ha! ha!"

"Don't drive me away!" I cried. "Don't reject my helping hand, for God's sake!"

"You want to take us down from our crosses?" said the crucified man in a grave, sad voice. "And then? The Germans will kill us like dogs. And you too — they'll kill you as they would a mad dog."

"They'll kill us like dogs," I repeated to myself, bowing my head.

"If you want to help us, if you want to shorten our agony . . . shoot us through the head, one by one. Come on — why don't you shoot us? Why don't you finish us off? If you really pity us shoot us, put us out of our misery. Come on — why don't you shoot us? Are you afraid the Germans will kill you for taking pity on us?" As he spoke he looked hard at me, and I felt those dark, glittering eyes boring into me.

"No, no!" I cried. "Have pity on me, don't ask me to do that, for God's sake! Don't ask me to do such a thing — I've never shot a man, I'm not a murderer! I don't want to become a murderer!" And I beat my head against my horse's neck, weeping and crying out.

The crucified men were silent. I heard them breathing, I

heard them whistling hoarsely through their teeth, I felt their eyes resting on me, I felt their flaming eyes burning my tear-stained face, piercing my breast.

"If you pity me, kill me!" shouted the crucified man. "Oh, put a bullet through my head! Oh, shoot me through the head, have pity on me! For God's sake kill me — oh, kill me, for God's sake!"

Then, grief-stricken and weeping bitterly, I put my hand to my side and seized the butt of my pistol, moving my arms painfully and laboriously, for they felt as if an enormous weight were pressing on them. Slowly I raised my elbow and drew the pistol from its holster. Standing up on the stirrups, and with my left hand grasping the horse's mane lest I should slip from the saddle, so weak and dizzy was I, so overcome by horror, I raised the pistol and pointed it at the face of the man on the cross; and at that instant I looked at him. I saw his dark, cavernous, toothless mouth, his hooked nose, the nostrils full of clotted blood, his disheveled beard, and his dark, glittering eyes.

"Ah, damn you!" shouted the crucified man. "Is this what you call pity? Can't you do anything else, you cowards? You nail us to trees and then kill us by shooting us through the head? Is this what you call pity, you cowards?" And twice, three times, he spat in my face.

I fell back on the saddle, while a horrible laugh echoed from tree to tree. Jolted by the spurs, the horse stirred, and moved off at a trot. My head down, I clung with both hands to the pommel of the saddle, and as I passed beneath those crucified men every one of them spat upon me, crying: "You coward! You damned Christian!" I felt their spittle lashing my face and hands, and I gritted my teeth as, bending low over my horse's neck, I passed beneath that shower of spittle.

Having in this way reached Dorogo, I fell from the saddle into the arms of some Italian soldiers who were on garrison duty in that forgotten village of the steppe. They were light cavalry of the Lodi Regiment, commanded by a very young

Lombard subaltern — he was almost a child. During the night I had a bout of fever and was delirious until dawn, the young officer meanwhile watching over me. I do not know what I shouted in my delirium, but when I regained consciousness the officer told me that I was in no way to blame for the horrible fate that had befallen those unhappy men. On that very morning, he said, a German patrol had shot a peasant who had been caught giving the crucified men something to drink. I began to shout. "I don't want to be a Christian any more!" I shouted. "I'm sick of being a Christian, a damned Christian!" And I fought to be allowed to go and take those wretches something to drink, but the officer and two of his men held me fast in bed. For a long while I fought, until at last I fainted. When I came to my senses I fell a victim to a fresh bout of fever, and I was delirious all that day and the following night.

Next day I stayed in bed, too weak to get up. I looked through the windowpanes at the white sky above the yellow steppe, and at the green clouds on the horizon. I listened to the voices of the peasants and the soldiers as they went past the fence that surrounded the orchard. That evening the young officer told me that as we could not help seeing those horrible things we ought to try and forget them, so as to avoid the risk of going mad. He added that if I felt better next day he would accompany me on my visit to the kolkhoz and the famous stud farm at Dorogo. However, I thanked him for his kindness, saying that I wanted to return to Constantinovka at the earliest possible moment. On the third day I got up and said good-bye to the young officer. (I remember that I embraced him, and that as I embraced him I was trembling.) Although I felt desperately weak I got into the saddle and, accompanied by two soldiers of the light cavalry regiment, set out for Constantinovka early in the afternoon.

We rode out of the village at a jog trot. When we entered the tree-flanked avenue I shut my eyes and, spurring on my horse, went forward at a gallop between the two terrible lines of crucified men. I crouched low on the saddle as I rode, shutting my eyes and gritting my teeth. Suddenly I reined in my horse. 'What does this silence mean?" I cried. "Why this silence?"

I had recognized that silence. I opened my eyes and looked. Those horrible Christs were hanging limply from their crosses. Their eyes were wide open, their mouths gaping, and they were staring at me. The black wind scurried hither and thither over the steppe like a blind horse. It stirred the rags that covered those poor mangled, twisted bodies, it shook the foliage of the trees — and not the faintest murmur passed through the leafy branches. Black crows were perched on the shoulders of the corpses, motionless, staring at me.

The silence was horrible. The light was dead, the smell of the grass, the color of the leaves, of the stones, of the clouds that drifted through the gray sky — everything was dead, everything was plunged in a vast, empty, frozen silence. I spurred on my horse; it reared, and flew off at a gallop. And I fled, shouting and weeping, over the steppe, while the black wind, like a blind horse, scurried hither and thither, under a cloudless sky.

I had recognized that silence. During the winter of 1940 I had sought refuge in a deserted house, situated at the end of one of the most beautiful and most deserted streets in the exquisitely beautiful, deserted city of Pisa. I had done so in order to escape from the war and from men, and to cure myself of that loathsome malady to which war exposes the human heart. With me was Febo, my dog Febo, whom I had picked up, dying of hunger, on the beach at Marina Corta, on the island of Lipari. I had tended him, reared him, brought him up in my lonely house on Lipari, and he had been my sole companion during my lonely years of exile on that sad island, which is so dear to my heart.

I have never loved a woman, a brother, a friend, so much as I loved Febo. There was an affinity between us. It was in his honor that I wrote the tender pages of *Un cane come me*. He was a noble creature, the noblest I have ever come across in my life. He belonged to that breed of greyhounds — a rare and delicate breed today — which came long ago from the shores of Asia with the first Ionic immigrants, and which are known to the shepherds of Lipari as cerneghi. These are the dogs which Greek sculptors used to represent on the bas-reliefs of sepulchres. The shepherds of Lipari say that they drive away death.

His coat was the color of the moon, between pink and gold; it was the color of moonlight on the sea, the color of moonlight on the dark leaves of lemon and orange trees, on the scales of the dead fish which the sea used to throw up on the shore outside the door of my house after a storm. He was the color of the moonlight on the Grecian sea that laps the shores of Lipari, the color of moonlight in the poetry of the *Odyssey,* the color of the moonlight on that wild Liparian sea which Ulysses sailed in the course of his voyage to the lonely shore of the realm of Aeolus, ruler of the winds. He was of a pale color, like the moon just before dawn. I used to call him Caneluna.

He never strayed so much as a yard from my side. He followed me like a dog. *He followed me, I say, like a dog.* There was something wonderful about his presence in my wretched house on Lipari, a house lashed without respite by the wind and the sea. At night the darkness of my bare room was lit by the bright warmth of his moon-eyes. His eyes were pale blue, the color of the sea when the moon sets. I was conscious of his presence as one is conscious of the presence of a shadow, of one's own shadow. He was, as it were, the mirror of my soul. His mere presence helped me to acquire that contempt for mankind on which the serenity and wisdom of a human being primarily depend. I felt that he resembled me, that he was in very truth the image of my conscience, of my secret life — a portrait of myself, of all that is deepest, most intimate and most characteristic in me. I felt that he was my subconscious and, so to say, my ghost.

From him, far more than from men, with their culture and

their vanity, I learned that virtue is its own reward, that it is an end in itself, and that it does not even aspire to save the world (not even that!), but only to invent ever new justifications for its disinterestedness and its liberty of action. The relationship of a man and a dog is always a relationship of two free spirits, of two forms of dignity, of two types of virtue each of which is its own reward. It is the most disinterested and the most romantic of relationships, one of those relationships which death illuminates with its own wan radiance — a radiance tinged with the color of the pale moon that hangs above the sea at dawn, when the sky is green.

I saw reproduced in him my most mysterious impulses, my secret instincts, my doubts, my fears, my hopes. The dignity of his attitude toward mankind was mine, the courage and pride of his attitude to life were mine, his contempt for the fickle passions of men was mine. But he was more sensitive than I to the obscure portents of nature and to the invisible presence of death, which ever lurks about us, silent and suspicious. He sensed the approach of the sad spirits that haunt our dreams as they come from afar through the night air, like dead insects that are borne on the wind, none knows whence. And on some nights, as he lay curled up at my feet in my bare room on Lipari, he followed with his eyes an invisible phantasm as it hovered around me, advancing and receding, and lingering long hours watching me through the windowpane. Every so often, if the mysterious presence came so close to me that it brushed my forehead, Febo would snarl menacingly, the hair on his back would bristle; and I would hear a mournful cry receding into the night, and gradually dying away.

He was the dearest of brothers to me, a true brother, one who betrays not, nor humiliates. He was a loving, a helping, an understanding, a forgiving brother. Only the man who has suffered long years of exile on a desert island, and who, on his return to the haunts of men, finds himself shunned and avoided as if he were a leper by all those who one day, when the tyrant is dead, will pose as heroes of freedom — only he knows what a dog can mean to a human being. Often Febo would gaze at me with a sad, noble expression of reproach in his loving eyes. At such times my sadness made me feel strangely ashamed, almost remorseful, and I was conscious as I faced him of a kind of heightened moral susceptibility. I felt that at those moments Febo despised me. True, he grieved for me, he was tender and loving; yet his eyes certainly held a suggestion of pity and, simultaneously, of contempt. He was not only my brother, but my judge. He was the guardian of my dignity, and at the same time, to use the expression of the old Greeks, he was my δορυφόρημα.

He was a sad dog, with grave eyes. Every evening we used to spend long hours on the high windswept threshold of my house, looking at the sea. Ah! the Grecian sea of Sicily, ah! the red crags of Scylla, yonder, facing Charybdis, and the snow-capped peak of Aspromonte, and the white shoulder of Etna, the Olympus of Sicily! Truly, as Theocritus sings, life offers no more beautiful experience than to contemplate the Sicilian sea from a vantage point on the shore. We used to see the shepherds' fires flaring up on the mountains, and the boats sailing forth into the deep to meet the moon; we used to hear the mournful wail of the sea shells, through which the fishermen call to one another over the water, receding into the silvery, moonlit haze. We used to see the moon rising over the crags of Scylla, and Stromboli, the high, inaccessible volcano that stands in the middle of the sea, blazing like a solitary pyre within the deep blue forest of the night. We used to look at the sea, inhaling the pungent salt air, and the strong, intoxicating perfume of the orange groves, and the smell of goats' milk and of juniper branches burning in the hearths, and that warm, heavy scent of women which pervades the Sicilian night when the first stars climb wanly above the horizon.

Then one day I was taken with handcuffs on my wrists from Lipari to another island, and from there, after long months, to Tuscany. Febo followed me at a distance, hiding among the casks of anchovies and the coils of rope on the deck of the *Santa Marina,* the little steamer which crosses every so often from Lipari to Naples, and among the hampers of fish and tomatoes on the motorboat that plies between Naples, Ischia and Ponza. With the courage that is peculiar to cowards — it is the only positive claim that slaves have to share the privileges of the free — the people stopped to look at me with reproving, contemptuous expressions, hurling insults at me through clenched teeth. Only the lepers who lay in the sun on the benches in Naples harbor smiled at me surreptitiously, spitting on the ground between the shoes of the carabinieri. I looked back now and again to see if Febo was following me, and I saw him walking with his tail between his legs, hugging the walls, through the streets of Naples, from the Immacolatella to the Molo Beverello, a wonderfully sad look in his bright eyes.

In Naples, as I walked handcuffed between the carabinieri along Via Partenope, two ladies smilingly approached me. They were Benedetto Croce's wife and Minnie Casella, the wife of my dear friend Gaspare Casella. They greeted me in the motherly, kindly fashion that is characteristic of Italian women, thrusting flowers between the handcuffs and my wrists, and Signora Croce asked the carabinieri to take me to some place where I might get a drink and some refreshment. It was two days since I had eaten. "At least let him walk in the shade," said Signora Croce. It was June, and the sun beat down on one's head like a hammer. 'Thank you, I don't need anything," I said. "I only ask you to give my dog something to drink."

Febo had stopped a few yards from us and was looking into Signora Croce's eyes with an intensity that was almost painful. This was his first experience of human kindness, of womanly pity and consideration. He sniffed the water for a long time before drinking it. When, a few months later, I was transferred to Lucca, I was shut up in the prison, where I remained for many weeks. And when I came out, escorted by my guards, to my new place of banishment, Febo was waiting for me outside the door of the jail. He was thin and mud-stained, and there was a horribly gentle expression in his eyes, which shone brilliantly.

Two more years my exile lasted, and for two years we lived in a little house in the heart of a wood. One room was occupied by Febo and myself, the other by the carabinieri who were my warders. At last I regained my freedom, or what in those days passed for freedom, and to me it was like going from a room without windows into a narrow room without walls. We went to live in Rome; and Febo was sad — he seemed to be humiliated by the spectacle of my freedom. He knew that freedom is alien to humanity, that men cannot and perhaps do not know how to be free, and that in Italy and in Europe freedom is discredited no less than slavery.

Throughout our stay in Pisa we used to remain indoors nearly all day. Not until noon or thereabouts did we go out for our walk by the river, the fair river of Pisa, the silver Arno, strolling along the beautiful Lungarni, so light and cold. Then we would go to the Piazza dei Miracoli, where stands the leaning tower for which Pisa is world-famous. We used to climb the tower, and from the top look out over the Pisan plain as far as Leghorn and Massa, gazing at the pine forests, and the sea below, the shining lid of the sea, and the Apuan Alps, white with snow and marble. This was my own soil, my own Tuscan soil, here were my own woods and my own sea, here were my own mountains and fields and rivers.

Toward evening we would go and sit on the parapet overlooking the Arno (that narrow stone parapet along which Lord Byron, in the days when he was an exile in Pisa, used to gallop every morning on his beautiful alezan, amid the terrified shouts of the peaceful citizens). We used to watch the river as it flowed along, carrying with it in its bright career leaves blighted by the frosts of winter and mirroring the silver clouds that drift across the immemorial sky of Pisa.

Febo used to spend long hours curled up at my feet, and every so often he would get up, walk over to the door, and turn and look at me. I would go and open the door for him, and he would go out, coming back after an hour or two, breathless, his coat smoothed by the wind, his eyes bright

from the cold winter sunshine. At night he used to lift his
head and listen to the voice of the river, to the voice of the
rain beating down on the river; and sometimes I would wake
up, and feel his warm eyes resting gently upon me, feel his
vital, affectionate presence there in the dark room, and his
sadness, his desolate foreboding of death.

One day he went out and never came back. I waited for
him until evening, and when night fell rushed through the
streets, calling him by name. I returned home at dead of
night and threw myself on my bed, facing the half-open door.
Every so often I went to the window and called him again and
again in a loud voice. At daybreak I again rushed through the
deserted streets, between the silent façades of the houses
which, under the leaden sky, looked as though they were
made of dirty paper.

As soon as it was daylight I rushed to the municipal dog-
prison. I went into a gray room where I found a number of
whining dogs, shut up in stinking cages, their throats still
bearing the marks of the noose. The caretaker told me that
my dog might have been run over by a car, or stolen, or
thrown into the river by a gang of young hooligans. He advised me to go the round of the dog shops: Who could say
that Febo was not in some dog shop?

All the morning I rushed about from one dog shop to another, and at last a canine barber in a dirty little shop near
the Piazza dei Cavalieri asked me if I had been to the University Veterinary Clinic, to which dog thieves were in the
habit of selling cheaply the animals that were subsequently
used for clinical experiments. I rushed to the University, but
it was already past midday and the Veterinary Clinic was
closed. I returned home. I felt as if there were something
cold, hard and smooth in my eye-sockets: my eyes seemed to
be made of glass.

In the afternoon I returned to the University and went into
the Veterinary Clinic. My heart was thumping, I was so weak
and in such an agony of mind that I could hardly walk. I
asked for the doctor on duty and told him my name. The

doctor, a fair-haired, shortsighted young man with a tired smile, received me courteously and gazed at me for a long time before replying that he would do everything possible to help me.

He opened a door and we entered a large, clean, bright room, the floor of which was covered with blue linoleum. Along the walls, one beside the other, like beds in a children's clinic, were rows of strange cradles, shaped like 'cellos. In each of the cradles was a dog, lying on its back, with its stomach exposed, or its skull split, or its chest gaping open. The edges of those dreadful wounds were held apart by thin steel wires, wound round wooden pegs of the kind that in musical instruments serves to keep the strings taut. One could see the naked heart beating; the lungs, with the veins of the bronchial tubes looking like the branches of a tree, swelling exactly as the foliage of a tree does when the wind blows; the red, shining liver very slowly contracting; slight tremors running through the pink and white substance of the brain as in a steamy mirror; the coils of the intestines sluggishly disentangling themselves like a heap of snakes waking from their deep slumber. And not a moan came from the half-open mouths of the tortured dogs.

As we entered all the dogs turned their eyes upon us. They gazed at us imploringly, and at the same time their expressions were full of a dread foreboding. They followed our every gesture with their eyes, watching us with trembling lips. Standing motionless in the middle of the room, I felt a chill spreading through my limbs; little by little I became as if turned to stone. I could not open my lips, I could not move a step. The doctor laid his hand on my arm. "Courage," he said. The word dispelled the chill that was in my bones; slowly I moved, and bent over the first cradle. As I proceeded from cradle to cradle the color returned to my face, and my heart dared to hope. And suddenly I saw Febo.

He was lying on his back, his stomach exposed and a probe buried in his liver. He was staring at me; his eyes were full of tears, and they had in them a wonderful tenderness. He was breathing gently, his mouth half-open, and his body was trembling horribly. He was staring at me, and an agonizing pain stabbed my heart. "Febo," I said in a low voice; and Febo looked at me with a wonderfully tender expression. In him I saw Christ, in him I saw Christ crucified, I saw Christ looking at me with eyes that were full of a wonderful tenderness. "Febo," I said in a low voice, bending over him and stroking his forehead. Febo kissed my hand, and not a moan escaped him.

The doctor came up to me and touched my arm. "I can't interrupt the experiment," he said. "It's not allowed. But for your sake . . . I'll give him an injection. He won't suffer."

I took the doctor's hand in mine. "Swear to me that he won't suffer," I said, while the tears rolled down my cheeks.

"He'll fall asleep for ever," said the doctor. "I would like my death to be as peaceful as his."

I said: "I'll close my eyes. I don't want to see him die. But be quick — be quick!"

"It will only take a moment," said the doctor, and he moved noiselessly away, gliding over the soft carpet of linoleum. He went to the end of the room and opened a cupboard.

I remained standing before Febo. I was trembling horribly, the tears were running down my face. Febo was staring at me, and not the faintest moan escaped him. He was staring at me with a wonderfully tender expression. The other dogs, lying on their backs in their cradles, were also staring at me They all had a wonderfully tender expression in their eyes, and not the faintest moan escaped them.

Suddenly I uttered a cry of terror. "Why this silence?" I shouted. "What does this silence mean?"

It was a horrible silence — a vast, chilling, deathly silence, the silence of snow.

The doctor approached me with a syringe in his hand. "Before we operate on them," he said, "we cut their vocal cords."

I awoke, dripping with sweat. I went to the window and

looked at the houses, the sea, the sky above the hill of Posilipo, the island of Capri drifting on the horizon in the pink haze of dawn. I had recognized the voice — the black voice — of the wind. I dressed hastily, sat down on the edge of the bed, and waited. I knew that I was waiting for something sad and painful to happen: some sad and painful experience was coming to me, and I could not prevent it.

At about six o'clock a jeep stopped under my window, and I heard a knock at the door. It was Lieutenant Campbell, of the P.B.S. During the night a telephone message had arrived from General Headquarters at Caserta instructing me to go and join Colonel Jack Hamilton outside Cassino. It was already late, and we had to start at once. I threw my haversack across my shoulder, put my arm through the sling of my Lewis gun, and leapt into the jeep.

Campbell was a tall, fair-haired young man; he had blue eyes, flecked with white. I had accompanied him to the front on various occasions, and liked him for his smiling nonchalance and his noble bearing in the hour of danger. He was a sad boy, a native of Wisconsin, and perhaps he already knew that he would never return home, that he would be killed by a mine a few months later on the road between Bologna and Milan, two days before the end of the war. He talked little, he was shy, and he blushed when he spoke.

Immediately after crossing the bridge at Capua we met the first convoys of wounded. These were the days of the futile, bloody assaults on the German defenses at Cassino. Presently we entered the battle zone. Heavy missiles were falling on Via Casilina, and the din was terrific. At the check-point two miles from the outskirts of Cassino a sergeant in the military police stopped us and made us shelter under an embankment while we waited for the storm of shells to subside.

But time was passing, and it was getting late. In order to reach the artillery observation post where Colonel Jack Hamilton was awaiting us we decided to leave Via Casilina and drive through the fields, where the hail of missiles was less concentrated. "Good luck!" said the M.P. sergeant.

Campbell drove the jeep into the ditch and climbed the embankment at the side of the road. He then began to crawl up a stony slope, through the vast olive plantation which sprawls among the barren knolls on the far side of the hills that face Cassino. Several other jeeps had passed that way before us, and the impressions of their wheels on the ground were still fresh. In some places, where the soil was of clay, the wheels of our jeep revolved furiously and ineffectually, and we had to thread our way very slowly between the large boulders that blocked our ascent.

Suddenly, ahead of us, in a hollow between two bare ridges, we saw a fountain of earth and stones shoot into the air, and the dull crump of an explosion reverberated from hill to hill. "A mine," said Campbell, who was trying to follow the wheel tracks so as to avoid the danger of mines, which were very numerous in that area. Presently we heard voices and groans, and through the olive trees, a hundred yards ahead, we distinguished a group of men gathered round an overturned jeep. Another jeep stood a little way away, its front wheels smashed by the blast from the mine.

Two wounded American soldiers were sitting on the grass, while others were attending to a man who was lying face upward on the ground. The soldiers looked contemptuously at my uniform, and one of them, a sergeant, said to Campbell: "What the hell's he doing here, this bastard?"

"A.F.H.Q.," answered Campbell. "Italian liaison officer."

"Get out," said the sergeant, turning brusquely in my direction. "Make room for the wounded man."

"What's the matter with him?" I asked, jumping out of the jeep.

"He's wounded in the stomach. He's got to be taken to a hospital at once."

"Let me see him," I said.

"Are you a doctor?"

"No, I'm not a doctor," I said, and I bent over the wounded man.

He was a fair-haired, slim young man, almost a lad, with a

boyish face. There was an enormous hole in his stomach, and from it protruded his intestines; they were slowly oozing down his legs and coiling themselves into a big bluish heap between his knees.

"Give me a blanket," I said.

A soldier brought me a blanket, and I spread it over the wounded man's stomach. Then I took the sergeant aside and told him that the wounded man could not be removed, that it was better not to touch him but to leave him where he was, and meanwhile to send Campbell in the jeep to fetch a doctor.

"I was in the other war," I said. "I've seen dozens and dozens of wounds like this, and there's nothing one can do. They are mortal wounds. Our only concern must be not to let him suffer. If we take him to the hospital he will die on the way in frightful agony. It's better to let him die where he is, without suffering. There's nothing else we can do."

The soldiers had gathered round us and were gazing at me in silence.

Campbell said: "The Captain is right. I'll go to Capua to fetch a doctor, and I'll take the two walking cases with me."

"We can't leave him here," said the sergeant. "They may be able to operate on him at the hospital. We can do nothing for him here. It's a crime to let him die."

"He'll suffer frightful agony, and he'll die before he reaches the hospital," I said. "Do as I say — let him stay where he is and don't touch him."

"You aren't a doctor," said the sergeant.

"I'm not a doctor," I said, "but I know what the trouble is. I've seen dozens and dozens of soldiers with stomach wounds. I know that they mustn't be touched and that they can't be removed. Let him die in peace. Why do you want to make him suffer?"

The soldiers stared at me and were silent. The sergeant said: "We can't let him die like that — like a beast."

"He won't die like a beast," I said. "He'll fall asleep like a child, painlessly. Why do you want to make him suffer?

He'll die just the same, even if he reaches the hospital alive. Have confidence in me — let him stay where he is, don't make him suffer. The doctor will come, and he'll say that I was right."

"Let's go," said Campbell, turning to the two wounded men.

"Wait a moment, Lieutenant," said the sergeant. "You're an American officer, it's up to you to decide. In any case you are a witness that if the boy dies it won't be our fault. It'll be the fault of this Italian officer."

"I don't think it'll be his fault," said Campbell. "I'm not a doctor, I don't know anything about wounds, but I know this Italian captain and I know he's an excellent fellow. How can it be to his advantage to advise us not to take this poor boy to the hospital? If he advises us to leave him here I consider that we should have confidence in him and follow his advice. He isn't a doctor, but he has more experience of war and wounds than we have." And turning to me he added: "Are you prepared to accept the responsibility for not having this poor boy taken to the hospital?"

"Yes," I answered, "I assume the entire responsibility for not having him removed to the hospital. Since he has to die, it's better that he should die without suffering."

"That's all," said Campbell. "And now let's go."

The two walking cases leapt into Campbell's jeep, which set off down the stony slope and very soon disappeared among the olive trees.

The sergeant gazed at me in silence for some moments, his eyes half closed. Then he said: "And now? What do we have to do?"

"We must amuse that poor boy — entertain him, tell him some stories, leave him no time to reflect that he's mortally wounded or to realize that he's dying."

"Tell him some stories?" said the sergeant.

"Yes, tell him some funny stories, keep him happy. If you leave him time to reflect he'll realize that he's mortally wounded and he'll feel bad, he'll suffer."

"I don't like play acting," said the sergeant. "We aren't

Italian bastards, we aren't comedians. If you want to act the buffoon, go ahead. But if Fred dies, you'll answer for it to me."

"Why do you insult me?" I said. "It isn't my fault if I'm not a thoroughbred like all the Americans . . . or like all the Germans. I've already told you the poor boy will die — but he won't suffer. I'll be responsible to you for his sufferings, but not for his death."

"O.K.," said the sergeant. And turning to the others, who had listened to me in silence with their eyes glued upon me, he added: "You are all witnesses. This dirty Italian maintains — "

"Shut up!" I cried. "That's enough of these stupid insults! Have you come to Europe to insult us or to fight the Germans?"

"Instead of that poor American boy," said the sergeant, half closing his eyes and clenching his fists, "it ought to be one of you. Why don't you chase the Germans out by yourselves?"

"Why didn't you stay at home? No one asked you to come. You ought to have let us fight it out with the Germans ourselves."

"Take it easy," said the sergeant with an unpleasant laugh. "You Europeans are no good, the only thing you're good for is to die of hunger."

All the others began to laugh, and they looked at me.

"We certainly aren't well enough fed to be heroes like you," I said. "But I'm here with you, I'm running the same risks as you. Why do you insult me?"

"Bastard nation," said the sergeant.

"A fine nation of heroes you are," I said. "It's only taken ten German soldiers and a corporal to keep you at bay for the last three months."

"Shut up!" cried the sergeant, taking a step toward me. The wounded man uttered a groan, and we all turned.

"He's suffering," said the sergeant, turning pale.

"Yes," I said, "he's suffering. He's suffering, and it's our fault. He's ashamed of us. Instead of helping him, here we are covering each other with insults. But I know why you're insulting me. It's because you are suffering. I'm sorry about some of the things I've said to you. Don't you think I'm suffering too?"

"Don't worry, Captain," said the sergeant with a shy smile, and he flushed slightly.

"Hello, boys!" said the wounded man, raising himself on to his elbows.

"He's jealous of you," I said, indicating the sergeant. "He wishes he was wounded like you, so that he could go back home."

"It's a gross injustice!" cried the sergeant, slapping his chest. "Why should you go back home to America, and not us?"

The wounded man smiled. "Home," he said.

"In a little while the ambulance will come," I said, "and take you to the hospital in Naples. And in a couple of days you'll be off to America by air. You really are a lucky guy!"

"It's a gross injustice," said the sergeant. "You'll go home, and we'll stay here and rot. That's what'll happen to all of us if we stay just a little longer in bloody Cassino!" And bending down he picked up a large handful of mud, rubbed it into his face, rumpled his hair with both hands, and began pulling faces. The group of soldiers all laughed, and the wounded man smiled.

"But the Italians will come and take our place," said a soldier, stepping forward, "and we'll go home." And stretching out his hand he seized my cap, which had a long black plume, signifying that I was an officer in the Alpine Regiment, jammed it on his head and began jumping about in front of the wounded man, pulling faces and shouting: "Vino! Spaghetti! Signorina!"

"Go on!" cried the sergeant, giving me a push.

I blushed. It was distasteful to me to act the clown. But I had to play my part in the game. It was I who had suggested the idea of this sad comedy, and I could not refuse now to act the clown. If it had been a question of acting the clown in order to save my country, or humanity, or freedom,

I should have refused. All we Europeans know that there are hundreds of ways of acting the clown. Acting the hero, the coward, the traitor, the revolutionary, the savior of one's country, the martyr in the cause of freedom — even these are forms of clowning. Even putting a man against a wall and shooting him in the stomach, even losing or winning a war, are among the many forms that clowning can take. But I could not now refuse to act the clown when it was a question of helping a poor American boy to die painlessly. In Europe — let us be fair — one often has to act the clown for reasons much less compelling! And after all, this was a noble and generous reason for acting the clown, and I could not refuse: it was a question of preventing a man from suffering. I would eat earth, chew stones, swallow dung, betray my mother, just to help a man, or an animal, not to suffer. I am not afraid of death. I do not hate it, it does not repel me. Fundamentally, it does not concern me. But suffering I do hate, and I hate the suffering of others — men or animals — more than my own. I am ready for anything, ready to perform any act of cowardice, any act of heroism, just to prevent a human being from suffering, just to help a man not to suffer, to die painlessly. And so, although I felt the color rising to my temples, I was glad to be able to act the clown, not, indeed, for the sake of my country, or of humanity, or of national honor, or of glory, or of freedom, but for my own sake — so that I might help a poor boy not to suffer, to die painlessly.

"Chewing gum! Chewing gum!" I shouted, and I began jumping about in front of the wounded man. I grimaced, pretending that I was chewing an enormous piece of gum, that my jaws were stuck together by its twisted strands, that I could not open my mouth, or breathe, or speak, or spit. At last, after many efforts, I succeeded in disengaging my jaws, opening my mouth and uttering a shout of triumph: "Spam! Spam!" The ejaculation, which conjured up a picture of that frightful imitation pork which is known as Spam — the pride of Chicago and the habitual and universally detested food of American soldiers — provoked a general outburst of laughter,

and even the wounded man smilingly repeated "Spam!
Spam!"

In a sudden fit of frenzy, one and all began prancing about,
waving their arms and pretending that their jaws were stuck
together by twisted strands of chewing gum and that they
could not breathe or speak. Seizing their lower jaws with
both hands they tried to force open their mouths; and I too
pranced about, shouting "Spam! Spam!" in chorus with the
others. Meanwhile, from the far side of the hill, came the
fierce, hollow, monotonous, resonant "Spam! Spam! Spam!"
of the guns of Cassino.

Suddenly we heard a gay, sonorous, laughing voice. It proceeded from the depths of the olive grove, and echoed among
the bright, sun-splashed tree trunks. We all stopped our
antics and looked in the direction from which it came. Amid
the silver-dappled leafy branches of the olive trees, silhouetted against the sky, whose grayness was relieved by occasional patches of green, we saw a Negro. He was slowly
making his way down the slope, over the reddish stones and
through the blue, mist-shrouded junipers. He was a tall, thin
young man, with very long legs. He carried a sack on his
shoulders, and he stooped slightly as he walked, so that the
rubber soles of his shoes barely touched the ground. "Oho!
Oho! Oho!" he shouted, opening his red mouth wide, and
he jerked his head from side to side as if he were in the
throes of some tremendous, acute, heart-searing agony. The
wounded man slowly turned his head in the direction of the
Negro, and a childish smile rose to his lips.

Having come within a few yards of us the Negro halted
and put down his sack, from which there came the clink of
bottles. He passed his hand across his brow and in his
boyish voice said: "Oh, you're having a good time, aren't
you?"

"What have you got in that sack?" asked the sergeant.

"Potatoes," said the Negro.

"I like potatoes," said the sergeant; and turning to the
wounded man he added: "You like potatoes too, don't you?"

"Oh, yes!" said Fred, laughing.

"The boy is wounded, and he likes potatoes," said the sergeant. "I hope you won't refuse a wounded American!"

"Potatoes are bad for wounded men," said the Negro in a whimpering voice. "Potatoes are death to a wounded man."

"Give him a potato," said the sergeant in a menacing voice, and meanwhile he turned his back on the wounded man and made mysterious signs to the Negro with his mouth and eyes.

"Oh, no, oh, no!" said the Negro, trying to understand the sergeant's signs. "Potatoes are death."

"Open the sack," said the sergeant.

The Negro started to wail, jerking his head from side to side. However, he bent down, opened the sack and took from it a bottle of red wine. He raised it, looked at it against the murky glimmer of sunlight that filtered through the mist, and clicked his tongue. Slowly he opened his mouth and eyes wide and uttered an animal cry which they all imitated with boyish glee.

"Give it here," said the sergeant. He uncorked the bottle with the point of a knife and poured a little wine into a tin mug which a soldier handed him. Raising the mug he said to the wounded man: "Your health, Fred," and drank.

"Give me a little," said the wounded man. "I'm thirsty."

"No," I said, "you mustn't drink."

"Why not?" said the sergeant, looking at me askance. "A nice mug of wine will do him good."

"A man with a stomach wound shouldn't drink," I said in a low voice. "Do you want to kill him? The wine will burn his intestines, it'll make him suffer agony. He'll start to scream."

"You bastard," said the sergeant.

"Give me a mug," I said out loud. "I want to drink that lucky chap's health too."

The sergeant handed me a mug full of wine. I raised it and said: "I drink your health, and the health of your loved ones and of all those who will be waiting for you on the airfield. Your family's health!"

"Thank you," said the wounded man, smiling. "And Mary's health too."

"We'll all drink Mary's health," said the sergeant; and turning to the Negro he added: "Out with the other bottles."

"Oh, no, oh, no!" cried the Negro in a plaintive voice. "If you want some wine go and look for it like I did. Oh, no, oh, no!"

"Aren't you ashamed to refuse a little wine to a wounded comrade? Give it here," said the sergeant in a stern voice, removing the bottles from the sack one by one and handing them to his companions. They had all taken mugs out of their haversacks, and we all raised our mugs.

"A health to Mary, so fair, so beloved, so young!" said the sergeant, raising his mug; and we all drank the health of Mary, so fair, so beloved, so young.

"I want to drink Mary's health too," said the Negro.

"Of course," said the sergeant. "And then you'll sing a song in honor of Fred. Do you know why you've got to sing in Fred's honor? Because in two days Fred will be leaving for America by air."

"Oh!" said the Negro, opening his eyes very wide.

"And do you know who will be waiting for him on the airfield? You tell him, Fred," the sergeant added, turning to the wounded man.

"Mummy," said Fred in a feeble voice, "Daddy, and my brother Bob . . ." He broke off and turned slightly pale.

". . . your brother Bob . . ." said the sergeant.

The wounded man was silent; he was breathing with difficulty. Then he said: ". . . my sister Dorothy, Aunt Leonora . . ." and fell silent.

". . . and Mary," said the sergeant.

The wounded man nodded assent, and slowly his lips parted in a smile.

"And what would you do," said the sergeant, turning to the Negro, "if you were Aunt Leonora? Naturally, you'd go to the airfield as well to wait for Fred, wouldn't you?"

"Oho!" said the Negro. "Aunt Leonora? I'm not Aunt Leonora!"

"What! You're not Aunt Leonora?" said the sergeant, giving the Negro a menacing look and making strange signs to him with his mouth.

"I'm not Aunt Leonora!" said the Negro in a whimpering voice.

"Yes! You are Aunt Leonora!" said the sergeant, clenching his fists.

'No, I'm not," said the Negro, shaking his head.

"But you are! You are Aunt Leonora," said the wounded man, laughing.

"Oh, yeah! Why, sure I'm Aunt Leonora!" said the Negro, raising his eyes to heaven.

"Sure you're Aunt Leonora!" said the sergeant. "You're a very charming old lady! Look, boys! Isn't it right that he's a dear old lady — dear old Aunt Leonora?"

"Of course!" said the others. "He's a very charming old lady!"

"Look at the boy," I said to the sergeant. "Look at Fred."

The wounded man was gazing at the Negro intently, and he was smiling. He seemed happy. His brow glowed red, and great beads of perspiration were rolling down his face.

"He's suffering," said the sergeant in a low voice, forcibly gripping my arm.

"No, he's not suffering," I said.

"He's dying — can't you see he's dying?" said the sergeant in a strangled voice.

"He's dying peacefully," I said, "without suffering."

"You bastard!" said the sergeant, looking at me with hatred in his eyes.

Just then Fred uttered a groan, and tried to raise himself on to his elbows. He had turned horribly pale, and the color of death had suddenly suffused his brow, removing the light from his eyes.

All were silent — even the Negro was silent — as they gazed at the wounded man, their eyes full of terror.

From behind the hill came the deep, hollow boom of the cannon. I saw the black wind meandering among the olive trees, casting a melancholy shadow over the leafy branches,

the stones and the shrubs. I saw the black wind, I heard its
black voice, and shuddered.

"He's dying — oh, he's dying!" said the sergeant, clenching his fists.

The wounded man had fallen on to his back. He had
opened his eyes again and was looking about him with a smile.

"I'm cold," he said.

It had started to rain. It was a fine, icy drizzle, and it
descended upon the leaves of the olive trees with a continuous
soft hissing sound.

I took off my greatcoat and wrapped it round the wounded
man's legs. The sergeant did the same, and covered the dying man's shoulders.

"Do you feel better? Are you still cold?" said the sergeant.

"Thanks, I'm better," said the wounded man, giving us a
smile of gratitude.

"Sing!" said the sergeant to the Negro.

"Oh, no," said the Negro, "I'm afraid."

"Sing!" cried the sergeant, raising his fists.

The Negro drew back, but the sergeant seized him by the
arm. "Ah, you won't sing?" he said. "If you don't sing I'll
kill you."

The Negro sat on the ground and began to sing. It was a
sad song, the lament of a sick Negro, sitting on the bank of a
river, amid a shower of white flakes of cotton-wool.

The wounded man started to groan, and the tears poured
down his face.

"Shut up!" shouted the sergeant to the Negro.

The Negro stopped singing, and gazed at the sergeant
with the eyes of a sick dog.

"I don't like your song," said the sergeant. "It's sad, and
it's got no tune. Sing another."

"But . . ." said the Negro, "that's a marvelous song!"

"I tell you it's got no tune!" cried the sergeant. "Look at
Mussolini. Even Mussolini doesn't like your song." And he
pointed his finger at me.

They all began to laugh, and the wounded man turned
his head and looked at me in amazement.

"Silence!" cried the sergeant. "Let Mussolini speak. Go on, Mussolini!"

The wounded man laughed; he was happy. They all pressed round me, and the Negro said: "You're not Mussolini. Mussolini is fat. He's an old man. You're not Mussolini."

"Ah, you think I'm not Mussolini?" I said. "Look at me!" And I stood with legs apart and arms akimbo, swaying my hips. I threw back my head, puffed up my cheeks, thrust out my chin and pouted my lips. "Blackshirts of all Italy!" I cried. "The war in which we have been gloriously defeated is at last won. Our beloved enemies, in fulfilment of the prayers of the whole Italian nation, have at last landed in Italy to help us fight our hated German allies. Blackshirts of all Italy — long live America!"

"Long live Mussolini!" they all shouted amidst laughter, and the wounded man drew out his arms from under the blanket and feebly clapped his hands.

"Go on, go on!" said the sergeant.

"Blackshirts of all Italy . . . !" I cried. But at that point I stopped, and followed with my eyes a group of girls who were walking down toward us through the olive trees. Some were full-grown women, others were still children. They were dressed in scraps of German and American uniforms, and their hair was held in place above their brows with handkerchiefs. The sound of our laughter, the singing of the Negro, and perhaps the hope of food had induced them to venture forth from the caves and ruined houses which in those days sheltered the inhabitants of the Cassino district, who lived in them like wild beasts. Yet they did not look like beggars. They had a proud, noble appearance, and I felt myself blushing, I was ashamed of myself. Not, indeed, that I was humiliated by their wretched state and wild aspect. I felt that they had sunk more deeply than I into the abyss of humiliation, that they were suffering more than I was; yet their eyes, their demeanor and their smiles expressed a pride that was more robust, more downright than my own. They approached and stood in a group, silently looking now at the wounded man, now at one or other of us.

"Go on, go on!" said the sergeant.

"I can't," I said.

"Why can't you?" said the sergeant, giving me a menacing look.

"I can't," I repeated. I felt myself blushing, I was ashamed of myself.

"If you don't . . ." said the sergeant, taking a step forward.

"Aren't you ashamed of me?" I said.

"I don't see why I should be ashamed of you," said the sergeant.

"He has ruined us, dragged us through the mire, covered us with shame. But I have no right to laugh at our shame."

"I don't understand you. Who are you referring to?" said the sergeant, looking at me in amazement.

"Ah, you don't understand? It's better so."

"Go on," said the sergeant.

"I can't," I answered.

"Oh, please, Captain," said the wounded man, "please go on!"

I looked at the sergeant with a smile. "Forgive me," I said, "if I don't make myself clear. It doesn't matter. Forgive me."

"I don't like it," said the sergeant; and going up to the girls he cried: "Signorine! Dance!"

"Yeah, yeah!" said the Negro. "Wine, Signorine!" And pulling a small mouth organ from his pocket he raised it to his lips and began to play. The sergeant put his arm round a girl and began to dance, and all the others followed his example. I sat on the ground beside the wounded man and laid my hand on his brow. It was cold and dripping with sweat.

"They're having fun," I said. "To forget the war one must dance now and again."

"They're swell guys," said the wounded man.

"Oh, yes," I said. "American soldiers are swell guys. They are simple and good-natured. I like them."

"I like Italians," said the wounded man, and stretching out his hand he touched my knee, and smiled.

I clasped his hand in mine and averted my face. I felt a lump in my throat, and I could hardly breathe. I cannot bear to see a human being suffer. I would rather kill him with my own hands than see him suffer. The color rose to my temples as I reflected that this poor boy lying in the mud with his stomach ripped open was an American. I would have preferred that he had been an Italian, an Italian like myself, rather than an American. I could not bear the thought that we were to blame, that I myself was to blame, for the suffering of this poor American boy.

I averted my face and contemplated that strange rustic carnival, that miniature Watteau painted by Goya. It was a lively, exquisite scene, with the wounded man lying on the ground, the Negro leaning against the trunk of an olive tree playing the mouth organ, the ragged, pale, thin girls in the arms of the handsome, pink-faced American soldiers, in the silver olive grove; and all around the bare hills, whose green grass was strewn with red stones, and, above, the gray, immemorial sky, ribbed with narrow blue streaks, a sky that was flabby and puckered like the skin of an old woman. And little by little I felt the hand of the dying man turning cold in mine; little by little I felt it going limp.

Then I raised my arm and gave a shout. They all stopped dancing and looked at me, then approached and bent over the wounded man. Fred lay inert on his back; he had closed his eyes, and a white mask covered his face.

"He is dying," said the sergeant in a low voice.

"He is sleeping. He has fallen asleep without suffering," I said, stroking the dead boy's brow.

"Don't touch him!" cried the sergeant, seizing my arm and roughly pulling me back.

"He's dead," I said in a low voice. "Don't shout."

"It's your fault if he's dead!" cried the sergeant. "It was you who let him die, you killed him! It's your fault that he's died in the mud, like a beast. You bastard!" And he struck me in the face with his fist.

"You bastard!" cried the others, closing upon me menacingly.

"He died without suffering," I said. "He died without realizing that he was dying."

"Shut up, you son of a bitch!" cried the sergeant, hitting me in the face.

I fell to my knees, and a stream of blood spurted from my mouth. They all threw themselves upon me, punching and kicking me. I let them knock me about without defending myself; I did not cry out, I did not utter a word. Fred had died without suffering. I would have given my life to help that poor boy to die a painless death. I had fallen to my knees, and they were all punching and kicking me. And I was thinking that Fred had died without suffering.

Suddenly we heard the sound of a car and a screeching of brakes.

"What's happening?" shouted the voice of Campbell.

They all retreated from me and were silent. I remained on my knees beside the dead man, my face streaming with blood, and said nothing.

"What has this man done?" said Captain Schwartz, a doctor from the American hospital at Caserta, coming up to us.

"It's this Italian bastard," said the sergeant, looking at me with hatred in his eyes, while the tears rolled down his face. "It's this dirty Italian who let him die. He didn't want us to take him to the hospital. He let him die like a dog."

I rose with difficulty and remained standing in silence.

"Why did you stop them from taking him to the hospital?" said Schwartz. He was a small, pale man, with dark eyes.

"He would have died just the same," I said. "He would have died on the way in the most terrible agony. I didn't want him to suffer. He was wounded in the stomach. He died without suffering. He didn't even realize he was dying. He died like a child."

Schwartz gazed at me in silence, then went over to the dead man, lifted the blanket and took a long look at the fearful wound. He let the blanket fall, turned to me and silently gripped my hand.

"Thank you for his mother's sake," he said.

GENERAL

CORK'S BANQUET

● "Exanthematous typhus," said General Cork, "is becoming disturbingly prevalent in Naples. Unless the violence of the outbreak diminishes I shall be forced to ban the city to American troops."

"Why worry so much?" I said. "It's obvious that you don't know Naples."

"It's possible that I don't know Naples," said General Cork, "but my medical service is familiar with the bug that spreads exanthematous typhus."

"It isn't an Italian bug," I said.

"It isn't American either," said General Cork. "As a matter of fact it's a Russian bug. It was brought to Naples by Italian soldiers returning from Russia."

"In a few days," I said, "there won't be a single Russian bug left in Naples."

"I hope not," said General Cork.

"I'm sure you don't think the bugs of Naples, the bugs of the alleys of Forcella and Pallonetto, will let themselves be fooled by those three or four miserable Russian bugs."

"Please don't talk like that about Russian bugs," said General Cork.

"My words carried no political implication," I said. "What I meant was that the Neapolitan bugs will swallow those poor Russian bugs alive, and exanthematous typhus will disappear. You'll see. I know Naples."

All the guests began to laugh, and Colonel Eliot said, "We shall all end up like the Russian bugs if we stay in Europe for long."

A decorous laugh rippled down the table.

"Why?" said General Cork. "Everyone in Europe likes the Americans."

"Yes, but they don't like Russian bugs," said Colonel Eliot.

"I don't get your meaning," said General Cork. "We aren't Russians, we're Americans."

"Of course we are Americans, thank God!" said Colonel Eliot. "But once the European bugs have eaten the Russian bugs they'll eat us."

"What?" exclaimed Mrs. Flat.

"But we aren't . . . hm . . . I mean . . . we aren't . . ." said General Cork, pretending to cough into his table napkin.

"Of course we aren't . . . hm . . . I mean . . . of course we aren't bugs," said Colonel Eliot, blushing and looking around him with a triumphant air.

They all burst out laughing and, goodness knows why, looked at me. I felt more like a bug than I had ever felt in my life.

General Cork turned to me with a gracious smile.

"I like Italians," he said, "but . . ."

General Cork was a real gentleman — a real American gentleman, I mean. He had the naïveté, the artlessness and the moral transparency that make American gentlemen so lovable and so human. He was not a cultivated man, he did not possess that humanistic culture which gives such a noble and poetic tone to the manners of European gentlemen, but he was a "man," he had that human quality which European men lack: he knew how to blush. He had a most refined sense of decorum, and a precise and virile awareness of his own limitations. Like all good Americans, he was convinced that America was the leading nation of the world, and that the Americans were the most civilized and the most honorable people on earth; and naturally he despised Europe. But he did not despise the conquered peoples merely because they were conquered peoples.

Once I had recited to him that verse from the *Agamemnon* of Aeschylus which runs, "If conquerors respect the temples and the Gods of the conquered, they shall be saved"; and he had looked at me for a moment in silence. Then he had asked me which gods the Americans would have to respect in Europe if they were to be saved.

"Our hunger, our misery, and our humiliation," I had replied.

General Cork had offered me a cigarette, had lit it for me, and had then said to me with a smile: "There are other gods in Europe, and I appreciate why you haven't mentioned them."

"What are they?" I asked.

"Your crimes, your resentments — and I am sorry I cannot also say your pride."

"We have no pride left, in Europe," I said.

"I know," said General Cork, "and it's a great pity."

He was a serene, just man. His appearance was youthful. Although he was now past fifty years of age he did not look more than forty. Tall, slender, active, muscular, with broad shoulders and narrow hips, he had long legs and arms and slim white hands. He had a thin, pink face, and his aquiline nose, which was perhaps too large by comparison with his childishly small and narrow mouth, afforded a contrast to the youthful softness of his blue eyes. I liked talking to him, and he seemed to have for me not only sympathy but respect. He was certainly dimly aware of what I, from a sense of decorum, sought to hide from him — that to me he was not a conqueror, but simply "another man."

"I like Italians," said General Cork, "but . . ."

"But . . . ?" I said.

"The Italians are a simple, good-natured, warmhearted people — especially the Neapolitans. But I hope all Europe isn't like Naples."

"All Europe is like Naples," I said.

"Why Naples?" exclaimed General Cork with profound astonishment.

"When Naples was one of the most illustrious capitals in Europe, one of the greatest cities in the world, it contained a bit of everything. It contained a bit of London, a bit of Paris, a bit of Madrid, a bit of Vienna — it was a microcosm of Europe. Now that it is in its decline nothing is left in it but Naples. What do you expect to find in London, Paris, Vienna? You will find Naples. It is the fate of Europe to become Naples. If you stay in Europe for a bit you will become Neapolitans yourselves."

"Good gosh!" exclaimed General Cork, turning pale.

"Europe is a bastard continent," said Colonel Brand.

"The thing I don't understand," said Colonel Eliot, "is what we have come to Europe to do. Did you really need our help to drive out the Germans? Why didn't you drive them out by yourselves?"

"Why should we put ourselves to so much trouble," I said, "when you ask nothing better than to come to Europe to fight on our behalf?"

"What? What?" cried all the guests in unison.

"And if you go on at this rate," I said, "you'll end up by becoming the mercenaries of Europe."

"Mercenaries are paid," said Mrs. Flat severely. "How will you pay us?"

"We shall offer you our women in payment," I answered.

They all laughed. Then they became silent, and looked at me with embarrassed expressions.

"You're a cynic," said Mrs. Flat, "an impudent cynic."

"It must be very unpleasant for you to have to say that," said General Cork.

"Undoubtedly," I said, "there are some things which a European finds it distressing to say. But why should we lie among ourselves?"

"The strange thing," said General Cork, as if apologizing for me, "is that you are not a cynic. You are the first to feel the sting of your own words. But you like hurting yourself."

"Why are you surprised?" I said. "It's always been so, unfortunately. The wives and daughters of the conquered always go to bed with the conquerors. The same thing would have happened in America if you had lost the war."

"Never!" exclaimed Mrs. Flat, flushing with indignation.

"It's possible," said Colonel Eliot. "But I like to think that our women would have behaved otherwise. There must be a certain difference between us and the peoples of Europe, and in particular between us and the Latin peoples."

"The difference," I said, "is this — that the Americans buy their enemies, and we sell ours."

They all looked at me in amazement.

"What a funny idea!" said General Cork.

"I have a suspicion," said Major Morris, "that the peoples of Europe have already begun to sell us so as to get even with us for having bought them."

"You're dead right," I said. "Do you remember what was said of Talleyrand — that he had sold all those who had bought him? Talleyrand was a great European."

"Talleyrand? Who was he?" asked Colonel Eliot.

"He was a great bastard," said General Cork.

"He despised heroes," I said. "He knew from experience that in Europe it's easier to act the hero than the coward, that any excuse is good enough for acting the hero, and that fundamentally political life is nothing more or less than a school for heroes. The raw material is certainly not lacking: the best, the most fashionable heroes are bums. Many of the heroes of today who shout 'Long live America!' or 'Long live Russia!' were also the heroes of yesterday who shouted 'Long live Germany!' The whole of Europe is like that. The real sahibs are those who don't profess to be either heroes or cowards, who didn't shout 'Long live Germany!' yesterday and who don't shout 'Long live America!' or 'Long live Russia!' today. If you want to understand Europe, never forget that the real heroes are dying, the real heroes are dead. Those who are alive . . .'"

"Do you think there are many heroes in Europe today?" asked Colonel Eliot.

"Millions," I replied.

They all began to laugh, leaning right back in their seats.

"Europe is a strange continent," said General Cork when his guests' laughter had subsided. "I began to understand Europe the very day we landed at Naples. The crush of people in the city's principal streets was such that our tanks couldn't get on with the job of chasing the Germans. The crowd strolled serenely down the middle of the streets, chatting and gesticulating as if nothing was the matter. It fell to me to arrange for the hurried printing of some large posters in which I politely asked the population of Naples to walk on the footpaths and leave the roadways clear, so that our tanks could get after the Germans."

A burst of laughter greeted General Cork's words. There is not a nation in the world that knows how to laugh as heartily as the Americans. They laugh like children, like schoolboys on holiday. A German never laughs on his own account, but always on someone else's. When he is at table he laughs on his neighbor's account. He laughs just as he eats: he is always afraid that he will not eat enough, and he always eats on someone else's account. And in the same way he laughs as if he feared he would not laugh enough. But Germans always laugh either too soon or too late — never at the right moment. This gives their laughter that air of being ill-timed, or rather untimely, which is so characteristic of their every action and sentiment. I would say that a German always laughs on behalf of someone who did not laugh at the right moment, or someone who did not laugh before him, or someone who will not laugh after him. The English laugh as if only they knew how to laugh, as if they alone had the right to laugh. They laugh in the way all islanders laugh — only when they are quite certain they cannot be seen from the shores of any continent. If they suspect that from the falaises of Calais or Boulogne the French are watching them laugh, or are laughing at them, they at once assume a studied gravity of expression. The traditional English policy toward Europe consists entirely in making it impossible for those damned Europeans to watch them laugh, or to laugh at them, from the falaises of Calais or Boulogne. The Latin peoples laugh for the sake of laughing, because they like to laugh, because "laughter makes good blood," and because — suspicious, vain and proud as they are — they believe that since they always laugh at others, and never at themselves, it follows that no one can laugh at them. They never laugh to please. Like the Americans, they laugh on their own account; yet, unlike that of the Americans, their laughter is never gratuitous. They always laugh for a reason. But the Americans — ah, the Americans — though they always laugh on their own account, often laugh for no reason, and sometimes more than necessary, even if they know that they have already laughed enough. And they are never concerned, especially at table, in the theatre or at the cinema, to know whether they are laughing for the same reason as their companions. They all laugh at the same time, whether there are twenty of them or a hundred thousand or ten million; but always each of them laughs on his own account. And what distinguishes them from every other nation on earth, the thing that reveals most clearly the spirit underlying their manners and customs, their social life and their civilization, is that they never laugh by themselves.

But at this point the laughter of the guests was interrupted. The door opened, and in the entrance appeared a number of liveried waiters, each holding aloft with both hands an immense tray of solid silver.

After the soup, which consisted of cream of carrots seasoned with Vitamin D and disinfected with a two per cent solution of chlorine, came Spam. It lay in purple slices on a thick carpet of boiled corn. I recognized the waiters as Neapolitans, not so much by the blue livery with red revers of the house of the Duke of Toledo as by the masklike expressions of horror and disgust that were imprinted on their faces. I have never seen faces in which contempt was written larger. It was the contempt — inscrutable, historic, deferential, serene — of the Neapolitan servant for the uncouth foreign master in his every shape and form. Peoples that have an ancient and noble tradition of servitude and hunger respect only those masters who have refined tastes and lordly manners. There is nothing more humiliating to an enslaved people than a master with uncouth manners and coarse tastes. Of all their foreign masters the people of Naples remember with approval only the two Frenchmen, Robert of Anjou and Joachim Murat, the one because he could choose a wine and appraise a sauce, the other because he not only knew what an English saddle was but could fall from a horse with supreme grace. What is the use of crossing the sea, invading a country, winning a war, and crowning one's brow with the victor's laurel, if afterwards one cannot comport oneself properly at table? What kind of heroes were these Americans, who ate corn in the manner of hens?

Fried Spam and boiled corn! The waiters supported the trays with their two hands; each averted his face as though he were serving up a Gorgon's head. The reddish violet hue of the Spam, which frying had, as always, made rather dark in color, like meat that has gone bad through exposure to the sun, and the pale yellow of the corn, which was covered with white streaks — corn is softened by the process of cooking, and becomes like the grain with which the crop of a drowned hen is sometimes found to be stuffed — were dimly reflected in the tall, clouded Murano mirrors, which alternated with ancient Sicilian tapestries on the walls of the hall.

The furniture, the gilded picture frames, the portraits of Spanish grandees, the "Triumph of Venus," depicted on the ceiling by Luca Giordano, the whole vast hall of the Duke of Toledo's palace, in which General Cork was that evening giving a dinner in honor of Mrs. Flat, temporarily in command of the Wacs of the American Fifth Army, little by little became tinged with the lurid violet of the Spam and the moonlight pallor of the corn. The ancient and glorious house of Toledo had never known so tragic a humiliation. This hall, which had witnessed the "triumphs" of Aragon and Anjou, feasts in honor of Charles VIII of France and Ferrante of Aragon, the balls and love-pageants of the brilliant nobility of the Two Sicilies, gradually became suffused with a pale, auroral half-light.

The waiters lowered the trays and offered them to the guests, and the frightful meal began. I kept my eyes fixed on the waiters' faces: the spectacle of their disgust and contempt absorbed my attention. These waiters were wearing the livery of the house of Toledo; they recognized me and smiled at me. I was the sole Italian present at that strange banquet; only I could understand and share their humiliation. Fried Spam and boiled corn! And as I perceived the disgust which numbed their white-gloved hands I suddenly noticed that the edge of each tray was embossed with a diadem. But it was not the diadem of the Dukes of Toledo.

I was wondering from what house, and by virtue of what marriage, what right of inheritance, what alliance, those trays had found their way into the palace of the Dukes of Toledo, when, looking down at my plate, I thought I recognized it. It formed part of the famous porcelain service of the Gerace family. Sadly and affectionately I thought of Jean Gerace, of his beautiful mansion on the Monte di Dio, which had been wrecked by bombs, and of his art treasures, now scattered to the four winds. I looked along the edge of the table, and there in front of the guests, in all its splendor, I saw the celebrated Pompeian porcelain of Capodimonte, on which Sir William Hamilton, His Britannic Majesty's Ambassador at the Court of Naples, had bestowed the name of Emma Hamilton;

and — a last, pathetic tribute to the unhappy Muse of Horatio Nelson — "Emma" is the name given, in this same city of Naples, to those plates which the craftsmen of Capodimonte have copied from the single specimen discovered by Sir William Hamilton during the excavations at Pompeii.

I was moved and gladdened by the knowledge that the worthy General Cork's table was graced by this porcelain, whose origin was so ancient and illustrious, and whose name was held so dear. And I smiled with pleasure as I thought that Naples, conquered, humiliated, destroyed by the raids, ravaged by suffering and hunger, could still offer its liberators such delightful evidence of its former glories. A gracious city, Naples! A noble country, Italy! I was proud and moved as I saw the Graces, the Muses, the Nymphs, the Venuses and the Cupids that chased one another round the edge of each of those beautiful pieces of china mingling the delicate pink of their flesh, the pale blue of their tunics, and the warm gold of their hair with the lurid ruby red of that terrible Spam.

That Spam came from America — from Chicago. How remote Chicago was from Naples in the happy years of peace! And now America was there in that hall, Chicago was there on those porcelain plates from Capodimonte that were sacred to the memory of Emma Hamilton. Ah, what a misfortune it is to be made as I am made! To me that dinner, served on those plates, in that hall, at that table, was like a picnic above a tomb.

I was saved from giving way to my emotions by the voice of General Cork.

"Do you think," he asked me, "that there is a more exquisite wine in Italy than this delicious Capri wine?"

That evening, in honor of Mrs. Flat, besides the usual tinned milk, the usual coffee, the habitual tea and the habitual pineapple juice, there was wine on the table. General Cork entertained an almost amorous affection for Capri, so much so that he described as "a delicious Capri wine" that light white wine which is a product of Ischia, and takes its name from

Epomeo, the high, extinct volcano situated in the heart of that island.

Whenever the situation on the Cassino front allowed him a brief respite from his cares General Cork would summon me to his office and, after telling me that he was tired, that he was not well, and that he needed two or three days' rest, would ask me with a smile if I was not of the opinion that the air of Capri would do him good. "Why, of course!" I would answer. "The air of Capri is just the thing to put an American general on his feet!" And so, after this little ritual comedy, we would set out for Capri in a motorboat, accompanied by Colonel Jack Hamilton or some other staff officer.

We used to follow the strip of coast dominated by Vesuvius as far as Pompeii and cut across the Gulf of Castellammare to the heights of Sorrento. And as he gazed at the vast, deep caves that open into the sheer cliff face General Cork would say: "I don't see how Sirens could live in those damp, dark caves." And he would ask me for information about those "dear old ladies" with the same shy curiosity with which, before inviting her to dinner, he had asked Colonel Jack Hamilton for information about Mrs. Flat.

Mrs. Flat, that "dear old lady," had discreetly given General Cork to understand that she would very much like to be invited to a dinner "in the Renaissance style." And General Cork had spent two sleepless nights trying to understand what a dinner in the Renaissance style implied. That evening, shortly before we took our places, General Cork had summoned Jack and me to his office and had proudly shown us the menu.

Jack had pointed out to General Cork that at a dinner in the Renaissance style boiled fish ought to be served before the fried course, not after it. In point of fact, the boiled fish came after the Spam and corn on the menu. But the thing that disturbed Jack was the name of the fish, which was "Siren mayonnaise."

"Siren mayonnaise?" said Jack.

"Yes, Siren . . . I mean . . . not an old lady of the sea, of course!" replied General Cork, somewhat embarrassed. "Not one of those women with fishtails . . . I mean . . . not a Siren, but a siren . . . I mean . . . a fish, a real fish, the kind they call sirens in Naples."

"A Siren? A fish?" said Jack.

"A fish . . . a fish," said General Cork, blushing. "An excellent fish. I've never tried it, but they tell me it's an excellent fish." And turning to me he asked me if that kind of fish was suitable for a dinner in the Renaissance style.

"To tell you the truth," I replied, "it seems to me that it would be more suitable for a dinner in the Homeric style."

"In the Homeric style?" said General Cork.

"I mean . . . yes . . . in the Homeric style. But a siren can be eaten with any kind of sauce," I answered, solely in order to dispel his embarrassment. And meanwhile I was wondering what sort of fish this could be.

"Of course!" exclaimed General Cork with a sigh of relief.

Like all the generals in the U.S. Army, General Cork lived in mortal dread of the senators and the women's clubs of America. Unfortunately, Mrs. Flat, who had arrived by air from the United States a few days before to assume command of the Fifth Army's contingent of Wacs, was the wife of the famous Senator Flat and president of the most aristocratic women's club in Boston. General Cork was terrified of her.

"It will be as well if you invite her to spend a few days at your beautiful house on Capri," he had said to me, as if he were giving me a piece of advice, and hoping perhaps to keep Mrs. Flat away from G.H.Q. at least for a few days.

But I had pointed out to him that if Mrs. Flat liked my house she would undoubtedly requisition it and turn it into a women's club or a rest camp for her Wacs.

"Ah, I hadn't considered that danger," General Cork had replied, turning pale.

He regarded my house on Capri rather as his own personal rest camp, and he was more jealous of it than I was myself. When he had some report to write for the War Department or some operational plan to lick into shape, or when he needed a few days' rest, he would summon me to his office and ask me if I didn't think a little Capri air would do him good.

He liked to have with him only Jack and myself, and sometimes his aide-de-camp. From Sorrento we would follow the coast as far as the heights of Massa Lubrense, and from there cut across the Bocche di Capri with our bows pointing in the direction of the Faraglioni.

As soon as the promontory of Massullo emerged from the sea, and my house — situated at the very tip of the promontory — came into view, a boyish smile would light up the face of General Cork.

"Ah, I see why the Sirens made their home here," he would say. "This is the *real* country of the Sirens!"

And, his eyes shining with joy, he would scrutinize the caves that open into the side of the Monte di Tiberio, the enormous rocks that rise from the breakers at the foot of the sheer, dizzy cliff of Matromania, and the Sirenuse, which lie away to the east, off Positano. On one of these little islands, which fishermen now call the Galli, is an ancient tower, lashed by the winds and the waves. The property of Massine, Diaghilev's pupil, it is empty save for a silent, derelict Pleyel, the keyboard of which is green with mould.

"There's Paestum!" I would say, indicating the long sandy beach which bars the eastern horizon.

And General Cork would cry: "Ah, *here's* where I should like to live!"

For him there were only two Paradises in the world — America and Capri, which he sometimes affectionately called "little America." Undoubtedly he would have regarded Capri as a perfect Paradise but for the fact that even that blessed isle lay prostrate beneath the heel of female tyrants — an elect band of "extraordinary women," as Compton Mackenzie calls them. All of them countesses, marchionesses, duchesses, princesses and the like, and mostly no longer young, though still ugly, they constituted the feminine aristocracy of Capri. And as everyone knows, the moral, intellectual and social tyranny of old and ugly women is the worst tyranny of all.

Already on the downward path that leads to the age of regrets and memories, already oppressed by self-pity and prompted by this complex sentiment, which is of all the most pathetic, to seek in their narrow feminine society a sad consolation for the past, a vain recompense for the love which they had lost, these faded Venuses had grouped themselves around a Roman princess who in her youth had enjoyed many successes with both men and women. This princess was already close on fifty. Tall and fat, she had a hard face and a raucous voice, and already her flabby chin was darkened by the suspicion of a beard. Apprehensive of the threatened raids, she had fled from Rome, placing no confidence in the protection promised by the Vatican to the city of Caesar and Peter, or rather, to use the phraseology of the time, doubting whether the Pope's umbrella was adequate to shelter Rome from the rain of bombs. And she had sought refuge on Capri, where she had summoned into her company all that still remained of that band of Venuses, once resplendent but now humbled and withered, who in the golden age of Marchesa Luisa Casati and Mimì Franchetti had made Capri a citadel of feminine grace and beauty and of a form of love in which men had no share.

With the aim of establishing her tyranny over the island the Princess had skilfully exploited the eclipse — due to the war — of Countess Edda Ciano and her court of beautiful young women, who, owing to the great dearth of men from which Capri suffered during those years, had been reduced to making a pantomime of love and to competing for the favors of the four or five young men who had hastened to Capri from near-by Naples in order to secure, as they put it, the means to live in peace during the war. But what had helped the Princess more than anything else to assert her tyranny over the whole island was the announcement of the impending American landing in Italy. Countess Edda Ciano and her youthful court had quitted Capri in a great hurry and had sought refuge in Rome; and the Princess had been left sole mistress of the island.

Every day, in the afternoon, these faded Venuses met in a lonely villa situated on the Piccola Marina, halfway between the villas of Teddy Gerard and Gracie Fields. What occurred during their secret reunions we are not privileged to know. It seems that their chief delights were music, poetry, painting and, added some, whisky. What is beyond question is that, even during the years of war, these gentle ladies had remained faithful in taste and sentiment to Paris, London and New York, that is to say to the Rue de la Paix, Mayfair and *Harper's Bazaar;* and because of their fidelity they had endured insults and gibes of every sort. In matters of art they had remained faithful to D'Annunzio, Debussy and Zuloaga, whom they regarded as the Schiaparellis of poetry, music and painting. Old-fashioned, too, was their taste in dress, inasmuch as it was still inspired by the motifs which Marchesa Casati had made famous throughout Europe thirty years before.

They dressed in long tweed jackets, the color of burnt tobacco, and purple velvet capes, and they swathed their wrinkled brows in lofty turbans of white or red silk, richly decked with gold clasps, precious stones and pearls, so that they looked like Domenichino's Cumaean Sibyl. In addition, they wore not skirts but broad trousers of Lyonese velvet, green or blue in color, whence protruded their feet, which were small and shod with gilt sandals, like the dainty little feet of the Queens portrayed in the Gothic miniatures in the livres d'heures. So clad, and by reason of their hieratic postures, they had the appearance of Sibyls or witches, and so in point of fact they were commonly described. When they crossed Capri's square, stiff and inexorable, sombre-faced, firm of gesture, proud and preoccupied, the people watched them go by with a vague feeling of disquiet. They inspired not so much respect as fear.

On September 16, 1943, the Americans landed on Capri, and at the first rumor of that happy event the square filled with jubilant people; and now there arrived in a body from the direction of the Piccola Marina the severe Sibyls, who mingled with the crowd, cleaving a passage through the dense throng merely by moving their eyes, and grouping themselves around the Princess in the front rank. When the first American soldiers emerged into the square, walking with their bodies bent and their Lewis guns slung over their shoulders, as if they expected at any moment to come upon the enemy, and found themselves face to face with the group of Sibyls, they halted in consternation, and many of them recoiled a step.

"Long live the Allies! Long live America!" cried the wrinkled Venuses in their raucous voices, raising their fingers to their lips and blowing kisses at the "liberators." Rushing up to encourage his troops, who were already retreating, and imprudently pushing his way too far forward, General Cork was surrounded by the Sibyls, enfolded by a dozen arms, lifted up and carried bodily away. He disappeared, and nothing more was heard of him until late in the evening, when he was seen crossing the threshold of the Albergo Quisisana, wide-eyed and wearing a dazed and guilty expression.

On the following evening there was a gala ball at the Quisisana in honor of the "liberators," and on this occasion General Cork was responsible for a memorable exploit. It was his duty to open the ball with the first lady of Capri; and without a doubt the first lady of Capri was the Princess. While the Quisisana orchestra played "Stardust" General Cork gazed one by one at the mature Venuses grouped around the Princess, who was already smiling, already slowly raising her arms. The countenance of General Cork was still pale with fright following his experiences of the previous evening.

Suddenly his face lit up as he looked beyond the wall of Sibyls and fixed his gaze on a dark, saucy-looking girl with very beautiful dark eyes. She had a wide, red mouth, and a black down covered her neck and cheeks. She was standing at the door of the buttery with the hotel maids, enjoying the gay confusion. Her name was Antonietta, and she was employed at the Quisisana as wardrobe mistress. General Cork smiled, forced his way through the group of Sibyls, passed unseeingly between the lines of beautiful, bare-shouldered, bright-eyed young women who were massed behind the Princess and her wrinkled Nymphs, and opened the ball in the hairy arms of Antonietta.

It was a colossal scandal, and the Faraglioni are still quivering from its impact. What a splendid army the American Army was! What a wonderful general was General Cork! Not content with crossing the Atlantic to conquer Europe, landing in Italy, spreading confusion among the hostile armies, entering Naples as a liberator and conquering Capri, the island of love, here he was celebrating his victory by opening the ball with the wardrobe mistress of the Quisisana! The Americans, it must be acknowledged, are smarter than the British. When, a few months later, Winston Churchill landed on Capri, he went and had lunch on the rocks of Tragara, right under my house. But he wasn't as *chic* as General Cork. He ought at least to have sent a luncheon invitation to Carmelina, the maid at the Trattoria dei Faraglioni.

During the days that he spent at my house on Capri General Cork used to rise at dawn and go for a solitary walk in the wood situated near the Faraglioni, or climb the craggy precipice which overhangs my house on the Matromania side; or, if the sea was calm, he would go out in a boat with Jack and me and fish among the rocks under the Salto di Tiberio. He liked to sit at my table alongside Jack and me with a glass of Capri wine before him, pressed from the vines of Sordo. My cellar was well stocked with wines and liqueurs, but more than the best Bourgogne, the best Bordeaux, hock, Moselle, or the choicest Cognac he liked the pure, unadulterated wine that comes from the vineyards of Sordo, on the Monte di Tiberio. In the evening, after supper, we used to sprawl in front of the chimney piece on the chamois skins that cover the stone-paved floor. It is a vast chimney piece, and built into the back of the fireplace is a representation of Jena in quartz. Through the flames one discerns the moonlit sea, the Faraglioni rising from the waves, the crags of Matromania, and the forest of pines and holm oaks that lies behind my house.

"Will you tell Mrs. Flat about your meeting with Marshal Rommel?" said General Cork to me with a smile.

To General Cork I was neither Captain Curzio Malaparte, the Italian liaison officer, nor the author of *Kaputt:* I was Europe. I was Europe, the whole of Europe, with its cathedrals, its statues, its pictures, its poetry, its music, its museums, its libraries, its victories and defeats, its immortal glories, its wines, its foods, its women, its heroes, its dogs, its horses. I was Europe — cultured, refined, witty, amusing, disturbing and incomprehensible. General Cork liked to have Europe at his table, in his motorcar, at his headquarters on the Cassino or Garigliano front. He liked to be able to say to Europe: "Tell me about Schumann, Chopin, Giotto, Michelangelo, Raphael, that damned fool Baudelaire, that damned fool Picasso — tell me about Jean Cocteau." He liked to be able to say to Europe: "Give me in a few words the history of Venice, tell me the theme of the *Divine Comedy,* talk to me about Paris and Maxim's." He liked to be able to say to Europe, at any time — at table, in his car, in a trench, in an airplane: "Tell me something about the life the Pope leads, what his favorite sport is — tell me if it's true that the Cardinals have lovers."

One day, when I had gone to see Marshal Badoglio at Bari, which was then the capital of Italy, I had been presented to His Majesty the King, who had graciously asked me if I was satisfied with my mission to the Allied Command. In reply I told His Majesty that I was satisfied, but that in the early days my position had been a very difficult one. At the beginning I was merely "the bastard Italian liaison officer," then gradually I had become "this fellow," and now I was "the charming Malaparte."

"The Italian people," said His Majesty the King with a sad smile, "have undergone a similar transformation. At the beginning they were 'the bastard Italian people': now, thank God, they have become 'the charming Italian people.' As for me — " he added, and he stopped. Perhaps he had intended to say that to the Americans he was still "the little King."

"The hardest thing," I said, "is to make those fine American boys understand that not all Europeans are scoundrels."

"If you succeed in convincing them that there are some honest people even in this country," said His Majesty the King with a mysterious smile, "you will have proved your worth, and you will have deserved well of Italy and Europe."

But it was not easy to convince those fine American boys of some things. General Cork asked me what Germany, France and Sweden were really like. "The Comte de Gobineau," I replied, "has described Germany as les Indes de l'Europe." "France," I replied, "is an island surrounded by land." "Sweden," I replied, "is a forest of fir trees in dinnerjackets." "That's funny!" they all exclaimed, looking at me in amazement. Then, blushing, he asked me whether it was true that in Rome "there was a bro . . . hm . . . I mean . . . a maison de tolérance for the priests. "They say there's a very smart one in Via Giulia," I replied. "That's funny!" they all exclaimed, looking at me in amazement. Then he asked me why the Italian people had not had a revolution before the war to throw out Mussolini. "So as not to displease Roosevelt and Churchill, who were great friends of Mussolini before the war," I replied. "That's funny!" they all exclaimed, looking at me in amazement. Then he asked me what a totalitarian State was. "It's a State in which everything that isn't forbidden is compulsory," I replied. "That's funny!" they all exclaimed, looking at me in amazement.

I was Europe. I was the history of Europe, the civilization of Europe, the poetry, the art, all the glories and all the mysteries of Europe. And simultaneously I felt that I had been oppressed, destroyed, shot, invaded and liberated. I felt a coward and a hero, a "bastard" and "charming," a friend and an enemy, victorious and vanquished. And I also felt that I was a really good fellow. But it was hard to make those honest Americans understand that there are honest people even in Europe.

"Do tell Mrs. Flat about your meeting with Marshal Rommel," said General Cork to me with a smile.

One day when I was at my house on Capri my faithful

housekeeper, Maria, came to tell me that a German general, accompanied by his aide-de-camp, was in the hall, and wished to look over the house. It was the spring of 1942, not long before the Battle of El Alamein. My leave was over; the following day I was due to set out for Finland. Axel Munthe, who had decided to return to Sweden, had asked me to accompany him as far as Stockholm. "I am old, Malaparte, I am blind," he had said, to arouse my pity, "please come with me, we'll travel in the same plane." Although I knew that Axel Munthe, in spite of his dark glasses, was not blind (his blindness was an ingenious invention designed to excite the compassion of romantic readers of *The Story of San Michele;* when it suited him he could see very well), I could not refuse to accompany him; and I had promised to leave with him next day.

I went to meet the German general and took him into my library. The general, noticing my uniform, which was that of a member of the Alpine Regiment, asked me on which front I was serving. "On the Finnish front," I replied. "I envy you," he said. "I suffer from the heat. And in Africa it's too hot." He smiled a little sadly, took off his cap and passed his hand across his brow. I saw to my amazement that his skull was of an extraordinary shape. It was abnormally elevated, or rather it was prolonged in an upward direction, like an enormous yellow pear. I accompanied him all over the house, going from room to room, from the library to the cellar, and when we returned to the vast hall with its great windows, which look out on to the most beautiful scenery in the world, I offered him a glass of Vesuvian wine from the vineyards of Pompeii. "Prosit!" he said, raising his glass, and he drained it at a single draught. Then, before leaving, he asked me whether I had bought my house as it stood or whether I had designed and built it myself. I replied — and it was not true — that I had bought the house as it stood. And with a sweeping gesture, indicating the sheer cliff of Matromania, the three gigantic rocks of the Faraglioni, the peninsula of Sorrento, the islands of the Sirens, the far-away blue coastline of Amalfi, and the golden sands of Paestum, shimmering in the distance, I said to him: "*I* designed the scenery."

"Ach, so!" exclaimed General Rommel. And after shaking me by the hand he departed.

I remained in the doorway, watching him as he climbed the steep steps, carved out of the rock, which lead from my house to the town of Capri. All of a sudden I saw him stop, wheel round abruptly, give me a long, hard look, then turn and go away.

"Wonderful!" cried all the guests, and General Cork looked at me with eyes that were full of understanding.

"In your place," said Mrs. Flat with an icy smile, "I should not have received a German general in my house."

"Why not?" I asked in amazement.

"The Germans," said General Cork, "were the Italians' allies then."

"That may be," said Mrs. Flat with a contemptuous air, "but they were Germans."

"They became Germans after you landed at Salerno," I said. "Then they were simply our allies."

"You would have done better," said Mrs. Flat, raising her head proudly, "to receive American generals in your house."

"At that time," I said, "it wasn't easy to get hold of American generals in Italy, even on the black market."

"That's absolutely true," said General Cork, while everyone laughed.

"Your reply is too glib," said Mrs. Flat.

"You will never know," I said, "how hard it is to reply in such terms. At any rate, the first American officer to enter my house was called Siegfried Rheinhardt. He was born in Germany, he had fought from 1914 to 1918 in the German army, and he had emigrated to America in 1929."

"Then he was an American officer," said Mrs. Flat.

"Certainly he was an American officer," I said, and I began laughing.

"I don't see what you have to laugh about," said Mrs. Flat.

I turned toward Mrs. Flat and looked at her. I did not

know why, but it gave me pleasure to look at her. She was wearing a magnificent purple silk evening gown, very décolleté, with yellow trimmings. The purple and the yellow invested her pale pink complexion, whose dullness was redeemed by a faint suggestion of rouge at the top of her cheeks, the somewhat glassy brilliance of her eyes, which were round and green, her high, narrow forehead and her violet-tinted, once lustrous hair with a somewhat ecclesiastical and at the same time funereal air. Years before her hair had undoubtedly been black, but she had recently dyed it a brownish yellow, the color of the artificial locks with which wigmakers endeavor to conceal gray hair. But instead of cheating the years that vivid color betrays them, making wrinkles look deeper, eyes duller, and the anaemic pink coloring of the face more lifeless.

Like all the Red Cross nurses and Wacs attached to the American army, who were arriving by air each day from the United States in the hope of triumphantly entering Rome or Paris in all their sartorial splendor and of making a not unfavorable impression on their European rivals, Mrs. Flat had included in her baggage an evening gown, the latest creation — "Summer, 1943" — of some famous New York dressmaker. She sat stiff and erect, her elbows close to her side, her hands resting lightly on the edge of the table, in the favorite attitude of the Madonnas and Queens portrayed by Italian painters of the Quattrocento. Her face was lustrous and smooth; it was like old porcelain, here and there cracked with age. She was no longer a young woman, but she was not more than fifty; and as happens to many American women when they grow older, the pink bloom on her cheeks, far from being faded or dulled, had grown brighter and, as it were, purer and more innocent. As a result she resembled not so much a mature woman with a youthful appearance as a young girl made to look old by the magic power of cosmetics and the art of skilful wigmakers — a girl disguised as an old woman. Her face contained one absolutely natural feature, in which Youth and Age contended as in a ballad of Lorenzo the Magnificent, and that was the eyes. These were of a beautiful sea-green color, and as their expression changed one was reminded of the undulations of green seaweed as it comes to the surface of the waves.

Her generous décolletage afforded a glimpse of a round, very white shoulder. White, too, were her arms, which were bare to the elbows and above. She had a long, sinuous neck, the swanlike neck which to Sandro Botticelli signified the acme of feminine beauty. I looked at Mrs. Flat, and it gave me pleasure to look at her, perhaps because of her weary and at the same time childlike expression, or because of the pride and disdain that were reflected in her eyes, in her small, thin-lipped mouth, and in her slightly frowning brow.

The hall in which Mrs. Flat was sitting formed part of an ancient and noble Neapolitan palace. It was a solemn, ornate structure, belonging to one of the most illustrious noble families in Naples and in Europe; for the Dukes of Toledo do not yield pride of place to the Colonna, nor to the Orsini, nor to the Polignacs, nor to the Westminsters. Only on certain occasions are they eclipsed by the Dukes of Alba. Seated at that richly laden board, amid the splendor of the Murano mirrors and the Capodimonte porcelain, under a ceiling painted by Luca Giordano, between walls hung with the loveliest and most priceless Arabo-Norman tapestries from Sicily, Mrs. Flat was deliciously out of place. She realized to perfection the fanciful concept of an American woman of the Quattrocento, who had been brought up in Florence at the Court of Lorenzo the Magnificent, or in Ferrara at the Court of the d'Estes, or in Urbino at the Court of the Della Rovere, and whose livre de chevet was not the *Blue Book* but the *Courtier* of Messer Baldassare Castiglione.

For some reason — it may have been her purple gown or its yellow trimmings (purple and yellow are the dominant colors in the chromatic scheme of the Renaissance), or her high, narrow forehead, or the dazzling pink and white of her complexion — everything, even her lacquered nails, her hair style and the gold clips at her bosom, combined to make of her an American contemporary of the women of Bronzino, Ghirlandaio and Botticelli. Even the grace which in the exquisite and mysterious women portrayed by those famous painters appears to have in it a deeply ingrained streak of cruelty assumed in Mrs. Flat a fresh and innocent character, so that she seemed a monster of purity and virginity. And she would undoubtedly have appeared to belong to an earlier age even than the Venuses and Nymphs of Botticelli except that something in her face, in the brilliance of her skin, which resembled a porcelain mask, and in her round, green eyes, wide and unwavering, recalled those colored portraits, advertising some "Institut de Beauté" or somebody's preserves, which are a feature of *Vogue* and *Harper's Bazaar;* or rather, I would say — lest I wound Mrs. Flat's amour propre too deeply — a modern copy of an old picture, with its excessively shiny and new appearance, due to the varnish. She was, I venture to say, an "original," but spurious. If I were not afraid of displeasing Mrs. Flat I would add that she conformed to the Renaissance style — wherein the corrupting influence of the baroque was already evident — of the famous "white hall" of the palace of the Dukes of Toledo in which we were that evening enjoying the hospitality of General Cork. She was rather like Tushkevich, that character in Tolstoy's *Anna Karenina* who conformed to the Louis XV style of the Princess Betsy Tverskaya's drawing room.

But what betrayed the presence beneath Mrs. Flat's Renaissance façade of a modern woman, in tune with the times — a typical American woman — was her voice, her gestures, and the pride that was reflected in her every word, in her eyes and in her smile. Her voice was thin and incisive, her gestures were at once imperious and sophisticated. She had an intolerant pride, a pride quickened by that distinctive Park Avenue brand of snobbery which holds that the only beings worthy of respect are princes and princesses, dukes and duchesses — in a word the "nobility" — and a false rather than a genuine "nobility" at that. Mrs. Flat was there at our table, seated beside General Cork. Yet how remote she was from us! In spirit she was floating through the sublime realms in which the princesses, duchesses and marchionesses of old Europe scintillate like golden stars. She sat erect, her head slightly tilted back, her eyes fixed on an invisible cloud, drifting across an invisible blue sky. And as I followed the direction of Mrs. Flat's gaze I suddenly became aware that her eyes were riveted on a canvas that hung from the wall opposite her. It was a portrait of the young Princess of Teano, maternal grandmother of the Duke of Toledo, who in 1860 or thereabouts had illumined with her grace and beauty the last sad days of the Court of the Bourbons in Naples. And I could not suppress a smile when I observed that the Princess of Teano was also sitting erect, with her head slightly tilted back and her eyes turned heavenward, in an attitude identical with Mrs. Flat's.

General Cork caught me smiling; he followed the direction of my gaze and smiled in his turn.

"Our friend Malaparte," said General Cork, "knows all the princesses in Europe."

"Really?" exclaimed Mrs. Flat, flushing with pleasure and slowly lowering her eyes until they rested upon me; and as her lips parted in a smile of admiration I saw the flashing of her teeth, the white splendor of those marvelous American teeth which are impervious to the years and which actually seem unreal, they are so white, so even and so perfect. That smile dazzled me; it made me lower my eyelids and shudder with fear. It was accompanied by that terrible flashing of teeth which in America is the first happy augury of old age, the last glittering gesture of farewell which every American makes to the world of the living as he descends smiling into the grave.

"Not all of them, for heaven's sake!" I replied, opening my eyes.

"Do you know Princess Esposito?" said Mrs. Flat. "She is the first lady of Rome — a real princess."

"Princess Esposito?" I replied. "There is no princess with such a name."

"Are you suggesting that Princess Carmela Esposito doesn't exist?" said Mrs. Flat, knitting her brows and eyeing me with cold contempt. "She is a dear friend of mine. A few months before the war she was my guest in Boston, together with her husband, Prince Gennaro Esposito. She is a cousin of your king, and, of course, she owns a magnificent palace in Rome, right next to the Palazzo Reale. I can hardly wait for Rome to be liberated so that I can hurry to bring her the greetings of the women of America."

"I'm sorry, but no Princess Esposito exists or can exist," I replied. "Esposito is the name given by the Istituto degli Innocenti to foundlings — to the children of unknown parents."

"I hope you aren't trying to make me believe," said Mrs. Flat, "that all the princesses in Europe know their parents."

"I don't claim that," I replied. "I meant that, in Europe, when princesses are real princesses their origin is known."

"In the States," said Mrs. Flat, "we never ask anyone about their origin — not even a princess. America is a democratic country."

"Esposito," I said, "is a very democratic name. In the alleys of Naples everyone is called Esposito."

"I don't care if everyone in Naples is called Esposito," said Mrs. Flat. "What I do know is that my friend Princess Carmela Esposito is a real princess. It's very strange that you shouldn't know her. She is a cousin of your king, and that's enough for me. In Washington, at the State Department, they told me that she behaved very well during the war. It was she who persuaded your king to arrest Mussolini. She is a real heroine."

"If she behaved well during the war," said Colonel Eliot, "it means that she isn't a real princess."

"She is a princess," said Mrs. Flat, "a real princess."

"In this war," I said, "all the women of Europe, whether princesses or porteresses, have behaved very well."

"That's true," said General Cork.

"The women who have had dealings with the Germans," said Colonel Brand, "are relatively few."

"That means they have behaved much better than the men," said Mrs. Flat.

"They have behaved as well as the men," I said, "although in a different way."

"The women of Europe," said Mrs. Flat in an ironical tone, "have also behaved very well in the matter of their relations with the American soldiers — much better than the men. Isn't that true, General?"

"Yes . . . no . . . I mean . . ." answered General Cork, blushing.

"There is no difference," I said, "between a woman who prostitutes herself to a German and a woman who prostitutes herself to an American."

"What?" exclaimed Mrs. Flat in a hoarse voice.

"From the moral point of view," I said, "there is no difference."

"There is a very important difference," said Mrs. Flat, while all were silent, their faces red. "The Germans are barbarians, and the American soldiers are fine boys."

"Yes," said General Cork, "they are fine boys."

"Oh, sure!" exclaimed Colonel Eliot.

"If you had lost the war," I said, "not a woman in Europe would deem you worthy of a smile. Women prefer the victors to the vanquished."

"You are immoral," said Mrs. Flat in an icy voice.

"Our women," I said, "don't prostitute themselves to you because you are handsome and because you are fine boys, but because you have won the war."

"Do you think that, General?" asked Mrs. Flat, turning abruptly to General Cork.

"I think . . . yes . . . no . . . I think . . ." replied General Cork, blinking his eyes.

"You are a happy people" I said. "There are certain things that you can't understand."

"We Americans," said Jack, looking at me with eyes that were full of sympathy, "are not happy: we are lucky."

"I wish everyone in Europe," said Mrs. Flat slowly, "were as lucky as we are. Why don't you try to be lucky too?"

"It's enough for us to be happy," I replied. *"For we are happy."*

"Happy?" exclaimed Mrs. Flat, looking at me with stupefaction in her eyes. "How can you be happy when your children are dying of hunger and your women are not ashamed to prostitute themselves for a package of cigarettes? You aren't happy — you're immoral."

"With a package of cigarettes," I said in a low voice, "one can buy six pounds of bread."

Mrs. Flat blushed, and the sight of her blushing gave me pleasure.

"Our women are all worthy of respect," I said, "even those who sell themselves for a package of cigarettes. All the honest women in all the world, even the honest women of America, ought to learn from the poor women of Europe how one may prostitute oneself with dignity to satisfy one's hunger. Do you know what hunger is, Mrs. Flat?"

"No, thank God. And you?" said Mrs. Flat. I noticed that her hands were trembling.

"I have a deep respect for all who prostitute themselves because of hunger," I replied. "If I were hungry, and I could not satisfy my hunger in any other way, I would not hesitate for a moment to sell my hunger for a piece of bread or a package of cigarettes."

"Hunger, hunger — always the same excuse," said Mrs. Flat.

"When you go back to America," I said, "you will at least have learned this horrible and marvelous truth — that in Europe hunger can be bought like any other commodity."

"What do you mean when you talk of 'buying hunger'?" asked General Cork.

"I mean 'buying hunger,'" I replied. "The American soldiers think they are buying a woman, and they are buying her hunger. They think they are buying love, and they are buying a slice of hunger. If I were an American soldier I should buy a slice of hunger and take it to America, so that I could make a present of it to my wife and show her what can be bought in Europe with a package of cigarettes. A slice of hunger makes a splendid present."

"The unfortunates who sell themselves for a package of cigarettes," said Mrs. Flat, "don't look as if they were starving. They have the appearance of being in excellent condition."

"They do Swedish drill with pumice stone," I said.

"What?" exclaimed Mrs. Flat, opening her eyes wide.

"When I was deported to the island of Lipari," I said, "the French and English newspapers announced that I was very ill and accused Mussolini of brutality toward political prisoners. As a matter of fact I *was* very ill, and it was feared that I had tuberculosis. Mussolini ordered the Lipari police to have me photographed in an athletic pose and to send the photograph to the Ministry of the Interior in Rome, where it would be published in the newspapers as proof that I was enjoying good health. So one morning a police officer visited me, accompanied by a photographer, and ordered me to assume an athletic pose.

" 'I don't go in for athletics on Lipari,' I replied.

" 'Not even a little Swedish drill?' said the police officer.

" 'Yes,' I replied, 'I do a little Swedish drill with pumice stone.'

" 'All right,' said the police officer, 'I'll photograph you while you do some drill with pumice stone.' And he added, as though trying to give me a piece of advice in the interests of my health: 'It isn't very strenuous. You ought to exercise with something heavier to develop your chest muscles. You need to do it.'

" 'One gets lazy on Lipari,' I replied. 'After all, when one is deported to an island of what use are muscles?'

" 'Muscles,' said the police officer, 'are of more use than brain. If you had had a little more muscle you wouldn't be here.'

"Lipari has the largest deposits of pumice stone in Europe. Pumice is very light — so light that it floats in water. We went to Canneto, where the pumice deposits are, and I picked up an enormous block of the light, porous stone. It looked like a ten-ton block of granite, but in reality it weighed barely four pounds. Smilingly I raised it above my head with both arms. The photographer clicked the shutter and thus I was portrayed in that athletic attitude. The Italian newspapers published the photograph, and my mother wrote to me: 'I am happy to see that you are well and that you have become as strong as a Hercules.'

"You see, Mrs. Flat — to those unfortunates who sell themselves for a package of cigarettes prostitution is merely a form of drill with pumice stone."

"Ha! ha! ha! Wonderful!" cried General Cork, while a merry laugh echoed all round the table.

Bewildered, almost frightened, Mrs. Flat blushed and turned to General Cork.

"But I don't understand!" she cried.

"It's only a joke," said General Cork, laughing, "a marvelous joke!" And to hide his amusement at the joke he began coughing.

"It's a very stupid joke," said Mrs. Flat severely, "and I am amazed that an Italian can laugh at some things."

"Are you sure Malaparte is laughing?" said Jack. I saw that he was moved. He was looking hard at me with a sympathetic smile on his face.

"Anyway, I don't like jokes," said Mrs. Flat.

"Why don't you like jokes?" I said. "If everything that is happening around us in Europe weren't a joke do you think it would make us cry — do you think crying would be enough?"

"You don't know how to cry," said Mrs. Flat.

"Why should you want me to cry? Because you kindly invite our women to the dances which your Wacs organize for the amusement of the American officers and men, but forbid their husbands, fiancés and brothers to accompany them? Would you wish me to cry because there aren't enough prostitutes in America to send to Europe to amuse your soldiers? Or should I cry because your invitation to our women to come to dances *by themselves* is not an invitation à la valse but an invitation to prostitution?"

"In America," replied Mrs. Flat, looking at me in amazement, "it is not considered wrong to invite a woman to a dance without her husband."

"If the Japanese had invaded America," I said, "and had behaved toward your women as you behave toward ours, what would you say, Mrs. Flat?"

"But we aren't Japanese!" exclaimed Colonel Brand.

"The Japanese are men of color," said Mrs. Flat.

"To conquered peoples," I said, "all conquerors are men of color."

An embarrassed silence greeted my words. They all looked at me with amazement and distress written on their faces. They were simple, honest folk; they were Americans, the most righteous, the most ingenuous of men; and they looked at me with mute sympathy, amazed and distressed because the truth that was implicit in my words made them blush. Mrs. Flat had lowered her eyes and was silent.

After a few moments General Cork turned to me. "I think you are right," he said.

"Do you *really* think Malaparte is right?" asked Mrs. Flat in a low voice.

"Yes, I think he is right," replied General Cork slowly. "Even our soldiers are indignant because they *have* to treat the Italians — men and women — in a way they consider . . . yes . . . I mean . . . hardly correct. But it isn't my fault. The attitude that we *have* to adopt toward the Italians has been dictated to us by Washington."

"By Washington?" exclaimed Mrs. Flat.

"Yes, by Washington. Every day the Fifth Army's newspaper, *Stars and Stripes*, publishes a large number of letters from G.I.s on this very subject which repeat Malaparte's views almost word for word. The G.I.s, Mrs. Flat, are citizens of a great country — a country in which women are respected."

"Thank God!" exclaimed Mrs. Flat.

"Every day I carefully read the letters which our soldiers send to *Stars and Stripes;* and only last Sunday I gave orders that invitations to our dances should in future be issued not only to the women but also to their husbands or brothers. I think I did right."

"I think you did right too," said Mrs. Flat. "But I shouldn't be surprised if Washington blamed you for it."

"Washington has approved my decision," said General Cork with an ironical smile, "but even if I didn't have Washington's approval I should still think I had done right, especially after the latest scandal."

"What scandal?" asked Mrs. Flat, tilting her head slightly to one side.

"It certainly isn't an amusing story," said General Cork. And he related how a few days before a boy of eighteen had shot his own sister dead in the middle of Via Chiaia because, although forbidden to do so by her family, she had gone to a dance at an American officers' club. "The crowd," added General Cork, "applauded the murderer."

"What?" cried Mrs. Flat.

"The crowd was wrong," said General Cork, "but . . ." Two evenings before some Neapolitan girls of good family, who had imprudently accepted an invitation to a dance at an American officers' club, had been made to go from the vestibule of the club into a room used as a Pro Station, where they had been forcibly subjected to a medical inspection. A shout of indignation had echoed through the streets of Naples.

"At the court-martial," added General Cork, "I denounced the men responsible for this shameful incident."

"You did your duty," said Mrs. Flat, blushing.

"Thank you," said General Cork.

"Italian girls," said Major Morrison, "are entitled to our respect. They are nice girls, and they deserve respect just as much as our American girls."

"I agree with you," said Mrs. Flat, "but I can't agree with Malaparte."

"Why not?" said General Cork. "Malaparte is a good Italian, he is our friend, and we are very fond of him."

They all smiled at me, and Jack, who was sitting opposite me, gave me a wink.

Mrs. Flat turned and surveyed me with eyes in which irony, scorn and malice blended in an expression of benevolent amazement. "You are fishing for compliments, aren't you?" she said, smiling at me.

At that moment the door opened and four liveried foot-men appeared in the entrance, preceded by the major-domo. On a kind of stretcher, covered with magnificent red brocade on which was designed the crest of the Dukes of Toledo, they carried, in the traditional manner, an immense solid silver tray, containing an enormous fish. A gasp of joy and admira-tion passed down the table. "Here is the Siren!" exclaimed General Cork, turning to Mrs. Flat and bowing.

The major-domo, assisted by the footmen, deposited the tray in the middle of the table, in front of General Cork and Mrs. Flat, and withdrew a few steps.

We all looked at the fish, and we turned pale. A feeble cry of horror escaped the lips of Mrs. Flat, and General Cork blanched.

In the middle of the tray was a little girl, or something that resembled a little girl. She lay face upwards on a bed of green lettuce leaves, encircled by a large wreath of pink coral stems. Her eyes were open, her lips half closed; and she was gazing with an expression of wonderment at Luca Giordano's painting of the "Triumph of Venus" which adorned the ceiling. She was naked; but her dark, shining skin, which was of the same purple color as Mrs. Flat's gown, was exactly like a well-fitted dress in the way in which it outlined her still callow yet already well-proportioned form, the gentle curve of her hips, her slightly protruding belly, her little virginal breasts, and her broad, plump shoulders.

She might have been not more than eight or ten years old, though at first sight, owing to the precocious development of her body, which was that of a grown woman, she looked fifteen. Here and there, especially about the shoulders and hips, the skin had been torn or pulpified by the process of cooking, and through the cracks and fissures a glimpse was afforded of the tender flesh, which in some places was silvery, in others golden, so that she looked as if she were clad in purple and yellow, just like Mrs. Flat. And, like Mrs. Flat's, her face (which the heat of the boiling water had caused to burst out of its skin like an over-ripe fruit from its rind) resembled a shining mask of old porcelain, while her lips pouted, and her brow was deep and narrow, her eyes round and green. She had short, finlike arms, pointed at the ends and similar in shape to hands with no fingers. Hairlike bristles protruded in a tuft from the top of her head and grew sparsely down the sides of her small face. About her mouth the flesh was all puckered and, as it were, congealed in a kind of grimace that resembled a smile. Her flanks were long and slender, and terminated, exactly as Ovid says, *in piscem* — in a fish's tail. The little girl lay on her silver bier; she seemed to be asleep. But, owing to the unpardonable negligence of the cook, she slept as the dead sleep when no one has performed the merciful duty of lowering their eyelids: she slept with her eyes open. And she gazed at Luca Giordano's Tritons as they blew into their sea shells; at the dolphins as they galloped over the waves, dragging Venus's coach behind them; at Venus herself, sitting naked in her golden coach, and her retinue of pink and white nymphs; at Neptune, grasping his trident as he raced across the sea, drawn by his mettlesome white horses, still athirst for the innocent blood of Hippolytus. She gazed at the painting of the "Triumph of Venus" which adorned the ceiling — at the blue sea, the silvery fishes, the green sea monsters, the white clouds that drifted across the horizon; and she smiled ecstatically. This was *her* sea, this was her lost country, the land of her dreams, the happy kingdom of the Sirens.

It was the first time I had ever seen a little girl who had been cooked, a little girl who had been boiled; and I was silent, gripped by a holy fear. All the diners were pale with horror.

General Cork raised his eyes and looked at his guests. "But it isn't a fish . . . ! It's a little girl!" he exclaimed in a trembling voice.

"No," I said, "it's a fish."

"Are you sure it's a fish — a *real* fish?" said General Cork, passing his hand across his brow, which was dripping with cold sweat.

"It's a fish," I said. "It's the famous Siren from the Aquarium."

After the liberation of Naples the Allies, for military reasons, had prohibited fishing in the bay. From Sorrento to Capri, from Capri to Ischia, the sea was blocked by mine fields and infested with drifting mines which made fishing dangerous. Moreover, the Allies, especially the British, considered it unsafe to let the fishermen go out to sea, fearing that they might carry information to the German submarines, or supply them with oil, or in some way endanger the hundreds and hundreds of warships, troop transports and Liberty ships which were anchored in the bay. To think that they could distrust the fishermen of Naples — that they could believe them to be capable of such crimes! But there it was: fishing was prohibited.

In the whole of Naples it was impossible to find a fishbone, let alone a fish: there was not a sardine, not a hogfish, not a lobster, a mullet or a cuttlefish — there was nothing. Consequently, when General Cork gave a dinner in honor of some high Allied officer, like Field Marshal Alexander, General Juin or General Anders, or some important politican, a Churchill, a Vishinsky or a Bogomolov, or some commission of American senators who had come by air from Washington to hear what the soldiers of the Fifth Army had to say in criticism of their generals and to collect their opinions and suggestions with regard to the most serious problems of the war, he was in the habit of having the fish for his table caught in the Naples Aquarium, which, apart from that at Munich, is perhaps the most important aquarium in Europe.

It followed that the fish served at General Cork's dinners was always very fresh and of a rare species. At the dinner which he had given in honor of General Eisenhower we had eaten the famous "giant octopus" presented to the Naples Aquarium by the Emperor William II of Germany. The celebrated Japanese fish known as "dragons," a gift from the Em-

peror Hirohito of Japan, had been sacrificed on General Cork's
table in honor of a party of American senators. The enormous
mouths of those monstrous fish, their yellow gills, their black
and scarlet fins, which resembled the wings of a bat, their
green and gold tails, and their heads, bristling with prickles
and crested like the helmet of Achilles, had profoundly de-
pressed the spirits of the senators, who were already preoccupied with the progress of the war against Japan. But General Cork, who in addition to his military virtues possessed
the qualities of the perfect diplomat, had restored his guests'
morale by intoning "Johnny Got a Zero," the famous song of
the American airmen in the Pacific, and they had all sung
it in chorus.

In the early days General Cork had had the fish for his
table caught from the tanks in the Lucrine Lake — famous for
the ferocious and exquisite murries which Lucullus, whose
villa was near Lucrino, fed on the flesh of his slaves. But the
American newspapers, which lost no opportunity of harshly
criticizing the High Command of the U.S. Army, had accused
General Cork of mental cruelty in that he had compelled his
guests — "respectable American citizens" — to eat Lucullus's
murries. "Can General Cork tell us," some papers had ven-
tured to say, "on what kind of meat he feeds his murries?"

It was in consequence of this accusation that General Cork
had given orders to the effect that in future the fish for his
table should be caught in the Naples Aquarium. Thus, one
by one, all the rarest and most famous fish in the Aquarium
had been sacrificed to General Cork's mental cruelty, including even the heroic swordfish, a gift from Mussolini (which
had been served steamed with a border of boiled potatoes),
and the strikingly beautiful tunny, a gift from His Majesty
King Victor Emmanuel III, and the lobsters from the Isle of
Wight, the gracious gift of His Britannic Majesty King George
V.

The valuable pearl oysters which His Highness the Duke
of Aosta, Viceroy of Ethiopia, had sent as a gift to the Naples
Aquarium (they came from that part of the coast of Arabia
which lies opposite Massawa) had enlivened the dinner which

General Cork had given in honor of Vishinsky, the Soviet Vice-Commissar for Foreign Affairs, who at the time was representing the U.S.S.R. on the Allied Commission in Italy. Vishinsky had been much astonished to find in each of his oysters a pink pearl of the color of the new moon. And he had raised his eyes from his plate and looked at General Cork with the same expression with which he might have looked at the Emir of Bagdad had he been present at one of the banquets described in the *Thousand and One Nights*.

"Don't spit out the stone," General Cork had said to him. "It's delicious."

"But it's a pearl!" Vishinsky had exclaimed.

"Of course it's a pearl! Don't you like it?"

Vishinsky had gulped down the pearl, muttering between his teeth, in Russian: "These decadent capitalists!"

No less great, it seemed, was the amazement of Churchill when, having been invited to dinner by General Cork, he found on his plate a strange fish, round, slender and of a steely hue, like the quoits which the ancient discoboli used to throw.

"What is it?" asked Churchill.

"A fish," replied General Cork.

"A fish?" said Churchill, looking closely at the extraordinary fish.

"What is the name of this fish?" General Cork asked the major-domo.

"It's a torpedo," replied the major-domo.

"What?" said Churchill.

"A torpedo," said General Cork.

"A torpedo?" said Churchill.

"Yes, of course — a torpedo," said General Cork, and turning to the major-domo he asked him what a torpedo was.

"An electric fish," replied the major-domo.

"Ah, yes, of course — an electric fish!" said General Cork, turning to Churchill. And the two men smiled at each other, their fish knives and forks suspended in mid-air, not daring to touch the "torpedo."

"Are you sure it isn't dangerous?" asked Churchill after a few moments' silence.

General Cork turned to the major-domo. "Do you think it's dangerous to touch it?" he said. "It's charged with electricity."

"Electricity," replied the major-domo in English, which he pronounced with a Neapolitan accent, "is dangerous when it is raw. When it is cooked it is harmless."

"Ah!" exclaimed Churchill and General Cork with one voice; and heaving sighs of relief they touched the electric fish with the ends of their forks.

But one fine day the supply of fish in the Aquarium ran out. There only remained the famous Siren (a very rare example of that species of "sirenoids" which, because of their almost human form, gave rise to the ancient legend about the Sirens) and a few wonderful stems of coral.

General Cork, who had the praiseworthy habit of concerning himself personally with the smallest details, had asked the major-domo what kind of fish it would be possible to catch in the Aquarium for the dinner he was giving in honor of Mrs. Flat.

"There's very little left," the major-domo had replied. "Only a Siren and a few stems of coral."

"Is it a good fish, the Siren?"

"Excellent!" the major-domo had replied, without batting an eyelid.

"And coral?" General Cork had asked. (When he concerned himself with his dinners he was especially meticulous.) "Is it good to eat?"

"No — not coral. It's a little indigestible."

"Very well, then — no coral."

"We can use it as a border," the major-domo had suggested imperturbably.

"That's fine!"

And the major-domo had written on the menu: "Siren mayonnaise with a border of coral."

And now, pale-faced and dumb with surprise and horror, we were all looking at that poor dead child as she lay openeyed in the silver tray, on a bed of green lettuce leaves, encircled by a wreath of pink coral stems.

Walking along the miserable alleys of Naples one often catches a glimpse, through the open door of some basso, of a dead man lying on a bed, encircled by a wreath of flowers. And it is not unusual to see the corpse of a little girl. But I had never seen the corpse of a little girl encircled by a wreath of coral. How many poor Neapolitan mothers would have coveted such a wonderful wreath of coral for their own dead babes! Coral stems are like the branches of a flowering peach tree. They are a joy to behold; they lend a gay, spring-like air to the dead bodies of little children. I looked at that poor boiled child, and I trembled inwardly with pity and pride. A wonderful country, Italy! I thought. What other people in the world can permit itself the luxury of offering Siren mayonnaise with a border of coral to a foreign army that has destroyed and invaded its country? Ah! It was worth losing the war just to see those American officers and that proud American woman sitting pale and horror-stricken round the table of an American general, on which, in a silver tray, reposed the body of a Siren, a sea goddess!

"Disgusting!" exclaimed Mrs. Flat, covering her eyes with her hands.

"Yes . . . I mean . . . yes . . ." stammered General Cork, pale and trembling.

"Take it away — take this horrible thing away!" cried Mrs. Flat.

"Why?" I said. "It's an excellent fish."

"But there must be some mistake! Please forgive me . . . but . . . there must be some mistake . . . Please forgive me . . ." stammered poor General Cork, with a wail of distress.

"I assure you that it's an excellent fish," I said.

"But we can't eat that . . . that girl . . . that poor girl!" said Colonel Eliot.

"It isn't a girl," I said. "It's a fish."

"General," said Mrs. Flat in a stern voice, "I hope you won't force me to eat that . . . this . . . that poor girl!"

"But it's a fish!" said General Cork. "It's a first-rate fish! Malaparte says it's excellent. He knows . . ."

"I haven't come to Europe to be forced to eat human flesh

by *your* friend Malaparte, *or by you*," said Mrs. Flat, her voice trembling with indignation. "Let's leave it to these barbarous Italians to eat children at dinner. I refuse. I am an honest American woman. I don't eat Italian children!"

"I'm sorry — I'm terribly sorry," said General Cork, mopping his brow, which was dripping with perspiration. "But in Naples everyone eats this species of child . . . yes . . . I mean . . . no . . . I mean . . . that species of fish . . . ! Isn't it true, Malaparte, that that species of child . . . of fish . . . is excellent?"

"It's an excellent fish," I replied, "and what does it matter if it looks like a child? It's a fish. In Europe a fish doesn't have to look like a fish . . ."

"Nor in America!" said General Cork, glad to find at last someone who would stick up for him.

"What?" cried Mrs. Flat.

"In Europe," I said, "fish at least are free! No one says that a fish mustn't look like — what shall I say? — a man, a child, or a woman. And this is a fish, even if . . . Anyhow," I added, "what did you expect to eat when you came to Italy? The corpse of Mussolini?"

"Ha! ha! ha! That's funny!" roared General Cork, but his laughter was too shrill to be genuine. "Ha! ha! ha!" And all the others joined in, their laughter a strangely conflicting blend of dismay, doubt and merriment. I have never loved the Americans, I shall never love them, in the way I did that evening, as I sat at that table, confronted by that horrible fish.

"You don't intend, I hope," said Mrs. Flat, pale with anger and horror, "you don't intend to make me eat that horrible thing! You forget that I am an American! What would they say in Washington, General, what would they say at the War Department, if they knew that the guests at your dinners ate boiled girls?"

"I mean . . . yes . . . of course . . ." stammered General Cork, giving me a look of supplication.

"Boiled girls with mayonnaise!" added Mrs. Flat in an icy voice.

"You are forgetting the border of coral," I said, as if I thought thereby to absolve General Cork.

"I am not forgetting the coral!" said Mrs. Flat, giving me a devastating look.

"Take it away!" shouted General Cork suddenly to the major-domo, pointing to the Siren. "Take that thing away!"

"General, wait a moment, please," said Colonel Brown, the chaplain attached to G.H.Q. "We must bury that . . . that poor kid."

"What?" exclaimed Mrs. Flat.

"We must bury this . . . this . . . I mean . . ." said the chaplain.

"Do you mean . . . ?" said General Cork.

"Yes, I mean bury," said the chaplain.

"But . . . it's a fish . . ." said General Cork.

"It may be a fish," said the chaplain, "but it looks more like a little girl . . . Allow me to insist: it is our duty to bury this little girl . . . I mean, this fish. We are Christians. Are we not Christians?"

"I have my doubts!" said Mrs. Flat, gazing at General Cork with an expression of cold contempt.

"Yes, I suppose . . ." replied General Cork.

"We must bury it," said Colonel Brown.

"All right," said General Cork. "But where should we bury it? I would say, throw it on the ash heap. That seems the simplest thing to me."

"No," said the chaplain. "One never knows. It's not at all certain that it is a real fish. We must give it a more decent burial."

"But there are no cemeteries for fish in Naples!" said General Cork, turning to me.

"I don't think there are any," I said. "The Neapolitans don't bury fish — they eat them."

"We could bury it in the garden," said the chaplain.

"That's a good idea," said General Cork, his face clearing. "We can bury it in the garden." And turning to the major-domo he added: "Please go and bury this thing . . . this poor fish in the garden."

"Yes, General," said the major-domo, bowing, and meanwhile the footmen lifted the gleaming solid silver bier on which the poor dead Siren lay and put it on the stretcher.

"I said bury it," said General Cork. "I forbid you to eat it in the kitchen!"

"Yes, General," said the major-domo. "But it's a pity! Such a lovely fish!"

"We don't know for certain that it is a fish," said General Cork, "and I forbid you to eat it."

The major-domo bowed, the footmen set off in the direction of the door, carrying the gleaming silver bier on the stretcher, and we all followed that strange funeral procession with sad eyes.

"It will be as well," said the chaplain, rising, "if I go and supervise the burial. I don't want to have anything on my conscience."

"Thank you, Reverend," said General Cork, mopping his brow, and with a sigh of relief he glanced timidly at Mrs. Flat.

"Oh, Lord!" exclaimed Mrs. Flat, raising her eyes to heaven.

She was pale, and the tears glistened in her eyes. I was glad that she was moved; I was deeply grateful to her for her tears. I had misjudged her: Mrs. Flat was a woman with a heart. If she wept for a fish, it was certain that in the end, some day or other, she would also feel compassion for the people of Italy, that she would also be moved to tears by the sorrows and sufferings of my own unhappy people.

THE TRIUMPH

OF CLORINDA

● "The American army," said the Prince of Candia, "has the sweet, warm smell of a blond woman."

"You're very kind," said Colonel Jack Hamilton.

"It's a splendid army. So far as we are concerned it is an honor and a pleasure to have been conquered by such an army."

"You are really very kind," said Jack with a smile.

"You were very polite when you landed in Italy," said Marchese Antonino Nunziante. "Before entering our house you knocked at the door, as all well-bred people do. If you hadn't knocked, we shouldn't have let you in."

"To tell you the truth, we knocked a little too hard," said Jack, "so hard that the whole house collapsed."

"That's merely an insignificant detail," said the Prince of Candia. "The important thing is that you knocked. I hope you won't complain of the reception we gave you."

"We couldn't have wished for more courteous hosts," said Jack. "It only remains for us to ask you to forgive us for having won the war."

"I am certain you will ask our forgiveness in the end," said the Prince of Candia with his innocent and ironical air — the air of an old Neapolitan nobleman.

"We are not the only ones who should ask your forgiveness," said Jack. "The British have won the war too — but they will never ask your forgiveness."

"If the British," said Baron Romano Avezzana, who had been Ambassador in Paris and Washington and had remained loyal to the great traditions of European diplomacy, "expect us to ask their forgiveness for having lost the war, they are deluding themselves. Italian policy is based on the cardinal principle that there is always someone else who loses wars on Italy's behalf."

"I am curious to know," said Jack, laughing, "who has lost *this* war on your behalf."

"The Russians, of course," replied the Prince of Candia.

"The Russians?" exclaimed Jack in great astonishment. "And why?"

"A few days ago," replied the Prince of Candia, "I was dining with Count Sforza. Also present was the Soviet Vice-Commissar for Foreign Affairs, Vishinsky. At a certain point in the proceedings Vishinsky related how he had asked a Neapolitan boy if he knew who would win the war. 'The British and the Italians,' the boy had replied. 'And why?' 'Because the British are cousins of the Americans, and the Italians are cousins of the French.' 'And what is your opinion about the Russians? Do you think they will win the war too?' Vishinsky had asked the boy. 'Oh, no, the Russians will lose it,' the boy had replied. 'And why?' 'Because the Russians, poor guys, are cousins of the Germans.'"

"Wonderful!" exclaimed Jack, while all the guests laughed.

Tall, lean, his face bronzed by sun and sea winds, the Prince of Candia exemplified to perfection a Neapolitan noblesse — among the oldest and most illustrious of its kind in Europe — that combines with its splendid manners a spirit of freedom in which the pride of Spanish blood is tempered with the irony of the great French seigneurs of the eighteenth century. He had white hair, lustrous eyes and thin lips. His small, statuesque head and his delicate hands, with their long, slim fingers, contrasted with his broad, athletic shoulders and the virile elegance of a strong man accustomed to violent sports.

His mother was English; and to his English blood he owed the coldness of his expression and the sober and assured deliberation of his gestures. Having in his youth vied with Prince Jean Gerace not, to be sure, in bringing the modes of Paris and L•ndon to Naples, but in introducing the modes of Naples to London and Paris, he had long since renounced the pleasures of the world so as to avoid having dealings with that "nobility" of nouveaux riches which Mussolini had brought into the forefront of political and social life. For a long time he had shunned all publicity. His name had suddenly been heard once more on everybody's lips when, in 1938, on the occasion of Hitler's visit to Naples, he had refused to attend the official banquet given in honor of the Führer. After being arrested and imprisoned for some weeks in Poggioreale Jail he had been banished by Mussolini to his estates in Calabria. This had earned for him the reputation of being a man of honor and a free Italian — titles which, though dangerous, were in those days not to be despised.

Prestige of a more popular kind had accrued to him during the days of the liberation by virtue of his refusal to be included in the group of Neapolitan noblemen chosen to offer General Clark the keys of the city. He had justified his refusal without arrogance, simply and politely, saying that it was not the custom of his family to offer the keys of the city to those who invaded Naples, and that he was merely following the example of his ancestor, Berardo of Candia, who had refused to pay homage to King Charles VIII of France, the conqueror of Naples, even though in his day Charles VIII also had the reputation of being a liberator. "But General Clark is our liberator!" His Excellency the Prefect had exclaimed — he to whom the strange idea had first occurred of offering the keys of the city to General Clark. "I don't doubt it," the Prince of Candia had replied simply and courteously, "but I am a free man, and only slaves need to be liberated." Everyone expected that in order to humble the Prince of Candia's pride General Clark would have him arrested, as was the usual practice during the days of the liberation. But General Clark had invited him to dinner and had received him with perfect courtesy, saying that he was glad to make the acquaintance of an Italian who had a sense of dignity.

"The Russians too are extremely well-bred," said Princess Consuelo Caracciolo. "The other day, in Via Toledo, Vishinsky's car ran over the old Duchess of Amalfi's Pekinese and crushed it to death. Vishinsky got out of his car, picked up the poor Pekinese himself and, after telling the Duchess how deeply distressed he was, asked her to let him take her in his car to the Palace of Amalfi. 'Thank you, I prefer to walk home,' replied the old Duchess haughtily, throwing a contemptuous glance at the little red flag, bearing the sign of the hammer and sickle, which flew from the bonnet. Vishinsky bowed silently, re-entered his car and drove swiftly away. Only then did the Duchess realize that her poor dead dog was still in Vishinsky's car. The following day Vishinsky sent her a present of a jar of marmalade. The Duchess tried it, and uttering a shriek of horror fell to the floor in a faint: the marmalade tasted like dead dog. I tried it too, and I assure you that it tasted exactly like dog-marmalade."

"Well-bred Russians are capable of anything," said Maria Teresa Orilia.

"Are you sure it was dog-marmalade?" asked Jack in great astonishment. "Perhaps it was caviar."

"Probably," said the Prince of Candia, "Vishinsky wanted to pay homage to the Neapolitan nobility, which is among the oldest of its kind in Europe. Don't we deserve to be given dog-marmalade?"

"You certainly deserve something better," said Jack naïvely.

"Anyhow," said Consuelo, "I would rather have dog-marmalade than your Spam."

"Our Spam," said Jack, "is only pig-marmalade."

"The other day," said Antonino Nunziante, "when I got back home, I found a Negro sitting down to a meal with my caretaker's family. He was a handsome Negro, and very polite. He told me that if the American soldiers didn't eat Spam they would have conquered Berlin by now."

"I am very fond of Negroes," said Consuelo. "They at least reflect the color of their opinions."

"Leurs opinions sont très blanches," said Jack. "Ce sont de véritables enfants."

"Are there many Negroes in the American army?" asked Maria Teresa.

"Il y a des nègres partout," replied Jack, "même dans l'armée américaine."

"A British officer, Captain Harari," said Consuelo, "told me there are a lot of American Negro soldiers in England. One evening, during a dinner at the United States Embassy in London, the Ambassador asked Lady Wintermere what she thought of the American soldiers. 'They are very likable,' replied Lady Wintermere, 'but I don't see why they've brought all those poor white soldiers along with them.'"

"I don't see why, either," said Jack, laughing.

"If they weren't black," said Consuelo, "it would be very hard to tell them from the whites. American soldiers all wear the same uniform."

"Oui, naturellement," said Jack, "mais il faut quand même un oeil très exercé pour les distinguer des autres."

"The other day," said Baron Romano Avezzana, "I was standing in the Piazza San Ferdinando, close to a boy who was busily engaged in polishing the shoes of a Negro soldier. At a certain point the Negro asked the boy: 'Are you Italian?' The little Neapolitan replied: 'Me? No, I'm a Negro.'"

"That boy," said Jack, "has a strong political sense."

"You mean he has a strong historical sense," said Baron Romano Avezzana.

"I wonder," said Jack, "why the people of Naples like Negroes."

"The Neapolitans are nice people," replied the Prince of Candia, "and they like Negroes because Negroes are nice too."

"They are certainly nicer than white men — they are more generous, more human," said Maria Teresa. "Children are never wrong, and children prefer Negroes to white men."

"I don't see," said Antonino Nunziante, "why Negroes are ashamed of being black. Are *we* ashamed of being white?"

"Women are never wrong, either," said Baron Romano Avezzana, evoking cries of indignation from Consuelo and Maria Teresa.

"In order to persuade the Neapolitan girls to become engaged to them," said Consuelo, "the Negro soldiers say that they are white like the others, but that in America, before sailing for Europe, they were dyed black so that they could fight at nighttime without being seen by the enemy. When they go back to America after the war they will scrape the black dye from their skins and become white again."

"Ah, que c'est amusant!" exclaimed Jack, laughing so heartily that his eyes filled with tears.

"Sometimes," said the Prince of Candia, "I am ashamed of being a white man. Luckily I am not only a white man — I am a Christian too."

"What makes our behavior unforgivable," said Baron Romano Avezzana, "is the very fact that we are Christians."

I was silent, and listened, my heart heavy with a dark fore-boding. I was silent, and with an abstracted air contemplated the walls with their historical frescoes, superimposed on a surface of red Pompeian earth, the beautiful gilt furniture of the time of King Murat, the great Venetian mirrors, and the frescoed ceiling — the handiwork of some painter schooled to follow the Spanish style which prevailed at the Court of Charles III of Bourbon. The palace of the Princes of Candia is not among the oldest of its kind in Naples: it belongs to the splendid yet unhappy age when the Spanish domination was at its most austere — the age when the Neapolitan nobles, abandoning the old, gloomy palaces which surround the Porta Capuana and flank the Decumano, began to build their sump-tuous dwellings on the Monte di Dio.

Architecturally the palace of the Princes of Candia con-forms to that heavy imitation-Spanish baroque which enjoyed a great vogue in the Kingdom of the Two Sicilies before Van-vitelli brought back into favor the classical simplicity of the Ancients. Yet its interiors reveal the influence of the grace and the pleasing innovations associated with that imaginative spirit which in the Naples of those days derived its artistic inspiration not so much from French refinements as from the stuccoes and encaustics of Herculaneum and Pompeii lately brought to light as a result of the learned researches of the Bourbons. The paintings and the decorative effects pro-duced by the artists of the two ancient cities, which for so many centuries lay buried in their tomb of lava and ashes, were in fact the prototypes of those dancing Cupids portrayed on the walls, of those representations of the triumph of Venus, of Hercules leaning wearily against Corinthian columns, of Diana the huntress, and of those vendeurs d'amours which later became a favorite subject of French decorative art. Let into the doors are great mirrors, which cast blue reflections and, by way of a contrast to the brilliant red of the Pompeian stuccoes, throw an aquamarine shadow upon the pink flesh and black tresses of the nymphs and the elusive whiteness of the classical robes.

A transparent shaft of green light flooded down from the ceiling; and if the guests raised their heads they found themselves looking into the heart of a vast wood, through the intertwined leafy branches of which they glimpsed a brilliant blue sky, flecked with white clouds. On the banks of a river naked women, immersed in the water up to their knees, or lying on a dense carpet of vivid green (not the green beloved of Pussino, which merges into blue and yellow tints, nor the purplish green favored by Claude Lorrain), unconscious of, or perhaps indifferent to, the Fauns and Satyrs who watched them through the leafy branches of the trees. In the distance, beyond the river, crenellated castles could be seen, rising from the summit of thickly wooded hills. Plumed warriors with glittering cuirasses galloped through the valley; others with swords upraised fought among themselves; others yet, pinned to the ground beneath their fallen horses, pressed hard on the earth with their elbows in an effort to rise. And packs of hounds rushed in pursuit of white stags, followed from afar by knights clad in blue or scarlet jerkins.

The green radiance of grass and leaves which flooded down from the ceiling was softly reflected in the gilded furniture, in the yellow satin covers of the armchairs, in the pale pink and sky-blue tints of the vast Aubusson carpet, and in the white Sphinxes that adorned the Capodimonte chandeliers. These were suspended in a row above the center of the table, which was splendidly draped in an ancient Sicilian lace cloth. There was nothing in that magnificent hall to remind one of the anguish, the destruction and the grief of Naples — nothing, save the pale, thin faces of the guests, and the modesty of the fare.

Throughout the war the Prince of Candia, like many other members of the Neapolitan aristocracy, had refused to leave the unhappy city, now reduced to a heap of rubbish and ruins. After the terrible American air raids of the winter of 1942 no one had remained in Naples except the common people and a few of the oldest noble families. Of the aristocracy, some had sought refuge in Rome and Florence, others on their estates in Calabria, Apulia and the Abruzzi. The wealthy middle classes had fled to Sorrento and the sea front of Amalfi, and the poorer middle classes had scattered to the outlying districts of Naples, in particular to the little villages on the slopes of Vesuvius, in accordance with the universal conviction — and heaven knows why or how it originated — that the Allied bombers would not dare to brave the wrath of the volcano.

Perhaps this conviction had its origin in the ancient popular belief that Vesuvius was the tutelary divinity of Naples, the city's totem — a cruel, vindictive God, who sometimes shook the earth terribly, brought down temples, palaces and hovels, and burned his own children in his rivers of fire, burying their homes beneath a pall of red-hot ashes. A cruel God, but a just one, who punished Naples for her sins and at the same time watched over her destinies, over her misery and her hunger — father and judge, executioner and Guardian Angel of his people.

The common people had been left masters of the city. Nothing in the world — no fire from heaven, no earthquake, no pestilence — will ever be able to drive the common people of Naples from their mean dwellings, from their sordid alleys. The common people of Naples do not run away from death. They do not abandon their homes, their churches, the relics of their saints and the bones of their dead to seek safety far from their altars and their tombs. But when danger has been graver and more immediate, when cholera has filled their homes with sorrow, or the fire and ashes from the skies have threatened to bury their city, the common people of Naples have been wont for countless centuries to raise their eyes and scan the faces of the "gentry" in order to divine their sentiments, thoughts and intentions, and from their demeanor to measure the magnitude of the scourge, estimate their chance of salvation, and derive an example of courage, piety and confidence in God

After each of these terrible raids, which had afflicted the unhappy city for three years, the common people of Pallonetto and La Torretta used to see the true "gentry" of Naples coming forth at the usual hour from the portals of the ancient palaces on the Monte di Dio and the Riviera di Chiaia, now wrecked by the bombs and blackened by the smoke from the fires. These were the men who had not deigned to flee, who out of pride, and perhaps also partly out of indolence, had not condescended to put themselves out for so little, but stuck to the habits which had been theirs in the era of gaiety and security, as if nothing had happened or were happening. Impeccably dressed, their gloves spotless and with fresh flowers in their buttonholes, they met and exchanged affable greetings each morning in front of the ruins of the Albergo Excelsior, within the shattered walls of the Circolo dei Canottieri, on the mole of the little harbor of Santa Lucia with its surfeit of capsized vessels, or on the footpath outside the Caflisch. The appalling stench of the dead bodies that were buried under the ruins polluted the air, but not the slightest flicker of emotion crossed the faces of those old gentlemen, who on hearing the hum of the American bombers would look fretfully up at the sky and, with ineffably scornful smiles on their faces, murmur: "There they go, the rascals."

Often, especially in the mornings, one saw passing along the deserted streets — littered with abandoned and already bloated human bodies, the remains of horses, and vehicles that had been overturned by the explosions — a few old tilburies, pride of English coachmakers, and even an occasional antiquated horse-charabanc, drawn by a shrunken jade, one of the few that remained in the squalid stables after the last requisitions for the army. They passed by carrying old aristocrats of the generation of Prince Jean Gerace, accompanied by young women with pale, smiling faces. Coming out into the sordid alleys of Toledo and Chiaia, the poor people, ragged, gaunt-faced, their eyes bright from hunger and lack of sleep, their faces dark with anguish, would greet the "gentry" with smiles as they drove by on top of their coaches. Aristocrats and paupers would then acknowledge one another with those informal gestures of greeting, those mute looks and that affectionate arching of the brows, which in Naples mean so much more than words.

"We are glad to see you well, gentlemen," implied the informally deferential gestures of the paupers. "Thank you, Gennari', thank you, Cuncetti'," the affectionate gestures of the aristocrats seemed to reply. "We can't bear it any longer, gentlemen, we can't bear it any longer!" was the purport of the poor people's looks and bows. "Patience, children, have patience for a little longer! This trouble will pass as they all do," was the aristocrats' reply, conveyed by nods and gestures of the hand. And as they raised their eyes to heaven the paupers seemed to say: "Let us hope the Lord will help us!"

For in Naples princes and paupers, the aristocracy and the poor, have all known one another for countless centuries, and their acquaintanceship has been handed down from generation to generation, from father to son. They know one another by name, they are all blood-relations, in virtue of that family affection which has from time immemorial existed between the commonalty and the old nobility, between the hovels of Pallonetto and the palaces of the Monte di Dio. From time immemorial the aristocracy and the commonalty have lived together in the same streets, in the same palaces, the populace in their bassi, in those dark caves which open out on to the alleys, the aristocracy in the magnificent gilded halls of the piani nobili.[1] For countless centuries the great noble families have fed and protected the common people, huddled together in the alleys that surround their palaces, not, to be sure, in a spirit of feudalism, nor merely out of Christian charity, but in fulfilment, I would say, of the obligations of kinship. For many years the aristocracy too have been poor; and the populace almost seem to apologize because they cannot help them. Commonalty and nobility share the joy of births and marriages, the anxieties of sickness, the tears of mourning; and there is not a pauper who is not accompanied to the cemetery by the lord of his district, nor a lord whose bier is not fol-

---

[1] The "noble floors," i.e., the two floors immediately above the mezzanine. (Translator's note.)

lowed by a weeping crowd of paupers. It is an old saying among the populace of Naples that men are equal not only in death, but in life.

The traditional attitude of the Neapolitan nobility to death is different from that of the common people. They greet it not with tears but with smiles, almost gallantly, as one greets a beloved woman or a young bride. In Neapolitan painting, as in Spanish, weddings and funerals recur with a haunting regularity. The pictures have a macabre and at the same time a gallant character; they are the work of obscure painters who maintain even today the great tradition of El Greco and Spagnoletto, though in their hands it has lost its scrupulousness and its distinctive character. And it was an ancient custom, observed until a few years ago, that noblewomen should be buried with their white bridal veils about their heads.

Hanging on the wall directly in front of me, and behind the Prince of Candia, was a large canvas, on which was depicted the death of Prince Filippo of Candia, our host's father. Dominated by the balefulness and gloom of the dirty greens and blues, by the shabbiness of the faded yellows and by the excessive boldness of the crude, cold whites, this canvas contrasted strangely with the festive splendor of the table, brilliant with Angevin and Aragonese silver ware and Capodimonte porcelain, and draped in its vast cloth of old Sicilian lace, whose Arabian and Norman ornamental motifs were interwoven with the traditional themes of pomegranate and laurel branches, bending under the weight of fruits, flowers and birds, against a sky filled with twinkling stars. The old Prince Filippo of Candia, conscious of the approach of death, had illuminated the ballroom in festive style, donned the uniform of a high dignitary of the Sovereign Order of Malta and, supported by his servants, made a solemn entry into the vast, empty, brilliantly lighted hall, clutching in his palsied hand a bouquet of roses. The obscure painter, who by the manner in which he piled white on white revealed himself to be in some remote way an imitator of Toma, had portrayed him standing in the middle of the hall, in the bright solitude of the exquisite marble floor, which was embellished with scenes from history. He was offering the bouquet of roses to his un-seen Princess, bowing as he did so. And he had died where he stood, in his servants' arms, while the common people from the Vicolo del Pallonetto stood in the open doorway and in reverent silence witnessed the death of the great Neapolitan aristocrat.

Something in that canvas filled me with disquiet. It was not the waxen face of the dying man, nor the pallor of the servants, nor the ostentatious splendor of the vast hall, with its glittering mirrors, marbles and gilt ornaments. It was the bouquet of roses which the dying man was clutching in his hand. These roses were of a vivid, sensuous red color; they looked as if they were composed of flesh — the pink, warm flesh of a woman. They radiated an impression of restless sensuality, and with it a pure, tender sweetness, as if the presence of death did not detract from the delicious vitality and smoothness of the fleshlike petals, but enhanced their triumphant quality — the ephemeral yet eternal quality of the rose.

Roses of the selfsame variety, which had bloomed in the selfsame hothouses, protruded in fragrant bunches from the old, tarnished silver vases that had been set out in the middle of the table. And it was not the scanty, humble fare, con-sisting of eggs, boiled potatoes and black bread, nor the thin, pale faces of the guests, so much as these roses that cast a gloom on the whiteness of the table linen and on the very magnificence of the silver, the crystals and the porcelain, con-juring up an invisible presence and filling my mind with a painful apprehension, a foreboding of which I could not rid myself, and which profoundly disturbed me.

"The people of Naples," said the Prince of Candia, "are the most Christian people in Europe." And he related how on September 9, 1943, when the Americans landed at Salerno, the people of Naples, unarmed though they were, revolted against the Germans. The ferocious battle in the streets and alleys of Naples lasted for three days. The people, who had counted on the Allies' help, fought with a frenzy born of desperation. But General Clark's soldiers, who ought to have come to the aid of the city now that it had rebelled, were clinging to the beach at Paestum, and the Germans were trampling on their hands with the heels of their heavy hobnailed boots in an effort to make them relax their hold and to throw them back into the sea. Thinking they had been deserted, the people denounced their betrayal: men, women and children wept for rage and grief as they fought. After a frightful struggle lasting three days the Germans, who had been driven out by the infuriated populace and had begun to retreat along the road to Capua, returned in force, reoccupied the city, and indulged in horrible reprisals.

The German prisoners who had fallen into the hands of the people numbered many hundreds. The heroic and unhappy Neapolitans did not know what to do with them. Should they let them go free? Had they done so the prisoners would have slaughtered the very people who had captured them and given them back their freedom. Should they cut their throats? The people of Naples are Christians, not a race of murderers. So the Neapolitans bound their prisoners hand and foot, gagged them, and hid them in the depths of their hovels, pending the advent of the Allies. But meanwhile they had to be fed, and the people were dying of hunger. The responsibility of guarding the prisoners was entrusted to the women, who, their fury at the slaughter having subsided, and their hatred giving way to Christian compassion, took the poor and scanty food from their children's mouths in order to feed their prisoners, sharing with them their kidney-bean or lentil soup, their tomato salad and their meagre ration of miserable bread. And not only did they feed them, but they washed them and looked after them as though they were in swaddling clothes. Twice a day, before removing their gags in order to victual them, they knocked them out, lest, having been relieved of their gags, they should call for help, giving the alarm to their comrades as they passed along the street. But in spite of necessary blows and inadequate feeding the prisoners, who had nothing to do but sleep, waxed fat like fowls in the hen coop.

Finally, at the beginning of October, after a month of anguished waiting, the Americans entered the city. And on the following day there appeared on the walls of Naples large notices in which the American Commander urged the population to hand over their German prisoners to the Allied authorities within twenty-four hours, promising a reward of five hundred lire for each prisoner. But a committee of citizens went to the Commander and explained to him that in view of the increase in the cost of kidney beans, lentils, tomatoes, oil and bread the price of five hundred lire per prisoner was too low.

"Try to understand, Excellency! We can't let you have the prisoners for less than fifteen hundred lire a head. We don't want to make a profit — we don't even want to recoup our losses!"

The American Commander was inflexible. "I have said five hundred lire — not another cent!" he insisted.

"Very good, Excellency, then we keep them," said the citizens, and they left.

A few days later the Commander had fresh notices affixed to the walls, in which he promised a thousand lire for each prisoner.

The committee of citizens went back to the Commander and declared that more days had passed, that the prisoners had got hungry and were continuing to eat, that meanwhile the price of foodstuffs was increasing, and that a thousand lire a head was too little.

"Try to understand, Excellency! With every day that passes the price of the prisoners increases. Today we can't let you have them for less than two thousand lire a head. We don't want to indulge in a speculation — we simply want to cover our expenses. For two thousand lire, Excellency, a prisoner is yours!"

The Commander lost his temper. "I have said a thousand lire — not another cent!" he said. "And if you don't hand over the prisoners within twenty-four hours I'll send you all to jail!"

"All right, put us in prison, Excellency, have us shot if you like — but that's the price, and we can't sell you the prisoners for less than two thousand lire a head. If you don't want them we'll make soap out of them!"

"What!" shouted the Commander.

"We'll make soap out of them," said the citizens mildly, and they left.

"And did they really boil the prisoners to make soap?" asked Jack, turning pale.

"When they get to know in America, thought the Commander, that the Neapolitans are making soap out of German prisoners, and that it's my fault, the least that can happen to me is that I shall lose my job. And he paid two thousand lire for each prisoner."

"Wonderful!" cried Jack. "Ha! ha! ha! Wonderful!" He was laughing so heartily that it made us all laugh just to look at him.

"Why, he's crying!" exclaimed Consuelo.

But Jack was not crying. The tears were rolling down his face, but he was not crying. This was the childlike and warm-hearted way he had of laughing.

"It's a wonderful story," said Jack, wiping away his tears. "But do you think that if the Commander had refused to buy the prisoners at the price of two thousand lire a head the Neapolitans would really have boiled them to make soap?"

"Soap is scarce in Naples," replied the Prince of Candia, "but the Neapolitans are nice people."

"The Neapolitans are nice people, but for a piece of soap they will do anything," said Consuelo, stroking the rim of a Bohemian crystal chalice with her finger. Consuelo Caracciolo is Spanish; she has the soft, honey-like beauty characteristic of blond women, and the ironical smile, the cold smile of blond Spanish women. The lingering, smooth, vibrant sound that Consuelo produced with her finger from the crystal chalice spread into the hall and gradually became louder, acquiring a metallic tone. It seemed to penetrate the heavens, to vibrate far away in the green moonlight, like the whir of an airplane propeller.

"Listen," said Maria Teresa suddenly.

"What is it?" asked Marcello Orilia, putting his hand to his ear. Marcello had for many years been Master of the Naples Hunt, and it was his custom nowadays when he was at home, in his beautiful Chiatamone house overlooking the sea, to wear his faded pink coat as a dressing gown. The tragic end of his thoroughbreds, which had been commandeered by the Army at the beginning of the war and had died of hunger and cold in Russia, his nostalgic memories of the fox hunts at Astroni, the slow, proud decline of Hélène of Orléans, Duchess of Aosta, to whom he had been devoted for forty years, and who was growing old in her Capodimonte palace, her long head poised on top of her long frame like an owl on its perch, had aged him and broken his spirit.

"The Angel cometh," said Consuelo, pointing heavenwards.

As the voices of the guests died away, and everyone listened intently to that desultory beelike hum in the sky above Posilipo (an aquamarine sky, into which a pale moon was climbing like a jelly fish from the limpid depths of the sea), I looked at Consuelo and thought of the women portrayed by the Spanish painters, the women of James Ferrer, of Alonso Berruguete, of James Huguet, with their diaphanous hair, the color of a cricket's wings — the women who in the comedies of Fernando de Rojas and Gil Vicente stand up when they speak, making slow, leisurely gestures. I thought of the women of El Greco, Velasquez and Goya, whose hair is the color of cold honey — the women who in the comedies of Lope de Vega, Calderón de la Barca and Ramon de la Cruz speak in shrill voices, walking on tiptoe. I thought of the women of Picasso — women with hair the color of Scaferlati doux tobacco and dark, shining eyes like watermelon seeds, who peer obliquely out between the strips of newspaper pasted on their faces. Consuelo too looks at you obliquely, her cheek resting on her shoulder, her dark pupil peeping round the corner of her eye, as one peeps over a window sill. Consuelo has los ojos graciosos described in the song of

Melibea and Lucretia in *La Celestina,* eyes that make los
dulces árboles sombrosos quail. Consuelo is tall and thin, with
long, loose arms and long, transparent fingers, like some of
El Greco's women — those vertes grenouilles mortes with
open legs and splayed fingers.

La media noche es pasada
y no viene,

sang Consuelo softly, stroking the crystal chalice with her
finger.

"He comes, Consuelo — your beloved comes," said Maria
Teresa.

"Ah, yes, my novio comes — my lover comes," said Consuelo, laughing.

We sat in silence round the table, motionless, craning our
necks in the direction of the great windows. The whir of the
propeller would come nearer, then fade away into the distance, drifting hither and thither on the long waves of the
night wind. It was undoubtedly a German airplane that had
come to drop its bombs on the hundreds of American ships
crowded in the harbor. We were all rather white-faced as we
listened to the prolonged vibration of the Bohemian crystal, to
that desultory beelike hum in the green moonlit sky.

"Why don't the antiaircraft guns fire?" said Antonio Nunziante in a low voice.

"The Americans always wake up late," replied Baron
Romano Avezzana in a low voice. During his long stay in
America, where he had been Italian ambassador, he had come
to the conclusion that the Americans rise early in the morning
but wake up late.

Suddenly, in the distance, we heard a voice, a stupendous
voice, and the earth shook.

We rose from the table and threw open the windows. The
palace of the Princes of Candia stands on the Monte di Dio;
and we looked out over the deep chasm that yawns at the
foot of the mountain's rugged and precipitous slopes, on the

side facing Posilipo. Just as the watcher from the battlements of a castle that rises from a mountaintop surveys and explores the plain below, so did we take in the whole vast expanse of houses stretching down from the hill of Posilipo and along the shore right up to the great wall directly beneath the Monte di Dio. The moon shed its mild beams upon the houses and the gardens, gilding the window sills and the edges of the balconies. The mellow light was distilled like honey from the trees that grew within the walls of the orchards; and the birds, nestling amid the branches, in the lavender hedges, and among the bright leaves of the laurels and magnolias, had awakened at the sound of that stupendous, distant voice, and were singing.

Gradually the voice drew nearer. It filled the sky, like an immense cloud of sound, and became almost perceptible to the eye, making the faint moonlight misty and more substantial. It arose from the low-lying districts that fringe the sea, spreading from house to house, from street to street, until it became a clamor, a cry, a loud human lament.

We moved away from the windows and went into the adjoining hall, which overlooked the garden on the other side of the Monte di Dio — the side facing the harbor. Through the wide-open casements we could make out the green, gilded abyss of the sea, the smoky harbor and, there in front of us, rising out of the golden lunar haze, the pale outline of Vesuvius. The brilliant moon was halfway up the sky, poised on the shoulder of Vesuvius like a terracotta jar on the shoulder of a water carrier. In the distance, on the skyline, floated the island of Capri, which was delicately suffused with violet. The sea was a maze of currents — some white, some green, some purple; it filled the sad yet tender scene with a silvery resonance. In the tranquil night this sea, these mountains, these islands, this sky, and Vesuvius, whose deep brow was wreathed in flame, had the mellow, pathetic look of an old, faded print — the pale beauty that nature has when it has reached almost the limit of endurance. And the sight filled my heart with a lover's anguish.

Consuelo was sitting in front of me on the arm of a chair,

near one of the casements, which were open to the night. I could see her in profile. Her fair complexion, her golden hair and the dazzling snowy whiteness of her neck merged into the gilded radiance of the moon, so that to my eyes she was imbued with the immobile, melancholy grace of a headless statue. She was clad in an ivory-colored silk gown, and in the light of the moon that fleshlike tint assumed the dull, pale aspect of old marble.

I felt the presence of danger as an extraneous presence, as something outside myself, something intensely remote from me, as a thing that I could touch and see. I like to remain detached from danger — to be able to stretch out my arm blindly and lightly touch it, as one touches something cold with one's hand in the dark. And I was already on the point of stretching out my arm and touching Consuelo's hand lightly with my own, with no other thought in my mind than that of touching something extraneous to myself, something that was outside me, as if to transform the danger that threatened us, and my own alarm, into something tangible, when the tranquillity of the night was shattered by a fearful explosion.

The bomb had fallen in the Vicolo del Pallonetto, just beyond the wall that flanked the garden. For a few seconds only the dull roar of the collapsing walls was audible; then we heard a stifled groaning, a sound, vague and intermittent as yet, of voices calling to one another, a single yell, a single wail, the footsteps of panic-stricken men and women in headlong flight, a furious knocking at the main door of the palace, and the voices of the servants as they tried to make themselves heard above a confused clamor which gradually swelled and came nearer, until all of a sudden an earsplitting shout penetrated into the adjacent library. We threw open the door and halted in the entrance.

In the middle of the hall, which a candelabrum, carried by a frightened and indignant servant, filled with a reddish light, stood a crowd of disheveled women, many of them almost naked. They clung to one another, yelling and groaning, giving vent at one moment to shrill animal screams, at the next to hoarse, ferocious whines. They were all looking in the direction of the door by which they had entered, as if afraid that Death were pursuing them and that he would enter by that door. Nor did they look round even when, raising our voices, we tried to reassure them and to allay their terror.

When at last they turned, we drew back in horror. They had the faces of wild beasts — thin, bloodless, covered with incrustations and smears which at first I took to be clotted blood, but which I afterwards realized were mud-stains. They had bleary, staring eyes, and their mouths were running with saliva. Their tousled hair stood up on end above their sweaty brows, and hung down over their shoulders and breasts in coarse, untidy shocks. Many, whose sleep had been rudely disturbed, were almost naked, and with a crude show of modesty were trying to cover their emaciated bosoms and powerful shoulders with the edge of a counterpane or with their folded arms. Lurking in the midst of that bestial crowd of women were a number of children, who, looking pale and frightened, watched us from behind their mothers' skirts, with strangely turbulent expressions in their staring eyes.

Lying on a table was a pile of newspapers, and the Prince of Candia ordered the servants who had hastened to the scene to distribute these among the unhappy women, so that they might cover their naked bodies. These women were neighbors, if the expression is permissible, of our host, who addressed them by name as being old acquaintances of his. Reassured perhaps by the warm light of the candelabra, which the servants had in the meantime dotted about the library on the socle and the table, or by our presence, and still more by that of the Prince of Candia — "'o signore," as they called him — or else by the fact of finding themselves in that magnificent hall, whose walls were mellowed by the golden reflection of the bookbindings and by the softly gleaming marble busts ranged along the library shelves, they had gradually calmed down and were no longer shouting so wildly. Instead they groaned, or prayed half aloud, calling upon the Virgin to have mercy on them. At last they were silent; and only occasionally, if a child suddenly started crying or if a shout arose far away in the night, did they break into a muffled whine — no longer the whine of a wild beast, but that of a wounded dog.

In a loud, curt voice our host bade them be seated. He had chairs of all kinds and cushions brought in, and all those unhappy women quietly curled up and were silent. Our host had wine passed round, saying apologetically that he could not give them bread because he had none, so difficult were those times even for the aristocracy; and he ordered coffee to be prepared for the children.

But when the servants, having poured the wine into the glasses and placed the jugs on the table, had retired to the end of the hall to await their master's bidding, we were surprised to see a little crooked man suddenly emerge from a corner of the library. Going up to the table, he seized with both hands one of the jugs that were still full, and passing from one woman to another went on filling their glasses until the jug was empty. He then went up to our host, and bowing awkwardly said in a hoarse voice, "By your leave, Excellency," whereupon he poured himself out a glass of wine from another jug and drained it at a single draught.

We saw then that he was a hunchback. He was a man of about fifty, bald, with a long, thin face, a moustache, and dark eyes surmounted by bushy brows A few titters arose from parts of the hall and a voice called him by name: "Gennariello!" At the sound of the voice, which he must have known, the hunchback turned round and smiled at a woman — a woman past her prime, with a fat, flabby body but a very thin face — who was coming toward him with outstretched arms. In a twinkling they had all gathered round him. One held out her glass, another tried to snatch the jug from his hand, and finally a third, as if in the grip of some divine frenzy, kept rubbing her flabby bosom against his hump, laughing obscenely and shouting: "Look! Look! What luck! Look! I'm in for some luck!"

Our host had made a sign to the servants not to interfere. He was surveying the scene in amazement and disgust, though at any other time it might have made him smile or would perhaps even have amused him. I found myself standing next to Jack, and I watched him. He too was surveying the scene, but with a stern expression, in which amazement and scorn strove to prevail. Consuelo and Maria Teresa had concealed themselves behind our backs, prompted more by a sense of modesty than by fear. And meanwhile the hunchback, who knew everybody, and was, as we afterwards learned, an itinerant vendor of ribbons, combs and false hair who made a daily tour of the hovels of Pallonetto, had become inflamed, whether by the wine or with desire I cannot say, and had begun to act a private pantomime, based apparently on some episode from mythology — the earthly adventures of some god, or the metamorphosis of some handsome youth. I held my breath and gripped Jack tightly by the arm as a sign to him to pay attention, and in order to communicate to him something of the rare delight with which that unusual spectacle filled me.

First of all the hunchback turned to our host and bowed, murmuring "By your leave"; then he cut a few capers, accompanied by grimaces and little guttural cries. Gradually he became excited, and started running about the hall, waving his arms and beating his breast with his clasped hands, while from his filthy mouth there issued a series of obscene sounds, whines and broken words. He extended his arms, opening and closing his hands as if he were attempting to catch something that was flying through the air — a bird, or a cloud, or an angel, or a flower thrown from a window, or the fringe of some elusive garment; and first one woman, then another, then yet another, with clenched teeth, white faces and staring eyes, panting as though in the grip of some uncontrollable emotion, rose and pressed around him. And one kept bumping against him, another tried to caress his face, a third attempted to seize his enormous hump with both hands, while the other women, the children and even the servants laughed and goaded the actors on, applauding, gesticulating and uttering comments in clipped, raucous tones, as if they were witnessing a delightful and innocent comedy, of which they knew the story and understood the hidden meaning.

Meanwhile other women had followed the ringleaders, and

now the hunchback was hemmed in by a pack of frenzied females, all speaking at once. At first they talked in hushed tones; then their voices grew steadily louder and more rapid, rising at length to a frantic pitch as, foaming at the mouth, they poured forth a torrent of confused shouts. Pressing round the hunchback in a menacing circle, they kept striking him, treating him as a crowd of infuriated women would treat a satyr who had attempted to ravish a little girl.

The hunchback defended himself, shielded his face with both his arms, threw himself with lowered head against the circle that was steadily closing in on him, and butted one woman in the stomach, another in the bosom, all the time shouting his obscenities in a voice that was at once frenzied, terrified and exultant, until finally he broke into a long-drawn-out, deafening, despairing cry. Still howling, he suddenly threw himself to the ground, turning over on his deformed back as though to protect his hump from the fury of his persecutors, who hurled themselves upon him, tearing his garments, forcibly stripping him, biting his naked flesh, and trying to turn him over on his stomach; as a fisherman dragging a turtle up onto the bank tries to turn the turtle on its back. All of a sudden we heard a frightful roar, a cloud of dust came in through the windows, and the blast from the explosion blew out the candles.

In the abrupt silence nothing was audible save a hoarse panting and the din of collapsing walls. Then the hall was filled with confused yells, groans, heavy sighs, and loud, shrill wails, and with the aid of the candles, which the servants had hastened to relight, we saw a jumbled heap of women lying on the floor, motionless, pouting, wide-eyed. In their midst was the hunchback, blue in the face, his clothes torn to shreds. As soon as the light was restored he got up, climbed over the jumbled heap of women who lay around him and ran out through the door.

"Don't be afraid — don't move!" our host kept shouting to the unhappy creatures, who had seized their children and, clasping them to their bosoms, were rushing toward the door in a panic. "Where do you think you're going? Stay here —

don't be afraid!" Meanwhile the servants, who were standing
in the doorway, raised their arms to halt and turn back that
fear-crazed mob of women. But at that point a great com-
motion was heard in the antechamber, and a group of men
appeared at the door, carrying in their arms a young girl
who had apparently fainted.

As the she-wolf, pursued by hunters and hounds, retreats
with her wounded cub into the depths of the northern forests
that are her home and, prompted by a maternal instinct that
is stronger than fear, seeks refuge in a woodman's cottage,
scratching at the door and howling, and, showing the terrified man her bleeding offspring, implores him by voice and
gesture to admit her and to grant her sanctuary in the warmth
and security of his home: even so did those unhappy men
seek refuge from death in the palace of the signore, standing in the doorway and showing him the bloodstained body
of the young girl.

"Let them come in, let them come in," said our host to
the servants, waving away the crowd of women. And he
himself helped to force a passage for the group of men, and
led them into the hall, casting his eyes around for a place
where they might lay the poor young woman.

"Put her here," he said, clearing a space on the table with
his arm, regardless of the glasses and jugs, which rolled on
the floor.

As soon as they laid her on the table the girl appeared
devoid of life. She lay dead, one arm trailing at her side,
the other resting lightly on her left breast, which had been
crushed by the weight of a beam or a lump of stone. But
her horrible death had not distorted her face nor imprinted
on it that expression of mingled terror and wonder which
is seen on the faces of corpses newly dug out of the ruins of
buildings. Her eyes were soft, her brow serene, her lips
smiling. Everything in that lifeless body seemed cold and
limp save the expression and the smile, which were warm
and strangely alive. As it lay there on the table the corpse
invested the scene with an air of brightness and calm; it
transformed the hall and the people in it into a peaceful

tableau, dominated by the sublime, naïve indifference of nature.

Our host had felt the girl's pulse, and he was silent. All around him gazed in silence at the face of the signore, awaiting not, indeed, his opinion but his decision, as though he alone had to decide, as though he alone *could* decide, if the girl was still alive or if she was already dead — as though it were on his decision alone that the fate of the unfortunate young woman depended. Such is the confidence which the common people of Naples repose in the gentry, and so deeply ingrained is their age-old habit of relying on them in matters pertaining both to life and to death.

"God has taken her," said our host at last; and as he uttered the words they all began to yell, tearing their hair, beating their faces and breasts with their clenched fists, and calling the dead girl's name aloud: "Concetti'! Concetti'!" And meanwhile two hideous old women fell upon the poor young girl and kept kissing and embracing her with savage frenzy, every so often shaking her as if to rouse her, and crying: "Wake up, Concetti'! Oh, wake up, Concetti'!" The two old women sounded so furiously reproachful, so frenziedly despairing, so menacing, that I expected to see them strike the dead girl.

"Take her into the next room," said our host to the servants; and they, forcibly pulling the two old women away from the body of the unfortunate girl, and repelling the others with a violence that would have aroused my indignation had it not been inspired by pity, gently lifted the poor dead girl and carried her with extraordinary gentleness into the dining hall, where they laid her on the old Sicilian lace cloth which covered the vast table.

The young woman was almost naked, like a corpse that has been dug out of the ruins after an air raid. Our host lifted the edges of the precious tablecloth and draped it about the naked body. But Consuelo's hand was laid upon his arm, and Consuelo said: "Go away and leave it to us; this is women's work." We all withdrew from the dining hall with our host, leaving only Consuelo, Maria Teresa and a few of the women — relatives, perhaps, of the poor dead girl.

We sat in the darkness of the room that overlooks the garden and gazed at Vesuvius and the silvery expanse of the sea. The wind ruffled the golden moonlit waters, which glittered like fishes' scales. A strong odor of the sea came in through the open casements and mingled with the clean fresh breath of the garden, which was heavy with the dampness of sleeping flowers and the murmur of grass in the night. It was a red, warm odor, smacking of seaweed and crabs; and as it floated up through the keen air, which was already filled with the languid stirrings of approaching spring, it evoked a picture of a scarlet curtain billowing in the wind. A pale green cloud was rising from the distant heights of Agerola. I thought of the oranges in the gardens of Sorrento, which were already beginning to turn soft as they sensed the advent of spring, and I seemed to hear the song of a lonely sailor drifting sadly over the sea.

Dawn was already upon us. The air was so clear that the green veins at the edge of the blue vault of heaven could be seen in sharp outline; they formed strange arabesques, resembling the ribs of a leaf. The whole sky trembled like a leaf in the morning breeze; and the singing of the birds in the gardens below, that murmur which spreads among the trees as they sense the approach of day, made sweet, sad music. The dawn was climbing not, to be sure, from the horizon but from the bed of the ocean. It resembled an enormous pink crab in a setting of purple coral reefs like the antlers of a herd of deer, doomed to roam the deep pastures of the sea. The bay that divides Sorrento from Ischia looked pink, like an open shell. In the distance, the pale, bare rock of Capri diffused a faint pearly radiance.

The sea's red breath was vocal with a myriad gentle whispers, a chirping of birds, a beating of wings; the glassy waves appeared carpeted with young green grass. A white cloud drifted up from the crater of Vesuvius and rose into the sky like a vast sailing-ship. The city was still shrouded in the black mist of night; but already dim lights were burning here and there at the end of the alleys. They were the lights of the sacred images in the chapels, which had to be extinguished during the night because of the threat of air raids, and which the faithful used to rekindle at daybreak; and the statuettes of wax and painted papier-mâché at the feet of the blue-clad Madonnas, which represented the souls in Purgatory, enveloped in masses of flames like scarlet flowers, were suddenly beginning to glow. The moon, which by now was setting, shed its pale, silent beams upon the roofs, above which the smoke from the explosions still hovered. From the Vicolo di Santa Maria Egiziaca came a short procession of little girls, wearing snowy veils, each with a rosary wound round her wrist and a black prayer book clasped in her white-gloved hands. From a jeep which had drawn up outside a Pro Station two Negroes followed the procession of newly initiated communicants with their great white eyes. The Madonnas in the sanctuaries of the chapels shone like specks of blue sky.

A star crossed the firmament and was submerged beneath the waves between Capri and Ischia. It was the month of March, the sweet season in which the oranges, overripe and almost rotten, begin to fall from the branches with a soft thud, like stars from the lofty gardens of the sky. I looked at Vesuvius, which was all green in the pale light of the moon; and gradually a vague feeling of horror crept over me. I had never seen Vesuvius looking such a strange color: it was green, like the ravaged face of a corpse. And it was watching me.

"Let's go and see what Consuelo is doing," said our host, after a long silence.

We looked through the doorway, and an extraordinary scene met our eyes. The young woman lay completely naked; and Maria Teresa was washing and drying her, aided by a few of the women, who kept handing her the basin of warm water, the bottle of eau de cologne, the sponge and the towels, while Consuelo supported the girl's head with one hand and combed her long black hair with the other. We stood in the entrance and surveyed that tender, animated scene. The golden light of the candelabra, the blue reflection from the mirrors, the exquisite brilliance of the porcelain and the crystals,

and the green landscapes depicted on the walls, the distant castles, the woods, the river and the meadows, where
iron-clad knights, with long blue and red plumes waving
from their helmets, galloped toward one another, raising their
glittering swords, like the heroes and heroines of Tasso in the
paintings of Salvator Rosa — all this gave the scene the
melancholy air of an episode from the *Gerusalemme liberata*.
The dead girl lying naked on the table was Clorinda, and
these were Clorinda's obsequies.

All around were silent. There was no sound apart from
the muffled groans of the ragged and disheveled crowd of
women standing in the doorway of the library and the crying of a child, who wept, perhaps, not for fear but for wonder,
bewildered by that sad, tender scene, by the warm light of
the candles and the mysterious actions of the two richly
dressed and very beautiful young women who were bending
over the white, naked corpse.

Suddenly Consuelo took off her silk slippers and her stockings, and with a series of swift, easy movements put them
on the dead girl. Then she took off her satin blouse, her skirt
and her vest. She undressed slowly, her face very pale, her
eyes glowing with a strange, unwavering light. The women
who were standing in the doorway came in one by one,
clasped their hands and, laughing and crying, their faces
beaming with a wondrous joy, contemplated the young
woman as she lay on her rich deathbed in her splendid funeral
attire. Cries of "How beautiful! How beautiful!" in which
grief was mingled with joy, arose on all sides. Other faces
appeared in the entrance; men, women and children came in,
clasping their hands and crying: "How beautiful! How beautiful!" And many of them knelt in prayer, as if in the presence
of a sacred image or of some marvelous wax Madonna.

"It's a miracle! It's a miracle!" cried a shrill voice suddenly.

"A miracle! A miracle!" cried one and all, drawing back
as though afraid lest their miserable rags might brush against
the splendid satin garment that adorned the body of poor
Concettina, whom Death had miraculously transformed into
a Princess of the Fairies, a statue of the Madonna. Very

soon all the poor people from the Vicolo del Pallonetto, summoned by the news of the miracle, were crowding round the doorway, and the hall took on a festal air. Old women arrived with lighted wax candles and rosaries, chanting litanies. They were followed by women and boys carrying flowers and the sweetmeats which, in accordance with an ancient custom, are eaten in Naples at funeral wakes. Some women brought wine, some brought lemons and other fruits. Some brought babes in arms, or cripples, or invalids, so that they might touch the miracolata.

Others — and these were all very young, with wild eyes, unruly hair and pale, forbidding faces, and their bare shoulders were covered with vivid shawls — surrounded the table on which Concettina lay and intoned those immemorial funeral dirges with which the people of Naples accompany their dead to the grave, recalling and lamenting the good things of life, the only good thing, which is love, recollecting days of joy and nights of tenderness, kisses, caresses and loving tears, and taking leave of them on the frontier of the forbidden country. They were funeral dirges, yet they sounded like love songs, so sweetly modulated were they, and so warmly voluptuous in their sadness and resignation.

The joyously plaintive throng moved into the hall, as it might have moved into a square in one of the poorer parts of Naples on a day of carnival or mourning; and no one — not even the young singers, although they were grouped around her and were touching her — seemed aware of the presence of Consuelo, who, white-faced and trembling from head to foot, stood almost naked near the dead girl, gazing at her face with a strange expression, though whether it betokened fear or some secret emotion I could not tell. Nor did she move until Maria Teresa, supporting her with loving arms, dragged her out of the throng.

As the two merciful women, each with her arm around the other, slowly climbed the stairs, weeping without restraint and trembling in every limb, a terrible cry rent the night, and a tremendous blood-red glare filled the sky.

THE HOLOCAUST

● The sky to the east was scarred by a huge, crimson gash, which tinged the sea blood-red. The horizon was crumbling away, plunging headlong into an abyss of fire. Shaken by subterranean convulsions, the earth trembled; the houses rocked on their foundations; and already one could hear the dull thud of tiles and lumps of plaster as they came apart from the roofs and the cornices of the verandahs, and hurtled down on to the pavements below, like harbingers of universal destruction. A dreadful grinding noise filled the air, like the sound of bones when they are broken and crushed. And above the din, above the wails and terrified shrieks of the people, who were running hither and thither, groping their

way through the streets like blind creatures, there arose a terrible cry, which rent the heavens.

Vesuvius was screaming in the night, spitting blood and
fire. Never since the day that saw the final destruction of
Herculaneum and Pompeii, buried alive in their tomb of ashes
and lava, had so dread a voice been heard in the heavens. A
gigantic pillar of fire rose sky-high from the mouth of the
volcano — a vast, stupendous column of smoke and flames,
which penetrated deep into the firmament, so that it touched
the pale stars. Down the slopes of Vesuvius flowed rivers
of lava, sweeping toward the villages which lay scattered
amid the green of the vineyards. The blood-red glare of the
glowing lava was so vivid that for miles around the mountains
and the plain were lit up with unbelievable brilliance. Woods,
rivers, houses, meadows, fields and paths could be seen far
more clearly and distinctly than by day; and already the sun
was a remote and faded memory.

The mountains of Agerola and the ridges of Avellino were
suddenly seen to fall apart, uncovering the secrets of their
green valleys and woods. A distance of many miles lay between Vesuvius and the Monte di Dio, from the summit of
which, dumb with horror, we contemplated that marvelous
spectacle; yet our eyes, as they searched and explored the
Vesuvian countryside, which but a little while before had
been sleeping peacefully in the moonlight, picked out men,
women and animals as though they had been magnified and
brought closer by a powerful lens. We saw them fleeing to
the vineyards, the fields and the woods, or wandering among
the houses of the villages, which the flames were already lap-
ping on every side. And not only could we make out their
gestures and demeanor, but we could even distinguish their
tousled hair, their unkempt beards, their staring eyes and
wide-open mouths. We even seemed to hear the hoarse
whistling sound with which they expelled the breath from
their lungs.

The sea presented, perhaps, an even more horrifying picture than the land. As far as the eye could reach there was

nothing but a hard, livid crust, pitted everywhere with holes that resembled the pockmarks of some frightful disease; and beneath that motionless crust one sensed the explosive presence of a prodigious force, of a fury scarce repressed, as though the sea were threatening to rise from its bed, to break its hard, scaly back, that it might make war on the land and vent its dreadful fury. Outside Portici, Torre del Greco, Torre Annunziata and Castellammare boats could be seen retreating in great haste from the perilous shore, propelled in desperation by oars alone, since out at sea the wind had dropped like a dead bird, though it was blowing violently to landward. Other boats were to be seen hurrying from Sorrento, Meta and Capri to bring help to the luckless inhabitants of the seaside villages, trapped by the fury of the flames. Torrents of mud flowed sluggishly down the sides of Mount Somma, forming twisted, coiled heaps like black snakes; and where the torrents of mud met the rivers of lava clouds of purple vapor rose aloft, and a dreadful hissing sound reached our ears, like the sizzling of red-hot iron when it is immersed in water.

A huge black cloud, in shape resembling the ink sac of a cuttlefish, swollen with ashes and fragments of glowing lava, was struggling to break away from the crest of Vesuvius. Propelled by the wind, which, fortunately for Naples, was by some miracle blowing from the northwest, it trailed slowly across the sky in the direction of Castellammare di Stabia. The roar emitted by that black, lava-filled cloud as it rolled through the heavens was like the rumbling of a truck laden with stones when it enters a bumpy street. Every so often, from some gap in the cloud, a deluge of lava rained down upon earth and sea, landing on the fields and the hard sea-crust with a crash like that which is heard when the same truck tips up its load; and as the lava touched the ground and the hard surface of the sea it raised clouds of reddish dust, which spread into the sky, blotting out the stars. Vesuvius screamed horribly in the red darkness of that awful night, and a despairing lament arose from the unhappy city.

I pressed Jack's arm, and felt him tremble. His face was pale as he contemplated that vision of hell, and horror, dread and wonder mingled in his wide eyes. "Let us go," I said to him, tugging him by the arm. We moved away, and set off along the Vicolo di Santa Maria Egiziaca in the direction of the Piazza Reale. The walls of that narrow alley reflected such a blaze of crimson light that we walked like blind men, groping our way. Naked people were leaning out of all the windows, waving their arms and calling to one another with shrill cries and piercing wails. Others who were rushing panic-stricken through the streets raised their eyes, crying out themselves and weeping, without pausing or slowing down in their headlong flight. There were people everywhere, some looking miserable, others fierce, clad in rags or naked; some were hurrying to the chapels with wax candles and torches for the Madonnas and the Saints; others, kneeling on the pavement, were calling aloud upon the Virgin and St. Januarius to help them, beating their breasts, while frenzied tears poured down their ravaged cheeks.

It often happens at a time of great and desperate peril that a sacred image, or the feeble glimmer of a candle in a chapel, suddenly revives the memory of a faith long neglected, and fans the embers of hope, repentance, fear, and a trust in God that has been long denied or forgotten. The man who has forgotten God pauses; bewildered and deeply moved, he contemplates the sacred image, and his heart trembles in an ecstasy of love. So it was with Jack. All of a sudden he stopped outside a chapel, and covered his face with his hands, crying: "Oh, Lord! Oh, my Lord!"

In answer to his cry there came from the depths of the chapel a sound like the chirping of birds. We heard a feeble fluttering of wings, a stirring as of birds in a nest. Jack drew back in terror. "Don't be afraid, Jack," I said to him, pressing his arm. "They are the birds of the Madonna." During those terrible years, as soon as the air-raid sirens announced the approach of enemy bombers all the poor little birds of Naples took refuge in the chapels: sparrows, swallows, their feathers rumpled, their round eyes shining under their white lids. They used to hide in remote corners of the chapels, where, huddling together and trembling, they would nest among the wax and papier-mâché statuettes of the souls in Purgatory. "Do you think I've scared them?" Jack asked me in a low voice. And we moved away on tiptoe, so as not to scare the little birds of the Madonna.

Along the streets walked nearly naked old men with whitish, bony shins, leaning against the walls for support. Their snowy locks, ruffled by the wind of fear, hung in disarray over their foreheads, and they kept shouting at the top of their voices. Their words were clipped, and sounded to me like Latin; they were, perhaps, ritual magic formulas of malediction, or of exhortation to the people to repent, to confess their sins aloud, and to prepare for death like Christians. Bands of harassed-looking working-class women hurried along at frantic speed, almost at a run, keeping close together as if they were warriors assailing a fortress; and as they ran they hurled obscene insults and threats at the weeping, gesticulating groups of people in the windows, exhorting them to repent of the infamies for which all were responsible, since the day of judgment had come at last, and neither women, nor old men, nor children would escape the chastisement of God. To their insults and threats the people at the windows responded with loud wails, frightful abuse and vile curses, which the crowd in the street echoed with groans and cries, shaking their fists in the air and uttering dreadful sobs.

From the Piazza Reale we had climbed the hill to Santa Teresella degli Spagnoli; and as we walked down in the direction of Toledo the tumult increased, the demonstrations of fear, rage and pity became more frequent, and the demeanor of the people grew fiercer and more threatening. Near the Piazza delle Carrette, outside a brothel famous for its Negro clientèle, a crowd of infuriated women yelled and stormed, trying to break down the door, which the prostitutes had barricaded in furious haste. At last the crowd burst into the house, and came out dragging by the hair a bleeding, terrified mob of naked harlots and Negro soldiers, who at the sight of the flaming sky, the clouds of lava suspended above the sea, and Vesuvius, wrapped in its dreadful fiery shroud, became as meek as frightened children. While some were attacking the brothels others were invading the butchers' and bakers' shops. The people, as always, tempered their blind fury with manifestations of their traditional hunger. Yet the underlying cause of their fanatical rage was not hunger, but fear — a fear that was turning to class bitterness, vindictiveness, and a hatred of self and of others. As always, the populace ascribed to that awful scourge the character of a punishment from heaven; they saw in the wrath of Vesuvius the anger of the Virgin, of the Saints, of the Gods of the Christian Olympus, who had become incensed at the sins, the corruption and the viciousness of men. And side by side with repentance, with a melancholy desire to expiate their misdeeds, with the eager hope of seeing the wicked punished, with an ingenuous confidence in the justice of a Nature that was so cruel and unjust — side by side with shame at their own wretchedness, of which the people are sadly conscious, there was growing up, as always, in the minds of the populace a base feeling of impunity, the origin of so many deeds of wickedness, and a miserable conviction that in the midst of such great destruction, such widespread chaos, anything is lawful and just. And so men were seen in those days to perform deeds both base and sublime, inspired by blind fury or by cold reason, almost by a wonderful desperation. Such is the power exercised by fear, and by shame at their sins, over the souls of simple men.

Such, too, were the sentiments which determined my attitude of mind, and Jack's, in the face of this inhuman scourge. No longer were we united only in our friendship, our affection, and our pity for the conquered and the conquerors, but also in virtue of the fact that we too felt afraid and ashamed. Jack was humbled and appalled by that frightful upheaval of nature. And so too were all those American soldiers who but a moment before had been so sure of themselves, so disdainful, so proud of their status as free men, and who now were darting about in all directions among the crowd, forcing their way along with their fists and elbows, and expressing their mental confusion in the disarray of their uniforms and the craziness of their behavior. They rushed along, some in silence, their faces distorted by fear, others covering their eyes with their hands and groaning, some in brawling gangs, others alone, and all peering about them like hunted dogs.

In the maze of alleys that leads down to Toledo and Chiaia the mob grew thicker and more frenzied at every step; for popular disorders develop in the same way as disorders of the blood in the human body: in such cases the blood tends to collect in one place and to cause disturbances now in the heart, now in the brain, now in one or other of the intestines. People were coming down from the remotest quarters of the city and collecting in what from time immemorial have been regarded as the holy places of Naples — in the Piazza Reale, around the Tribunali, the Maschio Angioino and the Cathedral, where the miraculous blood of St. Januarius is preserved. There the uproar was terrific, sometimes assuming the proportions of a riot. Lost in that fearsome crowd, which swept them now this way, now that, as it surged to and fro, turning them round and buffeting them like the gale in Dante's Hill, the American soldiers looked as if they too were possessed by a primeval terror and fury. Their faces were begrimed with sweat and ashes, their uniforms were in rags. Now they too were humbled. No longer were they free men, no longer were they proud conquerors. They were conquered wretches, victims of the blind fury of nature. They too were seared to the depths of their souls by the fire that was consuming the sky and the earth.

From time to time a hollow, muffled rumbling, which spread through the secret recesses of the earth, shook the pavement beneath our feet and made the houses rock. A hoarse, deep, gurgling voice rose from the wells and from the mouths of the sewers. The fountains exhaled sulphurous vapors or threw up jets of boiling mud. That subterranean rumbling, that deep voice, that boiling mud caused a sudden efflux of people from their lairs in the bowels of the earth. For during those melancholy years the wretched populace, in order to escape the merciless air raids, had made their homes in the winding tunnels of the ancient Angevin aqueduct which runs beneath the streets of Naples. This aqueduct, say the archaeologists, was excavated by the first inhabitants of the city, who were Greeks or Phoenicians, or by the Pelasgians, those mysterious men who came from the sea. There is an allusion to the Angevin aqueduct and to its strange population in Boccaccio's tale of Andreuccio da Perugia. These unhappy creatures were emerging from their filthy hell-holes, from the dark caves, the underground passages, the wells and the mouths of the sewers. Each one carried on his shoulders his wretched chattels, or, like a modern Aeneas, his aged father, or his young children, or the pecuriello, the paschal lamb, which at Eastertide (it was actually Holy Week) brings joy to even the meanest Neapolitan home, and is sacred, because it is the image of Christ.

This "resurrection," to which the coincidence of Easter gave a dread significance, the resurgence from the tomb of these ragged hordes, was a sure sign of the existence of a danger both grave and imminent. For what hunger, and cholera, and earthquakes — which, according to an ancient belief, destroy palaces and hovels but respect the caverns and the underground passages beneath the city's foundations — cannot accomplish was possible to the rivers of boiling mud with which Vesuvius in its spite was gleefully driving those poor wretches like rats from the sewers.

Those crowds of mud-strained, spectral beings who were everywhere emerging from beneath the ground, that seething mob which was rushing like a river in flood toward the low-lying parts of the city, and the brawls, the yells, the tears, the oaths, the songs, the panic, the sudden stampedes, and the ferocious struggles that would break out in the vicinity of a chapel, a fountain, a cross, or a baker's shop, created a frightful, stupendous chaos of sound, which filled the city and was overflowing on to the seafront, into Via Partenope, Via Caracciolo, the Riviera di Chiaia, and the streets and squares that front the sea between the Granili and Mergellina. It was as if the people in their despair looked to the sea alone for salvation, as if they expected that the waves would quench the flames which were devouring the land, or that the marvelous compassion of the Virgin or St. Januarius would enable them to walk on the waters and escape.

But when they reached the sea front, where they were greeted by the fearsome spectacle of Vesuvius, red-hot, with streams of lava winding their way down its slopes, and the blazing villages (the blast from the prodigious conflagration spread as far as the island of Capri, which could be seen drifting on the horizon, and the snow-covered mountains of Cilento), the crowd dropped to their knees; and at the sight of the sea, which was covered with a horrible green and yellow film like the mottled hide of some loathsome reptile, they called upon heaven to help them, uttering loud wails, bestial yells and savage oaths. Many, spurred on by the curses and the frightful abuse of the infuriated, envious populace, plunged into the waves, hoping that they would provide a foothold and were ignominiously drowned.

After wandering round for a long time we finally emerged into the vast square, dominated by the Maschio Angioino, that opens on to the harbor. And there before us, swathed from head to foot in its purple mantle, we saw Vesuvius. That ghostly Caesar with his doglike head, sitting on his throne of lava and ashes, cleft the sky with his flame-crowned head, and barked horribly. The pillar of fire that rose from his throat penetrated deep into the celestial vault and vanished into the abyss of heaven. Rivers of blood streamed from his gaping red jaws, and earth, sky and sea trembled.

The faces of the crowd that filled the square were shiny and flat-looking; they were seamed with shadowy black and white lines, as in a flash-bulb photograph. There was something of the harshness and frozen immobility of a photograph in those wide, staring eyes and intent faces, in the façades of the houses and the other impersonal features of the scene, and almost, one felt, in the people's gestures. The fierce light of the flames beat down upon the walls and illuminated the gutters and cornices of the balconies; and the contrast between the bloodshot sky, which had a sombre, purplish tint, and the red-rimmed roofs was illusory in its effect.

Crowds of people were hurrying down to the sea, pouring into the square from the hundred alleys that converge upon it from all sides. As they walked they gazed up at the black clouds, swollen with glowing lava, that rolled across the sky immediately above the sea, and at the red-hot stones that ploughed their way noisily through the murky air like comets. A terrible clamor arose from the square; and every so often a deep silence would fall upon the crowd, broken at intervals by a groan, a wail, or a sudden cry — a solitary cry that died away instantly without leaving behind it a trace of an echo, like a cry that goes up from a bare mountain-top.

Over on the far side of the square hordes of American soldiers were making a violent assault on the railings that block the entrance to the harbor, trying to break the great iron bars. Hoarse, plaintive cries for help came from the ships' sirens. Pickets of armed sailors were rushing to take up their positions on the decks and along the sides of their vessels. Fierce scuffles were breaking out on the moles and gangways between the sailors and the hordes of fear-crazed soldiers who were rushing the ships that they might escape the wrath of Vesuvius. Here and there, lost in the crowd, were American, British, Polish, and French soldiers, wandering about in bewilderment and terror. Some tried to force their way through the press, clutching the arms of weeping women, whom they appeared to have kidnaped; others allowed themselves to be swept along on the tide, dazed by the ferocity and novelty of the awful scourge. They were surrounded by swarms of prostitutes, half-naked, or wrapped in the ceremonial cloaks of yellow, green and scarlet silk worn by the women in the brothels. And some chanted their own private litanies; others uttered mysterious phrases in loud, piercing voices; others in rhythmic tones invoked the name of God — "O God! O God!" — frantically waving their arms above the sea of heads and distorted faces, and keeping their eyes fixed on the sky as if, through the rain of ashes and fire, they were watching the slow flight of an Angel armed with a flaming sword.

By now the night was waning, and a delicate pallor was suffusing the sky over toward Capri and above the wooded slopes of the mountains of Sorrento. Even the fires of Vesuvius were losing something of their terrible brilliance and were beginning to appear green and transparent; the flames were turning pink, and looked like huge rose petals scattered by the wind. As the nocturnal mists gave way to the uncertain light of dawn the rivers of lava ceased to glow; they grew dim, and were transformed into black snakes, just as red-hot iron, when it is left on the anvil, gradually becomes covered with black scales, which emit dying blue and green sparks.

Slowly the dawn was lifting that infernal panorama, still dripping with red darkness, out of the deep bowl of the flaming night, as a fisherman raises a clump of coral from the bed of the sea. The virgin light of day was washing the pale green of the vineyards, the antique silver of the olive trees, the deep blue of the cypresses and pines, the voluptuous gold of the brooms. In such a setting the black rivers of lava shone with a funereal radiance, glowing darkly as some crustaceans do when they lie on the seashore in the sun, or like certain kinds of dark stones when the rain has restored their lustre. In the distance, beyond Sorrento, a patch of red was gradually climbing above the horizon. Slowly it dissolved into the air, and the sky, which was full of yellow, sulphurous clouds, was suffused with a transparent blood-red glow, until unexpectedly the sun, white as the eyelid of a dying bird, broke through the turbulent mists.

A tremendous clamor arose from the square. The crowd stretched out their arms toward the rising sun, shouting "The sun! The sun!," as if this were the first time the sun had ever risen over Naples. And perhaps the sun was indeed rising now for the first time on Naples from the abyss of chaos, amid the turmoil of creation, climbing from the bed of a sea whose creation was not yet complete. And as always happens in Naples after a time of terror, grief and tears, the return of the sun, following a night of such endless agony, changed horror and weeping into joy and jubilation. Here and there arose the sound of the first applause, the first glad voices, the first songs, and those sharp guttural cries, attuned to the age-old melodic themes of elemental fear, pleasure and love, with which the people of Naples, in the manner of animals, that is to say in a wonderfully naïve and innocent way, express joy, amazement, and that happy fear which men and animals always feel when they have rediscovered the meaning of joy and are astonished to be alive.

Gangs of boys were running among the crowd, chasing from end to end of the square and crying "E fornuta! è fornuta!" Those words — "It's over! It's over!" — announced the ending not only of the scourge but of the war. "E fornuta! è fornuta!" answered the crowd, for always the sun's appearance deludes the people of Naples, inspiring them with the false hope that their misfortunes and sufferings are about to end. A cart drawn by a horse entered the square from Via Medina, and the sight of that horse filled the crowd with joyous amazement, as though it was the first horse ever created. One and all shouted: "See that? See that? A horse! A horse!" And as if by magic there arose on all sides the voices of the itinerant vendors, offering for sale sacred images, rosaries, amulets, dead men's bones, postcards representing scenes from former eruptions of Vesuvius, and statuettes of St. Januarius, who with a gesture had halted the stream of lava at the gates of Naples.

Suddenly the hum of engines was heard high up in the sky, and everyone looked up.

A squadron of American fighters had taken off from the airfield at Capodichino and was attacking the enormous black cloud or "cuttlefish," which, swollen with fragments of glowing lava, was gradually drifting in the direction of Castellammare. After a few moments the rat-tat of machine guns was heard, and the horrible cloud seemed to stop and confront its assailants. The American fighters were trying to break up the cloud with the salvoes from their machine guns so that it would be forced to jettison its load of red-hot stones over the stretch of sea that lies between Vesuvius and Castellammare. In this way they hoped to save the town from certain destruction. It was a desperate enterprise, and the crowd held their breath. A profound silence descended on the square.

Through the gaps which the salvoes of machine-gun bullets tore in the sides of the black cloud torrents of glowing lava hurtled down into the sea, throwing up lofty jets of red water, columns of vivid green vapor, comet-like trails of red-hot cinders, and marvelous rosettes of flame, which slowly dissolved in the air. "See that? See that?" cried the throng, clapping their hands. But meanwhile the horrible cloud, propelled by the wind, which was blowing from the north, drew nearer Castellammare every moment.

Suddenly one of the American fighters, looking like a silver hawk, darted with the speed of lightning straight at the "cuttlefish," tore a gap in it with its nose, passed through the gap, and with a fearful explosion blew up inside the cloud, which opened like a huge black rose and hurtled down into the sea.

By now the sun was high in the heavens. Little by little the atmosphere was becoming thicker, a gray pall of ashes obscured the sky, and green lightning rent the blood-red cloud that was forming on the brow of Vesuvius. Streaks of yellow zigzagged across the black wall of the horizon, from behind which came the rumble of distant thunder.

In the streets surrounding the Allied General Headquarters the congestion was such that we had to use force to get through. The crowd, massed in front of the G.H.Q. building, mutely awaited a sign of hope. But the news from the districts stricken by the scourge was growing graver from hour to hour. The houses in the villages situated near Salerno were collapsing beneath the hail of lava. A blizzard of ashes had been raging for some hours over the island of Capri, and was threatening to bury the villages that lie between Pompeii and Castellammare.

During the afternoon General Cork asked Jack to go to the Pompeii area, where the danger was greatest. The ribbon-like main road was covered with a thick carpet of ashes, on which the wheels of our jeep revolved with a soft, silky, rustling sound. A strange silence was in the air, broken at intervals by the hollow rumbling of Vesuvius. I was surprised at the contrast between the movement and shouting of the people and the mute immobility of the animals, which stood firm beneath the hail of ashes and looked about them with eyes that were full of melancholy bewilderment.

Now and again we passed through yellow clouds of sulphurous vapor. Columns of American vehicles were slowly going back up the road, carrying help in the shape of food, medical supplies and clothes to the unfortunate people who lived on the slopes of Vesuvius. The sombre countryside was shrouded in a green murk. Just after we had passed Herculaneum our faces were lashed by a shower of warm mud, which persisted for a considerable time. Directly above us Vesuvius snarled menacingly, spewing up lofty jets of red-hot stones, which fell to earth with a roar. Shortly before we reached Torre del Greco we were taken unawares by a sudden shower of lava. We sheltered behind the wall of a house near the sea front. The sea was a wonderful green color; it looked like a turtle made of ancient copper. A sailing vessel was slowly ploughing its way through the hard sea-crust, from which the descending fragments of lava rebounded with a resonant crackling sound.

We were now in the vicinity of a small meadow, dotted with clumps of rosemary and flowering brooms, and backed by a high rock which sheltered it from the wind. The grass was of a very harsh green color, a crude, bright green so vivid, so unexpected and so fresh in its brilliance that it looked as if it had only that moment been created — a green still virginal, glimpsed without warning at the instant of its creation, in the first moments of the creation of the world. This grass descended almost to the edge of the water, whose greenness seemed in contrast already faded, as if this sea belonged to a world already old, a world created long, long ago.

The countryside about us lay buried beneath the ashes. It had been scorched in places and turned topsy-turvy by the mad violence of nature, by the return of chaos. Groups of American soldiers, their faces concealed behind masks of rubber and copper like the helmets of ancient warriors, were roaming about the countryside, carrying stretchers, assembling the injured, and directing groups of women and children to a column of vehicles parked in the roadway. A number of dead were lying on the roadside near the ruins of a house. Their faces were encased in shells of hard white ash, so that it looked as if they had eggs in place of heads. Their bodies were those of men still without form, men only partly created. They were the first dead in creation.

The cries of the injured came to us from a world that lay beyond the reach of love and pity, beyond the frontier set between chaos and nature in the divine order of creation. They expressed a feeling not yet known to men, a grief not experienced by the living beings hitherto created. They were a presage of suffering, coming to us from a world still in the process of gestation, a world still plunged in chaos.

And here, in this little world of green grass, that had but lately emerged from chaos, and was still fresh from the travail of its creation, still virginal, a group of men who had escaped the scourge lay on their backs asleep, their faces turned to heaven. They had very handsome faces, with skin that was not begrimed with mud and ashes, but clear, as though washed by the light: faces that looked new, as if they had just been modeled, with lofty, noble brows and bright lips. They lay sleeping on the green grass like survivors of the Flood on the summit of the first mountain to appear above the waters.

A girl stood on the sandy shore, at a point where the green grass merged into the waves. She was combing her hair and looking at the sea — looking at the sea as a woman gazes at herself in a mirror. Standing on the young, newly created grass, she who was herself young, she who had but lately been brought into the world, gazed at herself in the ancient mirror of creation with a smile of blissful wonder; and the faded green of the immemorial sea was reflected in her long, soft hair, her smooth white skin and her small, strong hands. Her movements as she slowly combed her hair were already those of a lover. A woman dressed in red sat beneath a tree suckling her child. Her snow-white breast protruded from her red blouse, splendid as the breast of the first woman in creation, or the first fruit from a tree that has but lately emerged from the earth. A dog lay curled up near the sleeping men, following the woman's slow, placid movements with its eyes. Some sheep were grazing, and every so often they would raise their heads and look at the green sea. Those men, those women, those animals were alive and safe. They had been purged of their sins. They were already immune from the degradation, misery and hunger, from the vices and criminal tendencies of men. They had already died the death, and descended into hell, and risen again.

We too — Jack and I — were survivors from chaos. We too were living beings newly created, newly called into existence, newly risen from the dead. The menacing voice of Vesuvius, that loud, hoarse bark, came to us out of the blood-red cloud that enveloped the monster's brow. It came to us through the crimson darkness, through the storm of fire. It was a pitiless, implacable voice. It was in truth the voice of a tumultuous malignant nature — the voice of chaos itself. We were on the borderland between chaos and creation, on the confines of "la bonté, ce continent énorme," on the outer fringe of the newly created world. And the terrible voice that came to us through the storm of fire, that loud, hoarse bark, was the voice of Chaos, who was rebelling against the divine laws of creation, and biting the hand of the Creator.

Suddenly Vesuvius uttered a terrible cry. The group of American soldiers standing near the vehicles parked in the roadway drew back in terror. They scattered, and many of them, seized with panic, rushed pell-mell toward the seashore. Jack too withdrew a few steps, and turned his back. I seized him by the arm. "Don't be afraid," I said to him. "Look at those men, Jack."

Jack turned his head and looked at the men who lay sleeping, at the girl who stood combing her hair and gazing at herself in the mirror of the sea, at the woman suckling her child. I would have liked to say to him: "God has just made them, yet they are the oldest human beings on earth. That is Adam, and that is Eve. They have just been born out of chaos, they have just returned from hell, they have just risen from the grave. Look at them — they are newly born, and they have already taken upon themselves all the sins of the world. All the men and women in Naples, in Italy, in Europe are like these. They are immortal. They are born in sorrow, they die in sorrow, and they rise again, purified. They are the Lambs of God, they carry on their shoulders all the sins and all the sorrows of the world."

But I said nothing; and Jack looked at me, and smiled.

It was evening when we returned to Naples. As we drove back the tempest roared, and fire rained down from heaven. Near Portici we beheld once more green grass and green leaves, the buds on the trees, the play of the light on the windowpanes — things that had been from time immemorial. I thought of the gentleness of those foreign soldiers as they bent over the injured and the dead, of their warm compassion, heightened by fear. I thought of those men who had lain sleeping on the shore of chaos, and of their immortality. Jack was pale; and he was smiling. I turned to look at Vesuvius, that dreadful monster with the doglike head, barking on the horizon amid the smoke and flame.

"Pity, pity. Even you are deserving of pity," I said in a low voice.

THE FLAG

● Threatened in its rear by the wrath of Vesuvius, the American army, which had been held up for so many months outside Cassino, at last made a move. It hurled itself forward, smashed the Cassino defense line and, pouring into Latium, advanced within striking-distance of Rome.

Stretched out on the grass at the edge of the Lake of Albano, which in ancient times was the crater of a volcano, and resembles a copper bowl filled with black water, we looked down on Rome, situated on the far side of the plain, where the sluggish river, flavus Tiber, lay sleeping in the sun. Occasionally the staccato sound of rifle fire floated toward us on the warm wind. The cupola of St. Peter's shimmered on the horizon, suspended beneath a huge castle of white clouds at which the sun was aiming its golden shafts. I thought of the golden shafts of Apollo, and blushed. In the distance one could see snow-clad Soracte rising out of a blue haze. The verse from Horace sprang to my lips, and I blushed. "Dear Rome," I said in a low voice. Jack looked at me, and smiled.

In the morning Jack and I had left General Cork's column and joined General Guillaume's Moroccan Division in the upper part of the woods of Castel Gandolfo. Seen from here Rome, in the dazzling sunlight reflected from the fleecy clouds, had the livid whiteness of chalk. It resembled one of those cities of shining stone which rise from the skyline in pictures representing scenes from the *Iliad*.

The cupolas, the towers, the steeples, and the severely geometrical houses in the new districts which stretch down from St. John Lateran into the green valley of the Nymph Aegeria, in the direction of the tombs of the Barberini, looked as if they were made of a hard white substance with shadowy blue veins. Black crows flew up from the red tombs beside the Via Appia. I thought of the eagles of the Caesars, and blushed. I tried hard not to think of the Goddess Rome, seated in the Capitol, of the pillars of the Forum and the purple of the Caesars. "The glory that was Rome," I said to myself, and I blushed again. On that day, at that moment, in that place I did not want to think of the eternity of Rome. I liked to think of Rome as a mortal city, inhabited by mortal men.

In the unwavering, dazzling light nothing seemed to move or breathe. The sun was already high, it was beginning to get hot, and a white, transparent mist veiled the vast red and yellow plain of Latium, where the Tiber and the Anio were intertwined like two snakes locked in an amorous embrace. In the meadows that flank the Via Appia riderless horses could be seen galloping about as in a canvas of Poussin or Claude Lorrain, and ever and anon, far away on the horizon, the green lid of the sea sparkled in the sunshine.

General Guillaume's goumiers were encamped in the wood of ash-colored olive trees and dark holm oaks which stretches down the gentle slopes of Mount Cavo and dies away amid the bright green of the vineyards and the gold of the corn. Below us, on the high, steep bank of the Lake of Albano, stood the papal villa of Castel Gandolfo. Sitting in the shade of the holm oaks and the olive trees, with their legs crossed and their rifles across their knees, the goumiers gazed with avid eyes at the crowd of women promenading among the trees in the park of the papal villa — many of them nuns and peasants from the Castelli Romani [1] destroyed in the war, whom the Holy Father had gathered under his protecting wing. A community of birds sang in the branches of the olive trees and holm oaks. The air was sweet to the lips, like that name which I kept repeating in a low voice: "Rome, Rome, dear Rome."

A smile, faint but immense, passed like a scurry of wind across the Roman Campagna. It was the smile of the Apollo of Veii, the cruel, ironical, mysterious smile of the Etruscan Apollo. I would have liked to return to Rome, to my home, not with my mouth full of sonorous words but with that smile upon my lips. I was afraid that the liberation of Rome would not be an intimate, family occasion but one of the usual pretexts for triumphal marches, high-sounding speeches and songs of praise. I tried hard to think of Rome not as a vast communal grave, where the bones of Gods and men are strewn indiscriminately about the ruins of the temples and the Fora, but as a human city, a city peopled by simple mortal men, where everything is human, where the pettiness and degradation of the Gods do not diminish the greatness of man nor invest human freedom with the significance of a heritage that has been betrayed, a glory that has been usurped and tarnished.

My last memory of Rome was of a fetid cell in the Regina Coeli prison. And now, as I returned home on a day of vic-

---

[1] Walled villages situated on the Alban Hills. (Translator's note.)

tory (a foreign victory, gained over foreign arms in a Latium that had been overrun and laid waste by foreign armies), old thoughts and emotions, simple and sincere, surged up within me. But already my ears were filled with the din of the trumpets and the cymbals, with the Ciceronian orations and the songs of triumph. And I shuddered.

Such were my thoughts as I lay in the grass, gazing at distant Rome; and I wept. Jack, lying at my side, pressed a tender leaf to his lips and with its aid imitated the voices of the birds, which were singing in the branches of the trees. A breath of peace passed lightly through the air, rustling the grass and the leaves.

"Don't cry," said Jack in tones of affectionate reproof. "The birds are singing — and you are crying?"

The birds were singing, and I was crying. Jack's words, so simple, so human, made me blush. This foreigner from beyond the seas, this American, this warmhearted, generous, sensitive man had found in the depths of his heart the right words, the true words, the words that I had been vainly seeking within my mind and without, the only words that were appropriate to that day, to that moment, to that place. The birds were singing, and I was crying! Through my tears I looked at Rome, trembling in the depths of the limpid mirror of light; and I was happy.

As we lay in the grass we heard the sound of merry voices coming from the wood, and we looked round. It was General Guillaume, accompanied by a group of French officers. His hair was gray with dust, his face was tanned by the sun and bore the marks of his exertions, but his eyes were bright and his voice youthful.

"Voilà Rome!" he said, baring his head.

It was not the first time I had witnessed that gesture; it was not the first time I had seen a French general bare his head as he gazed at Rome from the woods of Castel Gandolfo. I had seen the same thing in the faded daguerreotypes belonging to the Primoli collection, which old Count Primoli had shown me one day in his library. In the pictures to which I refer Marshal Oudinot, surrounded by a party of French officers in red trousers, is seen saluting Rome from the very wood of holm oaks and olive trees in which we were at that moment.

"J'aurais préféré voir la Tour Eiffel, à la place de la coupole de Saint Pierre," said Lieutenant Pierre Lyautey.

General Guillaume turned to him with a laugh. "Vous ne la voyez pas," he said, "car elle se cache juste derrière la coupole de Saint Pierre."

"C'est drôle, je suis ému comme si je voyais Paris," said Major Marchetti.

"Vous ne trouvez pas," said Pierre Lyautey, "qu'il y a quelque chose de français, dans ce paysage?"

"Oui, sans doute," said Jack. "C'est l'air français qu'y ont mis le Poussin et Claude Lorrain."

"Et Corot," said General Guillaume.

"Stendhal aussi a mis quelque chose de français dans ce paysage," said Major Marchetti.

"Aujourd'hui, pour la première fois," said Pierre Lyautey, "je comprends pourquoi Corot, en peignant le Pont de Narni, a fait les ombres bleues."

"J'ai dans ma poche," said General Guillaume, taking a book from the pocket of his tunic, "les *Promenades dans Rome.* Le Général Juin, lui, se promène avec Chateaubriand dans sa poche. Pour comprendre Rome, Messieurs, je vous conseille de ne trop vous fier à Chateaubriand. Fiez-vous à Stendhal. Il est le seul Français qui ait compris Rome et l'Italie. Si j'ai un reproche à lui faire, c'est de ne pas voir les couleurs du paysage. Il ne dit pas un traître mot de vos ombres bleues."

"Si j'ai un reproche à lui faire," said Pierre Lyautey, "c'est d'aimer mieux Rome que Paris."

"Stendhal n'a jamais dit une chose pareille," said General Guillaume, frowning.

"En tout cas, il aime mieux Milan que Paris."

"Ce n'est qu'un dépit d'amour," said Major Marchetti. "Paris était une maîtresse qui l'avait trompé bien des fois."

"Je n'aime pas, Messieurs," said General Guillaume, "vous entendre parler ainsi de Stendhal. C'est un de mes plus chers amis."

"Si Stendhal était encore Consul de France à Civita Vecchia," said Major Marchetti, "il serait sans doute, en ce moment, parmi nous."

"Stendhal aurait fait un magnifique officier des *goums*," said General Guillaume. And turning with a smile to Pierre Lyautey he added: "Il vous ravirait toutes les jolies femmes qui vous attendent ce soir à Rome."

"Les jolies femmes qui m'attendent ce soir, ce sont les petites filles de celles qui attendaient Stendhal," said Pierre Lyautey, who had many women friends in Roman society, and was expecting to dine that same evening in the Palazzo Colonna.

I listened with emotion to the French voices and the French words as they floated softly through the green air, to the rapid, fluent articulation and the urbane, warmhearted laughter, so characteristic of the French. And I felt ashamed and abashed, as if it were my fault that the cupola of St. Peter's was not the Eiffel Tower. I would have liked to apologize to them, to try to convince them that it was not *my* fault. Just then I too would have preferred that that city down there on the horizon had been not Rome but Paris — for I knew how happy they would have been had this been so. And I said nothing, but listened to those French words floating gently among the branches of the trees. I pretended not to notice that those tough soldiers, those gallant Frenchmen were moved, that their eyes were bright with tears, and that their small talk and their laughter were a cloak behind which they were trying to conceal their emotion.

For a long while we remained silent, watching the cupola of St. Peter's gently quivering on the skyline at the far end of the plain.

"Vous en avez de la veine!" General Guillaume said to me suddenly, clapping me on the shoulder; and I felt that he v as thinking of Paris.

"I am sorry," said Jack, "to have to leave you. But it's already late, and General Cork is waiting for us."

"The American Fifth Army will conquer Rome even without your help . . . and without ours," said General Guillaume, and there was a plaintively ironical inflection in his voice. Then he altered his tone and added, with a smile at once sad and mocking: "You will lunch at our table, and then I will let you go. With the Holy Father's permission, Colonel Granger's column won't move off again before two or three o'clock. Let us go, gentlemen — the kouskous awaits us."

In a small clearing stood a row of tables, which the goumiers had taken from some deserted farm dwelling. Shelter was provided by a number of great holm oaks, where myriads of birds had built their nests. We took our places, and General Guillaume indicated two dark-skinned monks, thin as lizards, who were moving about among the Moroccans. He told us that when the news of the goumiers' arrival spread through the district all the peasants had fled, crossing themselves as if they already detected the smell of sulphur, and that a number of monks had immediately hurried forward from the neighboring monasteries to convert the goumiers to the religion of Christ. General Guillaume had sent an officer to ask the monks not to annoy the goumiers, but the monks had replied that they had orders to baptize all the Moroccans because the Pope did not want Turks in Rome. The Holy Father had in fact sent a radio message to the Allied Command in which he expressed his desire that the Moroccan Division should be halted at the gates of the Eternal City.

"The Pope is wrong," added General Guillaume with a laugh. "If he consents to be liberated by an army of Protestants I don't see why he should object if his liberators also include some Mussulmans."

"The Holy Father," said Pierre Lyautey, "might show himself less severe in his attitude to the Mussulmans if he knew what a high opinion the goumiers have of his power." And he told us that those three thousand women refugees in the papal villa had made an enormous impression on the Moroccans. Three thousand wives! The Pope was undoubtedly the most powerful monarch in the world.

"It has devolved upon me," said General Guillaume, "to throw a cordon of sentries round the outer wall of the papal villa, so as to prevent the goumiers from going in to pay their compliments to the Pope's wives."

"I understand now," said Jack, "why the Pope doesn't want Turks in Rome."

We all began to laugh, and Pierre Lyautey said that a big surprise awaited the Allied forces in the Eternal City. It seemed, in fact, that Mussolini had remained in Rome, that he had prepared a triumphal reception for the Allies, and that he was waiting for his liberators on the balcony of the Palazzo Venezia, so that he could welcome them with one of his usual magnificent speeches.

"I should be much astonished," said General Guillaume, "if Mussolini were to neglect such an opportunity."

"I am sure the Americans will applaud him enthusiastically," said Pierre Lyautey.

"They have applauded him for twenty years," I said, "and there's no reason why they shouldn't go on applauding him."

"It is certain," said Major Marchetti, "that if the Americans had refrained from applauding him during those twenty years they wouldn't have found themselves faced one fine day with the necessity of landing in Italy."

Just then a goumier, his head covered by the fringe of his dark mantle, so that he looked like an ancient priest in the act of performing a sacrifice, came up to our table carrying a tray, decorated with softly gleaming slices of ham like the petals of a great rose. As he approached we heard a muffled explosion among the trees, and we saw some goumiers running through the wood behind the kitchens.

"Another mine!" exclaimed General Guillaume, getting up from the table. "Please excuse me, gentlemen. I must go and see what has happened." And he made off in the direction of the spot where the explosion had occurred, followed by several officers.

"That's the third goumier so far who's been blown up since this morning," said Major Marchetti.

The wood was sprinkled with German mines of the sort which the Americans called "booby traps." As they strolled among the trees the Moroccans stepped on them with incautious feet and were blown up.

"The goumiers," said Pierre Lyautey, "are incorrigible. They can't accustom themselves to modern civilization. Even booby traps are a part of modern civilization."

"Throughout North Africa," said Jack, "the natives got used to American civilization straightway. It's an undeniable fact that since we landed in Africa the peoples of Morocco, Algeria and Tunisia have made great progress."

"What sort of progress?" asked Pierre Lyautey in amazement.

"Before the American landing," said Jack, "the Arab used to go about on horseback while his wife followed him on foot, walking behind the horse's tail with her child on her back and a large bundle balanced on her head. Since the Americans landed in North Africa things have altered profoundly. The Arab, it is true, still goes about on horseback, and his wife continues to accompany him on foot as before, with her child on her back and a bundle on her head. But she no longer walks behind the horse's tail. She now walks in front of the horse — because of the mines."

A roar of laughter greeted Jack's words, and hearing the officers laugh the Moroccans who were scattered about the wood looked up, pleased that their officers were in a good humor. At that moment General Guillaume joined us. His brow was beaded with tiny drops of perspiration, but he seemed more exasperated than upset.

"Luckily," he said, resuming his seat at the table, "luckily no one has been killed this time — only wounded. But what can I do about it? Is it my fault? Should I tie them to the trees to prevent them from stubbing their toes against the mines? I certainly can't shoot that poor beggar to teach him not to get blown up!"

Fortunately, this time the imprudent goumier had come off lightly. The mine had only carried off one of his hands, which had been neatly severed.

"They haven't yet succeeded in finding the hand," added General Guillaume. "Who knows what will become of it?"

The ham was followed by miniature trout from the Liri, silvery blue in color with a faint green glint. Then came kouskous, the famous Arab dish, pride of Mauritania and Saracenic Sicily, consisting of mutton cooked in a crust of bran, bright as the gilded cuirasses of Tasso's heroines, and golden wine from the Castelli Romani — a rich Frascati wine, noble and heart-warming as an ode of Horace, which brought a glow to the cheeks and a sparkle into the conversation of the guests.

"Vous aimez le kouskous?" asked Pierre Lyautey, turning to Jack.

"Je le trouve excellent!" replied Jack.

"It certainly isn't to Malaparte's liking," said Pierre Lyautey with an ironical smile.

"And why shouldn't it be to his liking?" asked Jack in great astonishment.

I smiled but said nothing, keeping my eyes fixed on my plate.

"Judging from *Kaputt*," answered Pierre Lyautey, "one would say that Malaparte eats nothing but nightingales' hearts, served on plates of old Meissen and Nynphenburg porcelain at the tables of Royal Highnesses, Duchesses and Ambassadors."

"During the seven months that we have spent together outside Cassino," said Jack, "I have never seen Malaparte eating nightingales' hearts in the company of Royal Highnesses and Ambassadors."

"Malaparte undoubtedly has a very vivid imagination," laughed General Guillaume, "and in his next book you will find our humble camp meal transformed into a regal banquet, while I shall become a kind of Sultan of Morocco."

They all looked at me and laughed. I kept my eyes fixed on my plate and said nothing.

"Do you want to know," said Pierre Lyautey, "what Malaparte will say about this lunch of ours in his next book?" And he proceeded to give an extremely amusing description of a sumptuous banquet, the scene of which was not the heart of a wood on the high bank of the Lake of Albano but a hall in the Pope's villa at Castel Gandolfo. Seasoning his discourse with a number of witty anachronisms, he described the porcelain crockery of Caesar Borgia, the silver ware of Pope Sixtus — the handiwork of Benvenuto Cellini — the golden chalices of Pope Julius II, and the papal footmen, busying themselves about our table while a chorus of angel voices at the end of the hall intoned Palestrina's "Super flumina Babylonis" in honor of General Guillaume and his gallant officers. They all laughed amiably at Pierre Lyautey's words. Only I did not laugh. I smiled and said nothing, keeping my eyes fixed on my plate.

"I should like to know," said Pierre Lyautey, turning to me with an urbanely ironical air, "how much truth there is in all that you relate in *Kaputt*."

"It's of no importance," said Jack, "whether what Malaparte relates is true or false. That isn't the question. The question is whether or not his work is art."

"I would not wish to be discourteous to Malaparte, for he is my guest," said General Guillaume. "But I think that in *Kaputt* he is pulling his readers' legs."

"And I don't wish to be discourteous to you," retorted Jack warmly; "but I think you are wrong."

"You won't ask us to believe," said Pierre Lyautey, "that all that Malaparte relates in *Kaputt* actually happened to him. Is it really possible that everything happens to him? Nothing ever happens to *me!*"

"Are you quite sure of that?" said Jack, half closing his eyes.

"Please forgive me," I said at last, turning to General Guillaume, "if I am forced to reveal to you that a few moments ago, at this very table, I had the most extraordinary experience of my life. You were not aware of it, because I am a well-mannered guest. But inasmuch as you question the truth of what I narrate in my books, allow me to tell you what happened to me a few moments ago — here, in your presence."

"I am curious to know what happened to you that was so extraordinary," answered General Guillaume, laughing.

"Do you remember the delicious ham with which we began our meal? It was a ham from the Fondi mountains. You have fought over those mountains — they rise behind Gaeta, between Cassino and the Castelli Romani — and you will therefore know that in the Fondi mountains they breed the finest pigs in the whole of Latium and the whole of Ciociaria. These are the pigs that are referred to in such affectionate terms by St. Thomas Aquinas, who came, in fact, from the Fondi mountains. These pigs are sacred, and they root within the precincts of the churches in the little villages situated on the high ridges of Ciociaria. Their flesh has the perfume of incense, and their lard is as soft as virgin wax."

"C'était en effet un sacré jambon," said General Guillaume.

"After the ham from the Fondi mountains came miniature trout from the Liri. A beautiful river, the Liri. On its green banks many of your goumiers have fallen before the fire of the German machine guns — fallen face downward in the grass. Do you remember the Liri trout — slim and silvery, with delicate fins that diffuse a faint green radiance and have a darker, mellower silveriness? The miniature trout from the Liri are like those found in the Black Forest; they are like the Blauforellen of the Neckar — the poets' river, the river of Hölderling — and of the Titisee; they resemble the Blauforellen found in the Danube at Donaueschingen, where the Danube has its source. That regal river rises in the park of the castle of the Princes of Fürstenburg, in a white marble basin that looks like a cradle and is adorned with neoclassical statues. That marble cradle, pleasance of the black swans celebrated by Schiller, is frequented by stags and fallow deer, which go there at sunset to drink. But the Liri trout are perhaps brighter and more transparent than the Blauforellen of the Black Forest; and the silvery green of their light scales, which in color resemble the old silver candelabra that hang in the churches of Ciociaria, does not yield the palm to the silvery blue of the Blauforellen of the Neckar and the Danube, which diffuse the same mysterious blue radiance as the dazzling white porcelain for which Nynphenburg is famous. The soil that is washed by the Liri is ancient and noble; it is some of the noblest and most ancient soil in Italy; and just now I was moved when I saw the Liri trout curled up in the form of a crown with their tails in their pink mouths, even as the ancients used to represent the serpent, symbol of eternity, in the form of a wreath, with its tail in its mouth, on their columns at Mycenae, Paestum, Selinus and Delphi. And do you remember the flavor of Liri trout — delicate and elusive as the voice of that noble river?"

"Elles étaient délicieuses!" said General Guillaume.

"And finally an immense copper tray appeared on the table. It contained the kouskous, with its barbarous, delicate flavor. But the ram from which this kouskous is made is not a Moroccan ram from Mount Atlas or from the scorched pastures of Fez, Teroudan or Marrakesh. The Itri mountains above Fondi — where Fra Diavolo ruled — are its habitat. On the Itri mountains, in Ciociaria, there grows a herb similar to horsemint, but richer, with a flavor that reminds one of sage. The people who live among those mountains call it by the ancient Greek name of kallimeria. From it pregnant women make a potion that facilitates childbirth. It is a pungent herb, and the rams of Itri devour it greedily. It is, indeed, to this herb, kallimeria, that the rams of Itri owe their rich fat, so suggestive of pregnant women; because of it they have the feminine indolence, the fullness of voice and the weary, languid eyes of pregnant women and hermaphrodites.

You should look attentively at your plate when you eat kouskous. The ivory whiteness of the bran in which the ram is cooked is in fact as delightful to the eye as the flavor is to the palate, don't you think?"

"Ce kouskous, en effet, est excellent!" said General Guillaume.

"Ah, if only I had closed my eyes when I ate that kouskous! For a moment earlier I had suddenly become aware that the warm, strong flavor of the mutton had an unpleasant sweetness about it, and that I was chewing a piece of meat that was colder and softer than the rest. I looked at my plate, and was horrified to see a finger appear in the middle of the bran — first one finger, then two, then five, and finally a hand with white nails — a man's hand."

"Taisez-vous!" exclaimed General Guillaume.

"It was a man's hand. It was undoubtedly the hand of the unfortunate goumier, which the exploding mine had neatly severed and hurled into the great copper pot in which our kouskous was cooking. What could I do? I was educated at the Collegic Cicognini, which is the best college in Italy, and from boyhood I have been taught that one should never, for any reason, interrupt the general gaiety, whether at a dance, a party, or a dinner. I forced myself not to turn pale or cry out, and calmly began eating the hand. The flesh was a little tough. It had not had time to cook."

"Taisez-vous, pour l'amour de Dieu!" cried General Guillaume in a hoarse voice, pushing away the plate that lay in front of him. They all looked ghastly, and were gazing at me with wide-open eyes.

"I am a well-mannered guest," I said, "and it is not my fault if, as I silently nibbled the hand of that poor goumier, smiling as though nothing were amiss so as not to interrupt such a pleasant luncheon, you were imprudent enough to start pulling my leg. One should never make fun of a guest while he is devouring a man's hand."

"But it isn't possible! I can't believe . . ." stammered Pierre

Lyautey, who was green in the face, and he pressed his hand to his stomach.

"If you don't believe me," I said, "look here, on my plate. Do you see all these little bones? They are the knuckles. And these, ranged along the edge of the plate, are the five nails. You will forgive me if, in spite of my good breeding, I wasn't equal to swallowing the nails."

"Mon Dieu!" cried General Guillaume, gulping down a glass of wine at a single draught.

"That'll teach you," laughed Jack, "to question the truth of what Malaparte relates in his books."

At that moment we heard a report far out on the plain, followed by a second and a third. From the direction of Frattocchie, clear and crisp, came the thunder of a Sherman's cannon.

"Ça y est!" exclaimed General Guillaume, springing up.

We all jumped to our feet and, overturning the benches and leaping over the table, ran toward the edge of the wood, whence the eye could explore the whole of the Roman Campagna, from the mouth of the Tiber to the Anio.

We saw a blue cloud rising from the Via Appia, on the far side of the Bivio delle Frattocchie, and the distant roar of a hundred — a thousand — engines reached our ears. Jack and I uttered a cry of joy as we saw the endless column of the American Fifth Army bestirring itself and setting off in the direction of Rome.

"Au revoir, mon Général!" cried Jack, grasping General Guillaume's hand.

All the French officers around us were silent.

"Au revoir," said General Guillaume; and in a low voice he added: "Nous ne pouvons pas vous suivre. Nous devons rester là."

His eyes were moist with tears. I gripped his hand in silence.

"Come and see me whenever you like," General Guillaume said to me with a sad smile. "You will always find a place waiting for you at my table, and my hand outstretched in friendship."

"Votre main, aussi?"

"Allez au diable!" shouted General Guillaume.

Jack and I rushed down the wooded slope, making for the spot where we had left our jeep.

"Ah! ah! bien joué, Malaparte! un tour formidable!" cried Jack as he ran. "That'll teach them to question the truth of what you say in *Kaputt!*"

"Did you see their expressions? I thought they were all going to be sick!"

"Une sacrée farce, Malaparte! Ah! ah! ah!" cried Jack.

"Did you see how skilfully I arranged those little ram's bones on my plate? They looked just like the bones of a hand!"

"Ah! ah! ah! merveilleux!" cried Jack as he ran. "It looked just like a hand — the skeleton of a hand!"

And we roared with laughter as we ran among the trees. We reached our jeep, jumped in and drove at breakneck speed down the Castel Gandolfo road. We reached the Via Appia and overtook the column amid a cloud of dust. Eventually we took our place behind Colonel Granger's jeep, which, preceded by a few Shermans, was leading the Fifth Army's column on its way to the capture of Rome.

Now and then a burst of rifle fire rent the dusty air. The smell of mint and rue was wafted toward us on the wind; it was like the smell of incense, the smell of Rome's thousand churches. By now the sun was sinking and the purple sky was filled with swollen clouds, marshaled as in the cloud-scenes of the baroque painters. The roar of a thousand aircraft created vast whirlpools of sound, through which the sunset river of blood went coursing down.

Ahead of us the Shermans advanced slowly with a loud metallic roar, from time to time firing their cannon. Suddenly, as we rounded a bend, Rome came into view. There it lay, at the far end of the plain, behind the red arches of the aqueducts and the tombs of blood-red brick, beneath that baroque sky — very white in the midst of a vortex of smoke and flame, as if a terrific fire were consuming it.

A shout went up, and passed from end to end of the

column: "Rome! Rome!" From the jeeps, tanks and trucks thousands and thousands of faces, covered with white masks of dust, strained toward the distant city as it lay there, wrapped in the flames of sunset; and I could feel my hoarse voice expressing the hatred, the bitterness, the anguish, and all the sadness and happiness of that moment, which I had awaited so long and in such an agony of fear. At that moment Rome seemed to me harsh, cruel, impenetrable — it was like an enemy city; and an obscure feeling of apprehension and shame came over me, as if I were committing a sacrilege.

Outside the smoking ruins of the Ciampino airdrome the column came to a halt. Here two German Tigers lay on their sides, barring the road. Occasionally a rifle bullet whistled over our heads. Standing up in their tanks, trucks and jeeps the American soldiers laughed and chattered happily and carelessly as they chewed their gum.

"This road," I said to Jack, "is strewn with obstacles. Why don't you suggest to Colonel Granger that we should leave the Via Appia Nuova and take the Via Appia Antica?"

Just then Colonel Granger turned, and unfolding an ordnance map made a sign to Jack with his head. Jack jumped down from the jeep, and going up to Colonel Granger started to confer with him, indicating a point on the map with his finger.

"Colonel Granger," said Jack, turning to me, "would like to know if there's a shorter and safer route to Rome."

"If I were Colonel Granger," I replied, "I would turn left at that crossroad and enter the Via Appia Antica at a point about a mile from the Tombs of the Horatii and the Curatii. Then I would pass through Capo di Bove and enter Rome by the Via dei Trionfi and the Via dell'Impero. It's a longer route, but it's more picturesque."

Jack ran over to Colonel Granger and came back after a few moments.

"The Colonel," he said, "asks if you feel inclined to act as guide to the column."

"Why not?"

"Can you guarantee that we shan't fall into an ambush?"

"I can guarantee nothing. We are at war, I believe."

Jack resumed his conference with Colonel Granger, and after a few moments came to tell me that Colonel Granger wanted to know if the Via Appia Antica was, *generally speaking*, safer.

"What does *generally speaking* mean?" I asked Jack. "Does it mean *usually?* In time of peace it's as safe as houses. I don't know about now."

"Generally speaking," replied Jack, "probably means in this particular case."

"I don't know if it's the safer way in this particular case, but it's certainly the more picturesque. It's the noblest road in the world — the road that leads to the Baths of Caracalla, the Colosseum and the Capitol."

Jack ran off to confer with Colonel Granger, and came back shortly afterwards to tell me that the Colonel wanted to know which was the road by which the Caesars entered Rome.

"When they returned from the Orient, Greece, Egypt and Africa," I replied, "the Caesars entered Rome by the Via Appia Antica."

Jack rushed away, and came back to tell me that Colonel Granger came from America, and had therefore decided to enter Rome by the Via Appia Antica.

"I should have been astonished," I replied, "if he had chosen any other road." And I added that Marius, Sulla, Julius Caesar, Cicero, Pompey, Antony, Cleopatra, Augustus, Tiberius and all the other Emperors had passed along the Via Appia Antica, and that Colonel Granger might therefore pass along it too.

Jack ran over to Colonel Granger, and after he had spoken to him in a low voice the Colonel, turning to me with a broad grin, shouted: "Okay!"

"Let's go!" said Jack, jumping into the jeep.

We passed Colonel Granger's jeep and took our place at the head of the column, immediately behind the Shermans. We turned down the lane opposite the Ciampino airdrome which leads from the Via Appia Nuova to the Via Appia Antica.

Shortly afterwards we entered that noble road, the noblest road in the world. It is paved with great slabs of stone in which the two grooves dug by the wheels of the Roman chariots are still visible.

"What's that?" shouted Colonel Granger, indicating the tombs that stand at the side of the Via Appia Antica in the shade of cypresses and pines.

"Those are the tombs of the noblest families of ancient Rome," I replied.

"What?" shouted Colonel Granger, amid the frightful din of the Shermans' caterpillars.

"The tombs of the noblest Roman families!" shouted Jack.

"The noblest what?" shouted Colonel Granger.

"The tombs of the Four Hundred from the Roman *Mayflower!*" shouted Jack.

The word passed from vehicle to vehicle all the way down the column, and the American soldiers, standing up in their tanks, trucks and jeeps, shouted "Gee!" and clicked their kodaks.

I too stood up and, pointing my finger at each tomb, shouted at random: "That's the tomb of Lucullus, the most famous drunkard in ancient Rome. That's the sepulchre of Julius Caesar. That's Sulla's tomb, and that's Cicero's. That's the tomb of Cleopatra . . ."

The name of Cleopatra passed from mouth to mouth and from vehicle to vehicle, and Colonel Granger shouted: "A famous signorina, wasn't she?"

When we came abreast of the Actor's tomb I told Jack to stop for a moment. Indicating the marble stage-masks embedded in the high red brick wall that rises like a theatre scene or backcloth beside the great round mausoleum I shouted: "That's the tomb of Cotta, the most famous Roman actor!"

"Who's what?" shouted Colonel Granger.

"The most famous Roman actor!" shouted Jack.

"I want to autograph it!" shouted a G.I., and a crowd of American soldiers jumped down from their vehicles and made a dash for the wall, which in a few moments was covered with signatures.

"Go on! Go on!" shouted Colonel Granger.

Just then I raised my eyes and saw, sitting on the rough stone steps that lead up to the mausoleum, a German soldier. He was almost a boy. His fair hair was disheveled, his face covered with a mask of dust through which his bright eyes gleamed softly like the sightless eyes of a blind man. He sat there with a weary, abstracted look, his head thrown back and his two hands resting on the stone steps. He seemed remote from everything — from the war, from his surroundings, from time. He was breathing deeply, panting like a shipwrecked mariner who has just reached the shore. No one had noticed him.

"Go on! Go on!" shouted Colonel Granger.

From the summit of the mound Rome, now that the fires of sunset had spent themselves, looked at once sombre and kindly in the transparent green light of evening. A vast green cloud hung over the cupolas, the towers, the columns and the roofs with their countless marble statues. The green light streamed down from the sky, like one of those showers of green rain that sometimes fall on the sea at the beginning of spring. It seemed exactly as though a shower of green grass were pouring down from the sky on to the city, and the houses, the roofs, the cupolas and the marble statues shone like a damp meadow in springtime.

A cry of wonder burst from the lips of the soldiers who thronged the mounds. As if disturbed by the cry, a flight of black crows ascended from the distant red Aurelian Walls which form the boundary of Rome between the Porta Latina and the tomb of Caius Cestius. Their black wings sparkled now green, now blood-red. From that lofty vantage point we could distinguish the meadows and orchards of the Via Appia and the Via Ardeatina, the grove of the nymph Aegeria, the forests of canes surrounding the little church in which the Barberini sleep, the red arches of the aqueducts, and in the distance, beyond Capo di Bove and over toward the Porta di San Sebastiano, the great crenellated tower of the tomb of Caecilia Metella. At the bottom of the vast green bowl, sprinkled with pines, cypresses and sepulchres, which gradually falls away toward the Acquasanta golf links, the first houses of Rome suddenly came into view — those lofty white stuccoed walls with their flashing glass, against which the green and red breath of the Roman Campagna spent itself as in a billowing sail.

Groups of men were running hither and thither over the plain. Every so often they would stop and look uncertainly about them, then start running again, hesitant, like wild beasts pursued by dogs. Other groups of men would come forward in overwhelming numbers from every side, closing in upon them and blocking the paths of flight and salvation. The sharp crackle of rifle fire was wafted toward us on the sea breeze, which brought a sweet tang of salt to our lips. These were the last clashes between the German rearguards and the bands of partisans; and the evening air, transparent as an aquarium, gave a melancholy tinge to that scene of pursuit, which in its sound and its vague, elusive coloring touched a chord of memory. It was a mild, green evening, like the evening on which the Trojans looked down from the top of their walls and anxiously watched the last encounters of the bloody battle, even as Achilles rose from the river like a bright star and ran across the plain of the Scamander toward the walls of Ilium.

Just then I saw the moon rising behind the wooded slopes of the mountains of Tivoli — an enormous moon, dripping with blood — and I said to Jack: "Look over there. That's not the moon — it's Achilles."

Colonel Granger looked at me in astonishment. "It's the moon," he said.

"No, it's Achilles," said Jack.

And in a low voice I began to recite in Greek the verses from the *Iliad* in which Achilles rises from the Scamander "like the mournful star of autumn which men call Orion." When I stopped Jack continued, watching the moon rising over the mountains of Latium and scanning the Homeric hexameters with the sing-song cadence that he had learned in his own University of Virginia.

"I must remind you, gentlemen . . ." said Colonel Granger

in a severe voice. But he stopped; slowly he descended from the tomb of the Horatii, climbed back into his jeep and in a furious tone gave the order to start. "Go on! Go on!" he shouted, and he seemed not merely irritated but profoundly astonished. The column set off again, and near Capo di Bove, where stands the athlete's tomb, we had to slow down in order to give the G.I.s time to cover the boxer's statue with signatures. "Go on! Go on!" shouted Colonel Granger; but when we reached the famous inn at Capo di Bove called "Qui non si muore mai" I turned to him, pointed to the sign, and shouted: "Here we never die!"

"What?" shouted Colonel Granger, trying to make his voice heard above the metallic roar of the Shermans' caterpillars and the gay, noisy chatter of the G.I.s.

"Here we never die!" shouted Jack.

"What? We never dine?" shouted Colonel Granger.

"Never die!" repeated Jack.

"Why not?" shouted Colonel Granger. "I *will* dine — I'm hungry! Go on! Go on!"

Down we went to the Catacombs of San Callisto, then up once more in the direction of San Sebastiano. When we reached the little church called Quo Vadis I shouted to Colonel Granger that we ought to stop there even if it meant that we were the last of the conquerors to enter Rome, because this was the Quo Vadis church.

"Quo what?" shouted Colonel Granger.

"The Quo Vadis church!" shouted Jack.

"What? What does 'Quo Vadis' mean?" shouted Colonel Granger.

" 'Where are you going?' " I replied.

"To Rome, of course!" shouted Colonel Granger. "Where d'you think I'm going? I'm going to Rome!"

Standing up in the jeep I then described in a loud voice how at that very point in the street, outside that little church, St. Peter had met Jesus. The word passed all the way down the column.

A hush came over the column, and in reverent silence the G.I.s crowded round the door of the little church. They wanted to go in, but it was shut. Some of them then began to try to force an entry with their shoulders, others hammered with fists and boots on the door, and just as a mechanic from a Sherman was endeavoring to lever it off its hinges with an iron bar the window of one of the hovels opposite the little church suddenly opened and a woman appeared. She hurled a stone at the G.I.s, spitting at them and shouting: "Shameless creatures! Stinking Germans! Sons of whores!"

"Tell that good woman that we aren't Germans, but Americans!" Colonel Granger shouted to me.

"We're Americans!" I shouted.

At my words all the windows of the houses were suddenly flung open, a hundred heads popped out, and on all sides voices arose in a delighted chorus: "Long live the Americans! Long live freedom!" A crowd of men, women and boys, armed with cudgels and stones, came out of the doors and emerged from behind the hedges. Throwing aside these rough weapons they all made a rush for the G.I.s, shouting: "The Americans! The Americans!"

Amid scenes of confusion that beggar description the G.I.s and the crowd embraced one another, uttering loud cries of joy. In the meantime Colonel Granger, who while the uproar lasted had not stirred from his jeep, called me to him and asked me in a low voice whether it was true that St. Peter had met Jesus Christ at this very spot.

"Why shouldn't it be true?" I replied. "At Rome miracles are the most natural thing in the world."

"Nuts!" exclaimed Colonel Granger. And after a few moments' silence he begged me to describe to him exactly what had taken place. I told him about St. Peter, his meeting with Jesus Christ and his question: "*Quo vadis, Domine?* Where goest thou, O Lord?" It seemed to me that Colonel Granger was much disturbed by my narrative, and especially by St. Peter's words.

"Are you quite sure," he said to me, "that St. Peter asked the Lord where He was going?"

"What else could he have asked Him? If you had been in St. Peter's place what would you have asked Jesus?"

"Of course," replied Colonel Granger, "I should have asked Him where He was going, too." And he stopped. Then with a jerk of the head he added: "So this is Rome!" And he said no more.

Before ordering the column to start off again Colonel Granger, who did not lack a certain prudence, begged me to ask someone in the small, gay crowd that surrounded us "who was in Rome."

I turned to a youth who looked to me more wide-awake than the rest and repeated Colonel Granger's question to him.

"And who do you think is in Rome?" the fellow replied. "The Romans, of course!"

I translated the youth's reply, and Colonel Granger flushed slightly. "Of course," he exclaimed, "the Romans!" And raising his arm he gave the order to resume the advance.

The column stirred and moved off. Shortly afterwards we entered Rome through the arch of the Porta di San Sebastiano and proceeded along the narrow street on either side of which stand high red walls covered with the green mould of centuries. When we passed by the tombs of the Scipios Colonel Granger turned and cast a lingering look at the sepulchre of Hannibal's conqueror. "That's Rome!" he shouted to me, and he appeared deeply moved. Then we came out opposite the Baths of Caracalla, and at the sight of the stupendous mass of the imperial remains, transfigured by the moonbeams' marvelously delicate caress, a chorus of enthusiastic whistles went up from the column. The pines, cypresses and laurels threw luminous dappled shadows of a greeny-black hue over that prospect of purple ruins and shining grass.

Amid a terrific roar of caterpillars we came face to face with the Palatine, which seemed weighted down by the remains of the Palace of the Caesars. Up we climbed once more, along the Via dei Trionfi, and suddenly, immense in the peaceful moonlight, the mass of the Colosseum arose before our eyes.

"What's that?" shouted Colonel Granger, trying to make

his voice heard above the chorus of whistles that went up from the column.

"The Colosseum!" I replied.

"What?"

"The Colisée!" shouted Jack.

Colonel Granger stood up in his jeep and for a long time surveyed the gigantic shell of the Colosseum in silence. He turned to me, and with a note of pride in his voice shouted: "Our bombers have done a good job!" Then, spreading out his arms, he added apologetically: "Don't worry, Malaparte: that's war!"

Just then the column entered the Via dell'Impero. I had turned to Colonel Granger, and was pointing to the Forum and the Capitoline Hill, shouting "That's the Capitol!" when a terrific uproar cut me short. A vast, yelling crowd was coming toward us down the Via dell'Impero. It consisted largely of women, and they seemed to be preparing to assail our column. They came running down, disheveled, delirious, their clothes awry, waving their arms, laughing, weeping and shouting. In a twinkling we were surrounded, assailed, overwhelmed, and the column disappeared beneath an inextricable tangle of legs and arms, a forest of black hair, and a soft mountain of ripe breasts, full lips and white shoulders. ("As usual," said the young curate of the Church of Santa Caterina, in Corso Italia, when delivering his sermon next day. "As usual Fascist propaganda lied when it predicted that if the American army entered Rome it would assault our women. It is our women who have assaulted, and discomfited, the American Army.") And the roar of engines and caterpillars was drowned by the yells of that joy-maddened crowd.

But when we were on the heights of Tor di Nona a man who was running toward the column, waving his arms and shouting "Long live America!," slipped, fell and was dragged along beneath the caterpillars of a Sherman. A cry of horror arose from the crowd. I jumped to the ground and forcing my way through the mob bent over the shapeless corpse.

A dead man is a dead man. He is just a dead man. He is more, and perhaps less too, than a dead dog or cat. Many times, on the roads of Serbia, Bessarabia and the Ukraine, I had seen in the mud of the street the imprint of a dog that had been killed and crushed by the caterpillars of a tank. The outline of a dog drawn on the slate of the road with a red pencil. A carpet made of the skin of a dog.

In July, 1941, I had seen a carpet of human skin lying in the dust of the street right in the center of Yampol, a village on the Dniester, in the Ukraine. It was a man who had been crushed by the caterpillars of a tank. The face had assumed a square shape, and the chest and stomach were splayed out at the sides in the form of a diamond. The outspread legs and the arms, which were a little apart from the torso, were like the trousers and sleeves of a newly pressed suit, stretched out on the ironingboard. It was a dead man — something more, or something less, than a dead dog or cat. I cannot say now in what respect that dead man was more, or less, than a dead dog or cat. But then, on that evening, at the moment at which I saw his imprint in the dust of the street, in the center of the village of Yampol, I could perhaps have said what it was that made him something more, or something less, than a dead dog or cat.

Here and there gangs of Jews in black caftans, armed with spades and shovels, were collecting the dead whom the Russians had left behind them in the village. Sitting on the doorstep of a ruined house I watched the light, transparent mist ascending from the marshy banks of the Dniester, while in the distance, on the other bank, beyond the bend of the river, the black clouds of smoke that rose from the houses of Soroca slowly spiraled up into the air. The sun revolved like a red wheel in a whirlwind of dust at the far end of the plain, where cars, men, horses and wagons were clearly silhouetted against the brilliant, dust-filled sunset sky.

In the middle of the street, there in front of me, lay the man who had been crushed by the caterpillars of a tank. Some Jews came up and began to remove the outline of the dead man from the dust. Very slowly they lifted the edges of the pattern with the ends of their spades, as one lifts the edges of a carpet. It was a carpet of human skin, and the fabric consisted of a fine network of bones, a spider's web of crushed bones. It was like a starched suit, a starched human skin. It was an appalling and at the same time a delicate, exquisite, unreal scene. The Jews talked among themselves, and their voices sounded distant, soft, muffled. When the carpet of human skin had been completely detached from the dusty street one of the Jews impaled the head on the end of his spade and moved off, carrying the remains like a flag.

The standard-bearer was a young Jew with long hair that hung loosely over his shoulders. His eyes shone forth from his pale, lean face with a melancholy, unwavering stare. He walked with his head high, and on the end of his spade, like a flag, he carried that human skin, which flapped and fluttered in the wind exactly as a flag does.

I said to Lino Pellegrini, who was sitting beside me: "That's the flag of Europe. It's our flag."

"It isn't my flag," said Pellegrini. "A dead man isn't the flag of a living man."

"What is the inscription on that flag?" I said.

"It says that a dead man is a dead man."

"No," I said. "Read it carefully. It says that a dead man is not a dead man."

"No," said Pellegrini, "a dead man is just a dead man. What do you suppose a dead man is?"

"Ah, you don't know what a dead man is. If you knew what a dead man was you would never sleep again."

"Now I see," said Pellegrini, "what the inscription on that flag is. It says: The dead must bury the dead."

"No, it says that this is our country's flag, the flag of our true country. A flag made of human skin. Our true country is our skin."

Behind the standard-bearer, carrying their spades on their shoulders, came the procession of gravediggers, enveloped in their black caftans. The wind fluttered the flag, ruffling the dead man's hair, which was saturated with a mixture of dust and blood and stood up on end above the broad, square brow like the rigid mane of a plaster saint.

"Let's go and see our flag buried," I said to Pellegrini.

They were going to bury the remains in the communal grave that had been dug at the entrance to the village facing the bank of the Dniester. They were going to cast them into the filth of the communal grave, which was already full to overflowing with charred corpses and the bloodstained, mud-spattered remains of horses.

"It isn't my flag," said Pellegrini. "The inscription on my flag is 'God, Freedom, Justice.'"

I began laughing and, raising my eyes, looked across at the opposite bank of the Dniester. I gazed at the opposite bank of the river and thought of Tarass Bulba. Gogol was born in the Ukraine. He had passed through this place, through Yampol. He had slept in that house at the far end of the village. It was actually from the top of that high, steep riverbank that Tarass Bulba's faithful Cossacks rode headlong into the Dniester. Tied to the stake at which he was to die, Tarass Bulba urged his Cossacks to flee, to throw themselves into the river, to seek safety. From that very spot, opposite Yampol, a little way upstream from Soroca, Tarass Bulba watched his faithful Cossacks ride rapidly away on their lean, shaggy horses with the Poles in pursuit; he watched them throw themselves headlong over the precipice, over the edge of the cliff that flanks the Dniester; and he watched the Poles likewise throw themselves into the river, and break their necks on the riverbank, directly opposite where I was sitting. The horses of an Italian field battery kept appearing and disappearing among the acacia groves situated on top of the steep bank, and down below, beneath the corrugated-iron roofs of the sheds of the Yampol kolkhoz, lay the charred, still smoking remains of hundreds of horses.

The standard-bearer passed by, carrying his flag. His head was high, his eyes were fixed intently on some distant point. He had the fixed, glassy stare of Dulle Griet. His walk was exactly like that of Peter Breughel's Dulle Griet,

like that of Greta the Mad, returning from market with her
basket on her arm, her eyes fixed in front of her, seeming not
to see or hear the diabolical uproar that is going on around
her nor the pandemonium through which she is passing —
violent and obstinate, guided by her madness as by an invisible archangel. He walked straight ahead, enveloped in
his black caftan, seemingly oblivious of the stream of vehicles,
men, horses, baggage wagons and gun carriages that rushed
in furious haste through the village.

"Let's go," I said, "and see our country's flag buried."

And joining the procession of gravediggers we started to
follow the flag. It was a flag made of human skin, the flag
of our country: it *was* our country. And thus we went to
see our country's flag, the flag of the country of all peoples
and all men, cast into the filth of the communal grave.

The crowd was yelling; it seemed mad with horror. Kneeling beside that carpet of human skin, spread out in the middle
of the Via dell'Impero, was a woman. Wailing and tearing
her hair, she stretched out her arms — helplessly, not knowing
how to embrace the corpse. The men shook their fists at the
Shermans, shouting "Murderers!" They were brutally re-
pelled by some M.P.s, who whirled their truncheons round
in an effort to free the head of the column from the pressure
of the infuriated crowd.

I went up to Colonel Granger. "He's dead," I said.

"Of course he's dead!" shouted Colonel Granger. "You'd
do better to try and find out where that poor fellow's widow
lives," he added in a petulant voice.

I forced my way through the crowd, approached the woman, helped her to get up, and asked her what the dead
man's name was and where he lived. She stopped yelling
and, stifling her sobs, gazed at me with a frightened expression, as if she did not understand what I was saying to her.
But another woman came forward and told me the name
of the dead man, the name of the street in which he lived
and the number of the house. With a spiteful air she added

that the weeping woman was not the dead man's wife, nor even a relative, but merely a neighbor. On hearing her words the poor wretch began to wail more loudly, tearing her hair with a fury that was far more intense and genuine than her grief, until the thunderous voice of Colonel Granger was heard above the tumult, and the column started off again. A G.I. leaned out of his jeep as it passed and threw a flower on to the shapeless corpse, a second imitated his merciful gesture, and in a short time the wretched remains were covered with a heap of flowers.

In the Piazza Venezia a vast multitude greeted us with a deafening shout, which changed into frantic applause when a G.I. from the Signal Corps clambered on to the famous balcony and began to harangue the crowd in an Italo-American dialect. "You thought Mussolini was coming to speak to you, didn't you, you bastards?" he said. "But today I am speaking to you — I, John Esposito, a soldier and a free citizen of America — and I'm telling you that you'll never become Americans — never!" "Never! Never!" yelled the crowd, laughing and clapping their hands. The roar of the Shermans' caterpillars drowned the ear-splitting shouts of the people.

Eventually we entered the Corso, went up Via del Tritone, and halted outside the Albergo Excelsior. Shortly afterwards General Cork sent for me. He was sitting in an armchair in the middle of the hall, his steel helmet on his knees, his face still begrimed with dust and sweat. In an armchair next to his sat Colonel Brown, the chaplain attached to Headquarters.

General Cork had seen the accident, and asked me to accompany the chaplain on a visit of condolence to the unfortunate man's family, and to take a sum collected among the G.I.s of the Fifth Army to the widow and orphans.

"Tell the poor widow and the orphans," he added, "that . . . I mean that . . . I too have a wife and two children in America, and . . . No! My wife and children don't come into it at all."

At this point he stopped, and smiled at me. I saw that he was very much upset.

As I drove with the chaplain in his jeep in the direction of Tor di Nona I looked about me with a feeling of sadness. The streets were full of drunken American soldiers and yelling crowds. Rivers of urine flowed along the pavements. American and British flags hung from the windows — flags made of cloth, not of human skin. We reached Tor di Nona, turned off into an alley, and had almost come to the Torre del Grillo when we stopped outside a mean-looking house. We climbed a staircase, pushed open a door which was ajar, and entered.

The room was full of people, who were talking in low voices. On the bed I saw the horrible thing. A woman with eyes swollen from weeping was sitting by the pillow. I addressed myself to her, saying that we had come to express to the dead man's family the grief of General Cork and of the whole of the American Fifth Army. I added that General Cork had placed a considerable sum of money at the disposal of the widow and orphans.

The woman replied that the poor fellow had neither wife nor children. He was an evacuee from the Abruzzi who had sought refuge in Rome after his village and his home had been destroyed in the American air raids. She added at once: "Forgive me, I meant the German air raids." The poor fellow's name was Giuseppe Leonardi, and he came from a little village near Alfedena. All his family had been killed by the bombs, and he had been left on his own. "And so," said the woman, "he did a little business on the black market; but only a very little." Colonel Brown handed the woman a large envelope, which she, after some hesitation, took delicately between two fingers and laid on the pedestal. "It will do for the funeral," she said.

After this brief ceremony they all began talking among themselves in loud voices, and the woman asked me whether Colonel Brown was General Cork. I replied that he was the chaplain — a priest.

"An American priest!" exclaimed the woman, and she rose and offered him her seat. Colonel Brown, red-faced and embarrassed, sat down; but he immediately got up again, as if he had been pricked by a pin.

They all looked at the "American priest" with respectful expressions, and every so often they bowed and smiled at him sympathetically.

"What do I do now?" Colonel Brown whispered to me. And he added: "I think . . . yes . . . I mean . . . what would a Catholic priest do in my place?"

"Do what you like," I replied, "but above all don't for heaven's sake let them see that you're a Protestant minister!"

"Thank you," said the chaplain, turning pale; and going over to the bed he clasped his hands and stood for a while absorbed in prayer.

When he turned and moved away from the bed the woman, blushing, asked me how the body could be prepared for burial. At first I did not understand. She pointed to the dead man. He was in truth a pitiable and horrible sight. He looked like one of those paper patterns that tailors use, or a cardboard dummy such as is employed for target practice. What upset me most was his shoes. They were crushed flat, and here and there something white was sticking through them — perhaps some little bone. His two hands, which were clasped together on his chest (his chest!), looked like a pair of cotton gloves.

"What shall we do?" said the woman. "We can't bury him in this state."

I replied that perhaps they could try bathing him with a little hot water. The water might make him swell and give him a more human appearance.

"You mean sponge him," said the woman, "the same as you do with . . ." She broke off, blushing, as if a sudden feeling of shame had silenced her just as the word was on the tip of her tongue.

"That's it — sponge him," I said, blushing.

Someone brought a basinful of water, apologizing for the fact that it was cold. There had been no gas for days and days, nor even a little coal or wood to light the fire.

"Now then, we'll try with cold water," said the woman, and helped by a neighbor she began to sprinkle the water over the dead man with her hands. As it absorbed the moisture the body swelled, but not much; indeed, it became no thicker than a stout piece of felt.

In the distance we heard the proud blasts of the bugles and the triumphant shouts of the vanquished ascending from the Via dell'Impero, the Piazza Venezia, the Foro Traiano and Suburra. I looked at the horrible thing lying on the bed, and I laughed to myself as I thought how each of us that evening believed himself to be a Brutus, a Cassius, an Aristogiton, though all, victors and vanquished, were like that horrible thing which lay on the bed — skins cut to look like men, miserable human skins. I turned to the open window and saw, high above the roofs, the tower of the Capitol; and I laughed to myself as I thought how that flag of human skin was our flag, the true flag of us all, victors and vanquished, the only flag worthy to fly that evening from the tower of the Capitol. I laughed to myself as I thought of that flag of human skin flying from the tower of the Capitol.

I made a sign to Colonel Brown, and we moved toward the door. We turned in the entrance and bowed low.

When we reached the dark passage at the foot of the stairs Colonel Brown stopped. "If they had soaked him with hot water," he said in a low voice, "he might have swelled up more."

THE TRIAL

● The boys sitting on the steps of Santa Maria Novella; the
small crowd of onlookers gathered round the obelisk; the
partisan officer who sat astride the bench at the foot of the
flight of steps leading up to the church, with his elbows
resting on a little iron table, taken from some café in the
square; and the squad of young partisans from the Potente
Communist Division who were lined up on the close before
a jumbled heap of corpses, armed with automatic rifles —
all these looked as if they had been painted by Masaccio on
the gray plaster of the air. In the dull, chalky light that
filtered down from the cloudy sky above their heads all were
seen to be silent and motionless, and all were looking in the

same direction. A thin stream of blood trickled down the marble steps.

The Fascists sitting on the steps that led up to the church were boys of fifteen or sixteen — deep-browed, with unbrushed hair and dark, bright eyes set in long, pale faces. The youngest, who was wearing a black jersey and a pair of short trousers that left his spindly legs uncovered, was little more than a child. There was also a girl among them. Very young, she had dark eyes, and her hair, which hung loosely over her shoulders, was of that auburn color often encountered among Tuscan women of the lower class. She sat with her head thrown back, gazing at the summer clouds above the rain-bright roofs of Florence, at the sullen, chalky sky, in which here and there a crack appeared, so that it resembled Masaccio's sky-scenes in the frescoes of the Carmine.

We had heard the shots when we were halfway up Via della Scala, near the Orti Oricellari. Emerging into the square we had come to a stop at the foot of the flight of steps leading up to Santa Maria Novella, behind the partisan officer who was sitting at the little iron table.

At the screeching of the brakes of the two jeeps the officer did not move, he did not look round. But after a moment he pointed his finger at one of the boys and said: "It's your turn. What's your name?"

"It's my turn today," said the boy, getting up, "but some day or other it'll be yours."

"What's your name?"

"That's my business," replied the boy.

"Why do you answer the silly fool?" said a companion of his who was sitting next to him.

"I answer the idiot to teach him his manners," replied the boy, wiping his dripping brow with the back of his hand. He was pale and his lips were trembling. But he was laughing impudently as he looked at the partisan officer with unwavering eyes. The officer lowered his head and began to doodle with a pencil.

Suddenly the boys began talking and laughing among themselves. They spoke with the broad accent of San Frediano, Santa Croce and Palazzolo.

"What are those bums staring at? Haven't they ever seen a Christian killed?"

"They sure get a big kick out of it!"

"I'd like to see what they'd do if they was in our place, the bastards!"

"I bet they'd throw theirselves on their knees!"

"They'd squeal like a damn pig."

The boys were deathly pale, but they were laughing as they gazed at the partisan officer's hands.

"Ain't he cute with that red bandana round his neck!"

"Who is he?"

"Who do you think? He's Garibaldi!"

"What gripes me," said the boy standing on the step, "is the idea of being killed by those bastards!"

"Don't take all day over it, you brat!" shouted someone in the crowd.

"If you're in a hurry come and take my place," retorted the boy, thrusting his hands into his pockets.

The partisan officer looked up. "Buck up," he said. "Don't waste my time. It's your turn."

"If your time's so precious," said the boy in a mocking voice, "I'll get a move on." And stepping over his companions he took up his position in front of the partisans, who were armed with their automatic rifles, and stood beside the heap of corpses, right in the middle of the widening pool of blood on the marble paving of the close.

"Watch it you don't get yer shoes dirty!" shouted one of his companions, and they all began laughing.

Jack and I jumped out of our jeep.

"Stop!" yelled Jack.

But as he spoke the boy shouted "Long live Mussolini!" and fell, riddled with bullets.

"Good gosh!" exclaimed Jack, pale as death.

The partisan officer looked up and eyed Jack from head to foot.

"Canadian officer?" he said.

"No, American colonel," replied Jack, and indicating the boys who were seated on the steps leading up to the church he added: "That's a splendid occupation — killing boys."

The partisan officer turned slowly and threw a sidelong glance at the two jeeps, which were full of Canadian soldiers with Lewis guns in their hands. Then he rested his eyes on me, observed my uniform, and laying his pencil on the table said to me with a conciliatory smile: "Why don't *you* answer your American friend?"

I looked him in the face and recognized him. He was one of Potente's aides. Potente, the young commander of the partisan division which had supported the Canadian troops when they besieged and attacked Florence, had died a few days before in Oltrarno, in the presence of Jack and myself.

"The Allied Command has forbidden summary executions," I said. "Leave those boys alone if you want to avoid trouble."

"You're on our side — and you talk in this way?" said the partisan officer.

"I'm on your side, but I must see that the orders of the Allied Command are respected."

"I've seen you somewhere before," said the partisan officer. "Were you there when Potente died?"

"Yes," I replied, "I was just by him. What of it?"

"Do you want the corpses? I didn't know you'd become a gravedigger."

"I want the living ones — those boys there."

"Take the ones that are already dead," said the partisan officer. "I'll let you have them cheap. Have you a cigarette?"

"I want the living ones," I said, handing him a package of cigarettes. "Those boys will be tried before a military tribunal."

"Before a tribunal?" said the partisan officer, lighting a cigarette. "What a luxury!"

"You have no right to try them."

"I'm not trying them," said the partisan officer. "I'm killing them."

"Why are you killing them? By what right?"

"By what right?"

"Why do you want to kill those boys?" said Jack.

"I'm killing them for shouting 'Long live Mussolini!' "

"They shout 'Long live Mussolini!' because you're killing them," I said.

"What do those two idiots want?" cried a voice in the crowd.

"We want to know why he's killing them," I said, turning to the crowd.

"He's killing them for sniping from the roofs," shouted another voice.

"From the roofs?" said the girl, laughing. "Do they think we're cats?"

"Don't let 'er make you soft!" shouted a youth, stepping out of the crowd. "I tell you they were sniping from the roofs!"

"Did you see them?"

"*I* didn't — no," said the youth.

"Then why do you say they were sniping from the roofs?"

"*Someone* was sniping from the roofs," said the youth. "And there are others. Can't you hear?"

Occasionally from the bottom of Via della Scala there came the crack of rifle fire, punctuated by bursts from automatic rifles.

"It might even have been you firing from the roofs," I said.

"Listen to him," said the fellow in a menacing tone, taking a step forward.

Jack came up close to me. "Take it easy," he whispered in my ear, and he turned and made a sign to the Canadian soldiers, who jumped out of the jeeps and took up positions to our rear, grasping their Lewis guns.

"Now they're starting," said the girl.

"And you — why are *you* interfering in our business?" said one of the boys, looking at me with a malevolent expression. "D'you think we're afraid?"

"He's more afraid of us," said the girl. "Don't you see how white he is? Give him a stimulant, poor little thing!"

They all began laughing, and Jack said to the partisan officer: "I'll take those boys into custody. They will be tried in accordance with the law."

"What law?" said the partisan officer.

"Before a military tribunal," said Jack. "You ought to have killed them at once — on the spot. Now it's too late. Now the law must decide. You have no right to try them."

"Are they friends of yours?" asked the partisan officer, giving Jack a mocking smile.

"They are Italians," I said.

"Italians — them?" said the partisan officer.

"Does he think we're Turks?" said the girl. "Listen to him — as if it was something special being an Italian!"

"If they are Italians," said the partisan officer, "what's it got to do with the Allies? We settle our affairs among ourselves."

"Informally," I said.

"Yes, informally. And you — why do you take the part of the Allies? If you're one of us you should stand by me."

"They are Italians," I said.

"Italians should be tried before the tribunal of the people!" cried a voice in the crowd.

"That's all," said Jack, and at a sign from him the Canadian soldiers surrounded the boys and pushed them down the church steps, directing them toward the jeeps.

White-faced, the partisan officer stared at Jack, clenching his fists. Suddenly he stretched out his hand and seized Jack by the arm.

"Hands off!" shouted Jack.

"No," said the other, and he did not move.

Meanwhile a monk had come out of the church. He was a great big fellow — tall, stoutly built, with a round, ruddy face.

He had a broom in his hand, and he had begun to sweep the forecourt of the church, which was littered with dirty pieces of paper, straw and cartridge cases. When he saw the heap of corpses and the blood trickling down the marble steps he stopped, planted his feet wide apart and exclaimed: "What's this?" He turned to the partisans who were lined up in front of the corpses with their automatic rifles slung over their shoulders. "What does this mean," he shouted, "coming and killing people at the door of my church? Go away from here, you wasters!"

"Take it easy, Brother!" said the partisan officer, letting go of Jack's arm. "This is no time for kidding."

"Ah! This is no time for kidding, isn't it?" shouted the monk. "I'll show you whether it's a time for kidding or not!" And lifting his broom he started beating the partisan officer about the head. At first coolly, with calculated fury, but little by little warming to his task, he lavished blows upon him, shouting: "What does this mean — coming and defiling the steps of my church? Go and work, you wasters, instead of coming and killing people outside my house!" And imitating the method which housewives use to drive away hens, he brought his broom down now on the head of the partisan officer, now on his men, jumping from one to the other and crying: "Shoo! Shoo! Go away from here, you hooligans! Shoo! Shoo!" Finally, when he was left master of the field, he turned about and, still hurling abusive epithets and curses at the "wasters" and "good-for-nothings," began furiously sweeping the bloodstained steps.

The crowd dispersed in silence.

"I'll catch up with you some day!" said the partisan officer, gazing into my eyes with a malignant expression, and he slowly made off, every so often turning round to look at me.

I said to Jack: "I should like to meet *him* one day too, poor fellow." But Jack came up to me and with a sad smile laid his hand on my arm. As he did so I noticed that I was trembling all over and that my eyes were full of tears.

The monk leaned on the handle of his broom. "Do you

think it's fair, gentlemen," he said, "that in a city like Florence Christians should be killed on the steps of the churches? People have always been killed, and I can't help that. But right here, in front of my church, in front of Santa Maria Novella! Why don't they go and kill them on the steps of Santa Croce? There's a prior there who would let them do it. But not here. Am I right?"

"Not here — or there," said Jack.

"Not here," said the monk. "I won't have them here. Did you see how I deal with them? You certainly get nowhere if you use kid-glove methods. A broom is what's needed. I don't know how many times I've beaten Germans over the heads like that with a broom, so why shouldn't I do the same to Italians? And mark my words, if the Americans took it into their heads to come and splash blood all over the steps of my church I'd chase them away with a broom as well. Are you an American?"

"Yes, I'm an American," replied Jack.

"In that case, forget what I've said. But you understand me. I too have reason on my side. Take a lesson from me, and beat them with a broom."

"We are soldiers," said Jack. "We can't go about armed with brooms."

"That's a pity. War isn't fought with rifles," said the monk, "it's fought with brooms. This war, I mean. Those wasters are decent kids really. They've suffered, and in a way I understand their feelings. But winning the war has spoiled them. As soon as a Christian wins a war he forgets that he's a Christian. He becomes a Turk. As soon as a Christian wins a war it's good-bye to Christ. Are you a Christian?"

"Yes," said Jack, "I'm still a Christian."

"It's better to be that," said the monk. "It's better to be a Christian than a Turk."

"It's better to be a Christian than an American," said Jack with a smile.

"I see what you mean. It's better to be a Christian than an American. And then . . . Good-bye, gentlemen," said the monk, and muttering to himself he went off toward the door of the church with his bloodstained broom in his hand.

I was tired of the sight of people being killed. For four years I had done nothing but watch people being killed. To watch people die is one thing, to watch them being killed is another. You feel as if you were on the side of the killers, as if you were yourself one of the killers. I was tired of it, I could stand it no longer. By this time the sight of a corpse turned me sick — not merely with horror and disgust, but with fury and hatred. I was beginning to hate corpses. My pity was exhausted; it was giving way to hatred. The idea of hating a corpse! To appreciate the abyss of despair into which a man may sink one must appreciate what it means to hate a corpse.

During those four years of war I had never fired on a man, whether living or dead. I had remained a Christian. To remain a Christian during those years was to betray the cause. To be a Christian was to be a traitor, since this sordid war was not a war against men, but a war against Christ. For four years I had watched bands of armed men seeking out Christ as the hunter seeks out game. For four years, in Poland, Serbia, the Ukraine, Rumania, Italy and all over Europe, I had watched bands of pale-faced men eagerly searching houses, thickets, woods, mountains and valleys in an effort to drive out Christ and kill Him as one kills a rabid dog. But I had remained a Christian.

And now, for two months and a half — ever since, following Rome's liberation at the beginning of June, we had rushed along the Via Cassia and the Via Aurelia in pursuit of the Germans (Jack and I had the task of maintaining liaison between General Juin's Frenchmen and General Clark's Americans amid the mountains and woods of Viterbo, Tuscany, the maremme of Grosseto, Siena and Volterra) — I too had been growing conscious of a mounting desire to kill.

Almost every night I dreamed that I was shooting, that I was killing. I used to wake up dripping with perspiration, clutching the butt of my automatic rifle. Never had I experienced such dreams. Never before had I dreamed that I was killing a man. I would shoot, and see the man fall gently, slowly. But I never heard the report. The man would fall slowly, gently, into a torrid, yielding abyss of silence.

One night Jack heard me cry out in a dream. We used to sleep on the ground in a wood near Volterra, sheltered by a Sherman, beneath the warm July rain. Here we had joined the Japanese Division — an American division consisting of Japanese from California and Hawaii whose task it was to attack Leghorn. Jack heard me cry out in my dream, and weep, and gnash my teeth. It was exactly as if I were harboring, deep down within me, a wolf, which was slowly freeing itself from the fetters of my conscience.

I had begun to be consumed by this species of homicidal mania, this thirst for blood, when we were between Siena and Florence, at which stage we had awakened to the fact that among the Germans who were firing on us were some Italians. In those days the war of liberation against the Germans was gradually transforming itself, so far as we Italians were concerned, into a fratricidal war against other Italians.

"Don't worry," Jack would say to me, "the same thing, unfortunately, is happening in every country in Europe."

Not only in Italy, but all over Europe, a frightful civil war was festering like a tumor beneath the surface of the war which the Allies were fighting against Hitler's Germany. In their efforts to liberate Europe from the German yoke Poles were killing Poles, Greeks were killing Greeks, Frenchmen were killing Frenchmen, Rumanians were killing Rumanians, and Jugoslavs were killing Jugoslavs. In Italy, the Italians who sided with the Germans were firing not on the Allied soldiers but on the Italians who sided with the Allies; and, similarly, the Italians who sided with the Allies were firing not on the German soldiers but on the Italians who sided with the Germans. While the Allies were allowing themselves to be killed in the attempt to liberate Italy from the Germans, we Italians were killing one another.

The same old Italian disease was flaring up again in each one of us. It was the usual sordid war between Italians, begun on the usual pretext of liberating Italy from the foreigner. But the thing about that age-old disease which appalled and horrified me most of all was the fact that I felt as if I too had succumbed to the contagion. I too felt thirsty for the blood of my kinsmen. During those four years I had succeeded in remaining a Christian. And now — great heavens! — I found that my heart was rotten with hatred, that I too was walking about, pale as a murderer, with an automatic rifle in my hand, that I too felt a horrible lust to kill consuming my very soul.

When we attacked Florence, and entered the streets of Oltrarno from the direction of Porta Romana, Bellosguardo and Poggio Imperiale, I removed the clip from my automatic rifle and offered it to Jack, saying: "Help me, Jack. I don't want to become a murderer." Jack looked at me with a smile. He was pale, and his lips were trembling. He took the clip I was offering him and put it in his pocket. Then I removed the clip from my Mauser and offered him that. Jack stretched out his hand and, still smiling his sad, tender smile, took the clips that were sticking out of the pockets of my tunic.

"They will kill you like a dog," he said.

"It's a glorious death, Jack. I've always dreamed that one day it might be given to me to be killed like a dog."

At the end of Via di Porta Romana, at the point where that street runs at an oblique angle into Via Maggio, the francs-tireurs greeted us with furious volleys of rifle fire from the roofs and windows. We had to jump out of our jeeps and creep forward in the shadow of the walls, while the bullets rained down upon us, whining as they rebounded from the pavement. Jack and the Canadians who were with us fired back, and Major Bradley, who was in command of the Canadian soldiers, turned round every so often and looked at me in amazement, shouting: "Why don't you fire? Are you a conscientious objector?"

"No, he isn't a conscientious objector," answered Jack.

"He's an Italian — a Florentine. He doesn't want to kill Italians — Florentines." And he looked at me with a sad smile.

"You'll regret it!" Major Bradley shouted to me. "You'll never have another chance like this as long as you live."

The Canadian soldiers also turned round and looked at me in amazement. They laughed, shouting to me in their peculiar French, spoken with an old Norman accent: 'Veuillez nous excuser, mon Capitaine, mais nous ne sommes pas de Florence!' And they fired at the windows, laughing as they did so. But I perceived in their words and their laughter a warmth of sympathy in which there was a hint of sadness.

Not until the struggle in the streets of Oltrarno had lasted for fifteen days did we manage to cross the river and penetrate into the heart of the city. We had established ourselves securely on the top floor of the Pensione Bartolini, an ancient mansion on the Lungarno Guicciardini, and we had to bend down as we walked about the rooms to avoid being riddled by the fire of the Germans crouching behind the windows of the Palazzo Ferroni, which stood facing us across the Arno, at the approach to the Santa Trinita bridge.

During the night, as I lay beside the Canadian soldiers and the partisans from the Potente Communist Division, I pressed my face against the brick floor, forcibly restraining myself from getting up, going down into the street, and moving from house to house shooting in the stomach all those who were hiding in the cellars, tremulously awaiting the moment when, the danger over, they could run out into the square with tricolor rosettes on their chests and red kerchiefs round their necks, crying "Long live freedom!" I was nauseated by the hatred which consumed my heart, but I had to cling to the floor with my nails to prevent myself from going into the houses and killing all the false heroes who one day, when the Germans had abandoned the city, would emerge from their hiding places with cries of "Long live freedom!" looking at our bearded faces and tattered uniforms with contempt, pity and hatred in their eyes.

"Why don't you sleep?" Jack asked me in a low voice. "Are you thinking of tomorrow's heroes?"

"Yes, Jack, I'm thinking of tomorrow's heroes."

"Don't worry," said Jack. "The same thing will happen all over Europe. Tomorrow's heroes are the ones who will have saved the freedom of Europe."

"Why did you come and liberate us, Jack? You should have let us rot in slavery."

"I'd give all the freedom of Europe for a glass of cold beer," said Jack.

"A glass of cold beer?" cried Major Bradley, waking up with a start.

One night, as we were on the point of going out to patrol the roofs, a partisan from the Potente Division came to inform me that an Italian artillery officer was asking after me. It was Giacomo Lombroso. We embraced in silence, and I trembled as I looked at his pale face and his great eyes, which were filled with the strange light that appears in the eyes of a Jew when Death comes to rest on his shoulder like an invisible owl. We made a long tour of the roofs, our object being to start the francs-tireurs from their coverts behind the chimney stacks and skylights, and on our return we went and lay down on the roof of the Pensione Bartolini in the shelter of a chimney.

Stretched out on the warm tiles in the summer night, whose peace was broken by lightning flashes from a distant storm, we talked among ourselves in low voices, gazing at the pale moon as it slowly rose into the sky above the olive trees of Settignano and Fiesole, and the cypress woods of Mount Morello, and the bare ridge of Calvana. Down below, at the far end of the plain, I seemed to see the roofs of my native city shining in the faint light of the moon. And I said to Jack: "That's Prato, Jack — that's my native city. My mother's house is there. I was born near the house in which Filippino Lippi was born. Do you remember, Jack, the night that we spent hiding in that grove of cypresses on the hills of Prato?

Do you remember how we saw the eyes of Filippino Lippi's Madonnas and Angels shining among the olive trees?"

"It was the glowworms," said Jack.

"No, it wasn't the glowworms. It was the eyes of Filippino Lippi's Madonnas and Angels."

"Why are you trying to pull my leg? It was the glowworms," said Jack.

Perhaps it was the glowworms, but in the moonlight the olive trees and the cypresses looked exactly as if they had been painted by Filippino Lippi.

A few days previously Jack and I, together with a Canadian officer, had gone out on patrol behind the German lines, our object being to ascertain whether, as the partisans asserted, the Germans, rejecting the idea of defending Prato, the entrance to the valley of the Bisenzio, and the road that leads from Prato to Bologna, had abandoned the city. Since I knew the district I acted as guide, while Jack and the Canadian officer were to communicate by radio with the headquarters of the American Air Force if they thought a new and more terrible bombardment of Prato was necessary. The life of my native city depended on Jack, the Canadian officer and myself. We walked toward Prato as the Angels walked toward Sodom. Our mission was to save Lot, and Lot's family, from the rain of fire.

We had forded the Arno near Lastre a Signa, and at a certain point had begun to make our way along the bank of the Bisenzio, the river close to which I was born — the "happy Bisenzio" of Marsilio Ficino and Agnolo Firenzuola. Near Campi we had turned aside from the river in order to avoid the houses, and after a long detour had struck the Bisenzio once more near Capalle Bridge. From there, always following the riverbank, we had trudged on until we came in sight of the walls of Prato. With Querce as our starting point we had climbed the slopes of Retaia and, cutting across the mountain above the Capuchin monastery, had walked down to Filettole, where, hidden in a grove of cypresses, we had spent the night watching the glowworms as they flitted about among the leafy branches of the olive trees, diffusing a pallid radiance.

I said to Jack: "Those are the eyes of Filippino Lippi's Madonnas and Angels."

"Why are you trying to frighten me?" said Jack. "They are glowworms."

I laughed and said: "That faint glow over there, near the fountain that is singing in the shadows, comes from the veils of Filippo Lippi's Salome."

"To hell with your Salome!" said Jack. "Why are you trying to pull my leg? It's the glowworms."

"One must have been born in Prato," I said to him, "one must be a fellow citizen of Filippino Lippi, to realize that it isn't glowworms but the eyes of Filippino's Angels and Madonnas."

Jack said with a sigh: "Unfortunately, I'm only a poor American."

Then we were silent for a long while, and I felt full of affection and gratitude toward Jack and all those who, unfortunately, were only poor Americans, and were risking their lives for me, my native city, and Filippino Lippi's Madonnas and Angels.

The moon set, and the dawn lightened the sky over Retaia. I looked at the houses of Coiano and Santa Lucia, far away across the river, and the cypresses of Sacca, and the wind-swept summit of Spazzavento, and I said to Jack: "There is the country in which I spent my childhood. It was there that I first set eyes on a dead bird, a dead lizard, a dead man. It was there that I first set eyes on a green tree, a blade of grass, a dog."

Jack said to me in a low voice: "That boy down there, running along the riverbank — is that you?"

"Yes, that's me," I answered. "And that white dog is my poor Belledo. He died when I was fifteen. But he knows I've come back, and he's looking for me."

Columns of German vehicles were passing along the road to Coiano and Santa Lucia, climbing in the direction of Vaiano, Vernio and Bologna.

"They're leaving," said Jack.

However much we scanned the hills, valleys and woods

with our binoculars we did not see a sign of any barbed-wire entanglements, trenches or gun emplacements, nor any munition dumps, tanks or concealed antitank guns. The city seemed to have been abandoned not only by the Germans but even by the inhabitants. Not a single wisp of smoke ascended from the chimneys of the factories or from those of the houses. Prato looked deserted and dead. Yet in Prato, as in all the cities of Italy and of Europe, the false "resisters," the false defenders of freedom, the heroes of tomorrow, lay hidden, pale and trembling, in the cellars. The imbeciles and the madmen, together with the partisan groups, had taken to the maquis and were fighting at the side of the Allies or swinging from the lampposts in the city squares. But the wise and the prudent, all those who one day, with the danger over, would laugh at us and our mud-spattered and blood-stained uniforms, were there, cowering in their secure hiding places, awaiting the moment when they could come out into the square uttering cries of "Long live freedom!"

"I'm truly glad that the fair-haired man has married the dark woman," I said to Jack with a smile.

"I'm glad too," said Jack, and smilingly he began to transmit by radio the words of the conventional message, "The fair-haired man has married the dark woman," which signified: "The Germans have abandoned Prato." A horse was grazing on the green bank of the Bisenzio, a dog was running about, barking, on the gravel at the edge of the river, a girl, clad in red, was walking down to the fountain at Filettole, supporting a shining copper bowl on her head with upraised arms. And I smiled happily. The bombs of the Liberators would not blind Lippi's Madonnas and Angels; they would not break the legs of Donatello's Cupids that danced in the pulpit of the Cathedral, nor kill the Madonnas of Mercatale and Olivo, nor Tacca's Bacchino, nor the Virgins of Luca della Robbia, nor Filippo Lippi's Salome, nor the statue of San Giovanni delle Carceri. They would not murder my mother. I was happy, but my heart ached.

So too this evening, as I lay beside Jack and Lombroso on the roof of the Pensione Bartolini, watching the pale moon slowly climb the sky, I was happy; but my heart ached. An odor of death rose from the blue abyss of the alleys of Oltrarno and from the deep silvery gash of the river into the pale green vault of the summer night, and when I leaned over the edge of the roof I could see the bodies lying on the pavement below, between the bridge of Santa Trinita and the entrance to Via Maggio — a dead German, still gripping his rifle, a dead woman, her face resting on her shopping basket, which was stuffed with tomatoes and gourds, a dead boy with an empty bottle in his hand, a dead horse wedged between the shafts of a carriage, while the dead coachman sat on his box with his hands on his stomach and his head drooping on to his knees.

Those corpses — I hated them. I hated all corpses. It was they that were the *foreigners* — the only real *foreigners* in the universal country of the living, in the universal country that is life. Living Americans, living Frenchmen, Poles, belonged to my own race, a race of living men, to my own country — life. Like me they spoke a warm, living, sonorous language, they moved and walked, their eyes shone, their lips opened when they breathed and smiled. They were alive, they were living men. But the dead were foreigners, they belonged to a different race, a race of dead men, and to a different country — death. They were our enemies, the enemies of my country, of the universal country — life. They had invaded Italy, France, all Europe. They were the only real *foreigners* in a Europe which, though conquered and humiliated, was alive — the only real enemies of our freedom. We had to defend life — our true country, life — even against them — the dead.

Now I understood the reason for that hatred, that lust for killing which gnawed at my vitals and consumed the souls of all the peoples of Europe. It was that we felt impelled to hate something that was alive, warm, human, something *that belonged to us,* something that resembled us, something that was of our own kind, that belonged to our own country, life, instead of hating those foreigners who had invaded Europe, and for five years had lain motionless, cold, livid, with empty eye-sockets, oppressing our country, which was life, and crushing our freedom and dignity, love, hope and youth, beneath the appalling weight of their ice-cold flesh. Why was it that we were hurling ourselves like wolves against our brothers? Why was it that in the name of freedom Frenchmen were pitting themselves against Frenchmen, Italians against Italians, Poles against Poles, Rumanians against Rumanians? It was that we all felt impelled to hate something that resembled ourselves, something that belonged to us, *something in which we could recognize and hate ourselves.*

"Did you see how pale poor Tani was?" said Lombroso suddenly, breaking the long silence.

He too was thinking of death. Already he knew that a few days later, on the morning of Florence's liberation, as he returned home after so many long, tragic months and knocked at his door, a man hidden in the cellar of the adjoining house would fire at him from below, mortally wounding him in the groin. Perhaps he already knew that he would die alone on the pavement, like a sick dog, while overhead the first swallows greeted the dawn with cries of terror. He already knew, perhaps, that his brow was veiled in the pallor of death, that his face was pale and bright as the face of Tani Masier.

As we returned that same evening from our patrol of the rooftops of Oltrarno, we were walking through the Vicolo di Santo Spirito, which lies behind the Lungarno Guicciardini, when a sudden hail of mortar fire drove us to shelter in the entrance hall of a house. In the dark hall we saw a white shadow coming toward us — the gracious shadow of a woman, smiling through her tears. It was Tity Masier; and although she did not recognize me she invited us into a room on the ground floor, a kind of cellar in which there lay, on beds of straw, a number of shadowy human figures. They were men, and at once I scented the odor of death.

One of the shadows raised itself on to its elbows and called me by name. It was a most beautiful spectre, reminiscent of those youthful spectres which the ancients used to meet walking along the dusty roads of Phocis and Argolis in the midday sun, or sitting at the edge of the Castalian spring at Delphi, or in the shade of the vast forest of olive trees which stretches from Delphi down to Itea, from Delphi down to the sea, like a river of silvery leaves.

I recognized it: it was Tani Masier. But I did not know whether he was already dead or whether he was still alive, and was turning round to call me by name from the threshold of the night. And I scented the odor of death, that odor which is like a singing voice, a summoning voice.

"Poor Tani — he doesn't know that he must die," said Giacomo Lombroso in a low voice. He for his part already knew that Death was standing on the threshold of his house, leaning against his door, waiting for him to come.

Brunelleschi's cupola was shimmering high above the roofs of Florence. The moon shed its pale beams upon Giotto's white steeple. I thought of little Giorgio, my sister's son — I thought of that boy of thirteen, asleep in a pool of blood behind the laurel hedge in my sister's garden, yonder on the heights of Arcetri. What did they want of me, all those corpses that lay beneath the moon in the paved streets, on the tiles of the roofs, in the gardens beside the Arno — what did they want of us?

From the vast maze of Oltrarno's alleys an odor of death ascended, like a singing voice, a summoning voice. But why? Could it really be that the dead hoped to persuade us that it was better to die?

One morning we crossed the river and occupied Florence. From sewers, cellars, attics and cupboards, from under beds and from cracks in the walls, where for a month they had been living "clandestinely," there emerged, like rats, the latter-day heroes, the tyrants of tomorrow — those heroic rats of freedom who one day would overturn Europe in order to build on the ruins of foreign tyranny the kingdom of domestic oppression.

We passed through Florence in silence, with downcast eyes, feeling like intruders and spoil-sports beneath the scornful gaze of the clowns of freedom, with their rosettes, armlets, braid and ostrich feathers, and their red, white and green faces. We pursued the Germans into the valleys of the Apennines and up the mountains. Upon the still lukewarm ashes of summer descended the chill rain of autumn, and we passed long months in front of the Gothic Line listening to the murmur of the rain as it fell on Montepiano's forests of oaks and chestnut trees, the firs of the Abetone, and the white marble rocks of the Apuan Alps.

Then came winter, and every three days we used to leave Leghorn, where the Allied Command had its headquarters, and go up the line, into the Versilia-Garfagnana sector. Sometimes at night we were caught unawares and took refuge near the American Ninety-Second Negro Division in my house at Forte dei Marmi, which the German sculptor Hildebrand, helped by the painter Böklin, had built at the end of the last century on the barren slope between the pine forest and the sea.

We used to spend our nights sitting round the fireplace in the great hall, which was adorned with frescoes by Hildebrand and Böklin. Bullets from the German machine-gun nests on the banks of the Cinquale pinged against the walls of the house, the wind in its fury shook the pines, the sea roared beneath the cloudless sky, across which sped Orion of the beautiful sandals with his gleaming bow and sword.

One night Jack said to me in a low voice: "Look at Campbell."

I looked at Campbell. He was sitting in front of the fireplace among the officers of the Ninety-Second Negro Division, and he was smiling. At first I did not understand. But in Jack's eyes, which were fixed on Campbell's face, I read a timid valediction, an affectionate farewell; and when Campbell lifted his head and looked at Jack his eyes too expressed a timid valediction, an affectionate farewell. I saw them smile at each other, and I was conscious of a very mild sense of envy, a tender jealousy. In that moment I understood that Jack and Campbell shared a secret, that Tani Masier, Giacomo Lombroso and my little Giorgio, my sister's son, shared a secret, which they jealously, smilingly kept from me.

One morning a partisan from Camaiore came to ask me if I wanted to see Magi. When, a few months before, our pursuit of the Germans had brought us to Forte dei Marmi, I had immediately, without telling Jack, gone to look Magi up. The house was deserted. Some partisans told me that Magi had fled on the very day on which our advanced guards had entered Viareggio. If I had found him at home, if, when I knocked at his door, he had appeared at the window, I might have shot him — not because of the wrong he had done me, not because of the persecution I had suffered following his denunciations, but because of the wrong he had done others. He was a kind of local Fouché. He was tall, pale and thin, with bleary eyes. His house was the one in which Böklin had lived for many years at the time when he was painting his centaurs and nymphs and his famous "Isle of the Dead." I knocked at the door and looked up, expecting him to appear at the window. In the wall beneath the window is the tablet commemorating the years which Böklin spent at Forte dei Marmi. I read the words on the tablet and waited for the window to open, my automatic rifle in my hand. If he had appeared at that moment I might have shot him.

I went with the partisan from Camaiore to see Magi. In a meadow near the village the partisan indicated something that protruded from the earth. "There's Magi," he said. I scented the odor of death, and Jack said to me: "Let's go." But I wanted to see from close at hand what it was that was sticking out of the ground, and on approaching I saw that it was a foot, still encased in a shoe. The woollen sock covered a fragment of black flesh, and the mouldy shoe looked as if it were impaled on a stick.

"Why don't you bury that foot?" I said to the partisan.

"No," replied the partisan, "it's got to stay like that. His wife came, then his daughter. They wanted the corpse. Oh, no — that corpse is ours. Then they came back with a spade, and wanted to bury the foot. Oh, no — that foot is ours. And it's got to stay like that."

"It's horrible," I said.

"Horrible? The other day there were two little sparrows on that foot, making love. It was comical to see those two little sparrows making love on Magi's foot."

"Go and fetch a spade," I said.

"No," replied the partisan obstinately. "It's got to stay like that."

I thought of Magi, wedged in the ground with that foot sticking out. Why couldn't he curl up in his grave and sleep? It was as though he were suspended by that foot above an abyss. Why couldn't he tumble headlong into hell? I thought of that foot, suspended between heaven and hell, exposed to the air, sun, rain and wind, and of the chirruping birds that came and settled on it.

"Go and fetch a spade," I said. "I ask you to do it as a favor. He wronged me greatly when he was alive, but now that he's dead I should like to do him a good turn. *He* was a Christian, too."

"No," replied the partisan, "he wasn't a Christian. If Magi was a Christian, what am I? We can't both be Christians, Magi and I."

"There are many ways of being a Christian," I said. "Even a scoundrel can be a Christian."

"No," replied the partisan, "there's only one way of being a Christian. In any case — what does it mean to be a Christian today?"

"If you want to do me a favor," I said, "go and fetch a spade."

"A spade?" said the partisan. "If you like I'll go and fetch a saw. Rather than bury his leg I'll saw it off and give it to the pigs."

That evening, as we sat in front of the fireplace in my home at Forte dei Marmi, we listened in silence to the bullets from the German machine guns pinging against the wall of the house and the trunks of the pines. I thought of Magi, wedged in the ground with his foot sticking out, and I began to realize what those corpses wanted of us — all those corpses that lay in the streets, fields and woods.

Now I was beginning to realize why the odor of death was like a singing voice, a summoning voice. I was beginning to realize why all those corpses were calling us. They wanted something of us, only we could give them what they asked for. No, it was not pity. It was something else — something

deeper and more mysterious. It was not peace — the peace of
the grave, of forgiveness, of remembrance, of affection. It was
something more remote from man, more remote from life.

Then spring came, and when we moved forward for the
final assault I was sent to act as guide to the Japanese Division
during the attack on Massa. From Massa we penetrated as
far as Carrara, and from there, crossing the Apennines, we
went down to Modena.

It was when I saw poor Campbell lying on the dusty road
in a pool of blood that I realized what the dead wanted of us.
They wanted something that is foreign to man, something
that is foreign to life itself. Two days later we crossed the Po
and, repelling the German rearguards, approached Milan.
Now the war was coming to an end and the massacre was
beginning — that terrible massacre of Italians by Italians, in
houses, streets, fields and woods. But it was on the day when
I saw Jack die that I understood at last what it was that was
dying around me and within me. There was a smile on Jack's
face as he died, and he was looking at me. When the light
went from his eyes I felt, for the first time in my life, that a
human being had died for me.

On the day on which we entered Milan we ran into a yelling crowd which was rioting in a square. I stood up in the
jeep and saw Mussolini hanging by his feet from a hook. He
was bloated, white, enormous. I started to be sick on the seat
of the jeep: the war was over now, and I could do nothing
more for others, nothing more for my country — nothing except be sick.

When I left the American military hospital I returned to
Rome and went to stay with a friend of mine, Dr. Pietro
Marziale, an obstetrician, at No. 9, Via Lambro. The house
was situated at the end of the new suburb which extends,
squalid and cold, beyond Piazza Quadrata. It was a small
house, comprising barely three rooms, and I had to sleep in
the study, on a divan. The walls of the study were lined with
bookshelves full of books on gynecology, and on the edges of
the bookshelves were rows of obstetrical instruments — for-

ceps, spoons, large forks, knives, saws, decapitators, basio-
tribes, cranioclasts, trephines and various kinds of large
pincers, as well as glass jugs filled with a yellowish liquid.
In each of the jugs was a submerged human foetus.

For many days I had been living in the midst of that community of foeti, and the horror of it oppressed me; for foeti
are corpses, though of a monstrous species: they are corpses
which have never been born and have never died. If I looked
up from the pages of a book I found myself gazing into the
half-closed eyes of those little monsters. Sometimes, when I
awoke at dead of night, it seemed to me that those horrible
foeti, some of them standing, some sitting on the bottom of
their jugs, some crouching on their knees in the act of jumping, were slowly lifting their heads and looking at me with
smiling faces.

On the bedside table there lay, like a flower vase, a large
jug, in which floated the king of that strange community, a
fearsome yet friendly Tricephalus, a foetus with three heads,
of the female sex. Those three heads — small, round, wax-
colored — followed me with their eyes, smiling at me with
sad and rather timid smiles, full of shamefaced modesty.
Whenever I walked about the room the wooden floor trembled
slightly, and the three heads bobbed up and down in a horrible yet graceful way. But the other foeti were more melancholy, more preoccupied, more malignant.

Some had the pensive look of a drowned man, and if I happened to shake one of the jugs, teeming with their flottaison
blême et ravie, I would see the pensive foetus slowly sink to
the bottom. Their mouths, which were half closed, were wide,
like the mouths of frogs, and their ears were short and
wrinkled, their noses transparent, their brows furrowed with
venerable wrinkles, with a senility still virginal in point of
years, and not yet corrupted by age.

Others amused themselves by skipping over the long white
ribbons of their umbilical cords. Others yet were seated,
squatting on their haunches, in a state of watchful, timorous
immobility, as if they were expecting to emerge at any moment into life. Others were suspended in the yellowish liquid

as if in mid-air, and seemed to be slowly descending from a lofty, frigid sky — the same sky, I thought, as forms an arch above the Capitol, above the cupola of St. Peter's: the sky of Rome. What a strange species of Angels is to be found in Italy, I thought, what a strange species of eagles! Others were sleeping, curled up in attitudes of extreme abandon. Others were laughing, opening wide their froglike mouths, their arms folded across their chests, their legs apart, their eyes covered by heavy batrachian lids. Others strained their small ears of ancient ivory, listening to remote, mysterious voices. There were others, finally, that contemplated my every gesture, my pen as it slowly glided across the white page, my abstracted pacing about the room, my relaxed slumbers in front of the blazing fire. And all had the ancient aspect of men not yet born, men who never will be born. They were standing before the closed door of life, even as we stand before the closed door of death.

And there was one that looked like Cupid in the act of shooting his arrow from an invisible bow, a wizened Cupid with the bald head of an old man and a toothless mouth. On him my eyes would rest whenever I was seized with melancholy at the sound of women's voices floating up from the street, calling out and answering from window to window. To me at such moments the most real and most joyous personification of youth, of spring, of love was that fearsome Cupid, that little deformed monster which the obstetrician's forceps had wrenched from its mother's womb, that bald, toothless old man who had come to maturity in the belly of a young woman.

But there were some which I could not look at without a secret terror. Among them were two embryonic Cyclopes, one like that described by Birnbaum, the other like that described by Sangalli. Each gazed at me with a single round eye, sightless and immobile in the center of its great socket, like the eye of a fish. There were some Dycephali, their two heads bobbing up and down above their scraggy shoulders. And there were two fearsome Dyprosopi, monsters with two faces, like the god Janus. The face in front was young and smooth, the one behind was smaller and more wizened, contracted into a malignant grimace like that of an old man.

Sometimes, as I dozed in front of the fireplace, I heard them, or seemed to hear them, talking among themselves. The words of that mysterious, incomprehensible language floated in the alcohol and dissolved like bubbles of air. And I said to myself as I listened to them: "Perhaps this is the ancient language of men, the language men speak before they are born into life, the language they speak when they are born into death. Perhaps it is the ancient, mysterious language of our conscience." And sometimes, as I looked at them, I said to myself: "These are our witnesses and our judges. It is they who, from the threshold of life, watch us live, and, hidden in the shadows of the primeval cavern, watch us rejoice, suffer and die. They are the witnesses of the immortality that precedes life, the guarantors of the immortality that follows death. It is they who judge the dead." And I would say to myself with a shudder: "Dead men are the foeti of death."

I had come out of hospital in a state of extreme weakness, and I used to spend a great part of my days stretched out on the bed. One night I was seized with a violent fever. It seemed to me that that community of foeti had emerged from their jars, and that they were moving about the room, climbing on the writing desk and the chairs, up the window curtains, and even on to my bed. Gradually they all assembled on the floor, in the middle of the room, arranging themselves in a semicircle like judges in session; and they inclined their heads now to the right, now to the left, in order to whisper in one another's ears, looking at me with their round batrachian eyes, staring and sightless. Their bald heads glistened horribly in the dim light of the moon.

The Tricephalus sat in the middle of the council, and on either side of him were the two twin-faced Dyprosopi. To escape the obscure feeling of horror with which I was filled by the sight of that areopagus of monsters I raised my eyes to the window and gazed at the green celestial fields, in which the cold, untarnished silver of the moon glistened like dew.

Suddenly the sound of a voice caused me to lower my eyes. It was the voice of the Tricephalus: "Let the accused be brought in," he said, turning to a group of little monsters that stood apart, looking like hired ruffians.

I gazed into a corner of the room, toward which all had turned, and was stricken with horror.

I saw, slowly advancing between two of the ruffians, an enormous foetus. It had a flabby stomach, and its legs were covered with glossy whitish hairs, like the down on a thistle. Its arms were folded across its chest, its hands were bound with its umbilical cord. As it walked it swayed its plump flanks in time with its steps, which were slow, grave and silent, as if its feet were made of a softish substance.

It had a bloated, white, enormous head, in which there gleamed two huge, yellow, watery eyes, like the eyes of a blind dog. The expression on its face was proud and at the same time timid, as if ancient pride and a new foreboding of extraordinary events there contended and — with neither ever prevailing — mingled in such a way as to create an expression at once abject and heroic.

It was a face of flesh — the flesh of a foetus and at the same time the flesh of an old man, the flesh of a foetus created in the likeness of an old man. It was a mirror that reflected, in all their senseless glory, the grandeur and wretchedness, the pride and degradation of human flesh. What amazed me above all else in that face was the odd mixture of ambition and disappointment, insolence and sadness, typical of the countenance of man. And for the first time I saw the ugliness of the human countenance, the loathsomeness of the substance of which we are made. How squalid, I thought, is the glory of the flesh of man! How miserable is the triumph expressed in human flesh, even in the fleeting season of youth and love!

Just then the enormous foetus looked at me, and its livid lips, which hung down like eyelids, parted in a smile. Its countenance, lit by that timid smile, gradually changed, and became like the face of a woman, an old woman, in which the traces of the rouge that had contributed to her ancient glory emphasized the wrinkles of time, disappointment and betrayal. I surveyed the fleshy chest, the flabby stomach, which seemed weakened by childbirth, and the soft, swollen flanks, and at the thought that this man, once so proud and glorious, was now merely a kind of horrible old woman, I began to laugh. But suddenly I felt ashamed of my laughter; for if, in my cell in the Regina Coeli prison, or on the lonely shore of Lipari, I had sometimes, in moments of sadness and despair, delighted to revile him, humiliate him, lower him in my eyes, as the lover does to the woman who has betrayed him, now that he stood there before me, a naked, loathsome foetus, I blushed to think that I was laughing at him.

I looked at him, and felt a sort of affectionate compassion growing within me, such as I had never experienced when he was alive. It was a new sentiment, and it filled me with terror and wonderment alike. I tried to lower my eyes, to evade his watery stare, but in vain. The quality of insolence, pride and vulgarity which his countenance possessed during his lifetime had transformed itself into a wondrous melancholy. And I felt profoundly disturbed, almost guilty, not, to be sure, because I thought that my new sentiment might humiliate him, but because I too, for many years before I had rebelled against his senseless tyranny, had bent my back like all the rest beneath the weight of his triumphant flesh.

At that point I heard the voice of the Tricephalus calling me by name and saying: "Why are you silent? Are you by any chance still afraid of him? Look! See the substance of which his glory was made."

"What do you expect me to do?" I said, raising my eyes. "Laugh at him? Insult him? Do you think, perhaps, that the sight of his wretchedness offends me? What offends a man is not the sight of decayed human flesh, gnawed by the worms, but the sight of human flesh in its triumph."

"Are you so proud, then, to be a man?" said the Tricephalus.

"A man?" I replied with a laugh. "A man is something even sadder and more fearsome than this mass of decayed flesh. A man is pride, cruelty, betrayal, degradation, violence. Decayed flesh is sadness, shame, fear, remorse, hope. A man —

a living man — is a puny thing compared to a mass of putrid flesh."

A malicious laugh went up from the horrible assembly.

"Why do you laugh?" said the Tricephalus, moving his three bald and wrinkled heads from side to side. "Man is in truth a puny thing."

"Man is an ignoble thing," I said. "There is no sadder or more sickening sight than a man or a nation in the hour of triumph. But what nobler or more beautiful thing is there in the world than a man or a nation that has been conquered, humiliated, reduced to a heap of putrid flesh?"

While I was speaking the foeti had got up one by one and, moving their large whitish heads from side to side and reeling about on their gangrenous little legs, had grouped themselves in a corner of the room around the Tricephalus and the two Dyprosopi. I saw their eyes gleaming in the semidarkness, I heard them laughing among themselves and uttering shrill wails. Then they fell silent.

The enormous foetus had remained standing before me and was looking at me with eyes that were like the eyes of a blind dog.

"You see now what they are really like," it said after a long silence. "No one took pity on me."

"Pity? What good would pity have done you?"

"They cut my throat, they hanged me by the feet from a hook, they covered me with spittle," said the foetus very softly.

"I was at Piazzale Loreto too," I said in a low voice. "I saw you hanging by the feet from a hook."

"Do you hate me too?" said the foetus.

"I am not worthy to hate," I replied. "Only a pure being may hate. What men call hatred is simply moral turpitude. Everything human is foul and base. Man is a fearsome thing."

"I *was* a fearsome thing too," said the foetus.

"There is no more loathsome thing in the world," I said, "than man in his glory, than human flesh enthroned on the Capitol."

"Only today do I realize how horrible I was then," said the foetus, and it fell silent. "If on the day when all deserted me, if on the day when they left me alone in the hands of my murderers I had asked you to take pity on me," it added after looking at me for a long while in silence, "would you have harmed me too?"

"Be silent!" I cried.

"Why don't you answer?" said the monster.

"I am not worthy to harm another man," I replied in a low voice. "The power to do harm is sacred. Only a pure being is worthy to harm another man."

"Do you know what I thought," said the monster after a long silence, "when the murderer pointed his weapon at me? I thought that what he was about to give me was a foul thing."

"Everything that man gives to man is a foul thing," I said. "Even love and hatred, good and evil — everything. The death which man gives to man is a foul thing too."

The monster lowered its head and was silent. Then it said, "And forgiveness?"

"Forgiveness is a foul thing too."

Just then two foeti of ruffianly aspect approached, and one of them, resting its hand on the monster's shoulder, said, "Come on."

The enormous foetus raised its head, and looking at me began to weep softly.

"Good-bye," it said, and lowering its head it moved off between the two ruffians. As it walked away it turned and smiled at me.

THE DEAD GOD

● Every evening Jimmy and I used to go down to the harbor to read the list posted up on the gates outside the harbor master's office, giving the order of embarkation of the American units and the date of departure of the ships which sailed from Naples carrying the troops of the Fifth Army back to America.

"It isn't my turn yet," Jimmy would say, spitting on the ground. And we would go and sit on a small bench beneath the trees of the vast square situated in front of the harbor, and overlooked by the towering mass of the Maschio Angioino.

I had been eager to accompany Jimmy to Naples so that

I might remain with him until the last moment and bid him farewell on the gangway of the ship that would take him back to America. Of all those American friends of mine with whom I had for two years shared the dangers of war and the melancholy joy of liberation only Jimmy was now left to me — Jimmy Wren, of Cleveland, Ohio, an officer in the Signal Corps. All the others were scattered about Europe — in Germany, France and Austria — or had gone back home to America, or had died for me, for us, for my country, like Jack and Campbell. For me, the day on which I said goodbye to him forever on the ship's gangway would be like those other days on which I had said good-bye forever to poor Jack and poor Campbell. I should be left alone, among my own people, in my own country. For the first time in my life I should be left alone, truly alone.

As soon as the shadows of evening crept along the walls, and the vast black breath of the sea darkened the green leaves of the trees and the red façades of the houses, a dingy, sluggish, silent mob would emerge from the thousand alleys of Toledo and invade the square. It was the Neapolitan mob — legendary, primeval, pitiable. But something within it had died: its joy in the knowledge of its hunger, and even its wretchedness, were sad, pale, dead. Gradually the evening would climb out of the sea, and the mob would lift its tear-reddened eyes and watch Vesuvius loom up, white, cold and spectral against the black sky. Not a wisp of smoke ascended from the mouth of the crater, not the palest glimmer of fire illuminated the volcano's lofty brow. The mob would linger mutely for hour after hour, deep into the night, then silently disperse.

Left alone in the vast square, with the black expanse of the sea before us, Jimmy and I would move off, turning round every so often to watch the great white corpse on the rim of the horizon slowly dissolving into the night.

In April, 1944, having rocked the earth and spewed up torrents of fire for many days, Vesuvius had spent its fury. It had not subsided gradually, but abruptly. Its brow enveloped in a pall of icy clouds, it had suddenly uttered a great cry, and the chill of death had turned its veins of burning lava to stone. The God of Naples, the totem of the Neapolitan populace, was dead. An immense shroud of black crape had descended upon the city, and the bay, and the hill of Posilipo. The people walked about the streets on tiptoe, conversing in low voices, as if every house sheltered a corpse.

A doleful silence brooded over the mourning city. The voice of Naples, the ancient, noble voice of hunger, pity, grief, joy and love, the loud, hoarse, resonant, gay, triumphant voice of Naples was stilled. And whenever the fires of sunset, or the silvery radiance of the moon, or the rays of the rising sun appeared to inflame the white spectre of the volcano, a cry, a piercing cry, as of a woman in travail, went up from the city. All the people appeared at the windows, rushed into the streets and embraced one another, shedding tears of joy, intoxicated by the hope that by some miracle warmth had returned to the lifeless veins of the volcano, and that the crimson touch of the setting sun, or the radiance of the moon, or the shy glimmer of dawn, presaged the resurrection of Vesuvius, the dead god whose immense, naked corpse filled the sombre sky of Naples.

But soon this hope gave way to rage and disillusionment. Eyes were dried, and the mob, unclasping hands which they had joined in an attitude of prayer, raised threatening fists or cocked a snook at the volcano, mingling entreaties and laments with their imprecations and insults, crying: "Have pity on us, curse you! Son of a harlot, have mercy on us!"

Then came the days of the new moon; and when the moon slowly rose above the chill slopes of Vesuvius an oppressive melancholy descended upon Naples. The lunar dawn lit up the lifeless deserts of purple ashes and the livid rocks of cold lava, which looked like boulders of black ice. Sporadic groans and wails arose from the depths of the dark alleys, and the fishermen who lay along the beaches of Santa Lucia, Mergellina and Posilipo, sleeping on the warm sand beneath the keels of their boats, emerged from slumber, raised them-

selves on to their elbows and turned their heads toward the
spectre of the volcano, listening in trepidation to the moan-
ing of the waves and the sporadic sobbing of the seagulls. The
shells glistened on the sand, and at the edge of the sky, which
was covered with silvery fishes' scales, Vesuvius lay rotting
like a dead shark that has been cast ashore by the waves.

One August evening, as we were returning from Amalfi, we
saw a long line of reddish flames moving up the volcano's
slopes toward the mouth of the crater. We asked a fisherman
what these lights were. They came from a procession which
was carrying votive offerings to Vesuvius in the hope of allaying its wrath and persuading it not to abandon its people.
Following a day of prayer in the Sanctuary of Pompeii a long
column of women, boys and old men, headed by a band of
priests clad in sacred vestments and by young men carrying
the banners and standards of the Brotherhoods and great
black crucifixes, was advancing up the highway which leads
from Bosco Treccase to the crater. Some were weeping,
others were praying. Some were waving olive sprays, pine
branches, and vine-shoots rich with clusters of grapes. Some
carried jars of wine and hampers filled with goat's cheese,
fruit and bread, others copper trays laden with buns and
whey tarts, others yet lambs, fowls, rabbits and baskets filled
with fish. Having reached the crest of Vesuvius the bare-
footed, tattered multitude, whose faces and hair were begrimed with ashes, silently followed the chanting priests into
the vast amphitheatre of the old crater.

The russet moon climbed above the distant mountains of
Cilento, which appeared blue and silver in the green mirror
of the sky. The night was deep and warm. Here and there
the sound of weeping arose from the mob, and stifled groans,
loud, harsh cries, and voices hoarse with fear and grief.
Every so often one would sink to his knees and poke his
fingers into the cracks in the cold lava crust as if probing
the fissures in the marble flagstones of a tomb, in order to
feel whether the ancient fire still burned in the veins of the
volcano; then, withdrawing his hand, he would cry in a

voice broken with anguish and horror: "He's dead! He's dead!"

At the words a great wail would go up from the mob, accompanied by the thumping of fists on breasts and bellies and the shrill groans of the faithful as they mortified their flesh with their nails and teeth.

The old crater is in the form of a shell almost a mile across. Its jagged rim is black with lava and yellow with sulphur. Here and there the deposits of lava, after cooling off, have taken on human shapes, the aspect of gigantic men, intertwined like wrestlers in a dark, silent affray. These are the lava statues which the inhabitants of the Vesuvian villages call "the slaves," perhaps in memory of the hordes of slaves who had followed Spartacus and, while they awaited the signal to revolt, had lived in hiding for many months among the vineyards which covered the slopes and summit of peaceful Vesuvius before the sudden eruption that destroyed Herculaneum and Pompeii. The moon awoke that army of slaves, who slowly loosed themselves from the shackles of sleep and, raising their arms, moved through the red mist of the moon toward the crowd of the faithful.

In the middle of the vast amphitheatre of the old crater rises the cone of the new, which, now mute and cold, had continued for nearly two thousand years to spew up flames, ashes, stones, and rivers of lava. Clambering up the rugged slopes of the cone the mob had collected around the mouth of the extinct volcano and, weeping and shouting, were flinging their votive offerings — bread, fruit and whey tarts — into the monster's black jaws, while over the lava rocks they sprinkled wine and the blood of the lambs, fowls and rabbits, whose throats they had cut and which they afterwards threw, still quivering with life, into the depths of the abyss.

Jimmy and I had reached the summit of Vesuvius just as the mob, having performed that most ancient propitiatory rite, had thrown themselves to their knees and, tearing their hair and clawing their faces and breasts, were mingling liturgical chants and lamentations with prayers to the miraculous Virgin of Pompeii and invocations of their cruel and unfeeling god Vesuvius. As the moon, like a blood-soaked sponge, climbed into the sky, so the tone of the wails and litanies was raised and the voices became shriller and more heart-rending, until the mob, seized with a wild, despairing fury and hurling imprecations and insults, began to fling pieces of lava and handfuls of ashes into the mouth of the volcano.

Meanwhile a great wind had arisen, and a dense mass of clouds, accompanied by flashes of lightning, was emerging from the sea, propelled by the sirocco. Very soon it enveloped the crest of Vesuvius. Amid those yellow clouds, driven by the thunderbolts, the great black crucifixes and the banners, which the gusts of wind buffeted unmercifully, appeared enormous, and the men looked like giants. The litanies, the imprecations and the wails of the mob seemed to well up from the smoke and flames of an inferno which had suddenly opened up beneath it. At length, first the band of priests, then the standard-bearers of the Brotherhoods, and finally the crowd of the faithful rushed headlong down the sides of the cone, beneath the rain that was already hissing down through the rents in the clouds, and disappeared into the sulphurous darkness which had meanwhile invaded the vast shell of the old crater.

Left alone, Jimmy and I set off for the spot where we had parked our jeep. It seemed to me that I was walking on the cold crust of a dead planet. We, perhaps, were the last two men in creation, the only two human beings to have survived the destruction of the world. When we reached the crater's edge the storm had passed, and a pale moon was shining out of a deep green sky.

We sat down under the lee of a lava rock, surrounded by the crowd of "slaves" who had by now resumed the likeness of cold black statues. For a long while we remained where we were, contemplating the squalid face of the earth and the sea, the scattered houses at the foot of the extinct volcano, the islands that drifted far away on the horizon, and, down below, the heap of dead stones that was Naples.

We were living men in a dead world. I was no longer ashamed of being a man. What did it matter to me whether men were innocent or guilty? The earth contained only living men and dead men. All the rest counted for nothing. All the rest was nothing but fear, despair, repentance, hatred, bitterness, forgiveness and hope. We were on the summit of an extinct volcano. The fire which for thousands of years had burned the veins of this mountain, of this soil, of the whole earth, had suddenly been quenched, and now little by little the ground was cooling beneath our feet. That city down below us, standing on the shore of a sea covered with a shining crust, beneath a sky heavy with storm clouds, was inhabited not, indeed, by the innocent and the guilty, the victors and the vanquished, but by living men who were roaming about in search of the means to allay their hunger and dead men who lay buried beneath the ruins of the houses.

Down below, as far as my eye could see, the earth was covered with thousands and thousands of corpses. Those dead men would have been nothing but putrid flesh had there not been among them Someone who had sacrificed Himself for the others in order to save the world, in order that all, innocent and guilty, victors and vanquished, who had survived those years of blood and sorrow should not have cause to feel ashamed of being men. Assuredly among those thousands and thousands of dead there lay the body of some Christ. What would have become of the world, and of us all, if among all those dead there had not been one Christ?

"What need is there for another Christ?" said Jimmy. "Christ has saved the world already, once and for all."

"Oh, Jimmy, why won't you understand that all those men would have died in vain if there were no Christ among them? Why won't you understand that there must be thousands and thousands of Christs among all those corpses? Even you know it isn't true that Christ saved the world once and for all. Christ died to teach us that every one of us can become Christ, that every man can save the world by his own sacrifice. Christ too would have died in vain if it were not possible for every man to become Christ and to save the world."

"A man is only a man," said Jimmy.

"Oh, Jimmy, why won't you understand that it isn't necessary for a man to be the Son of God, to rise again from the dead on the third day, and to sit on the right hand of the Father, in order to be Christ? It is those thousands and thousands of dead men who have saved the world, Jimmy."

"You attach too much importance to the dead," said Jimmy. "A man counts only if he's alive. A dead man is merely a dead man."

"Here in Europe," I said, "only the dead count."

"I'm tired of living among the dead," said Jimmy. "I'm content to go back home to America, where I'll be surrounded by living men. Why don't *you* come to America as well? You're a living man. America is a rich and happy country."

"I know America is a rich and happy country, Jimmy. But I won't go — I must stay here. I'm not a coward, Jimmy. And then, even misery, hunger, fear and hope are wonderful things — more so than riches, more so than happiness."

"Europe is a dump heap," said Jimmy, "a wretched, defeated continent. Come with us. America is a free country."

"I can't desert my dead, Jimmy. You are taking your dead to America. Every day ships sail for America laden with dead — dead who are rich, happy and free. But my dead cannot pay their fare to America — they are too poor. They will never know the meaning of riches, happiness and freedom. They have always lived in slavery; they have always been victims of hunger and fear. They will always be slaves, they will always be victims of hunger and fear, even though they are dead. It's their destiny, Jimmy. If you knew that Christ was lying among them, among those wretched corpses, would you desert Him?"

"You're not suggesting," said Jimmy, "that Christ has lost the war too!"

"It is a shameful thing to win a war," I said in a low voice.